"Reminds us all over again wł
put words together to give us
remembers too that without cc.
thing—that writing is itself as important and necessary and as beautiful and terrifying an endeavor as it ever was. Emily Sterling and her story—first to last—matter to us, and this is because Larry Baker cares."
—Bret Lott, author, *Gather the Olives: On Food and Hope and the Holy Land*

"Quirky, wise and compelling, capturing the pace of life as it's lived, equal parts drama and introspection, lingering in all the right places. Should be on every book club list."
—Lettie Prell, author, *The Three Lives of Sonata James*

"Larry Baker's artfully conceived and meticulously crafted novel, with the abiding spirit of Emily Dickinson hovering tantalizingly in the background, concerns itself with whatever 'Truth' may be. I can tell you that I love it. Entranced, even. It's enigmatic, quirky, idiosyncratic...as moving and honest a human story as I've read in quite a while."
—Harry Owen, award-winning poet and author, *Thicket: Shades from the Eastern Cape*

"With Emmy Sterling Larry Baker has created a captivating narrator whose unique and authentic voice drew me in from start to finish. The story is told with a pleasing non-linearity linearity—telling it slant à la her namesake from Amherst—while Emmy reviews her life and unruly vocation in the moment as well as with hindsight and reflection. The secondary characters—Emmy's parents, lover, best friends, mentor—are all flesh and blood even while they serve Emmy's path to self-understanding. *Tell It Slant* is a page-turner in which character is paramount and poetry is always near."
—Alan Michael Wilt, author, *The Holy Family: A Novel*

Tell It Slant

Larry Baker

Ice Cube Press, LLC (Est. 1991)
North Liberty, Ia, USA

Tell It Slant

First Edition

ISBN 9781948509688

Library of Congress Control Number: On request

Ice Cube Press, LLC (Est. 1991)
1180 Hauer Drive
North Liberty, Iowa 52317 USA
www.icecubepress.com | steve@icecubepress.com

The paper used in this publication meets the minimum requirements of the American National Standard for Information Sciences—Permanence of Paper for Printed Library Materials, ANSI Z39.48-1992.

Cover photo courtesy of the Emily Dickinson Collection at Amherst College Archives and Special Collections. Colorized adaptation by Manos Athanasiadis.

For Mike

Mike Lankford…my best friend, the best writer I ever knew. I wrote the first paragraph to this story three years ago and immediately sent it to him for his approval. Nobody else ever got to read anything of mine until I was finished. Mike wrote back, "This might be good. Send more when you can." He died before I finished the first draft. Like priests and sinners, we knew each other's secrets. He was that kind of friend, and I miss him.

Tell It Slant

Dewy and Dawn

He wondered what his parents would have named him if he had been born a girl. He quickly corrected himself. What would his mother have named him if he had been born a girl. His absent father's opinion would not have mattered. He had asked himself this question when he turned fifteen. His exact words: "I hate my name. Anything would have been better than my name. I should have been a girl. At least I would have a different name."

His journals began. His first written entry: "I hate my name." His journals. A page a day was his goal, even in the most harried moments, depressed or joyous, continuous, a page a day for fifty years. He came very close. An improbable, almost unbelievable feat. His wife had known. She was dead, herself the subject of thousands of pages. His only child, the daughter who looked more like him than her mother, was a close second, and she would eventually eclipse her mother, as long as he could write. He would die, the journals would stop, and his daughter would eventually read them after hearing bits and pieces of them from him when he was most melancholy.

Near his death, he had been re-reading the first page of his life when his daughter phoned him, and he noted the serendipity of her call and his own wish to have a different name.

Emmy called to ask how I was doing. She wanted to know if I was still taking my blood pressure medicine. How the visiting nurse was treating me. I did not tell her the truth, but she figured it out. Her mother in her, knowing when I lied. She laughed, telling me that I was not rich enough to die yet. That she expected me to be worth a lot more than I was now. My Social Security and part-time job were not going to get enough money for a new beach house. She made me laugh too, like her mother.

De Witt Clinton Sterling. His mother Rose had never thought twice about her choice. "He was a great man, De Witt Clinton, as you will be." It made no sense to him.

"Mother, he was famous and great in New York. We live in Florida. Nobody has ever heard of him, much less be impressed by his name."

She was adamant. "Henry Morrison Flagler was famous in Florida, is buried here, if that is important to you, but he was not a great man. Would you rather be named Henry Morrison Sterling? Would you be mocked less?" It was a toss-up in his mind. "Hank" versus "Dewey." "Henny" versus "Dim-Wit."

His looks did not command respect, the face that was off-center at birth and almost freakish by the time he was a teenager, and so he turned fifteen in a mob of other insecure and awkward teenagers who had to find someone more inept or ugly than they were. De Witt Clinton Sterling was their village idiot, their ugly duckling, their Quasimodo, their Christ.

He wrote the first page of his journal and showed it to Dawn Rosemary Latona. She already knew all his other secrets, as he did hers. Dawn was only ten years old, so her secrets were not profound, nor was she as fraught with guilt as he was about his secrets, but she shared them only with him. Her biggest secret? She heard music when it wasn't there. His biggest secret was not his anger over his name. No, his biggest secret was his anger over who had named him. The woman who had delivered him into this world almost by herself, who delivered Dawn, and who would eventually deliver her own grand-daughter, the child of Dawn and De Witt. Rose Sterling, her son was convinced, had probably delivered the baby Jesus.

Dawn had heard all the names that De Witt had been called. She knew he was unhappy. She wanted him to hear the music she heard, but all she could do after he told her about his first journal entry was offer him a new name. "I'm going to call you Dewy." He misunderstood. "Everybody already calls me Dewey. I hate that name." He would always remember how she put her hands on her hips and puffed out her flat chest, took a deep breath through her nose, and almost snorted back at him. "Dewy Sterling, you aren't paying attention to me. You aren't hearing what I'm saying. You are not Dewey. You are D-E-W-Y. Like the morning grass, like your eyes. Do you understand?" He did not. "You are not hearing your name, Dewy. So, right now, spell it out for me. D-E-W-Y." He obeyed. "Do you hear the difference now," she snapped, her left eyebrow arched as if a warning to him. "Say it again." He did. "Now say your name out loud." As soon as he spoke, he heard his own music. "My name is Dewy." Nothing mattered after that. If the other kids kept tossing "Dewey" at him, assuming that they were mocking him, all he heard was "Dewy."

It became their favorite story, but shared with few people. It was their mutual secret. They had told their daughter on her sixteenth birthday, and she had cried. Her long-held opinion that her parents were bat-shit crazy was confirmed more and more. The daughter insisted on her own well-balanced sanity, but her mother reminded her, "I hear music. You hear voices. Tell me again how crazy you think me and your father are."

Dewy met Dawn when he was five years old. She was ten minutes old. Rose Sterling was a midwife in Alachua County, an unwed mother of two boys by different fathers, twenty years apart. Dewy, the younger son, was on-call as much as she was. Midnight labors meant he was wrapped up and brought along to witness a new arrival. The new arrival that night was named Dawn. She preceded the actual first dawn of her life by three hours.

In the corner of the kerosene-lit room, sitting close to a cauldron of boiling water, his vision blocked by the backs of giant women seeming to sway like pines in the wind, he heard his future wife squalling before he saw her red-blotched face. Her crying was harsh, but not as inhuman as her mother's grunts and screams had been during the final moments of delivery. A few minutes later, scissors were retrieved from the boiling water. He remembered his mother's quick glance at him, then her turning back to the new mother and child. More minutes, and then his mother turned to motion for him to come see the child. His strongest memory of that moment? The room was tomb quiet. Gone were strife and pain and the curse of God. Wrapped in a purple blanket, Dawn lay on her mother's breast. He stood beside the bed, looking at his future.

As she lay dying many years later, he told her the story of her birth again. He had told her that story many times over the years, but each time he had added another small detail. Dawn sometimes laughed and accused him of making things up. He had told her, *Qui narrat eligit veritatem.* The last time, as she was an hour away from dying, her eyes covered by bandages so she could not see the monster a fire had created, the fire that was killing her, he remembered another detail. He told her that as he had stared at her for the first time, he had noticed that the other women had stood back, almost in darkness, whispering to each other about mysteries not yet comprehensible to a five-year-old boy. Witnesses to some sort of initiation. He had looked for his own mother, but her back was turned toward him. Baby Dawn's eyes were closed, and then he saw a small wet bubble appear on her lips, as if by magic. He looked for his mother again. She was washing her hands, her huge hands, scouring blood and slime into the past.

Their daughter would never tell them, but she always felt like she had disappointed her parents. They had always seemed so happy with nothing while she had wanted everything. Most of all, she wanted what they had. Each other. The thing they were when they were together. Happy. Was it that simple? How many times had she watched them when they were not looking? The two of them in the same room, usually the kitchen, not even paying attention to each other. Perhaps her mother cooking, her father reading. Other times, outside. Him using a push mower on their yard, her sitting in a lawn chair, wearing sunglasses, but Emmy knew that her mother was watching him. Even her friends saw it. Slumber parties, teenage girls who were themselves students of her father, hormones-in-an-atom-smasher giddy, stuffed with ice cream and cookies, poking her and whispering, "Jesus, Emmy, all I want is for some guy to look at me like your dad looks at your mom." And then someone would add a variation, "As long as he was good-looking." Emmy understood. Her father was not a handsome man, but her mother was beautiful. In the genetic clash that produced Emmy, her father won. If he had only been plain, mixed with her mother's beauty, perhaps then Emmy might have at least been pretty. But her father was not plain. He was ugly. None of his "parts" fit together. Each was off in a small way, and that off-ness was compounded by their combination. Eyebrows too bushy, ears too large, a lower lip that did not line up with his upper lip, swollen nose, and his hands ... like his own mother's hands ... huge.

Her mother was breathtakingly beautiful. Everyone agreed. But nobody ever wondered why she eventually married Dewy, ugly or not. It had always been a "given." They had always been a couple, ever since she could walk. Dawn always said, "He is my first memory. Him looking at me in my crib, me enthralled by his face." Always together. Separated only when he went to college in Gainesville and she began high school. Surely, people said, with him gone and her surrounded by other young boys her age, other handsome boys; surely, she would free herself from his spell. It had to be a spell, right? How else to explain it? But it also seemed so… so inevitable.

But the daughter understood. She had seen his face when her mother entered the room. And her face too. How each smiled. Others had seen it too. The day that her mother had come to her father's classroom to bring him his bagged lunch which he had forgotten. A knock on the door as he was diagramming a Latin sentence on the board. He had turned to the door, not expecting her, and then the smile. Most of his students had never seen his wife, so they were confused. He married *her*? She married *him*? *Him*? He introduced her and she had done a mock curtsy. "Yes, the charming Mrs. Sterling, of whom you have no doubt heard Philemon here praise in Pindaric odes." Her father had merely waved his hand and pointed to his visitor. "*Mea uxor lepidissima, Baucis.*" His first term students had no idea what he said. But every female in the class never forgot what happened next. Dawn had put the bag on his desk and then leaned forward to give him a kiss on the cheek, then turned and walked away. The students were frozen. A beautiful woman had kissed their ugly teacher, right there in front of them. But it was what happened next that they never forgot. Just as her mother was in the doorway about to disappear, she had turned back to her father and smiled at him. With a piece of chalk in his hand, he had silently mouthed "I love you" to her, and she did the same to him. Every female in the room was a lip-reader.

How did the daughter know this story? It was not in her father's journals. It was a ritual story, one of those told at her mother's funeral, a joyful memory of the deceased. A woman in black lingered after the service and told the daughter that she had been a student of her father's, that she had witnessed it all. She and the other girls in class had all agreed. They never made fun of Mr. Sterling ever again. The daughter had listened to the story, not really surprised. The only surprise was that the woman had felt guilty about thinking that her father was ugly. The talk about that moment in her parents' past had been followed by an awkward pause, and then the woman had looked down as she said, "When are you coming back home?"

I
Emmy: The Beginning

Disclaimer: This is a work of fiction. Although inspired by real people and events, it is still not true. Neither the author nor the narrator is to be trusted.

If I told you that I hear voices, would you believe me? Would you just shrug or roll your eyes? Would you be like my ex-husband, shrug and roll your eyes but never really look at me? My first and only and long-gone husband. He was actually two husbands, the one I married and the one I divorced. He changed. My father warned me. I was a child, but he knew me.

"You live in your own world, Emmy. Don't ever lose it. And don't share it with a fool."

I was ten. I had no idea what he meant. A fool? Fools were an April thing. But I told all my friends that I had married a fool. I quoted my father. Heads nodded. I was bitter and I was hurt. It took time for me to understand that I was wrong. He was not a fool, but he had been foolish to marry me.

The voices? My mother and father mostly. After too much alcohol, I hear my grandmother, the harshest voice. Former friends and lovers. The teacher who thought I would be her student "success" story. When she talks to me, still encouraging me, I want to scream at her, "If I'm so damn smart, how come I'm here by myself, dying alone but with a spectacular view of the ocean?" Another voice...the agent I did not appreciate, reminding me that I should write better in every new book. Peter James Jefferson and Amy, how could I not? Voices? My own voice, too much.

You didn't ask me, did you? You didn't ask me if I heard voices. Doesn't matter. It's still a good question. I'm probably just going through that final molting phase, shedding dead skin, unpacking baggage, confessing my sins. I'm a writer. I'm allowed to use metaphors and allusions, even if they are clichés. I'm a one-hit-wonder writer. First novel bestseller and bad-movie-made-of-my-story kind of writer. One book, and I had money for the rest of my life. But I kept writing. My parents would understand, especially my father. As long as I was writing, I was alive.

So, I hear voices. I wish I could tell you that I see ghosts. But that would be crazy. Nope, just voices. The important question? Don't you?

Here I am, lining up my ducks. Start at the beginning, I'm on a one-way street. Talking to you, talking to myself.

My first novel, my "Barnes and Noble Great New Voice" award-winning novel, was about my parents. I fictionalized them and myself, changed all the names to protect the innocent, and there's the problem, as my under-appreciated agent told me after she met my father. "You sure you don't want to make this a memoir? Wouldn't the truth be a better story?"

I had to give my agent credit. I had prepared her for how my father looked, but nobody, really, was ever prepared for how my father looked. My father and I agreed that we were thankful that my mother died before she could see the nightmare he had become, a nightmare for which she was partially responsible. He had always joked about being "the ugliest man in Florida," and that was before the fire.

My father was a wonderful talker, especially after a few drinks, and my agent was spellbound. My father had read the manuscript. I never thought to hide it from him. He said he loved it. He was my father, how could he not? I had named his character "Alexander," and he was pleased with that. I made Alexander a cripple, but not ugly. More happy approval from my father. But then I sat across the table from him and my agent and listened to him describe other scenes, other facts, straight from the proverbial horse's mouth. Sometimes my agent would glance at me and give me that "Have you considered…" expression. But the deal was done. The agent had sold a novel to Windsor House. A novel it was to be. My novel. Windsor House was excited. Why drop the bird that was in our hands, hoping for two in the bush. (I warned you. Clichés, clichés, just about all I have left.) My novel had been optioned by HBO in a bidding war. I was the publishing world's new "hot" writer. I was finally my favorite teacher's success story.

Protect the innocent? Did I say that? My agent was right. My parents deserved the literal truth about their lives. They were innocent. The only guilty character in my novel was the daughter. Not even my father knew that. I lied in the creation of my fictional self because lying is always easier than telling the truth. You heard different? Honesty is the best policy? You'll never be a novelist.

My parents were the most wonderful people I ever knew in my life, past and present. My girlfriends agreed. Their parents agreed. It was so improbable, how much they loved each other, how they loved me. My first and only husband asked me the most obvious question: "To have been raised by those two people, how come you're so fucked up?"

My joints ache every morning, and I am nauseous for the first few hours of the day. My chest, where my breasts used to be, aches as well. I used to be able to walk on the beach in the dark and then watch the sun rise over the Atlantic. That's when I think about my parents the most. The sunrise. The closest I ever feel to a God they believed in, but whom I dismissed. In fact, they, more than me, had every right to curse their own God. But they were happy Christians, even at my mother's grisly end. But they had the solace I would never have. No death-bed conversions for me. Sooner more likely than later, I'll be ashes in a jar. I told Dorothy that I wanted some of those ashes spread in the ocean too. I look at the spot every morning, a quarter-mile away, in a direct line from my beach-house deck. I can see my grave, every morning. I wish I believed what my parents believed. They knew there was a heaven and that they would be there. I'd like to believe in it too, and, although I wouldn't pass the Golden Gate exam, I might get a few hours with them again. I have so many questions now.

My novel was published. An idyllic childhood was idealized even more. I'm surprised that Hallmark didn't want the film rights. But then my father died and joined my mother. I was their only child. I inherited a few thousand dollars, a decrepit house north of Ocala, which I still own but do not live in, and my father's journals. My agent had been right. My parents deserved the truth. If you have that first book of mine, burn it. If I could do it over again, I would tell it differently.

The difference between writers and other people? Other than our neurosis and vanity and desperation and goddam brilliance? We remember things. Until it all turns to mush, a condition knocking on my door right now, we hold on to the past. How do I know this important fact? I heard it on the Oprah show. Some guest of hers was telling a story about scientific research that was done on writers. A writer would be given a lengthy interview, asking all sorts of questions about her past, any answer would lead to another asking for more details. Every damn detail, as best they could recall. And then the researcher would interview that writer's parents and siblings. Ask the same questions, probe. And then the researcher would say, "Well, your sister said...." And, over and over again, that family member would pause, as if a blurry picture was coming into focus, pause and nod and blink and finally say, "Yes, yes, I had forgotten about that." Sometimes, a sibling would resist. "I'm sorry, that's not how I remember it." But they would be wrong.

My parents are dead. I was an only child. My ex-husband died a year ago. The past belongs to me. But I have a friend...a writer-friend, reader of my first-drafts, sharer of writer gossip, call me once a week now, a check-on-me kind of friend. Her name is Lorrie. She said she saw the same Oprah show. When I use it to justify my dominion over my own past, she reminds me, "Emily, it wasn't a researcher on that show. It was a writer. You ever think that she might have been lying just a little, fudging the facts?"

My father never had to remember anything. After he was fifteen, he wrote it all down when it happened. A lawyer's dream. Contemporaneous Documentation. The most reliable of witnesses. After he died, I read everything he wrote. The irony? I learned more about him and my mother, but it only confirmed what I already felt. No surprises, no shocking confessions of infidelity or alcohol abuse. Even when he wrote about me, he was accurate. But, only about what he knew, not who I really was.

Is that a delusion we all have, that nobody really knows the truth about us? Do as I say, not as I do? Believe what I say, not what I think? I once had a boyfriend, my second year of college, who insisted on being "honest" with me. I sat there as he treated my dorm room as a confessional, and I liked him less. Then again, in perfect terminally ill hindsight now, I see that I really didn't like him all that much to begin with. He was simply a disguise for me, to hide that fact that I was falling in love with somebody else, the great love of my life. No, not the man I eventually married. Somebody else, the memory I cannot erase. My failure to forget him is my own fault. How can you forget someone if you keep every letter that he wrote to you, every card, every picture, every gift, all arranged in chronological order? Contemporaneous Documentation, remember? I was keeping a journal all that time but didn't know it. After the book about my parents, some part of him was in every book I wrote. Some version of him, some event in our life together, but performed by other characters. Facts turned into fiction, and I kept thinking that I would write a book just about him. Put it all together in one story. Neither one of us would be heroic. Adultery is never heroic. Love? I'll tell you that story eventually, the first time he told me that he loved me. The details of that night. The music in the room, the food in front of us, the clatter of dishes and clinking of glasses, in public for the world to see us together, caution damned long before. I asked him if he loved me, expecting evasion. He sat still, and then he simply said, "Yes." I blinked and looked around the room, and it all began to blur, as watercolors bleed in the rain. I wanted to speak, my usual ironic self, my defense against disappointment, but in that moment, I finally understood how my parents felt about each other. More than understood, how I felt at that moment, but I cannot find the right words now. Death and love, are there really words for those two moments? I'm a writer. Stick around, I'll remind you over and over. The words don't exist for how I felt at that moment.

Here's one of those suggestions in all the parenting books: You want your child to appreciate music, let her hear it even before she's born. You know, Mozart in the womb. Put your belly next to a stereo speaker and let those sound waves go through your skin into the inner sanctum of your womb. My mother never did that. When I was ten, I wanted to learn to play the piano. Lessons were arranged. Practice was religiously observed. I was awful. I tried the violin. More lessons. By the time I was twelve, I was down to my last musical resort, the flute. I practiced with the intensity of a prisoner on death row. All I needed was one damn flawless routine and I would get a call from the governor's office. Sentence commuted. Free at last. Sorry, dead woman walking.

I tried joking with my parents, blaming them for my lack of musical talent. I told them about the music in the womb theory. In hindsight, it should have been proof to me that I am not a naturally gifted joke-teller. It was one of those moments I could tell my children about, if I ever had children, how my parents did not get the joke. The confused and then pained look on their faces, as if they had failed me. Almost as a defense, my father said, "But we talked to you." I think it was the first time I ever hurt their feelings, and I still had my diva-teen years ahead of me. And then they told me the most intimate thing I had ever heard from them.

Almost every night after my mother started "showing" her pregnancy, my father would kneel between her legs as she sat on the edge of the bed, that creaky metal-framed double-bed they had as long as I knew them, and he would put his mouth close to her stomach and... talk to me. After he died and I read his journals, I learned more about that ritual. He would recite nursery rhymes, his lips almost touching her skin. He would recite the lyrics to songs. You want to see me cry now? Go find almost any recording of "Fly Me to the Moon," not the Sinatra version, but the Tony Bennett or Johnny Mathis versions. I will go into some sort of cosmic trance. Sometimes, my mother would lie on the couch and he would rest his head on her bare stomach and talk to her, not to me, letting me eavesdrop. But, more. He found some sort of device where my mother could talk into some sort of microphone that was connected to some sort of receiver that could be pressed up against her stomach. And she would talk to me. Soon enough, they took turns reading to me. Their own ritual, an hour a night. Poems, simple children's books, stories. My father told me that he once started to talk to me in Latin. My mother had rolled her eyes. "He only did it once. I told him not to confuse you." That night, with puberty lurking, my hormone fuse about to be lit, as they told me about my introduction to words, I wasn't sure if they were adorable or just adorably crazy.

And you don't think I hear voices?

Fate or Free Will? Psychology or Physiology? I am at that point. You'll be here soon enough. How did I get here? Was there ever really a road that diverged in a yellow wood? I zigged when I should have zagged?

I was born in the same room in which I had been conceived. Grandma Rose at the helm. Before science made it possible to know the sex of a baby before it was born, parents usually had Plan-B and Plan-G. Plan-B was a boy name; Plan-G, a girl. Emily Opal was Plan-G for me. Plan-B? My parents simply ignored the question when I asked.

I dropped into my grandmother's hands, was cleaned up, wrapped in the ceremonial purple blanket, and handed to my father who then handed me to my mother. He loved telling the story.

"I handed you to your mother and made a big show of saying let me introduce you to your daughter Emily Opal Sterling."

At that introduction, however, my mother changed the course of history. "Your father and I had agreed on Emily, but as soon as I saw you, I knew that you weren't that girl. You were Emmy to me."

My father hated his name, so my mother changed it for him. She had a certain power. According to the State of Florida, I am Emily

Opal Sterling. My mother named me Emmy.

When I first heard the story of how "Emmy" was born, I was six. My parents had just dressed me for my first day of school and were admiring their creation. Both of them were sitting on the floor in front of me, looking up at me. In subsequent years, they would tell me the story again and again. They always liked to repeat their favorite stories.

This will not shock you. I was named after Emily Dickinson. My father and mother talking to me in the womb? Emily was always on the playlist. One great disappointment of my life? Of all the voices I have heard in the past, hear now, none of them is the saintly Belle of Amherst. Even after I was born, I heard her poems almost every night. A proper child reaction to such indoctrination, especially when said child became a self-conscious teenager, would be to rebel and secede from her parents' expectations. Emily was a cockeyed reclusive virgin who wrote sing-song stupid poems about flies buzzing and funerals in your brain. I am not Emily. I am me. Right?

But I loved Emily Dickinson. I loved hearing my parents quote Dickinson poems to each other. Their favorite game? One would cite an opening line, the other would have to do the second line, alternating. And they would pull me into that game by the time I could read anything. They also read the Bible every night, but never out loud.

Our house had one Bible, but three copies of the Thomas Johnson hardcover edition of Dickinson poems. Yes, Mama and Papa and Baby Bear each had a copy. I still have mine, although I have to keep big rubber bands wrapped around it to keep the pages from falling out. I memorized almost a hundred all by myself. They're mostly all gone now, my brain no longer a sponge, just a rusty sieve, but I can still win a bet on remembering first lines. Not a smart skill to use when your marriage is dissolving, the ability to throw a Dickinson line like... oh, just grabbing one out of thin air... "My Life had stood a Loaded Gun"... at your unhappy spouse, a man who considered Dickinson over-rated even before he met me. How could I have missed that when we were dating?

I dressed like her on Halloween when I was eight, confusing our neighbors but thrilling my parents. That particular spooky night, after accepting a treat, I would hand the treater a copy of "One need not be a chamber to be haunted..." that my father had xeroxed off for me at his school. (#670 in the Johnson edition, you can thank me later.) Long before parents were warned about razor blades in apples and poisoned candy corn, my parents always went with me on Halloween. I will admit, I was embarrassed, but at least they did not dress up in costumes themselves. Lord knows where that would have led. From that particular night, I will always remember how the adults at the door, treats still in hand, would first ask, "And what goblin do we have here?" I would curtsy and inform them that I was Emily Dickinson. A blank look would follow. But they would fork over the candy and then I would hand them the poem. Blankness became confusion, but then they looked past me to see my spectral parents hovering on the sidewalk. We were in a small town. Evidently, everyone knew my parents. Confusion became laughter. I was Dewy and Dawn's daughter.

It would have been a perfect childhood memory if it wasn't for Dorothy Fergus, whose parents dressed her up like Dorothy from *The Wizard of Oz*. Dorothy was a Heather before Heathers were a thing. She and her little covey of Dorothys were always one house behind me and as I was leaving one house they were arriving, and I could hear them snicker and whisper to themselves about me as we crossed paths.

The missing fact here? Until I finally had surgery to correct it, I suffered from amblyopia. A kind description would be lazy eye. A Dorothy description would be "retarded." From my earliest memories of being in front of a mirror, I knew that something was wrong. But

Dickinson had eye problems too, I had seen her few pictures, and I loved my bad eye. I felt closer to Dickinson all the time, more and more. My parents? They did the patches and the glasses and the drops, and surgery was inevitable, but that was the future. By the time I got home that Halloween night, I was crying. The next day, my parents took me to Gainesville to see a new doctor. Me, I was an eight-year-old coward. I had forsaken the only goddess I ever believed in. I still worshipped her, but only in my parents' home. I kept reading her poems, and copying them out in my scribbly cursive handwriting into a spiral notebook, memorizing as best I could. With modern medicine and time, I eventually no longer looked like her. I was still plain and drab, but I was not her. I was just plain and drab Emmy, and ahead of me was one more failure in my Dickinson universe.

How many times has somebody asked you, "What do you want to be when you grow up?" You're usually a kid when they ask, so the emphasis is on a future of possible goals. I grew up when the question implied different answers depending on whether you were a girl or a boy. I was a girl, so my future was a girl future. Times are different now. I think my parents would be alright with that. They knew what I wanted to be. I told them when I was thirteen. "I want to be a poet," I announced. None of that "ess" crap at the end. I wanted to be a p-o-e-t. My parents looked at each other, then at me. My father said what I wanted to hear. "You will be brilliant." My mother was more indirect about her feelings. "Can we see some of your poems?"

My father assumed the future. My mother assumed the past, a past in which I must have already been writing poems in some form, somewhere. She was right. I had been writing poems for a year. I did not know about my father's journals then. He did not know about my spiral notebooks full of poems. My mother had suspicions. She was calling my bluff. Not in a bad way, not maliciously. I think she assumed they were good, adolescent for sure, but showing some talent. If I shared them with her and my father, surely, they would see my talent and praise me, encourage me more. They wanted me to be a poet.

"Can we see some of your poems?"

I told them that I would show them when I felt that they were ready. I was close. I had hundreds. A year earlier I had given up on my musical future. My in-utero existence had not been introduced to music, but surely all the poems and stories and nursery tales, all the reading I had done since I learned to put letters and sounds together, my absorption and adulation for Emily... surely, I was gifted in poetry, right? I was gifted, surely. Wrong. I wrote poetry as well as I played the flute.

You see it coming, right? I could not write a good poem if my parents were being held for ransom and all the kidnappers wanted was one...one good...one good goddam poem from me. Fifty years into the future, interviewed on a public radio station, I was asked if I had ever written any poetry, since I seemed to include Dickinson so much in my prose stories. I was honest in my own way. "Oh, Lord, no. Writing poetry is much harder than writing prose. The right words in the right order, an idea purely crystallized. A single great poem is an achievement beyond me. Dickinson wrote hundreds of great poems. I would never attempt that. I knew I was a natural fiction writer. It's a lazy art. And you can write a good book a lot easier than you can write a good poem. Nope, I was always meant to be a novelist."

But I wrote hundreds of poems, and I'll be damned if any of them ever see the light of day. I thought I would honor Dickinson by becoming a pale version of her, but I gave it up before I finished high school, and my parents never asked me again. I wasn't going to be a poet. A novelist? I wrote one short story in high school. And then I went to college to become an English teacher.

Opal?

I had been left with my grandmother when I was ten, just for a week while my parents took a rare vacation without me. I was terrified of my grandmother. I could fake courage with anybody else, huff and puff and stand my ground in any schoolyard, but my grandmother had some sort of death-ray glare that could chisel stone. My strategy for surviving a week with her was to be as invisible as possible. But I was fascinated by her house. Midwife, herbalist, colonic provider (those were the most medieval rooms in her house), probably a shaman, certainly a witch. I was mystified about how my talkative father could have been raised by this almost always silent woman. When she did speak, it was either wrath or scorn.

She had left me alone late one night, called to a birth, and I was afraid that she would make me go with her, as she had done with my father the night my mother was born, but being ten-years-old made me responsible for my own food and safety because, as she told me on her way out, "I will be gone until I get back. This child is early." Evidently, "early" was code for difficult. Hours passed. Dawn came, then noon, then dusk. I had brought books to read. My grandmother had cats, so I entertained them by reading to them. I wrote a letter to my parents, making sure my cursive lettering was legible. My father was a stickler for that. I found a radio in the kitchen, but that was a short-lived diversion. Then, I resolved to go exploring in the most alien of territory. I went to my grandmother's bedroom, which was always shut, turned the knob and cracked open the door, and then, for some reason, I whispered, "Is anybody here?"

The room did not smell like sulfur, as I expected, but it was musty and stale and tinged with the odor of cheap scented soap, exactly like my grandmother smelled. I stepped inside and felt for a light switch next to the door, but there was nothing. It had gotten dark outside, darker in the room. I stood motionless, my eyes adjusting as best they could to the dark. Surely, I thought, there had to be a lamp somewhere, probably by the bed, right? But that required me to maneuver slowly through the room, hands in front of me, anticipating any obstacle. I found her bed. First impression? It was as hard as stone, just as cold, but that was a first impression shaped by the darkness. Running my hand along the edge of the bed, I felt a pillow, then, knowing I was at the head of the bed, tentatively moved my hand to the right until it touched something that felt like a caterpillar running across the back of my hand. I was ten. Of course, I screamed. I froze in that spot, hand snatched back to cover my mouth, my chest heaving, terrified. I was afraid to move in any direction. A minute passed. Less, or more, I don't remember. All I knew was that I had wet my panties. I had two choices. Find my way back to the door, or find a lamp. Wriggly creatures be damned. I sat on the bed and scooted my bottom toward where my hand had wandered. There was, indeed, a bed table where the wrigglies had been. I slid my hand across the table and found the base of a lamp. I told this story years later and elaborated on what I was thinking at the time. Well, not really elaborated…fabricated. I would tell people that I thought, "Jesus Lord, please let there be a switch right there so I wouldn't have to bump into that wriggling monster again." Truth is, I was in a trance, not thinking at all, but I felt a hard button and pushed it down.

It was not a bright light, but enough to explain the first mystery. There was no wriggly monster, simply a yellow lampshade with beaded tassels around the bottom. I had rubbed my hand under the tassels in the dark and discovered a monster. Light dispelled that monster, but created a new mystery. My grandmother. I was in a Sears catalog page from 1910. Nothing in the room was out of place. The cold hard bed was simply a bed with sheets and a quilt-cover tucked so tightly that there was no slack. The bed table had the lamp and a leather-bound Bible. That was odd because I always thought my grandmother was godless. A dressing table, complete with a giant swivel mirror, was on one side of the room. Assorted small bottles were on the dressing table, arranged an inch from each other, in ascending order of height. On the other side of the room was an armoire. I was about to open it when I noticed the one, the only, the small-framed picture on the wall.

Four bare walls except for that one small picture. Two old people, standing side by side in front of a white-washed wooden house. Black and white, almost sepia. The old man had white whiskers and looked like he was pushing a hundred. The old woman was thin, with white hair, but something about her face made her look much younger than the old man. He was smiling. So was she, but she was not looking directly at the camera. The lamp did not give off a lot of light, so, looking around to make sure I was still alone, I took the picture off the wall and went back to the bed and sat down so I could see it better. Why is all this important, these details? Simple, it was the first time in my life that I felt a story forming in my brain. A stupid picture of old people and I was sitting there writing a story about them. In a few years I would be in high school and my favorite teacher, who wanted me to be a success story, she asked us all to write a paragraph about somebody else in our family. It was an in-class exercise. We had fifty minutes. Paragraph, hell, I wrote five pages, a story about how I got my middle name. She told me later…that was when I actually became a future success story for her.

I sat there in that dim dusty bedroom, holding some sort of history in my hands, interpreting and re-interpreting, and then I heard my name.

"Opal."

I knew who was speaking even before I looked up. My grandmother loomed over me. If this was a fairy-tale story, I could describe her as having a butcher knife in each hand, as if waiting to slice and dice and eat the little girl who had intruded into her inner sanctum. The truth is better. And sadder. She wasn't talking to me. She was talking to the picture. She wasn't about to murder me. She simply wanted to tell me a story. It was the only time, before or after, that I thought she had a soft side, the only time I saw her cry, the only time she spoke in a whisper.

Opal had been her older sister, the one who had a baby but no husband. Cast out by her own parents, she had been taken in by her grandfather, my great-grandfather. My grandmother Rose was forbidden by her parents to have anything to do with her sister. The twentieth century had just arrived. Perhaps only ten miles apart, the two sisters were a million miles away from each other. The picture in my lap that night in my grandmother's bedroom was the only picture ever taken of Opal.

We sat close together, the closest contact we had ever had except for my actual birth. She was not a hugger, not a soft-toucher, not a patter-on-the-head kind of grandmother.

Opal?

"Your father asked if he could use Opal as your middle name. I was surprised. I assumed that he would do what Dawn wanted. But he told me that she had also thought it was a perfect middle name for you. I had told him about his Aunt Opal, but that was when he was young, so I assumed he had forgotten, but when it came time to name you, he wanted Opal to be part of you too. It was a kind gesture. From both of them. How could I object? Your father is the kindest man I have ever known. It is a puzzlement for sure. I am not a kind person, and his father was simply kind enough to disappear before he was born. Your father's kindness came from somewhere beyond me. If you are blessed, some of his kindness will be in you too."

Until my grandmother appeared in the room with me, I had imagined a different story for the picture, but I liked hers better. When I wrote for my teacher, I used her version.

From the kitchen window of my beach house, I can look out and see the Atlantic. Every day now. My place is valuable only for its location. It was run-down, a money-pit, but cheap enough that I could afford a down payment and the monthly mortgage, even before I wrote my first book. Even after I got upper-middle class rich, and could afford to do better, I stayed here. Tin roof, two bedrooms, tile floors, bathroom with a claw-foot tub, a big kitchen area that is also the main indoor living space, with sliding glass doors to the deck. A couple of late-season hurricanes did their best to blow me away, and I did have to replace those sliding doors more than once, but I never left my house. Evacuation orders be damned. My mother lived long enough to visit me once in this house, and we sat through a hurricane together. She was slowly dying from cancer. As she said, "What's the worst that can happen to me?" The power went out. Rain came in horizontal waves. Palm leaves and luckless gulls slammed into the tin roof, a roof which was iffy even on a good day, but my mother was thrilled. We were in the dark, holding hands, telling stories.

"I brought you a present," she said.

"And the occasion?"

"We're still alive. God is putting on a show for us, and we're as snug as bugs in a rug. What better occasion?"

I ignored the god-stuff. She was happy, that's all that mattered.

"So, when do I get it?"

"As soon as you find a flashlight and my suitcase. Open it and bring me the box in the bottom."

A minute later, I was back with the box and the flashlight. She was almost giddy, knowing what she had brought me. Part of my past. As I unwrapped it, she told me a story.

"Your grandmother died while you were away at college. Remember how big her funeral was, every child born in the county for the previous fifty years came out of the woodwork with their children and grandchildren. Your father and I were surprised. We did not expect her to have generated so much sentimentality and love."

"Oh, Lord, yes," I said, remembering that day. "But, as you always tell me, the Lord moves in mysterious ways."

My mother poked me as she almost laughed. "Emily Opal Sterling. You are a terrible person."

"I'm also your favorite daughter."

"And your grandmother's favorite grand-daughter. This is from her to you. She gave it to me before she died, told me to give it you before I died."

It was the picture of Opal and her grandfather. It's on a wall in my bedroom now. Next to the picture of my parents. Other pictures. The great failure of my life? Not books unwritten or people unloved. Not the people I have hurt or disappointed. Simpler than all that. The pictures on my wall have no home after I am gone.

When I was a child, I loved being an only child. I had my parents to myself. I was, sort of, the center of their universe. My only competition was how they felt about each other. It took me a lot of years and a lot of distance to come to the conclusion that they would have been just as happy if I had never existed. I'm okay with that. But, today, looking at that damn ocean, I wish I had a brother or sister, a lot of them, just so I could talk to them about "our" parents. If I had had siblings, would my parents have treated me differently? Was

I actually "special"? And why just me? They could have had more children. I asked them more than once, why only me, and my father would say, "You were all we needed." I was nit-picking back then, so I asked, "But was I all you wanted?" I'm the writer, I told you, the good-memory writer, and some memories are more painful than others. I was thirteen, a bad year for me, when I asked my father about my being an only child for the last time. I pressed him on need versus want. I was quibbling without an agenda, just showing off my semantic skills. I thought he would laugh, but he just stared at me.

"Emmy, I didn't want any children at all, even you."

My mother was standing in the doorway between the kitchen and the dining room. And here's where I want a brother or sister, where I need a brother or sister. Some witness other than me. My parents are dead. My perfect memory is my only witness, and I am perfectly lost. I am not sure what I said then, perhaps nothing, perhaps I simply shook my head, blinking and fighting tears, or not. But early in the mornings now, when I want to remember the past, I want to hear him say what I think he said, looking at his trembling daughter, his daughter he had cut adrift. I had turned to look at my mother, knowing that she would make me understand, reel me back home, but she stood there framed in that doorway and kept her arms folded across her chest. She wasn't looking at me. She was looking at my father, grieving for him, not me. He reached for me, trying to hug me, but I pulled away. I took a deep breath, then another, but I could not speak.

"Emmy, I was afraid any child of mine would look like me."

I exploded.

"But I do look like you, Daddy. I am your daughter. Your daughter. So, I'm a freak, right!"

My mother exploded, "Emmy!"

If I were scripting that scene, I would have had the mother come to comfort the lost-at-sea daughter. Make it all right, translate again. I turned toward my beautiful mother and watched her walk toward and then past me, to put her arms around my father, gently guide his head down to rest on her shoulder as he wept, tears probably saved up from a lifetime of being… a freak? I had just called him a freak. His swaying back to me, my mother was looking over his shoulder at me, almost glaring.

"For the record, Emmy, you don't look like your father. You look like us. When you figure that out, when you see that person in your mirror, when you grow up, you'll know how beautiful you are."

I was too young and shallow to hear a door closing. No, not a door between me and my father. Rather, the door between me and my past. My moods were a roller coaster of ups and downs. Acne was beginning to explore my face. It's all laughable now. The obvious. I was a month away from having my first period. I was a late bloomer. Hell, Dorothy Fergus had her first period in class a year earlier, and you would have thought she was Wonder Woman. I would have been mortified, the stain showing through her white slacks, but she was a warrior. Evidently, her mother had prepared her for the inevitable blood and cramps. How else to explain her casually waving our teacher away as she retrieved a bag from her desk. "It's okay, I have a pad. My mother took care of me."

What do you want to be when you grow up?

Your official warning here. I'm about to start talking like an old person, about how things were better in the old days, even though life was a trial and we walked a million miles in the snow to attend a one-room unheated shack of a school. I don't mean that life was easier back then than now. No, but it was better. This is not the start to a debate. You want proof it was better? There is no proof. There are only memories and opinions.

We were not rich, but we were far from poor. I knew poor kids. I eventually found out that Dorothy Fergus had been a poor kid, but her mother's second marriage changed that. I suppose it changed Dorothy too, from bad to worse for awhile. Being poor, to me, meant that there were things you needed but could not have. Food, warmth, good clothes. Some of the poorest kids I knew lacked the things that I already had. For others, their poverty was inside. They were afraid of being hurt. They never lacked pain or abuse. My mother explained it to me in simple terms. "Emmy, money can't buy you love. Even rich people know that." How about that for the worst of clichés? Money can't buy you love. Of course, it was hard for me to prove or disprove that cliché since we didn't know any rich people. But we knew poor kids who were invited into our home and fed, sometimes without their parents knowing.

My parents' God delusion? You probably assumed I meant they were textbook Christians. No, they were better than Christians. They were Quakers. But they probably weren't even good Quakers, if you consider their choice of Bibles. Not the old original Anthony Purver version, or the eventual *New English Bible*, my parents were closet King James idolators. The most glowering I ever saw my father was when I came home from college and told him that I had been assigned the Thomas Jefferson Bible in a World Religion survey course. Evidently, my most serious teenage rebellion phase had been delayed until I was twenty. He huffed at me, "You said it was a 'religion' class. Deism is not a religion." I was ready for that theological debate. Jefferson was already one of my early American heroes. That was, of course, before I learned about his racial history. An early flaw of mine? Mistaking brilliant writing for goodness in the writer. I told my father that although Jefferson had omitted the miracles, he had emphasized the good works of Jesus. My father, of all people, should have appreciated that. How often had the Sterlings fed the poor, even clothed a few of them. On one memorable occasion, my father took me in tow and went to the proverbial wrong side of our small town and confronted an abusive father. Dewy knocked him down and warned him to never abuse his child again. My father, I reminded him, was the poster child for good works.

We were in our kitchen. My mother was the audience, clad in a flour-dusted apron, kneading biscuit dough. How many times over the years did I make them laugh by reminding them how much they reminded me of a Norman Rockwell painting? I was home on my Thanksgiving break. I was no longer a virgin, my secret. I had been pregnant and then not pregnant, another secret. I had already met the future great love of my life. Home for the holidays.

It was perfect timing. A cold-for-Florida winter. A goddam tableau of Yuletide postcard schtick, a Thomas Kinkade painting, without the snow, competing with Rockwell. And the smell. Remember, the past is always better than now. More than any other room, the kitchen was where I had grown up, a kitchen of cinnamon cookies and pumpkin pie and deviled eggs, a kitchen in which I had sat reading to myself while my mother cooked and my father read to her. Any serious conversation between me and my parents had happened in that kitchen. So, where else would we be debating Jefferson and the concept of good works? I was at the table, my father had risen, as if to lecture me, and my mother sat quietly until she saw him rise. And then she did the thing she always was best at…she translated my father to me. "Emmy, I think that what your father is trying to say is that Deism is not a religion because it lacks imagination. It is not a story."

My father was standing, a wooden spatula in his hand, which he pointed at my mother.

"What she said."

Forgotten was my betrayal of seven years earlier. I had hurt my father then. It was the last time. Of course, I never lost the knack of disappointing him.

If I were writing a stage adaptation of my life growing up with my parents, I would pay special attention to where each stood. An actor told me, "Where I stand on stage determines how much attention I get from the audience, how much the writer wanted me to get." The drama of my parents' life? In the beginning, my father was always center stage, front. When I was thirteen, after that scene in our kitchen, I started moving my mother to center stage. More likely, she moved herself. The omnipotent author be damned. By the time I was in my thirties, I figured out that she had really emerged when I was thirteen, when I had my first period.

I knew what had been coming. Even in the dark ages of the pre-pill Fifties, every pre-teen girl in my school knew about puberty before it happened to them. Well, not all our information was accurate. We did not have sex-ed classes. But a lot of my classmates had older sisters. I had my mother. And here's one of those hindsight mysteries. My mother never prepared me. How could someone so…smart….so wise…simply let her daughter, only child, drift in a sea of menstrual misinformation? Simply say, when questioned, "You'll be fine. We can deal with it when it happens." Then again, she was smart enough to figure out it was about to happen as soon as I snapped at my father and called him a freak. A week after it happened, she and I had "the talk." A month after that, I started spotting, as if I had been repressing everything until she finally took me under her wing and showed me how to take care of myself. The great irony would become how Dorothy Fergus and I finally became friends, with almost parallel menstrual periods, each of us packing extra pads in case the other was out. Our code? "Emmy, you got any extra white bread for lunch?" How stupid was that, as if every other girl in hearing distance didn't know what we were saying? I wasn't angry with my mother, not even disappointed, just mystified. When she died, a life of secrets and mysteries died with her.

My father tried to make me understand my mother, her seemingly casual dismissal of preparing me for the first great female initiation. I had been by her side for her final week, my father there with me, in as much pain as their God could inflict on him. More than pain in the soul, pain of the flesh. His doctor had adamantly wanted him to stay in the hospital. The less movement his body made, the easier his healing would be. His face was covered in bandages, his burned flesh facing a future of skin grafts. His hands were covered too, with just the tips of his fingers showing. But he had made sure his mouth and eyes were not covered. My mother's face was covered, but morphine dulled her pain. So, how aware was she? Did she know that her death was only days away? She seemed oblivious to me, but I knew that she was aware that my father was there. She would whisper something to him, her breath its own punishment, and he would stand and lean over her and whisper in her ears, her eyes burned away. But they could not touch. I have always wondered what they were saying to each other.

Celebrations of Life. Friends and family gather to honor and … "celebrate" … a life? We all do it. Another human ritual. We tell stories about the dead. A lot of times, funny stories. We remember the past. The joy? In a darkening hospital room, my mother had her husband and daughter. Friends had come and paid their respects for the previous week, most of them former students of my father. And then it was just me and my father, and I was desperate not to lose him too, desperate to atone for everything I had done to disappoint him. My mother was still breathing, but she was gone. I started blubbering, going back decades to that moment when I had called him a freak. And out of nowhere, I told him about being about to have my first period, how I was a mess of hormones, and how my mother had come to me after that and then started explaining life to me. If his lips had been able to smile, I would have known that he was trying to laugh. I was gushing about how I did not understand her back then, her ignoring me for so long before my cycles started. His head was nodding, and he was trying to clear his throat. He reached for me but pulled his hand back, remembering his doctor's orders.

"I remember your mother's first period."

How was I supposed to respond to that?

"Daddy, I have …"

"You must remember. I was there at her birth. I was in her life almost every day after that. I'll tell you those stories later. When she was eleven, she announced that she had just started. You know, *started.* I was sixteen, as clueless about that as every other sixteen-year-old boy in America, probably in the world."

He had stopped talking to look back at my mother. It was obvious that he had also stopped so that he could catch his breath again.

"She told me all about your first period."

Was I blushing?

"It was easy for her. Her periods. She told me how she never suffered like her friends seemed to suffer. No melodramatics for your mother. It was all natural, so she just assumed you would be the same way. Emmy, you are as much her as me, remember. She never felt like there was a need to have a big build-up. It would come. The two of you would handle it, and you would be fine. Just like her. She just assumed that you would be like her. Everything was easy for her. Unlike her own birth, your birth was easy. She used to say that loving me was easy.

Life was easy. How could I not love her? Loving her was easy."

My mother's healthy life stopped being easy when she was fifty. First, the bladder cancer. Sixty, breast cancer. As we sat there in that room, I could have reminded him of that, but I wasn't that cruel. Cancer, and then the fire.

He was sitting in a chair next to the bed, his bandaged hand resting near her hand, but not touching.

"You know, you do owe your mother one favor for sure. As much as you think she did not prepare you like you thought she should have, she shot down my suggestion as soon as it left my lips, back when she first told me."

"About my period? Seriously?"

"I suggested that she ask my mother to explain everything to you. Your grandmother knew all about those things for sure."

"Daddy!"

Sitting in his chair, he started rocking side to side, trying not to laugh. Me? I was laughing out loud, a schoolgirl laugh, and crying, and I wanted to put my arms around him and hug him, but that would have only been excruciating pain for him. So, I hugged myself, holding myself tight.

Peggy Lee? Is that all there is? Pre-period and post-period. No, no, let's not forget about menopause. My mother had been right. I was just like her. I never really "suffered" before or during my "time of the month." Quotation marks? Euphemisms? "My friend." "Aunt Flo is visiting." My mother knew them all. She even gave me a few originals to try out on my few friends at school. "Stalin is in the house" was probably too esoteric. My father, the oldest of old-school fathers, always blushed when my mother and I would let menstrual jokes flow. He would usually leave the room. My mother defended him, letting me know that he already knew all sorts of personal information about me and my body, from menstrual discharge problems to constipation. Information served up to him from her without him asking for it.

"Emmy, he just thinks that you would be uncomfortable if he were part of discussions like that, in the room with us." Sometimes my mother surprised me. She told me about his concern for me, her thinking it was quaint but unnecessary. She was wrong. I loved my father even more. He was absolutely right. But my mother always redeemed herself. Without her, I would never have become a woman who could finally look in a mirror and like what she saw. Well, until I was pushing sixty. I had survived menopause. If my menstrual periods for thirty-seven years had been calm and predictable and envied by most of my girlfriends, menopause was cosmic payback.

Mirrors? I avoid them now if at all possible.

My transformation began when I was sixteen. I might have had too much of my father in my face, but I was my mother's daughter below the neck. My version of her breasts arrived with a flourish, marked by two upgrades in bra size in that year. Something positive about my father's physiology, his six-foot-three altitude, finally made a positive contribution. I weighed the same as I did when I was fifteen, but I went from five-two to five-five, growing pains galore. A big deal to me. Soft flesh tightened up. My hips widened and my waist seemed to shrink. The odd thing about my parents' photo album…yes, only one… was that it had very few pictures of them. It was almost all me. When I turned sixteen, I wanted to see what my mother had looked like when she was sixteen. I especially wanted to see a picture of her in a bathing suit. I found her ancient high school yearbook, but it mostly had her never-a-bad-picture face, her beautiful face, and I was certainly not in those pictures, but even the full-length pictures of her in a skirt did not really reveal anything about her body. When I was sixteen, she did not have her sixteen-year-old body. When I was sixteen, always making sure my parents were not in the house, I would stand naked in front of a mirror, wondering. Most of all, I wondered what I would look like if I had my mother's face as well as her body. What my father told me as she was dying, remember? It was all so easy for her, so natural. She had grown up pretty and became beautiful, all so easy. I wanted everything to be easy for me too. Once, standing in front of my mirror, I wanted to touch myself, but I couldn't feel anything. I had to lie on my bed and close my eyes, and then I felt all I wanted.

Years ago, my writer-friend Lorrie and I were confessing our secrets to each other, major and minor. Alcohol was probably involved. She had just broken up with a long-term boyfriend and all her friends were shocked. Especially me. We thought they were a perfect couple. But Lorrie was honest. "The sex never got any better. I loved him. It was good in the beginning, but it got boring. And I knew it wasn't going to get better. It was either dump him or cheat on him. I loved him too much to do that." I either blinked like a spastic or did a spit-take, that part of my memory is still fuzzy, but I did ask the obvious question: "You gave up love for sex?" And she had a profoundly simple response: "I want both. With the same goddam man."

Lorrie and my mother and my body and sex and secrets? So, if having your first period is the first step toward becoming a woman, is losing your virginity the second step? Is desire automatic? Even before I had that first period, I was wondering about sex. Mostly the mechanics. I did my best to not imagine how my parents created me.

You have to remember, I grew up before the internet, before progressive education hit the classroom. None of us knew anything about sex except what we told each other. And we didn't know a damn thing. Sex was a game of bases, and turning second heading for third put you on the slut team. Sex was not casual, sex was not your birthright as an American teenage female. Not like today. I know, I know, this all sounds so Dark-Ages. Emmy Sterling, the cloistered nun. How ignorant were we? The most experienced girl in our class was…drumroll… Dorothy Fergus. She was still a virgin, but not for lack of trying to slide home more times than any of the rest of us had reached second. She had a reputation. But down deep I admired her. She knew how others talked about her, and she did not care.

I once taught a fiction workshop when I was in my late fifties. My students were in their twenties. Mostly female. All of them wanted what I had, books published and a career. But I had the sneaking suspicion that none of them wanted to be me. The workshop covered the usual fiction topics: character development, setting, point of view, dialogue, theme, symbolism…yadda dadda doodad…topics that were chapter headings in a hundred books about writing fiction, but supposedly more interesting if a real writer talked about them in person. "Creative Writing" is an industry in colleges now. MFA grads producing more MFA grads. I did not have an MFA, but I actually wish I had accepted an offer I had when I was fifty, my only offer, to teach full-time in a writing program in Florida. I left high school planning to be an English teacher. I was attracted to the "teaching" as much as the subject. I knew that as soon as I started teaching fiction, I was probably not going to write much of it anymore. Others could do that, do it well, but I am not a multi-tasker. When I write, I want the rest of the world to disappear. And now I take a long time to write a single page.

Wait, wait, weren't we talking about sex? But there is a connection. Sex and writing. Me and writing. Me and sex. I was teaching that workshop, thoroughly enjoying myself. My first rule of writing, my only real rule? Announced on the first day of class. You write for yourself, nobody else. Writing is not a hobby. It is a compulsion. I would say that and pause, looking at their faces. Some looked back, almost never the men, but the women who looked at me and then looked away, looking at nothing, but thinking. They understood.

By the second week of the workshop, cream began rising. Their writing revealed a lot, but I also knew them by the questions they would ask, or the comments they would make about somebody else's writing. Not the petty catty bitchy digs that workshop seminars are infamous for, but a comment that might begin with, "Have you ever considered....?" Students like that made me glad to be their teacher (as if anybody, and I mean anybody, can really teach anybody else how to write). This particular workshop had one student in a league by herself, totally original, in prose so pure that I was already thinking about sending her to my own publisher. Her name was Lorrie, and I had met her when she was barely out of her teens. That story? Meeting her? Later.

This ever happen to you? You're in a group of people...say, hypothetically, a classroom... talking back and forth, not friends, so the conversation is perhaps a bit too formal, as if everything said is filtered through your brain knowing that your words are meant to be "public" on-the-record. Perhaps a dinner party? You are having a discussion, but not with friends, especially not close friends. You are the party host, your role is to make everyone feel welcome, keep their drinks filled, and always listen for the oven timer to go off. You are multi-tasking, right? And then a guest asks a question, the answer of which is nobody's damn business. Two things can happen. You can ignore the question and start changing the subject. Or, you can do as I did in that workshop. You can make everyone disappear, everyone except the person who asked the question.

The topic was "Is personal experience fair game for a writer?" The cosmic questions of where do characters come from, their situations and conflicts. And the answer is always yes, feel free to steal from your own life. The trick is in the masking. The student was the young woman who did not need a teacher. Lorrie Knight, she of blond hair, blue eyes, and tender mercies. She had been the most gracious of any of my students toward the others. I tossed her a softball as I ended my short intro to the topic, "Any questions?"

"Emily, are you a virgin?'

Luckily, I was sitting at my desk at the front of the room. I was dizzy, too shocked to be offended. I was also speechless. Only the second week of class. A few students gasped, a few laughed nervously, divided between those who were staring at me and those who were staring at Lorrie. But here's the thing. It took a few seconds, but I recovered and waited for Lorrie to be Lorrie. I tried to be ironic and mature, forcing a smile, but fascinated by her...presumption? I had met her only a few years earlier, in a bookstore, and she had been the most retiring of wallflowers.

"And this is relevant to the topic at hand?"

Lorrie waved a wand and the class disappeared. It was just me and her, future friends for life.

"I apologize for the nitroglyceric...my own word, nitroglyceric... question, I did that to get your attention, but here's why I'm confused. I've read all your books. You know that. Like them all, loved the first one, but they all have one thing in common."

"Lorrie..."

"They're full of passion, but almost no sex."

Poof, and that was the moment we were totally alone.

"I'm just curious as to why you chose to do it that way. I mean, my

God, the scene in your last book, with the professor and his student on that bench in a university chapel, two pages of them doing it and you never mentioned a private body part, except for kissing and breathing, and I still go back and read it again and again. Same with that sex scene on a beach."

"Lorrie…"

"No, no, my question is this…you always talk about 'decisions' that a writer has to make when she writes, every word a choice, you said that, and you always choose to avoid anything graphic. But your books are full of sex as an emotion, not an act. And, come to think of it, your books have very little profanity in general. If I were a critic, I'd say that was a weakness. A few goddams and fucks here and there might actually be real human dialogue."

"Lorrie…"

"I'm sorry. I think you're a wonderful writer, you know that, I just want to understand why you make the choices you make."

The classroom was empty, wasn't it? I suppose it's possible that Lorrie and I had that conversation after class, when we were alone. The conversation is real, but the setting, the scene? Was it at a bar, after the class was over? Such intimacy. Such broken boundaries between teacher and student? But permitted if in private?

"Lorrie, have you ever read *Wuthering Heights*?"

"Emily, do you seriously have to ask that dumb question? Read it? How about three times? And I thought about that Emily and you the last time I read it, months after finishing all your books. But that Emily was writing in the 1800s in England. She gets a pass for not throwing in a cock or tit, but when she says 'I am Heathcliff' we all know what she meant. All I want for me is to write one book as good as that one."

"Do you want to know a secret, Lorrie?"

"You *are* a virgin! An old lady virgin!"

I laughed hysterically. She laughed just as much. It must have been a bar. We must have been drinking. I'm sure of that now. The workshop was over, and I was already forgetting all the other students. Lorrie would remain, is still here. When her first novel was published, she asked me to blurb it, especially since I had liked the chapters she had presented in the workshop. I told her that I'd be honored, but she might check with her agent and publisher. Praise from a certain Emily Sterling might be wasted ink, and the back cover space used for a bigger, more well-known, name than mine. Lorrie had insisted: "Maybe your blurb will be your introduction to a new generation of readers." She had said it with a straight face, the same straight face I had first seen her use when we discussed Emily Brontë two years earlier.

"Here's a secret. What you said about *Wuthering Heights,* how all you wanted was to write one book as good as that?"

She leaned in toward me, a beer glass in her right hand, a detail I am sure of now.

"I said the same exact thing when I was seventeen, even before I seriously imagined myself a writer, all I wanted was to write that book."

Straight face, she asked me, "Are you my mother?"

"Lorrie, I can be your mother or a virgin, but not both."

Straight face, "All the books you read, you never read the Bible?"

You need to meet Lorrie. I suppose you will eventually. I might be forgotten, but not by her, or you. Lorrie will be there at the end for me. Dorothy Fergus has already told me that she is going to be the master-of-ceremonies at my Celebration of Life. Lorrie will like her a lot.

"Okay, I'll take you being my mother over you being a virgin. But you still owe me a story about when you lost it."

"Oh, Lorrie, you've read all my stuff, you know I don't write funny stories."

My mother, she told me later, saw all the signs. I was miserable. I was headed into my senior year of high school, and I wanted a boyfriend. Girls uglier than me had boyfriends. What was wrong with me?

"Emmy, do we need to talk?"

My response was profoundly original.

"I don't know...do we?"

My mother arched an eyebrow, but she stayed calm.

"You know, I suppose it's common for all of us, us old people, we forget what it was like to be young. All our fuses lit, all the time."

"Mother, I have no idea what you're talking about."

"Look at the calendar on the wall, Emmy."

"Mother!"

It was a ritual. We would bicker. I would pout. She would uncharacteristically steam. And that damn calendar on the kitchen wall made an obligatory appearance.

Look at the calendar. I want you to remember this date, Emmy. Write it down in your spiral notebook. The date your mother told you...and each time she did it I had another lesson for my future self.

"I want you to remember this date, Emmy. The date I promised that I would come back to haunt you. I might not even be dead. But sometime in the future when you have your own child, especially a daughter, and she talks to you like you are about to talk to me, I want you to remember yourself now. And as you listen to your daughter, I want you to remember me. Because I'll be there in that room, thoroughly enjoying myself, watching you turn into me."

"Mother!"

"Your father and I are worried about you."

I was melting, not exploding. And I'm pretty sure that my nose was dripping snot. Did I mention that I was miserable, and my mother was my best friend and sister at that moment. I see that now, but, back then I just wanted to go to bed.

"I'm invisible, mother. I was used to being ugly. But I've got one last year of school and I might as well be invisible. I don't exist. It's worse than being ugly…"

"You are not ugly."

"Yeah, right."

She got up from the table, went to the refrigerator, and came back with a bowl of leftover chocolate cake frosting and two spoons.

"Eat."

"This will do wonders for my complexion."

"Eat."

"You were popular in high school, right?"

"Oh, belle of the ball."

"You had boyfriends, surely."

"Your father was my boyfriend."

"But he was gone when you were in high school. I know that. So, you had boys after you, wanting to date you. Surely you at least went out on dates."

"Emmy, that was so long ago, I don't remember any of that. Your father is the only man I have ever loved."

I let it slide right by, that obvious lie about not dating other boys, I was so wrapped up in my own melodrama. Just like I had always missed the casual reference to my spiral notebooks, my secret notebooks. I want her back now, I want to know the truth, connect more dots. I had my father longer, I understand him better. My mother is still ahead of me, looking back over her shoulder as I chase her, always ahead, but making sure I am still with her.

"Mother, I don't care about love. I just need a boyfriend."

She had just put a spoonful of chocolate frosting in her mouth. She paused, spoon in mouth, after I blurted out my real agenda, my low-bar agenda. How did she manage to smile with a spoon in her mouth? She pulled the spoon out slowly and then licked both sides.

"Ah, now I see the problem. First, you *want* a boyfriend. Never in your life will you *need* one. But that's okay. High school is not real life. Preparation? Maybe. Do you remember when you wanted your father to differentiate between want and need?"

At that moment, I did not. I shook my head. She was obviously disappointed.

"I should have made you look at the calendar back then."

"Mother, please, stop it. I wish I had never started this conversation."

"No, no, it's long overdue. Your father and I owe you an apology. We forgot how it was to be young. And, I suppose, we just assumed that us loving you was all you needed. All I thought I ever needed was him loving me, and then you came along and I knew that I needed you to love me too. The three of us, all we needed. I wish it was that simple."

Whose mother is like that? Talks like that? Almost fifty years ago, who can remember it all? It was a scene in my past. I'm sure it happened. The three of us, all we needed. I wrote that line in my notebook that night, but that's all I have now, proof that it happened, and if I think about that line hard enough, the rest comes back. I'm a writer. I remember things, remember?

My mother would joke about her being…not my mother…my fairy godmother. I became a restoration project for her. Magic wands and little mice and pumpkin carriages, I was Cinderella. She even started calling me Cindy, our private joke, when we went shopping. I pointed out the fairy godmother role, but she reminded me, "Dear Cindy, if you want to toss around fairy-tale references, never forget that I am like a Sleeping Beauty. Your father is the Prince."

How did I resist the obvious comeback, the adolescent but probably more accurate comeback about how their life was more Beauty and the Beast, rather than Sleeping Beauty. Years later, after she died, after he was even more beastly looking with his red leathery skin, my father would make the comparison himself. And he would laugh.

My restoration did not take all that long. My mother admitted that she and my father had not paid attention to my appearance, my choices for clothing or hairstyle. As she said, "As long as you were clean and presentable, and didn't wear holey clothes, how you looked was your decision." This made perfect sense to me, since they themselves were oblivious to fashion or even modernity. My father, in particular, never had more than three dress shirts at any one time, never more than two ties, and maintained a pair of black and brown dress shoes forever, with matching socks. A small selection of casual clothes. His only indulgence? He expected a new pair of pajamas every Christmas, a shopping task that my mother shared with me, another ritual. As for a formal suit, he had one, his Sunday suit, which he insisted was to be kept for his funeral. When the time came, I ignored him.

We had a week before my senior year began. First, my hair. It was long and straight and dark. It became shorter, wavier, with a tinge of a tint. I wanted blond. My mother tapped me on the head and said, "Trust me, you do not. Blond is cheap. My daughter is not cheap." Next came a new wardrobe. I knew what I wanted, but was afraid to say it. My mother knew, "You want to be noticed, right?" Of course, I did, and she knew who I wanted to notice me. For the first time in my budding vampiness, my new clothes covered me up while at the same time showing my curves. They were not tight. My mother made the simple observation, "Emmy, they actually fit you. That makes a difference." She even allowed me a prehistoric version of a mini-skirt.

My father was not pleased.

The most surprising thing? My mother took me to a dentist and had my teeth cleaned. I had always been a religious brusher, with a great fear of becoming toothless like my grandmother was becoming, but I had never had my teeth scraped and polished. It was a "moment" for sure, the dentist handing me a mirror and me seeing…a different mouth, different teeth. I think my mother was as astonished as I was. "Let me see you smile," she said. A small gesture? I had never thought about it, how to smile, and do it without trying. I had never smiled with my mouth open, a revelation to me. Seventeen years of a smile that nobody noticed. A tight-lipped repressed smile. Me, repressed? Shocking, right?

The last transformation was the most delicate. I was introduced to makeup. Sunday afternoon, the day before the first day of class, a few hours after sitting through another one of those austere Quaker meetings, my mother put on her kitchen apron and sat me down at the table. The first thing she did was tell me the new rules.

"Emmy, none of this is magic. It is work. What you want is to be something that is not natural to you." (A lot of positive reinforcement, you would agree?) "It's not one and done. Your hair grows, roots show, teeth turn yellow if you don't keep them polished, your complexion will plague you if you do not wash your face and keep sugar away from you. Speaking of sugar, look at all the flabby children around you. They eat too much and waste too much. You can get flabby too, if you do not watch what you eat. Your clothes will fade and fray, and you will be replacing them all your life. This, today…," holding up a mascara brush, "… is the most self-indulgent vice I can teach you. But you want to be noticed, you want to be…"

I interrupted her. "I just want to be happy."

And there was the look that both my parents had for as long as they lived. A look that was a sigh, which always led to them saying something that I never understood, until they were gone.

"I'm sorry to hear that."

"Mother, that is mean."

Another look. My father would be home in an hour. Mother and daughter across from each other in a kitchen. I knew it was time to shut up. My mother had never had an insecure moment in her life when it came to her looks, I was sure of that, so how could she understand me? When I was in the fourth grade, my teacher stood in front of the class and told everyone about meeting my mother for the first time, their first parent/teacher conference, and my teacher was gaga. "Boys and girls, I just met Emmy Sterling's mother this morning and she is such a lovely woman, and so beautiful." It was all true, of course. My mother was that, lovely and beautiful, and my teacher was smitten, as most people were when they first met my mother. Meeting her was a surprise. But I knew the subliminal message. I closed my eyes as she talked, and I knew that everyone in class was turning to look at Emmy Sterling and they were thinking: *Her* mother? Emmy's mother? Beautiful?

"I'm sorry. I meant to say that it is sad to me that these are the things that you think will make you happy. Am I forgiven?"

Forgive her? I was tearing up, disappointed in myself for failing to meet some standard of hers that I never knew existed. I sniffled, and nodded, and she motioned for me to lean forward.

"You have my skin tone, so not much to do in that department. No need for a lot of powder or rouge. Just keep yourself hydrated for the rest of your life. No big deal, eh? Your eyebrows should have been trimmed five years ago. Too wild. I can trim them down and pluck open some more space between them, make them match each other, but you will be trimming for the rest of your life. Don't say I didn't warn you. And we need to darken them up just a little. Now, your nose..."

The Nose of Gibraltar, isn't that what Dorothy Fergus had called it when we were sophomores?

"Your nose is a bit too big, but your father is right. You have the nose of a good Roman woman. If it still bothers you when you are thirty, go ahead and break our hearts and get a nose job. Until then, we need a diversion. And that will be your eyes."

After fifteen minutes of brow plucking and trimming, eyeliner, mascara, and some eyelash work, my mother leaned back and surveyed her work. "I'll show you how to do all this for yourself later. Like I said, it's all up to you for the rest of your life, if it matters all that much to you in the long run. And now for the crème de le crème. And then my work here will be done. I've worked on the outside of you, Emmy, betraying every Quaker bone in my body. But, never forget the inside, where the good stuff ought to be."

She held up a tube of lipstick. I was almost giddy. I wrote about this moment in a book forty years later. A mother and daughter, and how the daughter felt like she was being immersed in some sort of baptismal font, to be drenched and then arise soaked and saved. Something like that, a transformational moment. A bit overwritten, but I used the passage as part of my public reading while on tour for that book. I even talked about the "inspiration" for the passage. Audiences always want to know your inspirations. But I never wrote about, or told anybody (except for the married man who knew all my secrets) about the most memorable moment of that afternoon with my mother. Holding that tube of lipstick, a few hours after sitting in a Quaker Hall communing with her and my father's invisible God, a surly and disbelieving me at their side, my mother said, "You know, Emmy, I would sell my soul to have your lips."

The most beautiful woman in God's universe wanted some part of me? Envied me? My mother? How many times had they told me, never convincing me, that I was beautiful? I felt worse when they would say it because I knew they were either lying to me or lying to themselves. But there I was then, my mother wanting something I had, to make her more than beautiful, to make her perfect.

She squinted at those lips, holding the lipstick a few inches away from them.

"The right color is important. And you will want two shades. One for day. One for night. And it has to be spread just right. Your lips are naturally puffy, but they have distinct borders. You want your lipstick to outline what is already there, not make it look bigger."

I could feel the lipstick rubbing across my lips as she spoke, and I marveled at how she seemed to have some sort of lipstick philosophy, so much thought put into its application. Were other women so precise? My mother, who seldom wore lipstick, knew all its secrets.

"We have time to try other colors if this is not the one we need."

We?

"Ta-da! Now, take this tissue and press your lips on it. Do not pull the tissue out until you open your mouth again. I know, common sense, but there is an important lesson here. Smears are not your friend."

I did as instructed, and then she held up the tissue, as if I was supposed to approve the result. I was spellbound with the emblem I had created, the art, my lips. Had they always been there, like that? My mother was pleased with my reaction, pleased with her work.

"So, Emmy, has a boy kissed you yet?"

"Mother! Of course not!"

"Daughter, why are we doing all this? I recall something about you wanting to be happy, wanting a boyfriend, and I hate to break the news to you, but a boyfriend will want a kiss. And after that first kiss, which I suspect he is going to like a lot, he will want more, and that's when you and I are going to have a serious conversation."

"Mother!"

She was thoroughly enjoying my discomfort.

"All that's in the future, but I suspect sooner than you think. For now, go try on that new skirt and blouse we bought yesterday."

She followed me to my room and watched me dress, and then she motioned for me to follow her to her and my father's bedroom. At the door, she told me to close my eyes. She took my hand and led me inside to stand in front of the full-length mirror.

"Open your eyes…and smile."

I wasn't beautiful, but I would never be ugly again.

Beauty—be not caused—It Is—
Chase it, and it ceases—
Chase it not, and it abides—
(Johnson Edition, 516)

You're right. I read it all again. First draft requires second. Too much of the whiny woe-is-me Emmy Sterling. My life was more than a nonexistent God raining on all my parades. You reminded me: writing is a matter of decisions. Not just which words, but which scenes. Let the reader interpret.

Until my senior year, I was unhappy in high school. Surprise, surprise, most kids are unhappy in high school. Flashes of fun, sure, but always the sense of inferiority. Somebody was always more popular, prettier, smarter, with richer parents, and green-lighted for adult success. Me, you? We were the silent surly majority. My unhappiness? Self-imposed, sometimes justified, but always transitory. I loved my parents, loved being at home, loved reading. I even loved high school football games. I was unpopular, but never ignored. I was the daughter of a teacher. My father taught Latin and History. I suppose the assumption was that if you made his daughter unhappy you would still probably end up in one of his classes eventually. The smart thing to do was simply leave her alone. It was a small school. So, I was unhappy and unpopular and also class Secretary for three straight years. I was smart. Secretary sounded like a job for a smart girl. Toss that bone to Emmy Sterling. President and Vice-President of the class? Ah, the domain of the popular boys who almost always wore a letter-jacket. It was tradition. It was a million years ago. All this makes sense to me now because I still have a distant friend left over from high school, a friend who has read all my books and who buys them by the boatload for gifts to other people. That friend writes all the time, email makes that easy now, and comes to see me at least twice a year. I complain about high school and she metaphorically slaps me and reminds me of alternative facts. Or, as she likes to say, "the rest of the story." Yes, she loved Paul Harvey too. She was a friend, but she was not my best friend.

Mysteries of my life? How did Dorothy Fergus and I become best friends? Was it simply my cosmetic and sartorial makeover? I was no longer ugly, so perhaps I could join her world? I wonder if she will like how I have re-created her in this story. I know she liked how her "character" in my first novel was portrayed. Over the years, we have laughed about everything I have already told you here, and most of the scenes from our past that I'll use are also comedy gold. All except the night she saved me from total self-hatred. We never laugh about that. It was a blood-bonding moment for both of us, complete with literal blood.

I suppose it all began on the first day of my senior year. I walked into the giant lobby of our school, lined with pictures of athletic events, trophy cases galore, and even some pictures of notable graduates, our alumni Hall of Fame. I'm in that Hall of Fame now, but my high school is gone. Demolished. Late-twentieth-century steel and glass and plastic architecture replaced wood and brick from the early twentieth. I was in the new building only once, to be inducted into that Hall of Fame. I'm the only member of my class to be on the wall. Dorothy nominated me.

Every day at the old school began in that lobby as buses emptied the distant students and cars dropped off everybody else. I always arrived with my father, and had usually gone in the back entrance restricted only to faculty, but he insisted that I go through the front door on that first day. He dropped me off at the curb and then drove off, leaving me to the barbarians I assumed were waiting for me, led by Dorothy Fergus. My father was proud of his wife's magic.

"Knock 'em dead, Emmy."

Any confidence I had had a half hour earlier, a minute earlier, disappeared as I opened the door to enter the lobby. Inside were a hundred throbbing humanoids, notebooks and textbooks in hand, juiced up on Coca-Colas and candy bars, gathered to witness a virgin sacrifice. The virgin entered. And nobody noticed. The virgin walked slowly through the crowd. Nobody cared.

My mother's magic had failed. I was still invisible. And then a nightmare spotted me and weaved itself through the crowd, parting bodies as it approached, those bodies turning and then following behind it. I was Frankenstein's monster, and the mob with pitchforks and torches was circling me. Virgins and monsters, I'll edit out all the mixed metaphors later.

Dorothy had found me.

"Fuck me running. Emmy Sterling?"

Was this what actually happened? Mostly. When Dorothy and I talked about it years later, she agreed about the facts, just not the description. We were sitting on my beach-house deck at two in the morning, a bottle of Grey Goose opened just for the occasion. I had called her the day before and told her about my diagnosis. She drove four hundred miles that night and knocked on my door at midnight, announcing, "You owe me a drink. And you are not allowed to do your usual martyr routine. I hated that in high school."

Getting old, were we the same persons we knew back then. Older, hopefully wiser, the same? I love Dorothy now. I hated her in the past. Same person? I told her how much I was afraid of her back then.

She raised her glass to give herself a toast. "You weren't the only one. I was a bitch for sure. Bitch with a heart of gold. Jake says I still am."

"I'm so glad you married him. You were lucky."

"I was lucky? Emmy, you ever heard of manna from heaven? I was pussy from heaven. Jake is the lucky one. But, yeah, you're right, I do like him, even after all these years."

We talked about the past and present, but not the future. That would have to be a daytime sober conversation.

"Well, this is interesting. But just remember, you're still a retarded turd."

I was saved by the first-class bell. A hundred teenagers scattered in a few seconds, off to torment or to be tormented. Dorothy? She turned to go to class, but then turned back and pointed her finger at me. "We need to talk." She turned again and went a few more steps, and then turned around again to mouth at me, "Returd." And then she grinned.

I would spend the rest of my life processing Dorothy Fergus, but I could even tell at that moment in a lobby surrounded by her minions,

I was making progress in her world. The next day, she showed up at school with her dark hair dyed a bombshell blond. Dorothy was again the center of attention, especially among the boys. Me, I had been a one-day wonder. But I was still not the Emmy I was the previous year.

My senior, final, year began with a bang. Even my parents were impressed. My classes were easy, or so it seemed. I was still class Secretary, but I also got elected President of the Future Teachers Club. I was in the National Honor Society. Homecoming Committee? Call Emmy. School newspaper…Editor. However, my expanding status did have limits.

I told Dorothy that I was going to join the Drama Club, in which she was not only the President but also The Star. We were in the cafeteria, scooting our lunch trays along the counter as we were being served by elderly women in plastic bonnets. She was ahead of me, her back to me as I casually dropped the bomb.

"I was thinking about getting in the Drama Club. Just to…."

She did not turn around. She did not speak. Still, she did not move. The line was stopped. She just stood there.

"Dorothy?" I whispered.

She did not move. I could hear murmuring behind me. The natives were restless and hungry. Was it obvious to me then, or am I much smarter in hindsight? We were at a crossroads, and I chose the right road.

"Then again, probably not. I've got a lot on my plate." I said it and looked at the plate on my tray, a plate full of vegetable side dishes, me and Dorothy in the food line, her ahead of me.

She started moving again, but she did not look back, nor did she speak.

Was I getting smarter, more intuitive, or just luckier? I wasn't the class spook anymore. I was having a great first week, and then I met

Miss Randall, the new English teacher.

I grew up surrounded by books, but none of them were new. I don't mean that I was surrounded mostly by old books. Okay, the books my father inherited from his mother, the ones he had read growing up, those were old. My grandmother dealt with poor people all the time, and when money was not there to be fetched, a new mother would be told that she owed Rose Sterling a book. But my grandmother eventually had her own mythology. Not only would she get one book at birth, but a book every year on that child's birthday, a reverse gift. I never understood it, the homage she was paid, how her services created some sort of lifetime ritual from those she served. I had witnessed the ceremony a few times myself as I was growing up. A mother, seldom a mother and father together, would come to her house with a book, a child tagging along. The times I remember, that child was either bored or terrified, feelings I empathized with. The inexplicable thing? I never saw my grandmother read a book. She merely collected them, tokens of some mysterious obligation she felt was owed to her. She was gracious, as best she could be, when accepting the book, more gracious when the boy or girl child handed it to her, but she did not read them. Nor did my grandmother give gifts. Period. Not even to her son, except for the final dispensation of her worldly possessions.

My mother brought her own old books to the marriage too, and those were more interesting in one important regard. My mother's family was poor, and my mother was farmed out early for babysitting jobs and errand work. Small-change payments, but also her introduction to homes with books. The books of hers that I grew up with? I began to notice that some of them were inscribed, but not to her. My future mother had been a thief.

It was after her second bout of cancer, but before the fire, when she was fading away right before the eyes of me and my father, when she told me the story of her private library. It was so not the mother I knew. But a much better story than anything I could imagine. When I heard it the first time, I thought I had a logical question.

"I can understand, sort of, you taking them, Mother. But after you read them, why not simply sneak them back to the homes where you got them? You got them out without anybody noticing, why not return them? Or just go tell the truth and apologize. Never steal, never steal, isn't that what you and Daddy always told me?"

My mother and father, always confusing me. The "sense" of their universe sometimes made no sense to me.

"Emmy, after I read them, they were mine."

"But some of them were inscribed to other people. Those were personal books, gifts to somebody else. You shouldn't have kept those."

"Emmy, you know how you know a book has been loved?"

"Mother, you are getting weird, I know that."

"All the inscribed books I took, they had never been read. Stiff un-cracked spines, pristine un-smudged pages, not a dog-ear in sight, no paper bookmarks anywhere between the pages. They had not been read. They were unloved. I read them. I loved them. They were mine."

My father was in the room. I turned to him. Surely the most upright man I had ever known would have sided with his upright daughter against her obviously tilted mother.

"Daddy, have you been listening to..."

He was in a rocking chair in the corner, reading a book. He turned to me.

"I'm sorry. Listening?"

My mother was dying. Her cancer treatments were laying waste to her body without curing it. I was in my late thirties. I was seeing my own future, but I did not know I was seeing it then.

"Did you know that my mother, your wife, was a book thief?"

He closed his book. I wish I knew now what he was reading then. It would be an important detail in a story I still want to write. He tilted his head to one side, looked at me and then at my mother, whose eyes were closed, and said, "Of course. I helped her."

In a world of cosmic suffering, the good dying young, the evil prospering, I was trying to remember a line from a movie I loved, something about "…the problems of three little people don't amount to a hill of beans in this crazy world…." Those lines. Me and my father and my mother were three little people. Stolen books didn't matter. Outside of that room, at that moment, nothing mattered. Just us, that's all that mattered to me.

"Those books we read to you. Sometimes even before you were born. Your mother told me that she knew when she took them that she would keep them for you, whoever you were, whenever you arrived. I suppose that you grew up on stolen words. You're a lucky girl, Emmy. We're both lucky."

Stolen words. I need more time to write that book. Stretch the metaphor. Stolen words. I received stolen words. I was part of the crime. Possession of stolen property. I aided and abetted. How about Child of Thieves? I need a title for everything. If my mother had stolen forks and knives and spoons, would I have a book titled Sterling Silverware?

Yes, you're right. I have to stop. Trivial, to turn that moment in my past into trivial word games. I'm wasting time, and right now I have more words than time.

Eventually, my parents started paying for books. A high school teacher's salary did not buy trips to Europe, but, in addition to a morning newspaper, it bought subscriptions to *Life, Look, The Satur-*

day Evening Post, and *Reader's Digest.* Best of all, it bought the *Reader's Digest Condensed Books* series. Abridged versions of novels and non-fiction, all in one volume, published four times a year. I loved those books. The novels were usually bestsellers from the previous year, and probably had the really salacious parts edited out. They were wonderful mid-brow writing, but I did not care. I had already read almost every other book in my parents' stock. I needed more.

I always finished the entire volume before the next one arrived. And the variety. Excuse my name-dropping here, but just from the Summer 1960 volume I got to read: *The Lovely Ambition* (Mary Ellen Chase), *Trustee from the Toolroom* (Nevil Shute), *The Leopard* (Giuseppe di Lampedusa), *Village of the Stars* (Paul Stanton), and *To Kill a Mockingbird.* The fact that most of these are forgotten today is not important. All of us are going to be forgotten. You too. Four volumes a year, at least four books to a volume, sixteen-plus for the year, and those stayed on our bookshelves at home. The public library books had to be returned, but at least two a week were checked out by me.

The point of my bragging here? I might not have been pretty, I might have had parents that my friends thought were weirder than I thought they were weird, but I was hot shit when it came to reading. Zero self-confidence about my looks, no lack of hubris about my brain. A book-slinger with more notches on my belt than anybody around me, probably even my parents, who had a head start on me. I was mediocre in math, fascinated but confused by science, but I could read and write like a prodigy. And I was progressively less and less humble. I was sure that I had read more books than any of my teachers.

Miss Randall?

Right there on her syllabus: Miss Randall. Did she even have a first name? Back before the internet, rules were rules. Nobody called a teacher by his or her first name. Hell, teenage store clerks never called any adult customer by their first name. But at least everybody had a first name. Everybody except Miss Randall. After my first class with her, I immediately cornered my father and asked him about her first name.

"That's a good question."

"Daddy, do you call her Miss Randall?

"Well, ask me that after I meet her."

Miss Randall had been an emergency hire by the school. A week before school was supposed to start, our old…and I mean *old*…senior English teacher had quit. I would not miss her. She had been easy to ignore, and she always gave me A's, sometimes, I was sure, without even reading my papers.

Ere I saw Elba? Ere I met Miss Randall? I walked into the classroom and she was sitting behind her desk, seemingly oblivious to me and the horde behind me. I sat in my favorite spot in every classroom, back row corner seat. Nobody behind me. For some reason, I had always hated voices behind me.

How old was she? Add that to the question about her first name. Married? She wore a ring, but not a wedding band. Where was she from? Not from anywhere near us, but her accent had a soft Southern lilt. I loved her voice from the very beginning. Was she pretty? No, not really. She did have smooth pale skin. That was pretty, I suppose. She had reddish-blond hair, pulled back and tied in a ponytail. Is all that supposed to matter? I was still in my shallow-soul phase. Looks mattered to me. I looked at her my first day in class and wondered what my mother could do with her. Eventually, my mother did meet her and I later joked about her doing a makeover for Miss Randall, but she shut me down immediately. "Emmy, there is not a single thing I would change about her."

It all began when she called roll that first day.

From Terry Abbott to Gary Smith, she finally got to me.

"Emmy Sterling?"

I raised my hand.

She stared at me and she did that one thing she became famous for by the end of the year. She put her ring and middle finger together, right hand, and used those two fingers to seemingly brush away an invisible speck on her cheek. Two strokes. And then she would speak. Eventually, we all learned to pay more attention to what was about to be said.

"Emmy Sterling." Not a question anymore, simply a fact. "Yes, I've heard much about you."

I did not quite freeze in my seat, but I'm sure I must have blinked. Eddie Morris and Chuck Warren were in my class, two of the biggest smart-ass boys in school, a problem for any teacher, and I was sure that they were headed to prison after...if...they graduated. Two boys who never missed an opportunity to take someone else's discomfort and turn it into a joke. If the past were prologue, Miss Randall's comment would have been a perfect setup for them. Eddie and Charles were mute. The entire damn class was mute, probably waiting for me to respond. I was mute. Was it her lilting Southern voice? Did I detect... imagine... something that was not really in her voice? A threat? Simple curiosity?

Leaving her knowledge of me hanging in the air, she went on to Carol Thomas and ended with Charles Yates. She had our attention, and then she got out of her chair and came around to the front of her desk and stood, syllabus in hand. She was a giant.

A giant? Do you think I've slipped into some sort of Magical Realism? Poetic license? Metaphor? Not really. Miss Randall was six feet tall. Not a giant, but taller than anybody in front of her, including Eddie Morris and Chuck Warren. Dorothy Fergus was in her next class, and years later, pre-cancer for me and during a trial separation phase for her, vodka indulgence for both of us, we talked about Miss Randall and we both agreed…if we had been teenage lesbians back then we would have both fallen in love or lust or something with Miss Randall, even though she wasn't, for all we ever knew, a lesbian. It was then that I confessed to Dorothy that I was probably one of the few people in that school who ever saw Miss Randall with her hair unbound. Dorothy spun around in her deck chair, almost spilling her drink.

"I always wondered about that. Tell me, was she…was she…a goddess? Were you alone with her?"

I told her the truth, and she was disappointed. Miss Randall and my parents had become friends. I mean, seriously, how could those three people not become friends? She would come to our house for dinner. I was alone with Miss Randall only in a classroom.

"But, yes, she was a goddess. A fair-skinned blond Nordic Amazon goddess."

I've always been puzzled that Dorothy, after finding out that Miss Randall had been to my house many times, had never asked me if I had ever learned Miss Randall's first name.

She stood in front of the class and told us what was going to happen for the rest of the semester.

"We'll use the Norton Anthology listed here…" shaking her syllabus, "…and which are stacked over there," using the syllabus as a pointer aimed at a table to her left. "These are not my choices, but I have to use what was already ordered by the woman I replaced. I'll be able to choose my own books for the Honors Course in the Spring."

I was already seeing myself in that class.

"I did get permission to add a few novels of my own choosing, and I'll announce those as soon as I confirm that the school will buy them. Sorry, *Peyton Place* is not on the list."

Everybody else was clueless. I had read the book two years earlier. I had hidden it from my parents, one of many that they never knew about. I assumed that Miss Randall was joking. But she had paused as she dropped that title, paused and looked all around the class, gauging her audience's potential for understanding future ironic references, and then she looked at me. She had been in my universe perhaps ten minutes? I was trying to pin her down. Then the creepiest of feelings. What if she were not joking? The "much" she had heard about me? I was seventeen, "too smart for my britches," as my mother would tease me. Was it possible that the woman in front of me was capable of crossing all sorts of educational red lines? More than that, I really wanted to know what she thought of that book.

"So, we'll probably stick with *The Scarlet Letter*."

I was let down. I had read about, and dismissed, Hester Prynne a year earlier. I made myself a mental note to ask Miss Randall if I could read something different. I was obviously still in my smarty-britches phase.

"But, first up, poetry. And your first assignment. Look through the table of contents for that section in your anthology. We'll start discussing the first ten poems tomorrow. But the real assignment is for next Monday. I want you to go find a poem that is not in the book, a poem that means something to you, and I want you to bring a copy to class next week and be prepared to read it out aloud and then discuss what you think it means and why you chose it."

Even without looking at the book, I had three in mind.

"Emmy Sterling."

Where did that come from? I was hiding in the back, paying full attention, but hiding.

"Emmy, in your case, you cannot use any Emily Dickinson poem."

Was that when it happened, the moment I started to fall in love with her, but not realizing it?

My mother asked me the standard parent questions when I got home late that afternoon.

"How was your first day of class? Your teachers? Pick your college major yet? Any boys ask you for a date? Nominated for Homecoming Queen?"

Throwaway, teasing questions, tossed out as she stood washing dishes in the sink, her back to me, wearing the apron that she and my father shared.

"Mother, it was odd. I met somebody very strange today."

That got her attention. She turned around.

"Boy...girl? A new student?"

"A new teacher."

Hands quickly wiped, the apron off, she went to the refrigerator, pulled out two half-pint cartons of chocolate milk, and sat at the table.

"We have an hour before your father gets home. Tell me all about it."

An hour later, as we heard my father's out-of-tune Ford Falcon pull into the driveway, my mother was beaming.

"We must have Miss Randall for dinner. Won't that be fun?"

"But, Mother, don't you think it's weird? Her knowing so much about me. Not letting me choose Dickinson to read?"

"Said the girl who dressed as Emily Dickinson for Halloween? Who drops Dickinson lines at a hat. That girl? Emmy, if your father is correct, and we know that he is always correct, you do have a bit of a reputation at school. This Miss Randall is not a mindreader. She probably just had another teacher warn her about you."

"Warn?"

"Go change clothes, Emmy. Help me with dinner and then we'll see what your father thinks."

"Mother!"

"And one other thing. More important than your spooky new teacher, who I'm betting will become your favorite. Did anybody notice your new look?"

Was I so easily distracted all the time back then? Oblivious teenager? Kitten chasing a laser beam? Smarter now? I immediately forgot Miss Randall and gushed nonstop about how I thought that I had made a good impression on everyone, especially Dorothy Fergus. How I thought my senior year was going to be my best. I was so very uncharacteristically optimistic, and my mother was, seemed to me, sublimely happy for me.

Hindsight? To be shared with Dorothy decades later. It was only after I went away to college that I realized that Miss Randall was the only dinner guest we ever had. I was always there, and I was almost always silent. They made no effort to include me in any conversation, but my feelings were not hurt. They talked about everything I cared about and even some things I did not care about. I was indifferent to politics, but they seemed to actually care who won the Presidency in 1960. Evidently, Miss Randall had a television. We did not. She invited my parents to come over to her place and watch the debates that were being planned. How did I sense that I was not invited? I did not care. Kennedy or Nixon? Irrelevant to me.

My world was expanding in other ways for sure. I was spending more and more time at school than I had in the past, more activities, more classroom work, even more friends. Transitioning? I was going to graduate in 1961 and leave home. I was more and more excited.

Still, I had to do that final year. I was still an un-kissed virgin.

If I was indifferent to most of my classes in the past, and my grades reflected it, one message was drummed into me by my mother and my school counselor and even Miss Randall: My GPA needed to come up. Colleges paid attention. My father? If I was happy, he was happy. I had the feeling that he would have been happy if I stayed at home for the rest of my life. My mother and Miss Randall had my future all planned for me. I was going to be a teacher. I did not rebel. I wanted to be a teacher anyway. I mean, seriously, was I supposed to run for President or own my own company?

I paid attention in all my classes, actually crammed for tests, and still had a social life. I even had my first kiss, a miserably disappointing moment in life, not worth writing about, and I never told my mother about it. It was after the last football game of the year, at a house party, the first time I had ever been invited to one, and my parents extended my curfew to midnight. I appreciated their gesture, and I appreciated the invitation from Dorothy, but I was obviously the odd duck. I did not have a date. Luckily for me, as I was assured by Dorothy, at least a dozen guys there were also solo acts. I could get lucky, right? I did not get lucky. I got Jason Jordan in a walk-in closet. For those last few seconds, as his head was descending toward me, I actually thought, *This is it.* He had talked sweetly up until then, telling me that I was pretty, which even then I took as perfunctory window dressing for romance, but he was himself cute in his own way, so perhaps magic was possible? His lips found mine in the dark, a feat all by itself, and I waited. Was this sex? Passion? I felt nothing. His hand found my bottom. My hand found his hand and yanked it off me. The moment had come and gone. Jason disengaged lips, hands, and bodily presence, and left me in the closet, where I groped in the dark, only to find a line of coats and shirts. I wanted to cry. I needed something to cry into. As I stood there sniffling, some soft sleeve of something in my hands, about to be used as a handkerchief, Dorothy opened the door and stepped inside and shut the door behind her.

"How was it?"

I told her the unromantic truth, and then realized that she had known what was going to happen before I did.

"Well, that asshole owes me fifty cents."

"Dorothy?"

"I gave him a half-dollar and told him to give you the best first kiss of a girl's life. I've kissed him before. He's not bad."

"Dorothy!" Evidently my teen years, as my mother told me later, were a series of names followed by exclamation points, as if life was nothing but surprise or anger or disappointment. Her description. I did not see a pattern, but that night in the closet my first reaction was surprise, and then anger, and then…laughter?

"You paid him to kiss me?"

"Look, you needed to get it out of the way. It's no big deal."

"Except that I'm going to be emotionally scarred for life."

"Oh, get over yourself. I'm the drama queen of this school."

"No, you're the bitch of this school!"

I was trying to be angry, I really was, but it hit me there in that closet with Dorothy, one of those epiphanies that are talked about but seldom actually experienced. My memory is shaky now about a lot of things, my writer's perfect memory, but I can still try to imagine how I looked at that moment, try to conjure up and re-experience how I must have felt and looked there in the dark with Dorothy, my head shaking and my eyes wide open, suddenly thinking…*this is a story*. I had been collecting stories all my life, but that was only the second time I actually thought that I would be telling them later. I want more than to remember that epiphany now, I want to see me again, but I was literally in the dark back then, so all I have is my imagination.

"Bitch or drama queen, same to me, retard, but just remember...I am your bitch, and you are mine."

We laughed then, and we actually hugged each other. We still laugh about it now. An hour later, Dorothy and Jake drove me home, an hour before curfew, and then they went parking. I went inside my house, finding my father in his pajamas at the kitchen table doing a crossword puzzle. Another of his baffling rituals to me, doing crossword puzzles late at night with only two big glowing candles on the table, like he was Abe Lincoln in a log cabin. How could he see all that small print? It was more of our history, me going out at night and coming home to find my mother upstairs asleep, but my father was always waiting for me. No interrogation, no suspicions. No electric lights.

"Have a good time, Emmy?"

"It was lame. I asked Dorothy to bring me home."

"You win tonight?"

I answered the question I heard.

"You know, I think I did. I think I finally have a best friend."

My father nodded and looked back down at his crossword.

"Did we win the football game too?"

Here I am now, almost fifteen-hundred pages of fiction in print, my so-called career. My mother and father were the first three hundred and forty. I have more stories to tell, but only a few are still important. I need to turn Miss Randall into a character. And then I need to find her. She's dead, but I want to find her grave. I still want her to be proud of me.

She once described herself to me as "an acquired taste." And slowly, casually, she added, “just like you.”

It’s all tied together. How did Dorothy and I become each other’s bitches? How did I become a writer? Both happened because of Miss Randall. As he lay dying, my father asked me if I had ever found her again, Miss Randall. Still looking, I told him. And I told him about that first kiss and Dorothy and Miss Randall and me becoming a writer, all the …ripples? His response? *Omnes viae Romam ducunt.* I did not understand him. In his last few weeks, it was very difficult for him to speak at all, his throat permanently seared by the fire. In those weeks, his words were slurred and breathy, disjointed from each other. In the end, he was silent, but his eyes still sparkled. It had always been there, that sparkle in his eyes, and it must have been there from the first moment my mother was old enough to see and remember him as the boy with sparkling dewy eyes. His face had always distracted others from those eyes, me too, but not her. At the end, in his last days at my beach house, his lips were almost useless, but he had one struggling hand, and he wrote it for me, barely legible: *Omnes viae Romam ducunt.* My high school knowledge of Latin was long gone, but I did recognize one word.

“*Romam*? Rome?”

He struggled to raise his hand and point at me, and I thought he was simply confirming my intuition. But he kept pointing at me, as if tapping his finger in air.

“I am…Rome?”

At that moment, daughter with dying father, I needed my mother to come back for one last time, to translate my father for me.

Back in class for the second week of school, I was prepared for my poetry recitation. If the new teacher was trying to intimidate me, show me who was in charge, I was on a counter-offensive. I chose

Andrew Marvell's "To His Coy Mistress." She had asked us to choose a poem we liked and to explain why. I did not like the Marvell poem all that much, but I wanted to call her bluff. She had dropped *Peyton Place* into the mix, I was coming back with seduction, as if I actually understood the concept of seduction. I had even asked my father to help me analyze it, and he supplied a handy phrase for me...*carpe diem*. He also questioned my choice, but, as usual, he let me walk off my own plank.

"Seize the damn day," as I bragged to Dorothy before class started. I was ready to go to jousting with Miss Randall. Dorothy was in Miss Randall's next class. She had chosen a Dickinson poem. Actually, she had called me the night before and asked for a suggestion. Her poetry range was somewhat narrow. I thought it was odd, her calling me. We were not friends. She had never called me at home before. I told her to go with "I'm Nobody! Who are you?" It was the ideal teenage angst poem. An hour later, she had called me back and was ecstatic. "Emmy, I love this poem. Love it. I owe you a favor." If Miss Randall had let me do Dickinson, as I wanted, "I'm Nobody" would not have been my choice, but it was perfect for somebody like Dorothy.

Class began. Miss Randall asked for a volunteer to go first. Nobody raised their hand, not even me. I was ready, of course, but I wanted her to come to me. We had fifty-five minutes. Twenty-two students. She announced that we would only do five readings a day, and then she would lecture about the poems in the book. She called on Terry Abbott, then Billy Cook... and then I realized that she was going in alphabetical order. I was let down. It would be Thursday before she got to me. I tuned out. And then, five names down, I heard my name.

"Emmy Sterling, I think we have time for you today."

I was slumping in the back of the room, but came to attention as everyone in class turned to look at me.

"Why don't you come up front and talk to us?"

Everybody else had been allowed to read from their desks. My brain turned to butterfly mush. I hated the thought of standing in front all those kids who had ignored me, laughed at me, resented me for all those years. I could imagine myself on a stage, acting as somebody else, as hammy as Dorothy Fergus, probably not as good as her, but I could "act," I was sure, but Miss Randall wanted me to be myself. How had I avoided this moment in all the years before? Surely, I had done this sometime somewhere. I figured it out later. It had not been the fear of being in front of my class. I actually *had* done that before. It was being in front of Miss Randall. The game had started and I was already behind.

"Yes ma'am," I said, more in control of my voice than my emotions.

She was sitting in a chair at the side of the room as I began.

"For my poem, I have chosen…" and I was off. I ignored the laughs of Eddie Morris and Chuck Warren when they heard the word "mistress," making myself a mental note to see how they reacted when I talked about breasts. Five minutes later, after reading the poem and offering a secondhand opinion from a book I had read, I exhaled. And then Miss Randall started removing bricks in my wall.

"An interesting choice."

And then silence. I waited.

"Why did you choose it?"

"You said to choose something that we liked."

"Why do you like this poem? Your presentation wasn't clear about that."

I hated her. She had been gracious to all the others, even as lame as they were. She had been encouraging, thanking them. For me, the tone of her voice was absolutely neutral. Surely, with me, just a chance for me to clarify myself? I hated her.

"I thought some of the lines were terrific." (Hindsight: What a stupid word to choose, *terrific*, a stupid imprecise word.)

"And your favorite lines?"

Did she actually think she could trip me up like that? I looked back down at the page in front of me.

"The grave's a fine and private place, But, none, I think, do there embrace."

"Ah, yes, often quoted. Memorable."

More silence, just her looking at me. Even the class noticed how odd it all was.

"Okay, very good. You can go back to your seat. But, if you're interested, we can talk more about this later. Perhaps after school?"

My decision? Seriously, if I was interested…my decision? She was actually saying, *I expect to see you after school, but it's your decision.* I knew it, the class knew it. I was supposed to do page layouts for the first issue of the school paper that afternoon. The entire staff would be waiting for me. Plenty of room for me to wiggle.

"I'd like that very much. Thank you."

Me and Dorothy, me and writing, me and Miss Randall.

I walked into her classroom at 3:30. She was standing at the window. Outside, a short row of yellow buses was waiting to be filled. I could hear teen drama in the halls. Teens shouting and teen lockers slamming. I was seventeen. I decided that I officially hated being a teenager.

"Miss Randall."

An hour later, I had a story for my future, and a story for my parents that night. Miss Randall turned and smiled at me. You know a fake smile when you see it, right? One of those click-on then click-off smiles. Writers say a character smiled, and you have to see if any irony or insincerity is lurking in the context. Are all smiles equal? My mother had a beautiful smile. Sadly, my father's smiles might have been as sincere and natural, but his face never cooperated. Me and my mother, we always saw it, but few other people figured it out. I think that was Miss Randall too. I saw her smile. She knew I saw it. Nobody else mattered.

We sat and she resumed, I expected, my humiliation in her class earlier.

"I was wondering about your choice of poems."

"I'm sorry. I think I misunderstood the assignment." Okay, I figured, admit defeat and change the subject. I wanted her to like me.

"No, Emmy, you misunderstood me."

Where was she going with that?

"I said I wanted you to choose a poem that meant something to you. It was not that poem."

"But you said I couldn't choose Dickinson!"

"Are hers the only poems you care about?"

"No, no, I love a lot of other poems. I just started reading Edna somebody and Sara Teasdale, and they have some great poems. But Dickinson is different."

"Yes, she is certainly that." Another smile from her. "And yet you chose a wonderfully written...shallow... poem from Marvell. If I thought it was really important to you, I would think that style is important, word play, but not substance or originality."

I was lost. I could talk about some poems, but I realized that I did not know enough to really talk about poetry. I was also beginning to feel like *she* had misunderstood *me*, that she had assumed I was smarter than I actually was, more well-read, and she had discovered that I was neither smart nor well-read, that I was a disappointment to her.

"You know Dorothy Fergus, right?"

I nodded, suspicious about where we were headed.

"She was in the class after you. She chose a Dickinson poem, but you already know that, right?"

"Miss Randall, it's not her fault. Please don't get mad at her."

"No, no, Emmy, I'm not mad at her…or you. It doesn't matter how she got to that poem. What matters is that she loved it. Sincerely loved it. And when I asked her why, she was able to go through almost every line and tell me how it affected her. And she talked about feeling like a…ready for it…a frog. That's what I wanted from you, Emmy. I wanted you to care about the poem you chose. I asked Dorothy why she chose that poem, and she was not embarrassed at all to admit that you had chosen it for her. She was happy that you did. And as I listened to her, I was proud of you."

I fumbled for words. "It's a good poem, not my favorite, but good."

"Emmy, it doesn't matter if you like it. All that matters is that Dorothy did."

I would sort all this out later. I was in a conversation with Miss Randall like I would often have with my parents, in over my head but trying hard to not show it.

"You said you liked the Marvell poem because you liked the lines, right?

"Yes, but obviously that's not a good enough reason to like a poem, or am I missing something here?"

Was I frustrated? Of course, and intimidated, and confused.

"It's never wrong to like a line, or even a single word. As long as the lines or words are real to you. So, let me ask you a question, and then I have a favor to ask of you. And you don't have to answer the question right away. Think about it and we can talk later. Deal?"

"Deal."

"You know Dickinson, right, and I'd guess that you know her famous line about how she knows if she is reading real poetry, as if the top of her head were taken off, exploding, something like that, right?"

A letter to somebody, of course I knew the line.

"So, tell me Emmy, is there a line for you that she..."

"Tell the Truth, but Tell it Slant."

"And?"

"I felt a Funeral in my Brain."

"And?"

"My Life had Stood a Loaded Gun."

"And?"

"I heard a Fly Buzz When I Died."

"And?"

"I heard a goddam fly buzz when I died! What do you want from me, Miss Randall! I'm seventeen goddam years old. I live with crazy parents. I have no real friends, I'm not pretty, and sometimes I hear voices. Is that what you want to hear? What is it? What do you want me to be?"

Where did that come from? I was trembling, almost in a rage. All she did was sit back and wait for me to calm down. I did not want to calm down, I wanted to get out of that room and never see her again. I started crying.

"Emmy, all I want you to be is the girl everybody told me about."

What do I remember about that moment, what specific detail? Not any precise words we spoke. But we sat there, her letting me cry, and I remember hearing Mr. Sexton, the school custodian, pushing a mop bucket on rollers down the hallway, singing to himself. That damn mop bucket had one wobbly wheel but he never fixed it. The wheel would wobble, not quite a squeak, for as long as I went to that school. You know, a wobbly sound. And then it would stop and he would plop a wet mop down on the floor. A heavy wet plop, and then the only sound would be him singing as he mopped for a minute or two, then the splash of the mop being dropped back into the soapy water in the bucket, but not a single break in his singing. I do remember his voice, a baritone. If I wrote about it, I suppose I could name a song for him to sing, but I cannot remember it now. I'd like to believe it was a love song, maybe something from his own past, a woman he loved once, but lost. I could make the mopping and singing into a story. But that afternoon in that classroom with Miss Randall, all the singing meant to me was that we would soon be interrupted as he came into the classroom to empty the trash cans. Our hour would be over. Miss Randall got out of her chair and came over to me and extended her hands. I reached for them and she helped me up out of my chair. I felt like I weighed a million tons.

"Time for us to go home. But we can talk again, if you want to."

Want to? At that moment, I would have died if I thought that she and I would never talk again. I did my best to descend from cloud hysteria and simply become a high school student again.

"You said you had a favor to ask of me?"

"Yes, yes, and we can discuss this more later. I think this school needs a Literary Club, and I'd like for you to help me organize it. I would be the sponsor, but it really has to be initiated by a student. You feel up to some initiating?"

I walked home from school. I seldom did that. It was three miles away. Most often, I went home with my father, or took a bus if he was working late, as he often did. That day, I needed to walk. I was already organizing a club in my mind.

I've visited classrooms a lot in the past twenty years, done a fair share of bookstore readings, and somebody always asks a question about my writing "process." Nuts and bolts stuff. Where and when, music on or off, notes or wing it fresh? Easy to answer: "I have my own routine, but all writers find out what works best for them." I give them details, and sometimes I see a young person writing it down. As if my life, my routine, was important. But there is an obvious question that doesn't get asked enough: "What is the most important decision a fiction writer has to make?" And the answer is simple: Who's telling the story? The author or the character?

Especially with very young people, I make it simple for them.

"Do your parents know everything about you? The person you love? Your friends? Of course not. They only know what you tell them or what they see firsthand. And you control that. That's first-person narration. And that is life itself. All of you are writers. Telling your own story. Are you a reliable source? How much do you say, how much do you not say? Whether consciously or not, you edit your own life. And nobody ever really knows you. If you're lucky, you know yourself, but look around this room. Everybody is a story, but you'll never know the whole story."

I went home that day later than usual, so my mother noticed. She asked how my presentation went in Miss Randall's class. "Fine," I said, and then I went to my room. A few days earlier I had been Chatty-Cathy about my new year and my new English teacher. Not after my hour with Miss Randall. Even I noticed the difference. I was shutting my parents out of my life. I suppose everybody does that as they grow up, but this was the day I realized that I was making a conscious choice, and that choice had consequences. I was seventeen. I would be leaving home in less than a year, and I wasn't sure who I was. Who was the Emmy Sterling that others had told Miss Randall about?

I went to school the next day and everything was different. I looked for Dorothy as soon as I got there. She spotted me first, rushed over, and ... hugged me?

"Emmy, Emmy, thanks so much for giving me that poem. I just know that if anybody could help me pick one, it would be you."

"Not mine to give." I was splitting verbal hairs again, being myself.

"Sure, sure, whatever. But I think Miss Randall was impressed. She's weird, but I think I like her."

I did not want Dorothy to like Miss Randall. I did not want anybody to like Miss Randall. I wanted her all to myself.

Second week of senior year. My first executive decision had nothing to do with me. As editor of the school paper, I had to assign underclassmen to various beats. Sports was always a plum. But I had a problem. The best writer I had was Mike Migdalovich. A junior who had talent and an attitude. He had been on the junior varsity football team his sophomore year, but he was...to put it diplomatically... small, slow, and uncoordinated. He was not allowed to even try out his junior year. Mike was not a forgiving person, a trait I did not recognize until it was too late. An assistant coach had come to the journalism lab and subtly suggested that perhaps Mike might not be a good choice for sports editor. Mrs. Kimball, the journalism teacher and faculty advisor for the paper, was there with me. I looked at her and she simply said, "You're the editor, it's your call."

Second week, remember? I had just gotten out of Miss Randall's class. I was a bit testy. I thanked the coach for his input and told him that Mike was my choice. He looked to Mrs. Kimball, who shrugged and told him, "She's in charge." Then she looked at me. "You're responsible."

Mike lasted for almost the entire football season, but then I shifted him over to student government coverage. He eventually spent years as a political reporter for the *New York Times*. I still see him on some morning cable shows. I wonder if he ever figured out that I probably kept him from losing his teeth in high school. Then again, it was my fault that I put his square peg in a round hole. He never went to a class reunion. Then again, neither have I.

It took a semester, but the paper was soon a responsibility of mine that was on cruise control. I was Class Secretary, but all that did was get me an extra picture in the yearbook. Class officers never met as a group, so no minutes to take. I was in Future Teachers, another photo opportunity. Best thing about FT was that we met once a month and had a teacher from some other school come to talk to us about the "profession." I was always taking mental notes. I was in choir, back row alto. It was my only school activity that my mother took an interest in. But, as my father liked to remind me, "Your mother hears music anyway."

I worked harder in all my classes. Gotta bring those grades up, remember? I even started to get invitations to sleepovers at other girls' houses. It never dawned on me that it would have been polite to have sleepovers at my house too. I just assumed that other girls thought my parents were too weird. After all, as much as everyone seemed to like my father as a teacher, after the first day shock, they still thought he was not "normal." I had told myself that I hated being a teenager, but I was actually starting to like it. I was waiting for that first kiss, not knowing that Dorothy would be lurking in the wings. I would be a virgin all year long, until the last day.

All that really mattered to me that year was Miss Randall. All I looked forward to was being in her class, talking to her afterwards. In the second week of the semester, we had our own private curriculum.

"I expect you to do all the assignments that everyone else is doing…"

"Do I still have to read *Scarlet Letter* again?"

"Emmy, it's over-assigned for sure, especially for high-schoolers, even smart girls like you, but, yes, you are going to read it again. And I expect you to lead the discussion in class."

Eye roll.

"But you and I are also going to meet once a week after school and you are going to talk to me about your outside reading. And for that I have a list of books for you. No need to write anything. Just talk to me."

I thought I was the most well-read teenager in America. How did I get to be seventeen and never had read Virginia Woolf? Emily Bronte? Who the hell was Zora Neale Hurston? As for my head exploding, how about reading Dylan Thomas and Gerard Manley Hopkins? How was I supposed to read all them and more, and still be a star in my teen universe? Miss Randall introduced me to my first addiction: Coffee. How had my parents hidden this from me? It was as if I had been raised in a slow-motion world. I slept less, read more, talked even more. All so fast that I missed the slow disappearance of my parents that year. Less time at home, fewer evenings with them, evenings of just the three of us by ourselves, like all of my life before. I was a goddam shooting star.

Astronomical metaphors? Astrological? Shooting star? Meteor? Comet? Or simply a planet revolving around the sun of Miss Randall? She wanted a Literary Club. She would have a Literary Club. It was the only project I cared about, and it was easy to organize. I had a reputation. I had a father who was a teacher. As Mike Migdalovich told me when I asked him if he was interested, "I suppose, but you gotta remember, Emmy, not all of us have books shooting out our butts."

Mike, a future Pulitzer Prize winner for sure.

All school organizations had to be approved by the Principal.

Check. Had to have a faculty sponsor. Check. Had to not be subversive or un-American. I'm serious. It was 1960. I looked at that line on the organization form and...checked it. Had to have support from at least thirty students who wanted to join. That took me two weeks, but...check.

And now we come back to Miss Randall and Dorothy and sex, a long arc. Pay attention. I'm only going to tell this story once. Pay attention.

Dedicated to my father: *Emmy Rubiconis transit.*

If the center of my home was the kitchen, the center of my high school was the lunchroom. I've been to school lunchrooms today. Vending machines, fast-food franchises in some of the bigger schools, menu options for vegans and diabetics and dieters. Not when I was in high school. But we did have old women serving us. Old to us then, but probably just in their forties or fifties. Cafeteria style. Get your tray, push it along the counter and hand your plate to the woman with the ladle or tongs, who always wore rubber gloves. You could always choose to not take something, but there wasn't a lot of variety. A lot of white bread, a lot of pint bottles of milk, glasses of ice tea. Mike Migdalovich's proudest accomplishment in high school, more than his terrific writing? He raised enough hell to finally get us chocolate milk as an option.

The thing I remember most now, perhaps not the best, but the most. The women serving us. I never saw them anywhere else in town. They were always Black. I think they were cheerier than I would have expected back then, daily serving hundreds of ungrateful teenagers who probably seemed oblivious to their existence. One of the things I did as editor of the paper was write a profile each week of some faculty member or some notable student. I never thought to ask one of those women about her own life. All that is left of them now is a half-page black-and-white group picture in the yearbook. Just the picture, not even their names. But there are signs and wonders in that picture if you look closely. The woman on one end of the front row is holding her ladle like a torch in front of her. Everybody else has their arms hanging stiffly at their sides. Another has one eye closed. Another has her tongue barely sticking out the side of her mouth. All of them are wearing plastic bonnets, but one of them has hers pulled down all the way to cover up her eyebrows. She's the one I wish I had interviewed.

Three weeks into the semester, Dorothy called me at home. She was nervous, I could tell.

"Emmy, you wanna have lunch with me tomorrow?"

I hesitated, thinking it was an odd request from her, and she noticed.

"I mean, no big deal, I'll see you around some time."

"No, no, Dorothy, I'm sorry. Sure, that would be great. What's up?"

"Just want to ask you a favor."

A minute later, I was trying to figure out why she had called. We always saw each other in the lunchroom anyway. Not at the same table, but close. I went back to reading *Scarlet Letter*.

Was it a Friday? I think it was a Friday, and that was pep rally morning, so the lunchroom would have been decorated with all sorts of banners about how our team was going to crush somebody somewhere. Even the women serving the food would have been wearing one of those school spirit ribbons that we all wore. Testosterone and estrogen would have been jacked up with adrenaline too, all after our orgy cheerfest in the gymnasium. Probably a hundred details to remember, but only one material detail means anything.

Dorothy Fergus was a cheerleader. If you are surprised by that, you have not been paying attention. How could she, in my story, in my life, not be a cheerleader? The head cheerleader. The long-legged, high kicking, bellowing, bouncing-bosom cheerleader. I was Emmy Sterling, the retarded turd in Dorothy's world. Ever since I was eight.

The important material detail? Dorothy's cheerleader outfit. Short sequined skirt, blazing blue and radiant red. Did I say short? Micro-mini short, a length only allowed in that school on six girls a year, the cheerleaders. White cowboy boots. A tight silver vest trying to contain her breasts, with the school emblem on the front, and this provided me with absolute proof that God existed and that the sonuvabitch had a cosmic sense of humor, unappreciated by me until that exact moment. I was in Alachua County High School. Dorothy Fergus was walking toward me and it hit me all at once. The giant scarlet "A" across her chest.

I write fiction. I could not make this up and have you believe me.

Nor this. Dorothy still has that uniform in her closet. It doesn't fit her anymore, and it is sealed in plastic, but it is hers forever.

"Emmy, here, here, come sit with me over here."

She had found a table in the corner, but it had two sophomores sitting there…until she told them to go sit somewhere else. A few minutes of small talk, she was always full of gossip about everyone and everything, and I had to admit that I had a prurient interest in who was kissing whom and which teachers were flirting with students, but it was also obvious that she was nervous. She had a tray full of food in front of her, not a bite taken.

"Emmy, I have a favor to ask." She was looking down at her tray as she spoke. "And I'll understand if you say no."

"Dorothy?"

"I know you are starting a Literary Club. If it's okay with you, I'd like to join."

Is it a typical human reaction, to be asked a question so profound that all you can do is blink, stalling for time? And to not even know how profound it was? I did not control who could join the club. You like books, come join. Dorothy was still looking down. Nine years of our mutual past had to be processed. Every encounter between us, everything I thought I knew about her. Seventeen years of my life leading to that moment. That moment in that same lunchroom, only weeks earlier, when I had told her that I was thinking about joining the Drama Club. Her back in front of me, her not turning around. Me collapsing. The names she had called me. The times I had felt her and her friends snickering at me as I walked past them. The times I had wished she was ugly or crippled or just plain stupid. I had earned my righteous indignation. She had her world. I had mine. I deserved to be the center of the universe I had created. But there she was in front of me, head down, and I thought about the poem she loved, from me to her, a giveaway poem to me, a gift to her. I thought about Miss Randall. I wondered if Miss Randall was a Nobody, just like me...and Dorothy. How long did it take you to read this paragraph? I am sure it took you longer than it took me to answer Dorothy.

"Absolutely, Dorothy. You didn't need to ask. I was hoping you would join."

Thing is, I was telling the truth, even if I didn't understand where it came from.

Still to come was that first awful kiss, and then a perfect kiss after the Christmas Dance, and then graduation night, when I lost my virginity, and Dorothy was there for everything. It was not how I would have predicted my future. Me and Dorothy, each other's bitch for life.

When I was seventeen, it was a very good year. A song lyric. Look it up. I was seventeen, and my senior year was going to be the best year of my life, up until then. My birthday is June first. We graduated

May thirty-first. I graduated at seventeen, and then it was all over at eighteen.

Initiation stories. Basic ground to till for most writers. The most universal. Love, sex, and death. Love and death were ahead of me, sex came the night before I turned eighteen. Love when I was twenty, with the wrong man, or so most people would say, wrong wrong wrong, and I adored him. Death was my first novel, the story of my parents. I had to wait until my mother died before I could write it. I'm still waiting to write about my first love. Still processing, even as I am dying, still processing. Sex? Still trying to forget.

My high school was torn down twenty years after I graduated. I miss that building. True, it needed to be torn down. It was built in the 1940s, thrown together with a miserly budget and institutional architecture. I miss it. I miss the house where I grew up. I miss the grocery store where my parents shopped. Places are important. You probably have your own list of places gone forever from your life. Memories? Sure, but sometimes memories are not enough. You want to go stand in the spot where you existed in the past. I want to go back to the kitchen where I watched my parents be in love. I want to stand in Miss Randall's classroom again. That damn lunchroom. The hallway outside the gymnasium, where we had our Christmas Dance, the hallway where I finally had my first good kiss, a kiss I could finally talk about with Dorothy, who assured me that she had not paid Mike Migdalovich to do it. Yes, *that* Mike Migdalovich, forever the only younger man in my life, who was also the only person to ask me for a date that year. I think he was as shocked as I was, how good the kiss was, but we never kissed again. I can't remember what I was wearing, but I do remember the music drifting into the hallway, a Brenda Lee song. I think that if I could go stand in that same spot in the same hallway, I could remember that song. But that spot no longer exists.

I was busy every day of my senior year, and, as my father told me years later, "It was as if your mother and I were simply spectators of your life. You were on a float in a parade and we were standing on the sidewalk watching you pass by." I was heartbroken when he said that, and I tried to apologize for my ignoring them, but he shook his head and then he patted me on the top of my head, like he did a million times as I was growing up. "Oh, Emmy, we were so proud of you back then. Lord knows we had wondered if you had grown too dependent on us. You needed to grow up, and we knew you were going to leave eventually. Your mother and I talked about that a lot, you leaving, it was going to be so rough for us."

If a hundred wonderful small things happened to me my senior year, I have forgotten most of them. But, the big things? I try to hold on to them, all except graduation night. But that refuses to go away.

The best memories? If Miss Randall was Robinson Crusoe, trapped on the desert island that was my high school, I became her Friday. Shining in her class, seeing her after school to talk, doing errands for her, but mostly talking about books. Dorothy told me that there were rumors that I was sweet on Miss Randall, to which I replied that, of course, I was. Dorothy was always surprised by how "fucking innocent" I was.

"Emmy, I mean they think you're a lesbian and that Miss Randall is a dyke."

How innocent was I? Lesbian I understood, but Dorothy had to explain what a dyke was. As best I can remember, there were no lesbians on American television in 1960. But they were starting to show up in some of the books I was reading.

I protested, "Dorothy, that's crazy. Do you think I'm a lesbian?"

I was smarter than Dorothy, even she agreed with that. I had read more books, knew more things, yadda yadda. But she still taught me some important lessons.

"Emmy, it doesn't matter what the truth is, it only matters what people think is the truth. I know you're a damn straight arrow, and Miss Randall is just...weird...but not lezzie weird."

"But, Dorothy, you like Miss Randall too, don't you?"

"Like her? Hell, I love her, but you can keep that to yourself. But, you have to admit. She's weird. You know what she asked me to do this week for when we discuss that boring *Scarlet Letter*?"

I shook my head.

"She asked me to wear my cheerleader uniform. No big deal, I would have worn it anyway since class is right before the pep rally, but she asked me? I'm only telling you because if I told anybody else, they would start talking about how Miss Randall just wanted to see my legs. But, you gotta admit...weird."

Thinking about the scarlet letter on Dorothy's cheerleader outfit, I tried to keep a straight face. "Oh, absolutely."

The next day, Thursday, was *Scarlet Letter* day. Miss Randall had been right. I had re-read it for her, and it was a different book. I expected her to call on me last, letting the others go first. I did not expect what happened first. We were seated in class, me in my usual back-row sanctuary, when she pulled a box from her desk and gave us a pop test, a quiz that we did not know we were taking. Perhaps more precise to say...she was giving us a lesson.

She had a box full of A's cut out of red silk. She laid them on her desk, four rows of red A's, ten across. Two rows of six-inch-high letters, two rows of three-inch-high letters.

"We're going to take a couple of days to discuss Hawthorne, and I want you each to come get a letter and pin it on your shirt or blouse." With a flourish, she seemingly produced a box of safety pins out of thin air, like a magic trick.

Forty letters, twenty-two students, twelve girls and ten boys. My response? I wanted to be the first, but she called us up one row at a time, front to back. We shuffled up when called, and gave our choice to Miss Randall, who pinned it on us one by one, but she also told us to not sit back down, to keep standing around her desk up front until everyone had a letter.

Then came our lesson, which I described to my father later, whose only response was, "I might love her too," to which my mother said, "Dewy, grow up."

Miss Randall was like that person who has given you a perfect present all wrapped up and was trying to not be too excited as you opened it, knowing what was in store for you, anxious for you to be surprised and then thrilled.

"Now, everyone who chose the large A go to one side of the room, everyone who chose the small A go to the other side."

The Red Sea parted. On one side were all the girls, on the other side were all the boys. Large letters on the girls, small letters on the boys. Miss Randall stood there, beaming.

Me, I'm sure my jaw dropped. How did she do that? Hell, I wasn't even sure what she had done. I wasn't sure what the lesson was, but I knew that I had learned something at that moment. All I had to do was figure out what. Everybody else? More clueless than me, but a nervous laugh started with Terry Abbott and then spread to all the other girls. The boys were blushing, as much as seventeen-year-old boys are capable of blushing.

"Okay, go back to your seats, and write me a page about what you think this all means."

Then Chuck Warren broke Miss Randall's heart, I could tell. I knew her. I could tell when her heart was broken.

"Miss Randall, I thought we were supposed to talk about the

book."

That was too much for me.

"Chuck, you're an idiot. This *is* all about the book."

He was three rows ahead of me, and he turned around slowly, so that Miss Randall could not see him glare at me and mouth silently, "S-u-c-k m-y d-i-ck, l-e-s-b-o."

"Emmy!"

Miss Randall was glaring at me. I knew what she wanted me to do, apologize, but I just glared back at her. Why couldn't she see that I was the only person in that room who cared about her? I was in a snit, Chuck was soon gloating, and Miss Randall then broke my heart.

"Perhaps Chuck is right. Perhaps we need to focus on the book itself. Forget my earlier assignment. Just write me a page about..." and I could sense her struggling, "...just write me a page about any character, anything about any character. Write whatever you want. You have the rest of the hour."

I stopped looking at her. I looked at the blank page in front of me and started writing. Two sentences, then I scratched them out. Two more, and then I kept writing. But, back in the blackest part of my mind, I was also making notes about Chuck Warren. I was going to crucify him sometime in the future. I was going to stab him in the eye with my goddam ballpoint pen. Go re-read my third novel. Chuck is in there. But for the remaining few minutes of class, I wrote about something else. I wrote about what had happened a few minutes earlier. I wrote about guilt and pride and innocence and the human heart. I had no idea what it all meant. It was spontaneous and unorganized and full of sentence fragments. All I knew was that I had to write those words at that exact moment, the assignment be damned.

Class over, papers collected, I knew that I only had about two or three minutes to be alone with Miss Randall before the next class started filing in. I stayed in my back-row seat. Miss Randall sat at her desk, looking through the papers, finding one in particular, the one I knew she would read first. I never took my eyes off of her. She finished reading it and then started writing on the last page. The next class was coming in. She ignored them. I was going to be late to my next class, but I kept sitting there as she kept writing. The bell rang for a new class to start. She was still writing. I was noticeably out of place in that new group. Weird Miss Randall and even weirder Emmy Sterling in the same room. I wasn't leaving. She stood up and walked to the back of the room and handed me my paper back. I did not read it then. I wanted to be alone.

What she wrote? Five long lines. I still have that paper in a file somewhere. I need to read it again, while I still can. I remember every word. But I would like to see her handwriting one more time.

I went home and told my parents about the day, but I did not tell them about Chuck Warren and my desire to maim and then murder him. I did not tell them about what I wrote, or what Miss Randall wrote. I told Dorothy, of course, and I showed her the paper. She had two responses.

"Emmy, sometimes you scare me."

"Sometimes I scare myself."

"Another thing. Lemme know when you want to cut off Chuck's dick. I'll hold your coat."

When I was seventeen. A good year, remember? But listen to that song again. The guy's life is over at thirty-five. After that, the damn autumn of his life. So, basically, I guess the song is saying that we all have just eighteen good years. Me, my first book was published when I was past fifty. But I still love that song. I loved it at fifty. I love it now. But there is still something missing. It's a song about a man's life. I've tried to find a comparable song, but about a woman's life. They're not the same. Youth, middle-age, the looming autumn. The Chill, the Stupor, the Letting Go. I was a virgin, then I was not. I was pregnant at one time, and then I was not. I was in love for ten years, and then cast aside. Married, and then not. A success, and then less and less. I never murdered Chuck Warren, but I did kill his character. I watched my mother die, and then my father. I held a dead baby in my arms one time, but it was not mine. Odd, the burden of ambition. I aspired to be a poet, but I had no talent. I am a writer, but it was never a goal for me. The song is about "stages" of life, universal stages, I suppose, but it is still not a woman's song. I write prose, but I wish I wrote lyrics. I want a song about me, a song that other women hear and they think about themselves.

You are not reading a memoir. There are rules for writing a memoir: some basic adherence to facts and a coherent narrative, an arc from birth to lights out. You write a memoir, you are allowed to leave out ninety-nine percent of your life, but you still have to give the reader a reason to buy your life in print. Your life has to be an interesting diversion from their own. Or, perhaps you are important, so your life story is important by default. Celebrities write memoirs all the time, or they have somebody else write them anonymously. I've read a lot of memoirs in my life, and I'm always thinking, why? Why does this other person's life matter to me? I knew that I would never write my own memoir. Too much about me that I do not want you to know. You don't know me, so does it really matter what you don't know about me? But I should do it. Write a memoir. I told myself that I would never do it as long as my parents were alive. They were the only audience that mattered. But I did not want to hurt them, and some of the truth about me would hurt them for sure. They're gone, so I should write that memoir, right? All I need is time.

The Literary Club was my first experience with what would become book clubs later. My agent kept telling me, "Write a book that will be chosen for a book club. There's your target audience." What a strange phrase: target audience.

Me, I had never thought of our school having a Literary Club. I didn't need a club to make me read, but Miss Randall suggested it, so I made it happen. A half-page picture in the yearbook, added to my other senior activities being splashed around the pages. I was President. I told my father at dinner one night and he was his usual droll proud. "You are the George Washington of your club, the obvious first choice for first President, by acclamation. The Mother of your Country." My mother was less impressed. "You have your father's nose, and I love it, but I pray that you don't end up with his sense of humor." My father's response? Well, he had none. He opened his mouth as if to speak, but then he just winked at me and started clearing off the table.

Dorothy was the Vice President. I nominated her and must have done some sort of Vulcan death stare to everyone else. There were no other nominations. Her most lasting contribution was when we had our group picture taken for the yearbook. She made herself a big lapel button, a white circle with a red-letter **VP** in the middle. Go find that yearbook. Look hard at that picture. Pay special attention to the expression on my face. I had just asked Dorothy why she needed to have posterity remember that she once had a high school office. Just as the photographer said "Smile," she whispered to me, "Virgin Pussy." And click went the camera.

Had I never laughed before my senior year? I was laughing every day that year. Drama, sure. Anger, sure. Relentless self-pity, sure. Was something happening around me, seeping into my psyche? I did not care about politics, but something about John Kennedy excited me. His damn New Frontier optimism? Old Man Ike was fading away.

Jack and Jackie were the future. Inexplicably, my father had supported Nixon. "Experience counts, Emmy. Good looks are merely window dressing," said the ugliest man in town. My mother said that, about him being the ugliest man in town. I could never even hint at how I felt, not since he had admitted to me why he never wanted any children. But my mother could say it and then say he was also the most handsome man in town. She insisted that there was no contradiction. I did not understand, but my father always laughed. "I rest my case, daughter, good looks are merely window dressing." We all laughed, the three of us at home, as if nothing was sacred and life was but a dream anyway. We laughed, even though, late at night, alone in my room, house quiet, an open book in my lap as I lay in bed, I worried about the future. It was my last year at home. I was going to go away from my parents. Still, I laughed at school, laughed with some people, laughed at others. Chuck Warren and Eddie Morris were laughable. Dozens of others. I was myself laughed at, but it did not matter. I was seventeen. It was a very good year.

The Club met every other Monday. Eighteen members, including three boys, but we seldom had all eighteen at one time. The general rule? Read a book, or a short story, and be prepared to talk about it. It was soon obvious that at least four members were there just to be seen in another picture in the yearbook. I did not care. Miss Randall was there. Dorothy was there, and a few other surprising people who I had never considered to be readers. Had they been hiding? A core group of about ten, and we even became friends outside of the Club. It was a very good year.

I once confessed to Dorothy that one of my guilty pleasures about being in the Club was that I felt like I was...important?

She poked me in the stomach when I said it. "You mean you feel like you're a Queen, right?" I thought she was making fun of me. She poked me again. "Because that's how I feel in the Drama Club."

After the first few meetings, Miss Randall changed the format. She wanted us to write our own stories or poems and then share our work with the group. No nasty nit-picking allowed. And no rules about what we wrote, no subject off-limits. The odd thing? I thought it was a bad idea. I sure as hell was not about to share any of my poems. We were teenagers. My father's words: Experience counts. What sort of experience did any of us have? Writers were adults. My skepticism was obvious, but Miss Randall was undeterred.

"Emmy, I assume you have read *Frankenstein*."

Dorothy raised her hand and jumped in before I could answer. "I saw the movie." And then she realized that Miss Randall and I were about to have one of our notorious "moments" together that others had heard about but seldom seen. She lowered her hand sheepishly and slumped down in her chair.

"Emmy?"

I had not read *Frankenstein*.

"Did you know that she was sixteen when she eloped with Percy Shelley, who happened to be married at the time?"

I thought I knew where Miss Randall was going.

"Did you know she was eighteen when she started writing her book?"

She and I were back in a ring together. Dorothy and the others had gotten in free of charge to watch.

"I think I knew that, but it just seemed like a reason to not read the book. How good could it be?"

Miss Randall did that head-tilt thing she always did, just like my parents, as if I, my brain in particular, was a carnival oddity.

"Emmy, a book doesn't always have to be good to be important. I think she was writing science fiction long before Jules Verne or Edgar

Allan Poe."

Okay, if she was trying to motivate me, it was sort of working.

"Her mother was Mary Wollstonecraft."

A name that meant nothing to me.

"Did you know that she learned to write her name by tracing letters off her mother's headstone?"

Interesting, but, so what?

"Did you know that after her husband died, she kept his heart in a silk purse in a desk drawer?"

That got everybody's attention. But that was nothing compared to what she did next. Still looking at me, she spoke to Dorothy.

"Dorothy, did you know that she lost her virginity on top of her mother's grave?"

Dorothy was sitting beside me. She coughed, tried to clear her throat, all the while Miss Randall and I never lost eye contact. The others? They did not exist.

"Dorothy, how old is Emmy Sterling?"

Dorothy was obviously still trying to process the information about sex on a grave with a married man. But she came through like a champion.

"She's seventeen, just like me."

Miss Randall nodded, still looking straight at me.

"Yes, and you have both lived long enough to write as well as read. And, for the record, diaries don't count."

I went home and told my parents, and I had another one of those moments when you realize that adults are in one giant conspiracy, hiding secrets from their children, talking about their children with other adults. My father spilled the beans.

"Yes, she told me a few weeks ago that she was going to get you to write."

"Daddy, we all have to do it."

"Emmy Opal Sterling, they don't matter. Not to Miss Randall. They're just a smokescreen to hide the fact that the entire club is for you alone."

"And you know this how?"

"I hope I'm around when you have your own kids, Emmy. You're going to finally appreciate how wonderful me and your mother were as parents. And how damn smart."

My mother was drinking a glass of red wine before dinner, and she started tapping the glass with a teaspoon. My mother stirred wine. One of a thousand details that come back to me late in my life. Nobody stirs wine, except my mother. "Hear, hear," she said, tapping that glass. Tap tap tap.

I went to my room and began writing. The assignment was simple: A single paragraph. Pick somebody from your own family, anybody on that tree, and describe that person. Write a character sketch, something that makes everybody else "see" that person. No need for a plot. Simply, create a character. I wrote a paragraph about my grandmother, then a page, and then five pages. I wrote about her banished sister. I wrote about a picture on a wall. And then I took my mint-green Royal typewriter, my most prized possession, gift from my parents on my thirteenth birthday, and I turned five pages of cursive scrawling into three pages of pristine print. I read it again. It seemed different to me, as if I was reading something from somebody else. I took a pen and crossed out lines and words, and re-typed. It was better. And then it was midnight.

The Literary Club was not supposed to meet again for another two weeks, but I had written, and I wanted a reader. I took the pages to Miss Randall and asked her to read them right away. School was over for the day. Was it November? Just after the Election? Or earlier? I remember that it was cold outside, and our high school was not built with insulation as a priority. We had steam heat, those freestanding radiator things that don't exist anymore. All along the wall under the windows, so the hot wet air inside, pumping out in waves, would hit the cold windows and condense on the glass. It was my favorite time of the year.

"Did you show this to your parents?"

"No, I didn't write it for them."

"You should show it to them."

Why was I so bitchy? She did not deserve the response I gave her.

"I just assumed that you would show it to them later, when the three of you are talking about me again."

I had not assumed anything of the sort. I had assumed nothing. But I spit out an accusation that must have been festering from the previous night when my father told me that he knew about the assignment before I did. I was seventeen. It's my only defense now. Miss Randall? She simply ignored me.

"Is your grandmother still alive?"

"Oh, God, Miss Randall, my grandmother will live forever. I think she's already a couple of hundred years old."

"I'd like to meet her."

"Excuse me?"

"I'd like to meet her. This makes me want to meet her."

My expression gave me away.

"Emmy, this is wonderful writing, an indelible scene. Even better than I expected. It would make a good short story eventually, perhaps a novel, her and your parents are already characters. I know your parents, but I'd like to meet your grandmother to see how much of what you've written here is true or just made up. Two different skills. Photography versus painting. How good is your writing? When I said I would like to meet her, I didn't mean I would like her to be my neighbor. That's the same feeling I got after I read Flannery O'Connor for the first time. I want to know her characters, but I'm not sure I want to *know* them. Know what I mean? But I still want to meet your grandmother."

I did not. But the distinction would become clear in time.

"Who is Flannery O'Connor?"

"Oh, Emmy, I have just the book for you."

Before it came time for the Literary Club discussion, Miss Randall stopped me in the hallway and told me that I was going to read last. Everyone had turned in their work ahead of time, so she had already read everything. My conclusion? She did not want me to go first and intimidate the others. Sometimes, yes, hard to believe, I could be insufferable. But the day was full of unplanned lessons.

My first epiphany? The obvious clue about the club profile, who was in and who was "out" even when they were there? Reading was easy. You could even fake like you had read something. Writing was different. Of eighteen members, only ten had turned in some writing. The rest were no-shows. As usual, nobody volunteered to go first. I waited, but I still kept my hand down. Teacher's orders. We had our chairs arranged in a circle. In college, years later, a professor had the same arrangement and he joked about it being a circular firing squad. He was an asshole. Even then, no hindsight needed, I knew he was an asshole.

Miss Randall waited until it became obvious that everyone but me was scared to go first. She waited perhaps thirty seconds and then pointed at Terry Abbott.

"Terry, you go first. It's a lovely piece of writing. Please share it."

I don't know if it was lovely. All I knew at the time was that hearing words and reading words was different. Terry was a sweet girl but an awkward reader. I felt bad for her. I closed my eyes. I tried to imagine the words on the page, to read them in my mind as she spoke. Mistake, Miss Randall told me later. Terry saw me with my eyes closed and assumed that I was simply not listening to her. That I thought she was boring. It was just the opposite. She was monotone. But there were lines that I "heard" that were very good. Now, looking back to then, I ask myself, "Who was the asshole?" I didn't mean to be, but I was. I was starting to get into some sort of flow with Terry, some sort of verbal sync with her, and then she stopped. It was a bad ending. The story had led nowhere. I opened my eyes. Terry was trembling. Miss Randall was glaring at me.

"Thank you, Terry. Any comments from anybody?"

I liked Terry. She had never been one of the girls who made fun of me in school, ever. I wanted her to feel better.

"I liked it, Terry. I wanted to hear more at the end. That's always a good sign, right?"

She was almost crying.

"I have another page. I just stopped because I thought you hated it."

Everybody was looking down, anywhere except at me. Miss Randall saved both me and Terry.

"Terry, I let Emmy read your work ahead of class. We both agreed that it was very good. And she told me that she wanted to talk to you personally about it after the meeting. I know that Emmy was just concentrating on your reading right now."

Terry blinked and beamed. "You really did like it?"

What could I say?

"Very much."

Miss Randall picked up the baton.

"Terrific, Emmy. The more everyone writes, the more we can help each other. And as soon as Emmy turns in her own work, Terry, I'll let you read it first."

Turn in my own work? The work that Miss Randall had already read? I was confused. I was seventeen. I was not an adult. Miss Randall was an adult.

Eight more presentations, with Dorothy going last. I was surprised by how genuinely good her writing was. I mean, compared to everyone else. A few pages about a distant uncle, a drunk who abused his family, but his family still loved him. One detail was painfully precise: how the uncle would always look down and then up, right before he slapped his wife. It was as if he was giving her a signal, a warning about what was coming, every time, but she never backed away. She knew it was coming, and she took it. Dorothy's final two lines killed me: "All happy families are alike. My uncle's family was unhappy in its own way."

Anna Karenina? "All happy families are alike; each unhappy family is unhappy in its own way." Dorothy had actually plagiarized Tolstoy? Dorothy, whose personal library I always thought was mostly Nancy Drew?

But, here's the thing. I had not read Tolstoy back then. That would be years ahead. Dorothy closed her story with "All happy families are alike. My uncle's family was unhappy in its own way." I thought it was a line better than anything I had written in my own story about my grandmother. When I finally read Tolstoy, I remembered Dorothy's story. But, by the time I read Tolstoy, I also knew that Dorothy's story was not about an uncle far away, but about her own father.

Years in the future, Dorothy and I would go on a road trip, looking for Miss Randall's grave. I asked her if she had ever read *Anna Kareni-*

na. She laughed. "Fuck, no. But Miss Randall read a draft of my story and then wrote that line on the board for me, telling me to think about it. Tolstoy, I had no clue who he was. But the line stuck with me, so I paraphrased what she wrote on the board and added it to my story. And you remember this after all these years?"

"So, the line that I thought was the best in your story was stolen from Tolstoy! And you had no idea who he was?"

"I wasn't stealing from *him*, I was stealing from Miss Randall. No, no, wait, I wasn't stealing. She gave it to me. Told me to think about it. That was her gift to me. I accepted."

Was I always so predictable back then, when I was seventeen? I stayed after the Literary Club meeting with some questions for Miss Randall. Of course, she knew I would. I always had questions. I'm guessing that she could predict my questions too.

"I have to wait two weeks before I read my story?"

"Yes, and you are going to talk to Terry about her story before then, and you are going to let her read your story before anybody hears it, and you are going to ask her what she thinks."

"Terry Abbott? She's very sweet, but she's not going to understand my story."

"Emmy, listen to yourself."

Were adults always so condescending? Pontificating? I did not want another parent, the two I had were more than enough. The scene? Just the two of us and then Dorothy stepped back into the classroom, saw us, and spun around to make a quick exit. Comedy gold. Miss Randall and I turned when we heard her open the door and then watched her spot us and turn around. We looked back at each other. We were both stifling a laugh.

"Now, where was I?"

"You were telling me that I was a snobby know-it-all brat."

"Right, right, as you are. But you can grow out of that. Not a sure thing, but I have high hopes for you."

"Miss Randall, okay, I'll do it for you, put my big mother hen wing around Terry and make her feel better."

"And when you decide that you are doing it for yourself, not me, then you might be starting to grow up. Terry will never be anywhere close to you in her writing, her mind, her potential, but I know this about her. She struggled to write her story, but she kept at it because it was important to her. I suspect that you did not struggle a bit. I suspect that you loved writing it. You worked to find the right words. Terry struggled to find any words. The same with Dorothy and the others. You are gifted, Emmy. Don't waste those gifts just on yourself."

Did that conversation happen? Yes. Were those the exact words? No, but are any words from our past the exact words? Was Miss Randall that perfect? Depends on your definition of perfect. But I do know this, will know with my last breath, how our conversation ended that day, as she was shooing me out of her classroom to go back home where my mother and father would be waiting for me.

"Emmy, if you ever become a teacher, which is a good fit for you, among other careers, I hope you have a student then like you are now. Here's a teacher secret for you. We all have our own lists of students who we think are going to be a success. In some way, a success, and we helped make that happen somehow. You, Emmy? I don't think you're going to be one of my success stories."

My heart started sinking.

"No, Emmy, and don't let this go to your head, but I think you are going to be *the* success story of my life."

Go to my head? No, it went straight to my sinking heart. From some sort of abyss, to bursting. I took a deep breath.

"Miss Randall, I want you to do a favor for me. You know I write a faculty profile every week for the school paper, even have Coach Rigsby going in next week's issue."

I guess I really was too predictable.

"The answer is no."

Was that meeting in October of 1960? Or after the election? I want to remember the exact date, so I can then count the number of days from then to May thirty-first. Graduation night. How many days between then and the night I lost my virginity? And I was eighteen the next day. To graduate? To leave something behind and begin something new? A graduate...somebody who has graduated? But there's another definition of graduate: "arrange in a series or according to a scale." There is no sharp break, just gradualism. At any one point in your life, you are still only slightly different than who you were right before. Evolution? Survival of the Fittest? Only the strong survive? I was headed to graduation, I was headed to college, and I was headed away from home.

March of 1961. I was on fire. I was bouncing off lockers in the hallway. Tests to take, papers to write, meetings to attend, lunches with Miss Randall on Saturdays, and my parents were waving to me as I circled past them again and again. I was still seventeen and, with absolutely no supporting evidence, I thought I was in control. However, as my father reminded me, Life had other plans.

"You hear anything about Miss Randall?"

It was an odd question from my father. It was just him and me sitting at the kitchen table while my mother was asleep upstairs. Two big candles burning. He had just finished a crossword puzzle in the newspaper and it was crumpled next to one of the candles.

"Daddy, you see her every day. She eats with us once a month. All

I know is what you know."

"Well, we both know *that* is not true."

You ever have conversations by candlelight? Not the clichéd romantic dinner candlelit conversations. I mean *conversations you have when your power goes out* kind of conversations. In a small circle of light, and the shadows on the wall are wavy, and the rest of the world is dark. In the first seventeen years of my life, I must have had hundreds with my father, even a lot with my mother. I did not think it was a big deal. It was just what we did. I told Dorothy once, about our candle conversations, and her eyes got blinky and wide. Years later, when she and her daughters were visiting me for Thanksgiving in Florida, she was describing my parents to her own children, who were as blinky and wide-eyed as she had been, but she finally just summed it up with, "Emmy here grew up in the Addams family." Her children shrieked, but they also laughed, and then her oldest, the teenager, the one she named Emily, my god-daughter, that daughter spread her arms wide, as if inviting an embrace, and said, "Well, that explains a lot." No, I wanted to say, it explained nothing. We were not the Addams. We were not macabre and gothic or spooky or anything...except ourselves. But I loved Dorothy and I loved her Emily. If cartoons and a television family explained me to them, I let it be. But I knew the truth about my father and candles. He thought he looked better in the shadows, even when he was alone.

"I was just wondering."

My father was a bad liar.

"Daddy, you want to explain the question?"

Usually, if we were going to have a father-daughter talk, it would sneak up on me. He would talk, I would talk, and then I would eventually realize that we were actually talking about something else. That night was different.

"There have been some complaints filed against her. Some of her students. I was wondering…"

"Who! What students?" I had been cocked and loaded even without knowing it. "And what are they saying?"

"They say that she plays favorites, that she has pets who get treated better, that ..."

I pulled my own trigger, exploding.

"Daddy, they all do that. You, you do it too. I know you do!"

I had risen with righteous indignation, righteous teenage indignation, slamming my fist on the table as I rose, my voice rising, my legs hitting the table as I rose … knocking a candle out of its holder, to fall on the crumpled newspaper, to ignite the paper and words. My father grabbed the burning paper and swiftly tossed it into the sink behind him. From accident to extinguishment, five seconds? And we were down to one candle. Blazing symbols, right?

I was hysterical, whether from fire or the attack on Miss Randall, I don't know, even now. I was yelling at my father.

"This is all bullshit, and you know it!" I don't think he had ever heard me curse before. My books, I am told a lot, have almost no profanity in them. It is not natural, they say. Real people curse, real people drop *hells* and *damns* and *shits* and *dicks* and *assholes* and every variation. I ignore the criticism. But, of course, it is not really criticism. Merely an observation. Right? An afterthought. I always have a response, but nobody takes me seriously: "Real people? My characters aren't real. They're fiction. They don't exist in your world. They exist in mine." In my real world, in the home I grew up in, raised by Dewy and Dawn Sterling, I never heard a profanity. Not even a *hell,* unless it referred to a place, nor a *damn*, unless it referred to a divine judgment.

My personal profanity? Dorothy gets credit for that. But I was raised in a world where language was never vulgar. My home world was real to me, but it was not the real world that was coming for me as soon as I left home.

"There's more."

I sat down. My father moved the remaining candle away from my side of the table. I did not speak.

"Some kids are saying that she says things to them, implies things, that make them feel uncomfortable. You probably know what I mean."

How many years before a child and parent are the same? Before they are equals? Ever? I think my father and I were the same in his last year, as I was taking care of him. We could talk then, about mother, the past, his own life. And I could tell him things I never told him before, as if I knew he would finally understand me. That was to come, but it was not happening in my senior year. He was still trying to protect me. Did I know what he meant that night when he told me about the complaints? Not at all. Miss Randall had "pets." Of course, she did. But, other things?

He asked me a question without looking at me.

"Has she ever made you…has she ever…done…"

"Daddy, what are you talking about?" Was he implying that Miss Randall was a lesbian? I might have been raised by them in a monastery, but I was also in high school. I knew Dorothy Fergus, who was the gold-standard conduit of gossip and innuendo from all her followers. Of course, I knew all about lesbians and homosexuals, sort of. But my father was asking an absurd question. What did that have to do with Miss Randall? That thing I said about him and me being equals? It happened eventually, but it absolutely happened for one single time before the future happened, it happened that night as I made him make a choice.

"Daddy, the answer is *never*. And I hate it that you even had to ask. I hate it that you don't know anything about me. Or her. She sits at our table. You and mother talk all the time. You see her at school. And you are asking me these questions as if you are not sure about her...or me."

"Emmy, I'm sure you are right," defensively, "and those kids are probably misinterpreting..."

"Daddy, those kids are lying."

"They went to their parents. The parents went to the principal. There's some discussion about not renewing her contract for next year."

"Based on a lie."

"Emmy, the truth doesn't matter here."

I suppose it would have been a perfect scene in a story if the candle had flickered out at the moment my father told me that the truth did not matter. *Finis.* Truth does not matter. Everything I had thought I knew about my father was a lie. The father I loved would never say that the truth did not matter. Lights out. But that damn candle kept burning.

"Daddy, do you believe all those things?"

"Not really."

"That's not good enough, Daddy. Yes or no, do you believe those things?"

It was another one of those looks, the look of Miss Randall, or him and my mother a million times in the past, the look directed at me as if I were a puzzle. Eyes a little bit squinty, focusing on me, more difficult that night in the candlelight, but staring hard.

"No."

"Okay, Daddy, what are you going to do about it?"

Would he have ever told me? All I know is what Miss Randall told me the next week.

"Your father is a remarkable man, Emmy."

Out of nowhere, no setup, no context, just a line about my father as we sat in her classroom after school. Unseasonably cool outside. Graduation in a couple of months. She always kept a hot plate in her classroom, two burners, I remember that, and we always had hot tea by ourselves. Hot tea with honey, and a squirt of lemon juice. I always imagined being properly British when we did it, sip tea in the afternoon, talking about … things.

"Yeah, I like him a lot."

I was not concentrating on my father or her at the time. I was thinking about whether I would have a date to the Senior Prom. The phone at home was not ringing off the wall.

"I will miss him."

I snapped back. I blinked. I looked around her classroom. Posters on the walls. JFK and Jackie at an Inaugural Ball. Norman Rockwell. Robert Frost. Eleanor Roosevelt. Emily Dickinson.

"Excuse me?"

"I'm going to teach somewhere else next year."

My father had failed, had done nothing, my first thought. I said the first thing that came to my mind, my seventeen-year-old mind.

"I don't want you to go away."

"Oh, Emmy, we're both going away. Sorry, I can't go to college and be your teacher for the rest of your life. Apron strings always have to be cut eventually."

She was right. I was going to lose her anyway. But I just assumed that she would be there whenever I came back. I assumed that my father would save her.

"My father was supposed…"

"Let me tell you a story about your father."

Holding my teacup, I listened to a story about my father slaying dragons. None of that tilting-at-windmills Quixote nonsense. Before she started, Miss Randall swore me to secrecy.

"You cannot tell your father that I told you this. Understand?"

How cruel was that, to deny me hearing his side of the story? I wasn't really upset. I understood and I agreed, but when I wrote my book about my parents, my fictionalized version of their lives, I included that scene, written as if I had been there. But, like all fiction, with only one version of the event to rely on, I had to make the facts fit the fiction I was writing. A problem in the narrative? Invent the facts. Miss Randall was in that book too, and morphed into other characters in other books. I could never really pin her down.

"I was called into the Phil Ellington's office two days ago. I wasn't really surprised, but I still felt like I was a student, not a teacher, called into the principal's office. I expected a lecture. I knew the rumors. I was used to rumors. But as soon as it was obvious that old man Ellington had a different agenda than I expected, I was bracing for the worst. And then your father walked in."

Just walked in? I was getting saucer-eyed.

"Not even a knock. Just walked in. Ellington was as shocked as I was. Nobody knew about the meeting, I assumed, and I guess that Ellington did too. Ellington, he did the *Dewy, this is a private meeting* thing, but your father ignored him. And then your father ran through a list of all the rumors about me. I mean, he was literally using the finger on one hand to count on the fingers of the other, and then switching hands. Ellington kept trying to interrupt. Your father then punched Ellington in his flabby gut with three words. *It's all bullshit*, he said."

My father cursed? I was in Wonderland.

"But, Emmy, as surprised as I and Ellington were about him defending me, neither one of us was expecting what he did next. Your father gave Ellington a choice. *You fire Miss Randall here, and I quit. Today. And I'm taking at least five of your teachers with me…because you are going to have to fire them. Seriously, Phil, you and I both know what…* and he named five names… *have been doing over the past twenty years. And I suspect that they will not go quietly into that good night, Phil, they will make sure that the school board knows that you knew too.*"

Sound familiar? Yes, my third book, the one about a college teacher. Not my father, not Miss Randall, but somebody who was a combination of three other teachers I had known. Dorothy said that Miss Randall had given her a gift of that line from Tolstoy. Her story about my father was a gift to me. The detail she did not mention? I remembered how my father dressed that day. It was odd. He was wearing his Sunday suit, the one he only wore to the Friends meeting. It was not his school wardrobe. Even my mother asked him why he was so dressed up. All he said was, "big meeting today." If I was writing allegories, I'd make up something about that Sunday suit being his armor.

"And then your father waited, looked at the watch on his wrist, and waited. Oh, Emmy, if your father was single, I'd marry him myself. He stormed in and sliced and diced Phil Ellington, saving me."

And then I said the dumbest thing a daughter can ever say about her father. "I'd marry him too. I mean…" instantly stuttering and backtracking, "… I mean if I was older…I mean older and he was not my father."

Miss Randall was gracious enough to ignore me.

"He and I talked yesterday, and I thanked him, but here's the thing, Emmy, I had already made up my mind to not come back next year. I needed to move on. Didn't know where, but I was leaving anyway. He had been brave and gallant and heroic, but I didn't need him."

"You'll come back, won't you? I can write to you, can't I?"

"I won't be that far away. Only over to Jacksonville. I didn't need your father to save my job here, but, when I told him I was going to leave anyway, he asked me if I had anywhere in mind. I didn't, so he made two calls, he told me later, and I had a job offer in Jacksonville. And he told me that Phil Ellington was going to write me a sterling letter of recommendation. I kidded him about calling it a "sterling" letter, and he gave me one of those weird looks of his...you know what I mean...and he said, *I'm going to write it. Phil is going to sign it, even though he doesn't know yet.*"

An out-of-focus future was coming into focus. The universe was making more sense. I was almost eighteen. I was going to graduate in two months. My father was a hero. Miss Randall was not going to disappear. I was still not pretty. It did not matter.

Three stages in a life? Three phases? An infinite number of scenes, but three big roles to play: sunrise, a blazing day, and sunset? No, no, compare it to the seasons. Spring is youth, summer is adulthood, autumn is old age, winter is...the ceramic vase on my mantel, the one holding the ashes of my mother and father. You accuse me of being too self-absorbed, too damn flowery for even a writer? Fair enough, go tell your own story. Pick your own words. See if your story ends any different than mine or anybody else's. Me, my Spring was almost over. I was graduating.

You want a day-by-day account? Not going to get it. Not going to get the stories about the two dates I had before graduation, the two boys who kissed me, but not better than Mike Migdalovich kissed me. Colleges applied to, the scholarships I was winning, the choices I had to make...not going to get those stories. The piss fights between me and Dorothy, our laughing reconciliations. The books I read in that final year. The times I had to call my parents to tell them that I was going to be late for dinner. I was skipping...no, running...down some yellow brick road toward graduation night and then my birthday and then the last few months I would live with my parents.

You want to know some odd research I did when I was first diagnosed with cancer ten years ago? I wanted to know when it had actually started. Genetic? Lifestyle choices? Was it there long before it was discovered, just waking up, waiting for me to be happy? I wasn't researching just for myself. I wanted to go back and look at my mother again. I was hearing her voice, and my father's, and Miss Randall's, but I needed to see them again, in the flesh. My mother was first diagnosed with bladder cancer when I was twenty-one. Had it been there when I was seventeen, there when she and I would talk about my future, her helping me pick out clothes for college, even before I graduated from high school? After I was diagnosed, sometimes I would be teaching a class, adults thirty years younger than me, and I would look at a young woman and see how excited she was to simply be...alive. Like me at seventeen, and I would wonder if the thing that would kill her was already in her. Yes, it was a bad time for me. I wanted my mother back. Her and all the others.

Graduation was more than the ceremony, all that pomp and circumstance, tassels turned, hats tossed in the air at the end. Graduation was cord cutting. That baby was born and pushed out into the world. My favorite memory? Phil Ellington had to hand my diploma to me and shake my hand, congratulate me, yadda yadda. My parents were in the front row. Principal Ellington had been his unctuous self, especially in his own speech, but I could see him naked on an ass. I could see him and Miss Randall and my father in his office. He had no reason to know that I knew about it, but as he shook my hand...I refused to let go. The next name had already been called. But I just looked him right in his bulging eyes. He tried pulling away from me, but I held on. Not long, how long was it, perhaps five seconds? And he figured it out. Close to my father dying, he asked me about that night. My handshake memory? I think I got it from him.

I remembered more. It was a special night. I was going to the after-graduation party at the lake, with Dorothy and Jake and then spend the night at her house. Even though he was a junior, Mike Migdalovich was going to the party too. That part is still clear, even now. When the ceremony was over, I rushed to meet my parents and have Dorothy take a picture of us together, me in that cap and gown, my father in his Sunday suit, my mother in her Sunday dress, her cancer slouching toward her. I still have that picture. Hugs and kisses and other parents milling around, sort of a collective adult communion. Dorothy yelled at me that it was time to leave, and my father kissed me again and whispered, "See you tomorrow. Big day. Have fun tonight."

I can tell you the story, but I am not a reliable narrator because I am telling you what others told me, mostly from Dorothy. Their memories, not mine. Keep that in mind as you listen to me. This is not just my story. This is how they remember it too. After my father died, and I could think about that night and not feel guilty, some of the details came back to me. Repressed memories are a real thing in psychiatry. But so are false memories. I have to be careful. All I know for sure is that I have never gone to another graduation of any kind, even if specifically asked by any of my students. I tell them a joke, and they laugh, but it is not a joke: "When I hear 'Pomp and Circumstance,' I want to get a gun."

Dorothy heard me screaming. And for years afterwards, she blamed herself for letting me out of her sight. And for encouraging me to drink. I was graduating, remember, about to be eighteen, time to do adult things. Break rules. Dorothy was a drinking pro. She poured the rum in my cup.

For the first few years after I started retrieving memories, I would do more than remember, more than "see" the past, I could feel it, smell it, and I would puke. But I'm better now. I can talk about it, as best I can. But I never write about it. If I write about it, it gets away from me. If I were to write about it, it would mean that there was just one version of what happened. In print on a page. Locked in. But that moment in my past…it is never clear to me.

"Hey, Emmy, you want to see my dick? Or are you still just a pussy girl?"

Words something like that. Words that Chuck Warren could have said.

"My parents gave me a Polaroid for graduation. I've got a gift for you now. Maybe we can take a picture of you?"

Is there anything in life that cannot be described in words? Abject terror? Or just the premonition of pain and humiliation to come? But if you cannot remember that moment clearly, or want to forget, how do you describe it? The hands on you, tearing your blouse, the voices around you, more than one, the stench of cigarettes and booze, the slapping, being forced to your knees, and then down on your back. The weight. The laughter. And then the numbness. You looking up at the night sky. The beautiful starry sky.

Afterwards, different voices.

"She's over here!"

Dorothy and Jake, Dorothy making Jake turn around and look away from me as she got down on her knees and starting putting me back together. I was an hour away from being eighteen.

How many times in the past five decades has Dorothy asked me to forgive her? I have to keep telling her, "What you did after that night...you earned all the absolution you'll ever need."

Details, damnable details.

Dorothy and Jake got me back to their car and told me that they were taking me home. I protested, "You can't do that. They can't know. Nobody can know. Especially my parents. It will kill them."

"Emmy, we have to get you some help. We can take you home or to the hospital, but you need help. And you can't keep this a secret forever. That asshole Chuck will be bragging tomorrow, saying that you threw yourself at him."

Dorothy told me later that was the moment she realized that she was in love with Jake. She and I were in the back seat, he was driving, and he said over his shoulder, "Don't worry about that bastard. I'll take care of him and Eddie."

"And we can't go back to my house. My folks are dim, but even they'll know something is wrong."

Midnight, we were driving in circles, and I was bleeding. I thought I was awake, but I was dreaming. Dorothy told me that I began to cry. Could not go home. We could not go to Dorothy's place. In my dream, I had a question for her.

"Do you know where Miss Randall lives?"

"No, but I have her phone number. Jake, can you find us a pay phone?"

It was all a dream, right? Miss Randall, as much as I had kidded her about living in her classroom, rented a house near the school. Walking distance. We were there and I remember, I am told, that Jake actually carried me to her front door, handed me over to her, and then turned to leave. Dorothy was confused.

"Jake, aren't you going to stay?"

"I'll be back. First, I have to go find Chuck Warren."

Dreams don't have rules. No need to make sense. You interpret later. Miss Randall and Dorothy took me into the bathroom and took off my clothes. The bleeding had seemed to stop, but I had bruises on my wrists and thighs. I was too numb to be embarrassed. They put me in a clawfoot tub filled with hot water, washed me, and were about to lift me out when I asked them to just let me lie there, submerged up to my neck as my head rested on the back of the tub. The overhead light was too bright, I wanted that starry night back.

"Can you turn off the light?"

I did not get stars, but I did get candles. Miss Randall went to find them while Dorothy stayed with me. Then, as I lay in the water, in a room lit by three candles, Dorothy and Miss Randall stayed with me. None of us spoke for who knows how long. I was probably asleep. Finally, Miss Randall woke me up.

"Emmy, we need to get you to a doctor in the morning. You need to see somebody, to be on the safe side."

I couldn't do it. I did not want anybody to know. A doctor would tell my parents. Miss Randall was adamant.

"I'm not a doctor, Emmy. I can't help you."

Dorothy motioned to Miss Randall, pointing to the door. I was left alone. I wanted to slide down into the water. How long? I heard them whispering. I heard the front door open. Jake was back. A shriek from Dorothy, "You did what?" Laughter. How could they laugh at that moment? More whispering. I think they were whispering. I went back to sleep in the water. I woke up, and only Miss Randall was in the room with me. Where was Dorothy?

"She went to get somebody to help you."

I wanted to get angry, but I was too tired to care anymore. I was less than a Nobody. I closed my eyes. I woke up in a bed, wearing a robe that was too big for me. Standing around the bed were Jake, Dorothy, Miss Randall, and my...grandmother.

That did not happen. I told Dorothy years later that it did not happen. I did not remember it. It did not happen. She had sighed. "It doesn't matter what you remember. It happened."

Not candles, but only a small lamp beside the bed. I was looking up. Jake was taller than Miss Randall but not by much. Had my grandmother always been that short? My father was tall, but there in that bedroom Miss Randall towered over my grandmother. Who was my father's father?

"Young man, you must leave us alone," my grandmother said to Jake. I was not her grand-daughter for the next half hour. I closed my eyes and looked at a starry sky.

When it was over, I was warm again. Arrangements were being made. I would still go home tomorrow, for my birthday party. Dorothy would go with me and make a big deal about how she and I had done some childish things at the lake, like drink too much. We were both hungover. Sorry sorry sorry about being such party-poopers, but all was well and let's eat cake and open presents and celebrate. My grandmother would never mention this to them. My secret would die with her in a year. Jake would have his own secrets too, like finding Chuck and Eddie and breaking a finger on each of their right hands after he destroyed their Polaroid, telling them that if they ever said a word about me then he would be back and break their arms, that if he even heard a rumor about me and them, he would be back, for the rest of their lives. He kept twisting Chuck's arm, closer and closer to breaking it, relenting only when he was convinced that he had all the pictures they had taken. Were all men like Jake, like my father...capable of courage and wrath, of being almost noble? That has not been my experience in general.

I never saw Chuck and Eddie again. Did I tell you that I never went to a reunion? Dorothy has kept my secret. Miss Randall is dead now. I went through a lot of therapy, so that therapist knows. My mother never knew. I always wondered about my father. Sometimes, for years, he would look at me like he saw…I don't know. But he never asked me. Who else? Well, *you* know, but I trust you. Who else? I haven't introduced you to him yet.

I slept in Miss Randall's bed that night. Jake slept on the couch in the living room. My grandmother sat in a chair near the bed, awake all night. Miss Randall and Dorothy? They slept with me, one on each side of me, our bodies touching. If I dreamed there between them, I do not remember it. Fifty years later, here I am. Talking to you, putting my affairs in order.

Does any one thing explain everything? Me today, the sum of my life, explained by one night when I was seventeen? Would I be a different me now if it had never happened? If that is true, wouldn't that also mean that my life stopped then? Who I was going to be… died that night? I was raped. And so, I lost control of my future? Free Will up to that point, Fate afterwards? You figure it out. I tried. All I know is that what happened to me has happened to millions of women. Some cases not so bad as mine, many others much worse. Each is their own story.

I once wrote a book in which one of the minor characters had been raped. A reviewer focused on that minor character as a major flaw in the book. I did not "capture" the essence of that character's experience. I was "dismissive." The reviewer was right. I could have written the book without that character even being included. I originally thought there was a reason for her inclusion, some story line that would circle back to her, but I just deserted her. In my first draft, she was raped by a man the narrator was involved with, part of his past, and it was the narrator/rapist relationship that I tried to develop. But that was a dead-end so I dropped the male character and took the narrator in a different direction. But I kept his victim. It was sloppy writing, and the reviewer called me out. I wanted to contact that reviewer, an idea my publisher adamantly opposed. How could I explain it to him, my desire to admit my own failure to a person who had missed the many other strengths of the book?

Dorothy read my book, read the review, and she saved me from myself.

"Emmy, unless you're willing to be totally honest with her about your own experience, don't contact her. I'm surprised your editor didn't ask you about it. You gave that girl a full three pages, and then you never mentioned her again. And, maybe, you ever think, maybe the reviewer saw something in the character that you missed?"

"Such as?"

"Herself. And you abandoned her. And the thing is, Emmy, I knew why that character was there. I'm just surprised that she's the only one you ever wrote about."

Abandoned? Sometimes Dorothy was more insightful than she realized. Even years after that night, she was still redeeming herself with me.

I turned eighteen and became an actress. Acting as if it had not happened. Dorothy helped write the script. She had an aunt who lived in St. Augustine. Lots of room at her beach house on the Atlantic coast. How about Dorothy and I go down there. Her real agenda was therapeutic. She told me that I needed to get away from anything connected to graduation night...people and places.

My parents were skeptical, but my father still thought it might be a good idea.

"A couple of weeks of freedom before you get back to the grind of school. Go get a tan. Take some time in the mornings to get up and watch the sun rise, just like we did when we took you."

Dorothy and I had looked at each other. When did that happen? My mother motioned for my father to stand aside. Her palm toward him, waving back and forth, pointing to the kitchen table.

"Emmy, your father is a notorious tightwad, as you know. But he did actually spend money...thirteen or fourteen years ago?... on a real vacation for us. Neither one of us had ever seen the ocean. All those years, so close, but we never went. I wanted to see the ocean. I was surprised how easy it was. I simply asked, realizing that I should have asked sooner. He was such a pushover...a cheap pushover."

Those moments I love to remember about my parents? Their habit of interrupting each other when one was telling a story that the other also wanted to tell. Not a bad thing, they each riffed off each other as more and more details would come out, one added to the other, as if the real audience was themselves, not whoever else was in the room, as if they we reliving the past again, but always a happy past. The first two weeks after my eighteenth birthday had not been happy in my house. Did they sense that too? Did they decide to go back to a happy time, the past?

"I might be cheap, but I used up everything in our savings to make that trip. I decided that I wasn't going to live forever..."

"...especially if you did not take your wife to the beach."

"But we made it late on a Saturday night."

"I was exhausted, your father was exhausted, and you, Emmy, you were a bawling brat."

"But the next morning was a new start for us. Up in the dark, a walk to the beach. It was worth the drive."

He stopped talking. Another one of those moments. Dorothy and I might as well not have been in the kitchen with them. I had told

Dorothy about those moments between my parents, but she had never seen one until then. My father and mother were finishing their story, looking at each other, but not talking, both of them back on that beach with their only child in tow. Both knowing what the other was remembering at that moment. Both of them back in time.

"Daddy, I remember none of this."

"You were barely out of diapers, Emmy. You could walk and talk a little, but you were just a baby. It's okay, not to remember. But you have to promise me that when you get down there you will go to the beach before the sun rises, and watch. Okay? Dorothy, you make sure she does that. Promise?"

"Yessir, Mister Sterling."

Details, these details? Dorothy was there, and years later when my father would talk about the past, he would tell his version of that moment too. Dorothy even remembers what she said to me after we left my parents that night.

"Emmy, no wonder you're so damn weird."

Dorothy and I went to St. Augustine in July. Two weeks turned into a month. My parents were not worried. Florida in the summer of 1961 is not the Florida of today. Five million people versus sixteen million today. Not a Spring Breaker destination yet. Disney World was ten years away. A different world. But the ocean is the same.

Dorothy kept her promise to my father. Her aunt's run-down house was right on the beach, less than fifty yards from the ocean at high tide. We would get up every morning and take our folding chairs to the water's edge. Two eighteen-year-old girls, who had always been capable of cynicism and snark and irreverence, we sat silently and waited for the sun to rise. It was everything my father had promised, but I still never remembered seeing it in my past, me standing on the sand with my mother and father. I did not remember it. It never happened. I was in their memories, not mine.

I went back home in August, started college in September, and came back home in October. I dropped out. My father drove to the school to get me. It would become the last year of the first phase of my life. I would have to learn how to leave home a second time.

October of 1960, I came home. I went back to college in September of 1962, and that was when the first third of my life was over. It had not ended on graduation night. The middle of my life began with my first day of class in 1962. Those eleven months between October and September were recorded in my father's journals, but not in my spiral notebooks. His memories, Dorothy's, even my mother's memories of that time...are all I have.

I did not have to justify my desire to come home. I called my father and told him, "Daddy, I can't do this. I want to come home." He did not argue with me, ask me to reconsider or to give it a few more weeks. He came to my dorm room and helped me pack a single suitcase. That small task had been too much for me. When I got home, my mother carried the suitcase in for me and then I went to sleep in my old bedroom, which had not been touched since I left.

Dorothy was away at her own college. Miss Randall was gone. My grandmother was almost an invalid and seldom seen. Then again, even in the uneventful past, she seldom came to our house. Nobody else knew that I had dropped out. My parents wrapped me in some sort of emotional cocoon and waited for me to emerge whenever I was ready. Butterflies gonna fly eventually, right?

Eleven months. I quit wearing makeup. I cut my hair short. I gained weight. I lost weight. But here's the thing. Those eleven months might have been the most important eleven months of my life. That small window of time was when I discovered my mother. Those moments eventually became memories much later. My father was gone most of the day, and my mother and I had the house to ourselves. In the past, my life was home, and then home and school, and when at home I had almost always had both parents around me. My mother's "life" was always as an attachment to my father. At school, I saw my father as an independent actor, not a husband or father, but as an individual. At home, my mother was always his wife and my mother, but I wasn't sure that she was ever herself. Does that make sense? I needed to live with her, as damaged and off-kilter as I was, for those eleven months, just her and me.

My mother never had a job. My father's teacher salary wasn't much, but we had enough. How had I never asked her what she did with all that time to herself? Years later, as feminism evolved, I watched it all change, women in the world, at least in America. I read all the books, Friedan and Greer and Steinem and others. I had grown up reading women writers, novelists and poets, who were not polemic, but whose work was molding my own view of myself. "The problem that has no name"? Was that my mother? I kept looking for somebody to explain her. All I have now are hazy memories from those eleven months.

If I told you that, for the first six months I was home, my mother ignored me...would that make her look bad to you? Selfish? Indifferent? The only time she seemed to acknowledge me was when my father came home, but I never felt slighted. If I wanted lunch, I went to the kitchen. If I stayed in my room, she never asked me if I was hungry. Was our house immaculate and orderly because she had so much free time? Not really. I had grown up doing my own laundry, as my father had done his. Cooking was mostly her domain, but not exclusively. Cleaning the kitchen was absolutely his domain. In the evenings, they would sit and read. And talk to each other, looking up from a page, sometimes reading a passage to each other.

Those six months at home are the haziest, but I did, finally, emerge in April, and my mother was waiting for me. I discovered one afternoon that I was more than just hungry, I was famished. I went to the kitchen, but she was not there. I called out for her, but no answer. I went to her bedroom, not there. Not in the house at all. Two in the afternoon. I went to the back screen door. There she was, on her knees in her flower garden, her back to me, wearing a frayed straw hat.

"Mother, you okay?"

Why would I ask that? I had seen her a thousand times in that garden. She did not answer.

"Mother?"

Without turning around, she raised her hand and waved for me to come sit beside her. I had done that a hundred times too. I glided out the door, still in my ghost phase, as I called it later, dead but not gone, and plopped down beside her.

"What you doing?" Another dumb question.

"Pulling weeds, listening to music, playing in the dirt, waiting for you."

My father and I never heard the music she heard. I had to finally, after all the years of watching her sway to some silent music, ask the obvious question.

"Music?"

She reached over and cut a rose off a stem and handed it to me.

"Smell this, and rub it on your cheek."

I smelled the rose. I felt it. But I did not hear music. I shook my head but I did not hand the rose back to her. She seemed to go in a different direction.

"I'm a dirt person. I love putting my hands in the dirt. Your father does not. I'm not sure about you yet. Sometimes you're him. Sometimes you're me. Most of the time, you're just you. And that's a good thing."

Was that when it all began, the road back? I was suddenly tired. I wanted to go back to sleep, but I did not want to go back to my room. I did not want to leave my mother alone.

"Lie down on the grass, Emmy. I love that. Sleeping on the grass. One of the reasons I hate the winter. The grass is hard and cold. But a day like today…is perfect."

I do not remember this, but I think it happened. I lay on the grass beside my mother and looked up at the sky. Ever since graduation night, I had been afraid to go to sleep. I would have nightmares, but the worst part was the waiting to go to sleep, the anticipation of nightmares, and always the memory of looking up at a dark starry sky that particular night. I would see those stars again and I would know that a nightmare was coming. That afternoon with my mother, all I could see above me were puffy cumulus clouds, floating in a blue sky. I went to sleep. When I woke up, my mother and father were standing over me, looking down at me. My mother's hands were still covered in dirt. My father's fingertips were tinged with chalk dust. I think. But I do remember what he said.

"Hey, sleepyhead, you hungry? I'm cooking tonight."

Every day, just me and my mother, and we did nothing. I started to read again, even though I do not now remember much of what. She and I worked in her garden, and I did my best to like dirt, and she appreciated my obvious effort, but she was resigned: "You are your father's daughter." I discovered that my mother hummed a lot during the day, a habit that my father and I seldom heard when we were around. But that's the important thing I want you to think about. My mother did not change because I was there, when in the past I was not. She just let me into her world and let me roam free.

The most profound discovery?

My father kept a journal. I inherited them when he died. I was not surprised that he had written so much about his life, even if he kept it a secret from his daughter who was keeping her own notebooks. But my mother? I discovered that she wrote a note to my father every day. I surprised her in the kitchen one day when she thought I was asleep upstairs. It was a rare thing, to see her caught off guard, nervous, covering the small sheet of pink paper as if I would not see it. I did not think much at the time.

"If that's a grocery list, please put chocolate milk on it."

A weak smile. And then she made me a co-conspirator.

"Can you keep a secret?"

"Am I your daughter?"

She understood.

"I write a note to your father every day. Well, almost. Not a lot. Never on a weekend, when he is home. Sometimes only a couple of lines, perhaps a line of poetry. But I set aside time and write to him while he is gone. I put the date on them. And I save them for him."

"You mean to read later?"

"Much later."

"Mother…"

"You must not tell him."

"Mother…"

"They are for after I am gone."

My father, I would learn, kept a record of his life. I kept a record of mine, and my mother wrote notes every day to him. The three versions of our story.

"Will I get to read them?"

"They're for him, but I wouldn't be surprised if he showed them to you eventually."

"But he does not know now?"

"In our bedroom, at the bottom of the armoire, under a pile of old clothes, are the boxes."

"And he has never seen them!"

"Emmy, he has never looked."

"Mother, that's not fair, you keeping them a secret."

Fair? I had no idea what *fair* meant in a situation like that.

"When I am gone, I want you to tell him about them. Only then. Promise, for me?"

"Of course," I stammered.

"And I trust you to never look at them before he does. Do you promise that too?"

I had been too distracted…confused?... to see that she had folded the piece of paper in front of her. She was waiting for me to be her daughter forever.

"I truly promise."

The three versions of our story? I read my father's after he died. I told him about my notebooks, but I never showed them to him. He was happy with anything I did share when we talked. The story I am telling now? All I need are my mother's notes to finish it.

When the fire came for her, it took everything in her bedroom. The boxes of notes became smoke. My father was saving her, not thinking about, or even knowing about, anything else to save. I never told him that they existed. It is the most merciful thing I have ever done for anybody in my life.

Is two-thirds of a story still a story?

I suppose I could have gone back to school sooner, but I stayed at home for another year. Me and my parents, me and my books. I was in no hurry. Dylan wrote about time being a jet plane. I was on a slow boat.

II
Emmy: The Middle

I went back to college in 1962, but not the college where I started. If I have avoided my high school all these years, I also never went back to the scene of my breakdown. America, land of new beginnings. Call me Emmy the Lesser Gatsby. I lost my scholarships, and my father had to scrimp even more to pay my bills. But I did make Dorothy happy. She and I had gone to different schools after graduation, me to Florida State, her to the University of Florida. I had lasted two months at FSU, went home, slept for a year, and then decided to go to UF with Dorothy. Even her mother was happy that I was going to Gainesville, to be Dorothy's dorm roommate. Evidently, I was considered a good influence. Dorothy's mother was not happy that UF had finally integrated, admitting seven black Gators.

My father was happy that I had finally committed to a career as a high school teacher. My mother?

"Will you come back to teach with your father?" In her world, it all made sense. I would go away but I would come back. Thankfully, my father squashed that idea.

"Alachua County is not big enough for two Sterlings."

Truth was, I did not see my future. I would go to college, get a degree, get certified, and go teach. Where? I did not really care. I just needed a goal, one step at a time. Get out of bed, go to class, study... one step at a time, day by day.

Another truth? I thoroughly enjoyed college after I started over. That first semester was a bit traumatic, with the Cuban Missile Crisis offering the possibility that we would all be teaching in a cinderized world eventually. I would call home almost every day and talk to my father. My mother was calmer than he was. She assumed that John Kennedy would keep us safe. My father was not so sure. I thought Dorothy was going to have a nervous breakdown, but Jake would come up to Gainesville, rent a motel room, and the three of us would sit on the bed and watch the news on the black-and-white TV. After awhile, I would go back to the dorm. Dorothy would stay with Jake. I was sworn to secrecy.

Other than that threat of imminent incineration in October, my first year back was stress-free, as if graduation night had never happened. I even had a social life. Dorothy took care of that. I started wearing makeup again. I started drinking. I started smoking. I started reading again. I started writing in my notebooks again. On a two-thousand-acre campus of eight-thousand-four-hundred-sixty-six students, I was normal. I started having sex, but that was not normal. It was 1962. Dorothy and I were still in the minority. The birth control pill was approved by the FDA in 1960. Dorothy knew about it before I did. Me, I never worried about getting pregnant.

Sex? See how quickly that snuck into the conversation. And so casually, as if it were no big deal. Thing is, it wasn't. I wasn't promiscuous. I eventually taught in college in the '80s and '90s and beyond. I watched America turn into Sodom and Gomorrah. Do not misunderstand. I'm not judging, but I am using loaded language. Seriously, Sodom and Gomorrah? An apocalyptic overload.

I've lived long enough to see sex become an equal opportunity sport. But I grew up in the '50s. A lot of baggage in general, moreso in my history. *Nobody* was supposed to be having sex in the '50s. And only the boys were allowed to enjoy it. And there's the proverbial rub. I was having sex, but I wasn't enjoying it. Dorothy was lucky. She had Jake. I had four boys in one year. Borderline slut status. You want names? How about Curly, Larry, Moe, and Darrell? I don't remember their goddam names. Dorothy warned me. I was doing it for the wrong reason. She loved Jake, that was her reason. The bonus? Evidently, Jake was very good at it.

"You ought to at least care about them, Emmy."

"Dorothy, it doesn't matter."

"Well, you ought to at least like *it*."

I think that was the problem. I wanted to like *it*. But I always went somewhere else when I was doing it, leaving my body behind. I was doing my best to not think about starry nights. I wasn't having nightmares like I used to. I was getting better, right?

Who am I describing? That person named Emmy in 1962? Thirty-eight years until the end of the twentieth century. Remember the year 2000? We were told that a disaster was coming. The Y2K bug that was always there in our computers, waiting to short-circuit the future. The so-called greatest minds of our generation, and none of them were sure what was about to happen. What a perfect metaphor. The bug is always there, in my mother, in me, in all of us? We all eventually see the end, but it is just our end. Life goes on, without my mother, without my father, without me. I can tell you this now, but if I was talking to Dorothy, she would tell me to stop being so melodramatic. You, thankfully, are not my best friend.

Me? You reach a certain age, you talk about yourself in the past, and it is not you anymore. Not a profound insight from me now, but, like every person in their late sixties, you want to time travel to the past and slap who you were. Bitch-slap, is it okay to say bitch-slap now? I wanted to go back and watch the other me who was also there in 1962. Better things were happening to that girl, that first year, so many better things, happier things.

On some days, she would walk across campus as if she were on drugs, but she was straight as an arrow. She was walking but she felt like running. Every breath was a drug. The air was cool and fresh and the sun was warm. She was glad to be alive. She had a best friend in Dorothy, but for the first time in her life she had other friends too. She had good teachers, not as good as the one she had in high school, but better than she expected. Her parents would come visit and she would take them on a tour of the campus. Her father brought her more books to read. Her mother brought her seeds even though she had nowhere to plant them. No problem. They went shopping and bought clay pots and potting soil. Window sills and windows were all she needed. Trees might grow in Brooklyn, but she had geraniums and petunias in Gainesville. She went on a Virginia Woolf reading binge. She went to poetry readings. She volunteered as a tutor at the local high school. She wrote short stories and hid them, but at least they were written. She went to her first symphony orchestra concert, still wishing she had musical talent. She had her mother with her, and she wondered if the music in the auditorium was as good as the music in her mother's head. She re-read *Wuthering Heights.* She tried to read *Ulysses*, but stopped after fifty pages. That did not make her unhappy. She made A's in all her courses, except Spanish. Music and foreign languages, evidently, were not fated to be her strong suits. She was still happy. For Christmas, her parents gave her a new typewriter, a blue Royal "All-American." She still has it, in the original case, somewhere in her beach house.

"You're pregnant."

Are you responsible for your own life? The good things…kudos to you. The bad things...shame on you. Or, the bad things...you were tricked...you were lied to...you were too young? Shame on those other people.

Love? Love is real? The person you loved was not real, but the love was? What are the rules? And how do you describe it?

Of course, love is real. My parents prove it. Even Dorothy and Jake prove it, as up and down, in and out, sad and happy as they were from the beginning and still are now...they love each other. We all know people in love.

That happy girl in Gainesville in 1962, was she really in love in 1963?

Yes, I was.

Writing a memoir, you include real people. Sometimes you change a name or some detail to keep yourself out of court. Fiction also requires fictitious names. *This is a work of fiction. Any resemblance to any person, living or dead, is purely coincidental.* Yadda yadda. I am telling you a story now. Fiction or memoir, you figure it out. While you're at it, you should figure out who you are too.

I cannot tell this story, or my life, without including him. But there's the Shakespearean rub. I need him in the story, but I want to hide him too. I suppose you could go back to some UF annual from 1963 and find the faculty page for the History Department. You would see him immediately. You might fall in love with him by just looking at that black-and-white photo. I can't hurt him now. He's dead. His wife is dead. They are beyond my reach.

But I still need a name for him. The right name for a character. It's not a casual decision for a writer...picking names. I've written books with characters whose names I changed halfway through. My first choice no longer "fit" the character. But as soon as I knew I had to change the name, I knew the character was real and I knew how to write the rest of the story. So, what would be the right name for a married professor who would have a ten-year affair with a student who was hearing voices even before she met him?

Before I started this story, I started thinking about names. Up to now, the names have become the characters, perhaps vice versa. He was different. But he has to have a name now, so I can continue, even if it has to be changed later, I have to name him now.

His name is Peter James Jefferson.

Disappointed? You wanted something dramatic and profound, something "literary"? Let me see where Peter and that girl go, and I might see a different name.

"You're pregnant."

The Fall of 1963, I was excited about starting my second year. Dorothy had started a year before me, but I was already catching up. Thirty-six credit hours in my first two semesters. She only had fifty-two after two years. Even my father told me to slow down. Not me, I was in a big rush to finish college and start a teaching job and lead an obscure middle-class American Dream life. I wanted to be the next Miss Randall, emphasis on the *Miss*.

The Fall of 1963, a lot was going to happen. Kennedy shot, my mother's grief so bad that I went home early for Thanksgiving that year and stayed until December. I sat with her and watched television, a luxury I did not have when I lived with them before. We saw Ruby shoot Oswald, we saw the riderless horse, the veil of Jackie and salute of little John-John. The eternal flame lit. That week, my mother seemed to age before my eyes. Her cancer was coming. I was falling in love with Peter, thinking about him as I watched the funeral. I would not kiss him until 1964.

The Fall of 1963, I was majoring in English. Hardly original, I know. But I needed eighteen hours in some other elective. History. I know what you're thinking. It was also an obvious choice for me. I told Dorothy that I was going to take a survey course...American History: 1700-1877. She rolled her eyes,

"Boring. Who's the teacher?"

"I have no idea, but I think it will be an easy A."

"You remember those red A's in Miss Randall's class?"

"Dorothy, duh, I still have mine in an envelope at home."

She laughed.

"Me too. Those were the days, when we were still virgins."

"*You're pregnant.*"

Classes began the first week of September, 1963. The last week of August, I was nauseous every day, cramping, and I kept staring at the calendar. My period, my clockwork perfectly consistent period, had not started. I was over a month late. I confessed to Dorothy and she hustled me to the school clinic. A blood test, a vaginal smear, a doctor who had obviously graduated from a Catholic medical school.

"You're pregnant. Have you told your husband yet?"

How should I have answered that? *Sorry, how can I tell him if I only found out ten seconds ago? Sorry, I have no idea who the father is. Sorry, would you like to marry me?*

"I'm not married." Head down, staring at my shoes, Dorothy holding my hand.

The Church snorted, pulling off his rubber gloves and tossing them in the trash can.

"Then you have a decision to make. My nurse can give you a list of agencies who can help you. They handle situations like this all the time, more than you think. They can find a good home for your child."

That was my only decision to make? Thing is, I did know who the father was. Do I remember his name now? Not a chance. He was a non-factor. But I was still lost. Dorothy's tirade at me as she drove me back to the dorm did not help.

"Emmy, how many times did I tell you to be careful? How many times did I offer to show you how to take care of yourself? But, no, nobody tells Emmy Sterling, smarter-than-anybody-else-Emmy-Sterling, how to run her life."

I was trying not to cry. How many times could I break my parents' hearts? I was lost, getting more and more numb, hearing voices and doors slamming.

"I didn't think it could happen to me. I was careful, I really was, but it didn't happen after…that night. That would have been when it should have happened, but it didn't."

"Fuck Mary Mother of God, Emmy! You are the dumbest smart girl I know! Do you remember your grandmother being there that night, and then me taking you to see her a month later without your parents knowing? Right before we went to Florida."

Bits and pieces, details coming back. I did not remember, but Dorothy started irrigating my memory as she drove.

"Emmy, all I know is that I wish that old lady were still alive. She could help us now."

"Us?"

"Yes, dumb ass, you and me. You think you're in this alone?"

"Dorothy, you're not the one who is pregnant."

"Nope, but I was once."

She was staring straight as she drove. Had I never noticed how her profile was perfect?

"And, yes, Jake knew. He got the money. He drove me to a place in Jacksonville. He sat in the waiting room. Jake, aiding and abetting the crime. Him and the doctor over there. We could have all gone to jail. But Jake's still around, still crazy about me, still driving me crazy by being a lunkhead sometimes. But, here's the deal. You do have a decision to make. You call one of those agencies, or I make a call to Jacksonville. There is no third choice, Emmy. I do not see you as mother-material...ever. But it's your decision. If you want me to make the call, you have to trust me. You do not tell anybody else, you do not ask anybody else. A lot of goddam butchers out there."

I sat there in the front seat, thinking, not really noticing that Dorothy had slowed down and was driving in circles around Gainesville, killing time, letting me think about killing...something.

Killing. That's the word the pro-lifers use now. Killing babies. I was holding my thumb up, then down, then up. Back to my earlier question. Does one moment determine who you are for the rest of your life? I was raped. I was about to kill a baby, right? Still to come were my parents dying, Peter and his wife telling me that we were over. Other crushing moments, but less important as I got older. I would eventually become myself, harder to hurt. In 1963, I was twenty.

"Emmy?"

I kept looking out the front window. We had gone to the clinic at three in the afternoon. It was dark outside now.

"Emmy?"

"Yes, please, make the call."

It was Thursday evening. She made the call the next day. I had an appointment to go to Jacksonville on Monday. Sunday at midnight, I started cramping and bleeding. An hour later I was sitting on a toilet having a miscarriage, with Dorothy doing her best to keep me from screaming. I did not have to go to Jacksonville. I broke no laws. I did not sin. I did not have an abortion. Whatever came out of me did not look like a baby. I was not guilty of anything. Intent was not a crime.

A week later, still weak, still padded up, but doped up too, I went to meet Peter James Jefferson. I sat in the back of the lecture hall. I was invisible.

All my first-week impressions of Peter? I blame Valium. I was high as a kite...or numb as a rock? Dorothy was my dealer, and her mother was her source. Valium came out in 1963, and Dorothy's mother was first in line, and Dorothy was pilfering meds as soon as her mother entered nirvana. I was feeling miserable after my miscarriage, so Dorothy handed me two blue round pills and told me to thank her later.

If I had been in pain, would that first day have been different?

There were probably fifty other students between me and the front of the room. I was feeling light-headed and all I really wanted to do was sleep. Peter was already at the front of the room when we started drifting in, writing on the blackboard, oblivious to me and his mostly male class. When the clock on the wall over the blackboard hit precisely eleven, he turned and everything began.

"A short class today. We'll go over the syllabus and I'll call roll. I apologize for not knowing your names right away. As you can tell, this is a large class, but I'll do my best. My name is at the top of the syllabus: Mister Jefferson. You can call me Mister Jefferson."

Nobody laughed except me. He did not notice. Things I would learn: He had a PhD but did not want to be called *Doctor* Jefferson. He especially disliked any letter signed like "*John Smith, PhD.*" He was not a scholar, and he was struggling to publish enough to get tenure.

"This is not a difficult course."

That got everybody's attention.

"Passing is easy. Getting a B is easy. Forty percent of your grade will come from four general exams, for each of which I will give you a hundred multiple-choice questions ahead of time. Only forty will be on the actual test. Those study questions are all answered in the textbook, but I will not discuss the text in class. You are responsible for reading and answering the questions I choose for the test when the time comes. The other half of the tests will be questions I ask which are based on my lectures. My lectures will not be a repetition of the textbook. Pay attention to anything I write on the board. If I do not write it on the board, it will not be on the test."

I was almost confused. Surely, he knew that unless he was writing something on the board that nobody would pay attention to anything else he said? He was laying a trap, and I fell into it at first.

"Twenty percent of your grade will come from two essays to be written."

I was not a stellar test taker, but I wasn't worried about writing.

"Twenty percent of your final grade is based on the Final Exam. It will be comprehensive."

The hill just got steeper.

"And the remaining twenty percent of your final grade will be based on attendance."

???????

"Choose your seat carefully. At the beginning of the next class, I will make a seating chart. Where you are sitting then is where I expect you to be for the rest of the semester. If it is empty, you are not here. If you are not here, you are absent. Everyone starts with a hundred points. Twenty percent of your final grade is an A+ as of this first class. First absence is a five-point deduction. Second absence is a ten-point deduction. You are down to a B. Third absence is a fifteen-point deduction. You are down to a C-. All subsequent absences are each worth a ten-point drop."

A hand shot up with the obvious question.

"Mister Jefferson, what if we're sick?"

"A note from the hospital, or the coroner, will be a valid excuse."

Why was it that I knew he was serious when everybody else thought he was joking?

"Let me explain something. This course is based on a few assumptions. One, I know more about this subject than you do. Two, this is a lecture course, not a lit course where you are entitled to an opinion. I absolutely promise you that, if you come to class and pay attention you will walk out smarter than you were when you walked in. That is why attendance is so important and you get credit. If you're not here, you're not as smart as you would have been if you were here. Your grade should reflect that. Taking lecture notes is important, but..."

And then he paused, looked all over the room, as if looking for something or somebody in particular, and for the rest of my life I would remember not only what he said next, but how his voice changed, from firm to soft, how it was as if he had been reading from a script, an introduction he had given many times and knew by heart, but suddenly quit reading from his script and simply shared a revelation he was having all by himself at that moment.

"...paying attention is more important. Listening. Paying attention to the world. For three hours a week, this is going to be your world. Pay attention...please."

The boy next to me, there in the back row, leaned over and whispered to me, insuring that he would be a character in one of my future, unimagined at that moment, books, a character I would probably cripple and maim.

"This guy is full of himself for sure."

The Valium was numbing my pain, but not my contempt for that crew-cut young man next to me. I did not respond, but I really hoped that when the next class began, he would choose a different seat. I was actually considering a change for myself, to move closer to the front, but old habits are hard to break. I was safer in the back row. As always. I just needed to figure out how to not be so invisible.

It was not love at first sight. He was handsome in a generic-male kind of handsome way, certainly not movie-star handsome. His wardrobe was totally unmemorable. He was tall, but tended to stoop a little when he walked, odd for such a young man. His brown hair was thick and wavy, and he obviously saved money on haircuts because it was long and then too long and then cut. He had a small gap in his right eyebrow. He would tell me later that he had been hit by a rock when he was a teenager, his brow gashed, stitches required, and in that tiny space in his brow the hair never grew back. You could not see the gap from a distance. But if his face was very close to yours, so close you could feel his breath, you could see it. His hands? He talked with his hands during his lectures. He did not use notes, so both hands were free as he paced back and forth in front of the blackboard. He had two recurring gestures. Sometimes his right hand would move slowly back and forth, as if it was a wave of water, ebbing back and forth. He could do that as he walked. When he was standing still, he would sometimes put his two hands together, but just the fingertips touching. And then, in my favorite part of his performance, when he would wander off into another one of those "I'm here all by myself" moments that only I knew was happening, he would raise his hands as if to pray, the fingers still touching but spread apart, and he would touch his lips with just the two forefingers. My first mistake with him was telling him about those gestures late in the semester, which I thought he would take as proof of how attentive I was in class, but all it did was make him self-conscious and he stopped doing them for a few weeks, only to have them return. His lectures for those few weeks were not his best.

His lectures? How had I not heard the stories about him before I signed up for the class? Dorothy had even been out of the loop. He had fifty students in that lecture hall who were actually in his grade-book, but he always had more than fifty in the hall. Five or ten extra every class. Not always the same five or ten, but always more than fifty warm bodies in attendance. I even convinced Dorothy to come listen to him. She came back more than once. She also pointed out to me that almost all the extra sit-ins were female.

Peter James Jefferson loved American History. I suppose any good teacher must love their subject. But can any good teacher turn his subject into a story? Peter told stories. He turned the Constitutional Convention into a drama. He made us actors.

Anybody six-foot-four in class? Come up front and stand here while I talk about George Washington. And I need somebody who is five-four too. Madison was five-four. Who's five-four?

Was that the first time he actually noticed me? I was five-five. But he needed somebody five-four. I shortened myself by an inch and raised my hand. I was long past my Valium days. A minute later I was standing next to George Washington, aka Billy Mottern, in Philadelphia. Dorothy was in class that day. She said I was spectacular.

I've seen lots of movies about teachers. Actors acting like some sort of stereotypical inspirational teacher. None of them were as good as Peter. Was it a matter of inadequate scripts or inadequate acting? Nor, I suppose, were any as good as Miss Randall. Dorothy agreed, in all the years we processed the teachers in our past, that Miss Randall was the kind of teacher who could pull things out of you, bring out some sort of essence in you that others had never seen. Peter was the kind of teacher who filled you up. He made you bigger by filling you up with a world that had always existed outside of you before. He said it once in class, but I think he was only talking to me.

Life is an accumulation of experience. Your own, for sure. History is the experience of others who lived before you. You need to accumulate their history too, to be part of their experience, to make your own life more interesting, to use their experience just like you would use your own, to understand yourself.

I tell young writers now, "You need to experience the lives of your characters. You have to be there with them when you write. You have to be in their own history. Not at a desk at home or a table at a coffee shop, you have to be in the story, discovering their history first hand." It sounds totally grand, right? Or just pretentious?

Sometimes he would tell stories that had nothing to do with history, but he explained to me that it was all part of being a teacher. Explained to me years after we started having sex.

"Every teacher can tell when he is losing his audience, usually near the end of a long class. Sorry, Emily, short attention spans are the norm, not the exception, even in my classes. And, truth is, sometimes even I need a break from the Monroe Doctrine or the Mason-Dixon Line. I like to tell stories, so I stop history and announce that I am going to tell a story. That story gets their attention back on me, so when I have their attention back, it might take a few minutes, and..."

"You make up stories. Peter, I figured it out soon enough. You said they were stories from your past, but you were just making them up, weren't you?"

"Tell me again, how old are you?"

"Peter, you've already crossed that Rubicon."

Did it all inevitably lead to me falling in love? Go back to the truest love of your life. Inevitable? Like I said, I don't believe in love at first sight. Lust at first sight is possible, sure, and Dorothy got there long before I did. But love is a tough nut to crack, or so they say. Love is real, I believe that. You can actually love someone who is not real, but the love itself is real. True, deep, and mad love can be real. Falling in love, even if you think you're not, is real.

I fell in love with his voice first. Of everything that happened to me after that first class, I think it would not have mattered if he did not have the voice he had. Even in that very first class, I would close my eyes and just listen to him. And, yes, almost fifty years later, I can close my eyes and still hear that voice. Sometimes I think I can see that voice. My mother would understand.

Dorothy understood, in her own Dorothy way. After the first time she heard him lecture, humoring my insistence that she come visit the class and see who I had been gushing about. As we were walking to another class, she hit me on the shoulder and said, "I would fuck that man's voice. No, no, I want that voice to fuck me."

The attraction was growing, a desire that surprised me. I thought about having sex with him. Where did that come from? Not just wanting to have sex with him, but wanting to have sex. Even when I was having sex with those earlier boys, I wasn't interested in the sex itself. Fantasy sex with Peter James Jefferson was a totally new world for me. But it was all one-sided. As far as I could tell, I was just James Madison in a skirt to him.

For how it eventually turned out, I blame my father. Before he died, when all we had left of the beginning was each other, I told him more and more about my life after I left home. I never told him about graduation night, but I did tell him about Peter. We were drinking wine together at my place on the beach, after midnight. He would be gone in a few years.

"You slept with a married man? One of your teachers? The one I met at your graduation?"

"Your fault, Daddy. Without something you said to me, I wouldn't have had a question to introduce myself to him."

It was a warm night in August. Full moon. We were drinking wine in the dark. No candles allowed. Doors and windows open, you could hear the ocean.

"Emmy, I am responsible for your nose."

"No doubt about that." I raised my near-empty wine glass and offered a toast. "To our nose."

"And I absolutely forbid you to go all Freud on me."

"Daddy, Freud was full of shit."

"We agree. But, Hester Prynne, you still owe me an explanation as to how I led you into adultery. And a refill. And if we keep going like this, we can watch the sun come up."

My father taught World History and Latin. But he knew a lot about American History and he would salt any kitchen table discussion of politics with a reference to something from American history, especially when Miss Randall would come over for dinner. Me, I wasn't all that interested, but a few weeks into Peter's class, I remembered something my father had said about the Constitution. I thought it would be the perfect question to ask in class, to at least let him know that I existed as me and not James Madison. I was ready, and then I folded. I did not raise my hand. I left class kicking myself for my cowardice. The next class, the same.

Plan B? I wrote the question in a note, then went to the department office and asked the secretary to put the note in his mailbox. I did not sign the note. Again, kickable cowardice.

At the beginning of the next class, Peter looked around the room and then did something he never did. He pulled some pages out of his big notebook, took a few minutes to read them to himself while we waited, and then he began.

"I had an interesting question posed to me yesterday from someone in this class. An unsigned note in my mailbox. Whoever you are, thank you. It's not a fashionable question in these days, but still important. Let me read it to you: *I was told that the Constitution was written by a bunch of Capitalists who were simply protecting their wealth, and that they made even more money after writing the Constitution. It had nothing to do with freedom or checks and balances and all that. Is that true?*"

Was I blushing? Was I about to wet my pants? Was I thrilled?

"So, I am going to talk about something that's not in my usual lecture schedule. It should have been, and will be in the future, but I should discourage the rest of you from slipping me a lot of questions. I don't want to have to rewrite an entire semester of lectures."

I wished my father was there in class with me.

"I think the questioner is referring to the work of Charles Beard, his economic interpretation of American history. Beard is interesting. Yes, half the men who worked on the Constitution were slaveowners, and yes, the Constitution protected slavery. It was an essential compromise at the time. I've already mentioned, I think, the fact that the word 'slave' is never even mentioned in that document. And, yes, as I'll discuss more as we get closer to the Civil War, slavery was the economic engine of early America. So, it is fair to talk now about the Constitution and slavery and racism and wealth all being intertwined in American history."

An hour later, I felt ten years older.

He had said, "*I should discourage the rest of you from slipping me a lot of questions. I don't want to have to re-write an entire semester of lectures.*" What I heard was, *Whoever asked this question, feel free to ask another. But I do not want to hear from the rest of you.*"

A week later, he had another note in his mailbox: *Other than Betsy Ross, were there any other women in America before 1800?* I thought I had just the right blend of curiosity and irony, and to further hide my identity, I signed that note: *Your prettiest student.* A week went by. No acknowledgment. And then he answered the question in class, and disappointed me at the same time. Not in his answer, but because he simply acted as if my question did not exist.

"Historians have usually ignored women in American history, but prior to 1800..." and then he went through some women I already knew about and added new ones: Anne Hutchinson, Anne Bradstreet, Mary Dyer, Abigail Adams, Dolly Madison, Mary Rowlandson, and even George Washington's first love, Mary Philipse, "...some notable in their own right, others for how they influenced the men around them..."

What about me? That was the question in my mind. What about the pretty student who asked you the question in the first place? He did not even acknowledge that it was not his idea, this sudden inclusion of women in history. He was taking all the credit. I was twenty years old, and I was sulking like a fourteen-year-old.

And then my world tilted and never recovered, for a long time.

"Emily Sterling, would you please see me after class."

Class was ending, a minute before the end, and he called my name. As everyone else filed out, some stopped by his lectern to talk to him, delaying me, enraging me. I wanted them to go away.

There was not another class in that lecture hall after his, so we were finally left alone. I was still in my back-row seat. He was still standing down front, obviously waiting on me to come to him. It was not my plan, to stay in my seat, I had no grand dramatic gesture to make, I was simply scared to go to him. He looked at me and then shrugged as if to say, *And?* I did not move. So, he came to me, leaving the stage, walking up the steps to the back row, holding a manilla folder.

"I wanted to thank you."

My dumb response? "You're welcome." I had no idea what he was thanking me for.

"Those were two good questions. Thank you for asking them."

I was busted, I was joyous, and I'm sure I was blushing.

"How did you know?"

"You asked the secretary to put them in my mailbox. I asked her who had given them to her. She described you. And then you did it again, my same question to secretary, same description, and only you look like you. All I had to do after the first question was go to class, look for you, and see your name in that seating chart square. I wasn't sure if I should acknowledge you, since you obviously wanted to remain anonymous, but..."

The tilting began. I'm sure he probably kept talking without a pause, but I like to remember it differently, as if he said "but" and I had waited for him to finish the sentence, the thing that made him seek me out.

"...but I finished grading the first set of essays last night."

And with that he opened the folder and handed me my essay.

"This is exceptional. You sure you want to be an English major? The history profession is full of the deadest writers in the English language. You understand history, you write...well, better than I do."

How did he know I was an English major? How did I not realize that he was being serious and teasing me at the same time?

"I am teaching the second half of the survey next semester. I hope that you'll take it too."

I talk about my world tilting. I even told him later, years into sex and love, how the tilting had begun that day. He confessed to the same tilt, the same day, when I had responded to his asking about the next semester.

"I knew I was going to take your next class the first day of this one."

Was it true? I think so, as best I can remember.

And then I stood up. He stepped back and we walked down the steps together. He stopped at the edge of the stage. I waited, not sure we were actually finished with our first personal conversation. I wanted more.

"Emily, if you ever have any other questions for me, you should give them to me directly. Come see me in my office. I have office hours posted, but I can see you any time convenient for you. We can talk, okay?"

"Thank you, Mister Jefferson, I'd like that very much."

Wasn't that the moment when he was supposed to say, *No need for that between us now. You can call me Peter.*

"Great, I'll see you next week in class. Have a good weekend."

Did I immediately rush to tell Dorothy about what had just happened? Absolutely not.

I apologize for being gone so long. I have not been feeling well, but that's not the real problem. If I can sit in front of a keyboard, sniffling or aching, I can write. I have never understood the concept of "writer's block." My problem is the opposite. I cannot stop writing. I have been gone because I have been writing too much.

I am writing a story about my life, and I can break my life down into a beginning, middle, and end. Truth is, I ended the story. And I started again. I was up to a thousand pages, so I had to end it. A thousand pages and I was still talking about Peter James Jefferson. All the things I talked about when I had aspiring writers in front of me… narrative flow, pacing, addition or omission of details, especially dialogue…all those things. I had been ignoring my own guidelines. But I have also been honest with myself. First drafts are usually not perfect.

How's that for an understatement? You write, and then you rewrite. Different writers have different approaches. Some finish a complete first draft and then start surgery. Some work blocks at a time. Me, I'm a block reviser. A hundred pages, and then I reread and polish and continue, a block at a time, and then I take all the blocks and start over. Looking for the last, final, complete version of the story.

A thousand pages, almost all of it about him. But my life was not just one thing, even if that thing was Peter.

Peter James Jefferson, whose name I think about changing. Everyone else important...my parents, Miss Randall, Dorothy, the others...they never change because I think that I understand them. Their names are them. Peter James Jefferson? The great mistake of my life, the great delusion, the ten years I am supposed to regret but would live again if I could. A thousand pages just about him? A thousand pages about a man with no real name? Nope, he won't get that from me. He should have written his own life while he had the chance.

Still, it was a perverse pleasure, those thousand pages about him, because I got to go back and live it again. Go back and read all the correspondence, the notes in my own notebooks, even talk to Dorothy about him, so she could remind me that I had been foolish at the time, and that she had told me I was foolish as it was happening. A perverse pleasure, to have her remind me about how foolish I had been, and then to remind her what she also said back then.

"You're being very foolish, Emmy, but I know that you're going to do whatever you want. But, damn, girl, you don't have to be so fucking happy being such a fool."

I wrote a thousand pages and I could still not pin him down, understand him. So, I had to start over. You are reading the third draft. I figured out that my understanding Peter was not important. No, I was really writing all those pages to understand who I was. To understand that girl who would become the woman I am. Or, considering how other things are rushing toward me, the woman I was.

Peter James Jefferson was something, but not everything.

I'm going to start my story over.

It feels a shame to be Alive—/When Men so brave—are dead

Remember how I said I collected every piece of correspondence between us? The very first thing? My second essay for him that first semester. A grade in red ink, A+, and then just two words in his handwriting: *See me?* A question or a command or a wish? See him when? Right after class? Go to his office? I went to his office after class. If I had paid attention, and been objective, that visit should have stopped me from ever seeing him in private again.

"You wanted to see me?"

Is everyone's office an extension of themselves? I ask that and then I realize that most people aren't lucky enough to have an office all to themselves. Their own private room, a room of their own. Thank you, Virginia. A room to help you think, a room with artifacts of your life. The things that matter to you? Peter's office was a mess, an absent-minded professor mess. Stacks of papers on his desk, books stacked in chairs, diplomas on the wall, each slightly tilted. A giant window behind him, west side of the building, so at certain times of the day, as I would eventually discover, the setting sunlight would go around him and almost blind the person facing him. Perhaps not, perhaps I was the only person who was blinded.

"Emily, yes, please come in."

In all the time we knew each other, he never lied to me. On his desk were two framed pictures: his wedding picture, and a picture of his wife all by herself, a picture of her when she was younger than I was at that moment. I had always known that he was married. I had noticed his wedding ring the first time he spoke to me after class. He had even mentioned her in class in passing, something about errands he had to run, a faculty party that he and she both wanted to avoid, or having to leave class early because he had to get his wife early from her salon visit. Small toss-away talk. He had an adult life, a wife life, but none of it was real until I saw the pictures on his desk. I was headed into the future with my eyes wide open.

"You wanted to see me, Mister Jefferson?"

"Yes, yes, and just between us, you can call me Peter out of class."

Finally.

Intuition? I knew that when he said "out of class" he actually meant "when we're alone."

"I just wanted to compliment you on your writing…again. Some remarkable insights, some of them not quite relevant to the actual topic, but always interesting."

I had been flattered the first time he complimented my writing, but I was irritated the second time.

"Thank you."

I had obviously been constructing a fantasy about him all those weeks, but there he was just being a good teacher, throwing a crumb of positive reinforcement to a bright student. Sometimes words don't matter, though. Sometimes it's a look or a tone of voice, especially when the teacher doesn't look at you when he speaks, but somewhere else, somewhere in the future?

"You know, I've never had a student quote some lines from Emily Dickinson in an essay about the Gettysburg Address."

I was back to mush again.

"You only cited the first two lines, but I went to Johnson's collection and found the entire poem."

He was looking at his messy bookshelves, so I followed his eyes to see Thomas Johnson's edition on the top shelf.

I hesitated before asking, "You like Dickinson?"

"I love her."

How utterly adolescent was I? Utterly bug-eyed adolescent.

"Really?"

He tilted his head down but kept eye contact with me.

"Are you seriously surprised? I mean, seriously, I thought you knew me better than that."

Where did that come from?

"Peter, I don't know you at all."

He looked up, then down again, losing eye contact. I kept staring at him. Sometimes, I bet you know, a few seconds seems like an hour. Neither one of us spoke for a few seconds. Me, I was trying very hard to memorize the moment, how his face looked, his hair, his hands. He started to slowly nod his head. I wanted him to say something that would make me stop falling in love with him. Hindsight, sure. Literary embellishment, a little. He looked back at me, then across his desk, past the picture of his wife, then back at me.

"We have time."

I took a deep breath. Time? If I could resurrect him now, as I tell you this story, I would educate my dearly loved favorite former history teacher about the absolute lack of enough time for him or me or Dorothy, or for my mother and father, or his wife. Not enough time for any goddam person in the universe. Sure, now, knocking on heaven's door, I've had "time" to know him, almost enough time to know myself. Time to find another Dickinson poem.

Forever – is composed of Nows – 'Tis not a different time –

He told me three years later, naked in bed with a very naked me at the Dupont Circle Hotel in Washington, lying on his side, propped up by his right arm, about the first time he actually thought I was romantically interested in him, a line he loved but I had forgotten, what he called my first *adult* line, responding to him saying that "we have time."

"Peter, I'm not getting any younger."

Without me having time to take another breath, he responded, "Nor, Juliet, am I."

How could I not laugh? And then he said something I think ought to be on my tombstone.

"You know, Emily, you're a very strange young woman. I'd love to know you when you're fifty or sixty, when your life sorts itself out."

"Yeah, me too, Peter. I hope I'm around."

"Well, until then, you have to get through this semester and my class next semester. But, for now, one reason I wanted to see you is that I have a list of books you might be interested in, based on what you wrote in your essays."

"Extra credit?"

I was joking. He knew it.

"You don't need extra credit, Miss Dickinson. No, these are books you ought to read before you die, or before I die. No hurry. I think we're both in good shape for now."

It was then that I wished I had thought to get him a gift before I went home for Christmas. But I had a month, from holiday break until first day of classes in January, to figure out what. You know the oddest thing about that first time in his office? From entrance to exit, I was probably there less than fifteen minutes.

"And one more thing, when you get back, I'd like to take you to lunch sometime. Is that okay with you?"

"A drink?"

"Lunch. You're barely old enough to drink."

Christmas in 1963. Kennedy was dead. Jackie was a widow. My mother was starting to die, a fact unknown to her or me or my father, but it had begun.

Quakers seem to have a reputation for being austere in word and deed. Not big on ceremonies and holidays. Worse than the Catholics in their choice of music. Evidently, my parents were not Quaker role models. True, we did not spend a lot on gifts. My parents always seemed indifferent to getting things for themselves or each other, but they would make an exception for me. Me, trying to shop for them? You ever try to buy a gift for two adults who have all they want?

Not with material things, my parents were decadent with simple pleasures. For Christmas week, our house was five degrees warmer than the week before or after. Winters in Florida were seldom actually cold, but coolness drove us indoors. Heating bills be damned. The lights might not be blazing, but a hundred candles were. And the food? There was not a cow or pig or chicken or pumpkin safe in central Florida, and our kitchen was a culinary version of Dante's inferno. A lot of roasting and baking going on. And that was our tradition. My parents cooked for an ark and we gave it all away. More precisely, we opened our doors to anybody who needed food and I was there with my parents every year. My mother hated going outside in the winter, so let the hungry come to us, right?

Christmas Day dinner was our personal family meal, excess epitomized, leftovers given away the next day. It was also one of the few meals that my grandmother would eat with us. I sometimes had the feeling, especially when I was very young, that she looked at her son and daughter-in-law as sinners in their excess. A perennial scowl. Only after her death was I told that she had been a lifelong atheist. Why had it not been obvious to me all along, her future atheist grand-daughter?

Christmas Day dinner was opulent, but the Christmas Eve supper was more important to me, the tradition I would have copied with my own children if I had had any. Our meal? It was never opulent. It was not even a meal. We ate desserts. We had popcorn balls. You want fudge? Fudge you got. We drank Coca-Colas. We filled up on anything bad for us. And we each opened one present, always the same present every year for each of us...our new pajamas. My father loved this tradition. Not only would we open the present, we would then put on the new pj's and wear them the rest of the night. My favorite memory? The Christmas that my father found matching pajamas for the three of us. Christmas Eve was always good, but if I had to choose only one to relive, it would be that one in 1963, the Sterlings in their red flannel pajamas, sugared almost into a coma, a kitchen filled with future memories of the aroma of spices and glazed hams baking. And my parents singing. My mother's pristine alto. My father's warm baritone. Christmas carols? Not a chance. They sang show tunes and ballads from the '40s, bubble-gum pop from the '50s. My Quaker father imitating Johnny Mathis singing "Chances Are" was worth the price of admission all by itself. That was the night that I almost wept from happiness. I remembered a lot of all those songs. They had sung them to me before I was born. Christmas Eve, I was a baby waiting to be born.

Christmas Eve, 1963. I was falling in love with Peter James Jefferson.

"Welcome back to reality. I hope you had a good Christmas, and I assume that you all brought me a gift, right? See me after class. Until then, let's go over the syllabus. Basic theme for the first week: How the North won the War but lost Reconstruction."

How did he know that I had a gift for him? I should have thought about it before I went home for the Christmas break, but I was still… not sure? Not sure about a lot of things, particularly him. How was I supposed to feel about being attracted to, obsessed with, a married man? Especially since he had done nothing to encourage me. Nothing except talk to me after almost every class the previous semester. Nothing except look at me in class at the oddest moments. We would be taking an exam, everybody's head down, focusing on the test in front of us, and I would feel something, so I would look up and he would be looking at me. We became the only people in the lecture hall. Eye contact made, I would quickly look down again. Nothing except tell me that he wanted to take me to lunch when I got back from home after Christmas. Nothing except tell me that we had time to get to know each other. No, he never encouraged me, right?

I had told my father that I wanted to get a gift for my history teacher. Shouldn't that have been a red flag to any father? His college-age daughter was buying gifts for a young male history teacher whose class she had described over and over at the kitchen table, about how his lectures were inspiring and…no, in my father's world, teachers like Peter James Jefferson did not exist. The classroom version, sure, but how was my father to know what Peter was like outside of a classroom. *That* Peter James Jefferson?

Dorothy had enrolled in his Spring class, telling me that she was going to become the angel on my shoulder who had to work against the devil on my other shoulder.

"Can you be any more obvious, Emmy?

"It's just a late Christmas gift."

"I rest my case."

"Remind me to not tell you anything else about my life, okay?

"Right, right. Just remember…you are my bitch."

"And you are trying too hard to be my Jiminy Cricket."

"I hate it when you do that, make some comment that makes sense to you but nobody else."

That first day of class, she had seen the gift in my purse. She did an exaggerated vocal mime.

"Fooouuur Paaaaayyyyter?"

I wrote a note to her: *Be nice to me and I will make sure you get an A in this class.*

She put her middle finger in her nose. Both of us in our twenties, acting twelve.

After class, I went to his office, gift in hand.

"You do realize that I was kidding about expecting a gift from anybody, right?"

You ever have one of those hindsight lightbulbs go off in your head? You see who you were a million years ago. You wish you had seen it then. Dorothy and I were almost women, by all the legal and social rules. Almost old enough to vote and drink. We had broken the sex stereotypes, neither one of us a virgin. But we weren't really adults. True, being twenty-one wouldn't mean we could get our own credit cards. A lot of that other pre-Nineteenth Amendment garbage was in its death throes, even if we did not see it then. No, something was different with me, between me and Dorothy. Together, she and I, kids like us, we were growing up. When I was with Peter, I already felt grown up. I felt like I was not in Dorothy's world anymore. My hindsight is not that I was wrong. I might have been delusional. No, the hindsight is that I felt like that at all. I think I felt it first when I went to his office that afternoon.

"Peter, you weren't expecting a gift from anyone else, but I know you were expecting something from me."

"Excuse me, but who are you?"

"I am your favorite and prettiest student."

"Well, favorite and prettiest student, prove it."

I had the perfect gift for him, a copy of the latest Richard Hofstadter book, *Anti-Intellectualism in American Life.* How could he not be impressed? I watched intently as he unwrapped it, focusing on his face, wanting to see him smile, as I knew he would. Book in hand, he remained blank. He was at a loss for words, but for the wrong reason.

"This is very...generous...of you."

The odd thing about that moment. I wasn't hurt. I wasn't crushed like a child who gave a parent a handmade puppet for Christmas, something like that, full of love but not made with any skill or talent. The parent would react with genuine gratitude but also, deep down, you could see him or her thinking, *What the hell do I do with something like this?* Peter wasn't that obvious, but something was wrong with my gift, and I was, at that moment, profoundly curious as to what I got wrong. I kept staring at him, and his expression finally changed.

"I have a gift for you too."

He went to his book shelf and pulled down a pristine, unopened, spine not cracked, copy of the same book.

"Peter?"

"Here's some sort of cosmic irony...I've heard you use that term before, right...cosmic irony. I bought this book for myself last week. I had been looking forward to reading it this summer. But now I can give this one to you and maybe you'll read it too."

I'm sorry to sound stupidly sappy here, and in no so-called adult world would the work of Richard Hofstadter ever be considered "romantic," but there we were, me giving him a gift he had already bought for himself and him giving me the same damn book. A stupid O. Henry story on stage in Florida. Hair combs and pocket-watch fobs floating in air. But, if it's true, how am I supposed to understand it? Not just the exchange, but Peter? He did not have to tell me that he already had a copy. My girl heart could have been broken, right? He could have accepted mine and simply put the other copy away, never to be acknowledged. But here's what I think happened back then. I think that as soon as he saw what I had given him, he intuitively knew, immediately, because he cared about me more than he wanted to admit, that the moment required some sort of…gesture… from him, some reciprocal gesture of both honesty and…affection? He did not have time to think about all that. He had a few seconds to react, and it had to be emotional, not rational. I've rewritten this scene a dozen times, but I always come back to the same conclusion: Peter James Jefferson was falling in love with me.

"I guess I owe you something else, uh?"

"No, Emily, this is perfect. Thank you."

"But you already have it. You wanted it. You bought it."

I wasn't upset. I was just still curious.

"I do now," he said, holding the one I gave him. "This is the one I wanted. And the fact that you would know that I wanted it…that is why it's the one I want now. Makes sense to me. But I'm serious about you taking this and saving for later. I might make a History major out of you yet."

"Peter, that train has left the station. My English teacher in high school got to me first."

That point in any conversation where you're not sure where to go, what to say, next? The elephant in the room? It was finally time for me to go there.

"One more thing, you might want to keep this in your office and not take it home. I inscribed it for you."

The Emmy that Dorothy knew would have never said that. Then again, the Emmy she knew would not have written the inscription that she did for her older married history teacher.

He gave me one of those *Are you for real?* looks, sat down, and opened the book. How to describe his expression as he read it? I'll figure it out for the final draft. But I can tell you what he did next. He motioned for me to give him the book that he had given me and then he wrote his own inscription to me: *January 10, 1964—Never stop asking questions. The right answers are not always obvious. Mister Jefferson.*

He handed the book back to me and I read the inscription. The ending was perfect.

"Yessir, Mister Jefferson."

Before he could stand up, I walked around his desk and leaned down to kiss him on the top of his head, and then I walked out. Three months later, I would kiss him on the lips.

An hour later, Dorothy was grilling me about what happened in the office and I told her the truth…about the same book being exchanged, about our small talk, but I did not tell her about the kiss. I showed her his inscription to me, the Mister Jefferson inscription, but I did not tell her about my inscription to him.

Dorothy had no illusions about where Peter and I were headed, and she never let me forget for the rest of our lives together. More than once, she had the same question.

"You seriously thought you were in love with him? That he loved you?"

She never accepted either possibility. But she was wrong. She gave me hell, but she was wrong. To her, I was a misguided cliché, the Trifecta of clichés. I had an affair with an older man, a married man, and my teacher. That it lasted so long was irrelevant.

After many years she finally granted me a small absolution.

"Well, if it was real, I'm happy for you. But just remember, I warned you. I told you about the rumors about him and other students."

"Dorothy, yes you did, but when I asked you to name a single girl, point to anybody who you or anybody else knew for sure had slept with him…all you could say was 'well, I heard…' and all you had was a goddam rumor, and remember all those rumors about Miss Randall? Did you believe those? No, you didn't, when I told you what had happened with her and my daddy and the principal, all you said was something along the lines of 'those fucking bitches'… so don't talk to me about rumors now."

I kept insisting that Peter was not to blame for what happened, that nothing would have happened between us if I had not wanted it to happen.

"Dammit, Emmy, that doesn't make it right. He was your teacher. It was his responsibility to not let himself get involved with you. He was wrong."

"It was my choice."

"Emmy, you were twenty-one. Barely old enough to vote, much less choose to sleep with a married man. An irritatingly smart twenty-one, old lady mature in a lot of ways, but he should have had better judgment, to stop you from hurting yourself."

"So, it wasn't my decision to make?"

"No! You were too young. He was your teacher. He took advantage of you, whether you believe that or not."

"You knew it all along, Dorothy. I told you when it started. You didn't discourage me then."

"No, Emmy, you're right. I was a lousy friend. Who knows, maybe I was jealous. Sexy older man liked you and not me. Maybe I was just stupid like you. Who knows?"

"Ten years older was not older."

She finally granted me a point.

"You know, I could see that age wasn't really an issue even then, but he was still your teacher…and he was still married. And you didn't care. You did it anyway. That's on you as well as him. I don't know about other wives, but if Jake ever cheated on me, I would lock his balls in a freezer and go after the bitch he screwed."

I loved Dorothy, and I could have kept quiet at that moment, but she was attacking me, so…fair game, right? It was fair, but I was cruel.

"But you cheated on Jake, Dorothy. He never knew, but I do. You were the bitch that somebody else's husband screwed."

She went ballistic.

"That was different, Emmy! It didn't mean anything! You know that!"

I did not respond. I just waited. We had been in my house on the beach, waiting for a phone call from her son in Atlanta to tell us about the birth of her first grandchild. An ultrasound had indicated a baby girl on the way, and Dorothy's first grand-daughter was going to be named Dorothy.

"Emmy, I know, fuck do I know, I was stupid for a few years, no excuse, but never stupid enough to think that those men loved me, or that I loved them. So, we okay?"

"Oh, hell, Dorothy, we've had bigger piss fights. We're okay. I just wish I could explain me and Peter better. It was complicated…Peter and his wife…and me. Complicated."

Rumors? Let me tell you about a rumor, about me. But it begins with my first flash of jealousy for a man who was married to somebody else. He wasn't even sleeping with me. Except for that platonic peck on the top of his head, Peter and I had never touched, much less kissed. I had no right to be jealous, right? Dorothy had already told me that Peter had a "reputation." As if we were back in high school again. I dismissed her simply because I did not want it to be true. I was possessive but had no title of ownership. He was married.

But, two months after exchanging books in his office, I was in class watching Jessica Wyman flirt with Peter. It was obvious. Class was over, essays turned in, and there she stood at his lectern, leaning forward to whisper something to him. Suspicious enough to me, but then he put his hand over hers and patted it, leaning forward himself to whisper to her. Daggers, I was throwing daggers. His guilt was obvious ten minutes later when I went to his office and Jessica was there with him, her eyes red and wet. Had he broken her heart? Or was she blissfully in love?

How's this for a cliché. Life is full of teachable moments. You just have to be teachable.

His office door was open, so I had just walked in, acted surprised, apologized for the intrusion, and left. She might have been oblivious to my anger, but I'm sure he wasn't. It was the next day that I became teachable. She was enrolled in another class of mine, a Fundamentals of Teaching class required of anybody thinking of being a public school teacher. She wasn't there. I skipped class and went looking for her. Where? I had no idea. I just went looking for her, and I found her on a Quad bench. I sat beside her and started another faux apology.

"I'm sorry again about yesterday. It was rude of me to barge in like that."

She was visibly nervous. She was also, up close, very pretty, the kind of creamy-skin, flawless-complexion, high-cheekbone, blue-eyed kind of pretty that was never in my future. She kept looking down, and then, dammit, started crying. I was suddenly her older sister.

"Hey, let's go get a snack, okay?"

Fifteen minutes later, we were in the dining hall, squirreled away in a corner. It was soon obvious that she had our awkward meeting from the previous day on her mind. I let her confess.

"He told me to not tell anyone, that it was our secret, but I know it looked bad, and I hope you don't think I was…that anything was going on. I know that you and him are…friends."

The rumor was me.

"But he is such a wonderful man."

"Jessica, are you okay? Did he…"

"No, no, Emily. I'm dropping out of school. I was just telling him. I hadn't turned in the essay that was due, and my last test was a failure. Before then, I was doing better in that class than I expected. I really wanted him to think I was smart enough to at least get a B. I mean, I know I'm not as smart as you, nobody else in class is either, but I'm smarter than I look."

Even now, almost fifty years later, I could kick myself, but not as much as I wanted to kick myself back then.

"What's wrong, Jessica? Are you sick?"

And then the waterworks started again.

"My father is sick. He's going to die, and he's all by himself. I go home as much as I can, to take care of him, but it's all too much, and I'm failing all my classes, so I went to Mister Jefferson to tell him that I was dropping out. I wanted to apologize to him."

Her father is dying, her grades are in the toilet, and she was apologizing to her teacher? Even then, I completely understood her.

"Maybe I could help you in some of your classes? Try to salvage something?"

She grabbed my hand and I thought she was going to kiss it. Jessica Wyman was evidently a "touching" person.

"Thank you, thank you. Mister Jefferson even suggested that I talk to you about helping me. But it's too late. I'll try to start over after… after…"

He was thinking of me when he was talking to her?

"…but he did something for me that I am supposed to keep a secret. But you're okay, aren't you? Everybody knows you're special to him. You'll keep his secret too?"

She said it without condemnation or innuendo. It was just a fact.

"Jessica, I'm not sure where you're going with this…"

"He told me to not worry about the class. I should go home and take care of my father, and he said to take care of myself too. He was going to give me a B for the course anyway. No more tests or papers. He said I deserved a B, that I was headed there anyway. That I should not worry about my grade. In the big picture, or something like that, it was irrelevant. I'm not supposed to tell anybody, but I'm sure he won't mind you knowing."

Little bits and pieces about Peter James Jefferson. Topics of future conversations.

Jessica and I parted, hugging each other, promising to keep in touch, and we did until she died thirty years later. All in the future. That day, I went looking for Dorothy. If everybody thought that Peter and I were one of those academic clichés of prof and mattress-mate student, if Jessica thought that, and Dorothy had told me about "rumors," why hadn't my best friend told me that I was the inspiration for all those rumors? When I cornered her later, she had an answer.

"Emmy, you were his pet, that was obvious, but nobody ever thought you were the kind he would sleep with. And that drove a lot of people crazy. You're in a rumor category all by yourself. The kind that makes the rest of us jealous."

I've lived long enough to know how women are abused by men, especially young women. Even in college back before social media and the internet, we all knew stories about coeds being seduced by older men. Professors who were beasts, who coerced insecure girls into sex, or who simply offered grades for sex. Predatory. It was just part of the culture. And, unless they were criminally stupid about their behavior, there were no consequences. Dorothy was propositioned more than once. It never happened to me. I was not surprised. I did not look like Dorothy. But there was another part of the academic culture that was also true, then and now. When I taught in college, I could see it all around me, and a few of my male colleagues would confirm it, but only after they were sure I was a safe audience. Young women away from home, away from restraints, young women who wanted to experience sex with older men. Seductress, not the seduced. I am sure it is more common now. Sexuality is for women as well as men, right? Thank you, Hugh Hefner. Thank you, feminism. Thank you, birth control pill. Young women are freer now. But, were there ever rules for that sort of thing? There are laws now, and thank God for that, to protect women, punish men, sometimes punish them when they are innocent. Science to protect women's bodies. Indeed, more women going to college than men, more female professors in the ranks. But, moral rules? Emotional rules? I think about this now, more clearly than I did back then, but I still wonder.

Sometimes, when I am the most tired, when I just want to go to sleep and not wake up, I want to stop writing. My father had journals. My mother had notes that became smoke and ashes. I have journals. I could just point you to the shelves in my tiny home office where everything is, and tell you, "There you have it, go crazy, read it all without me trying to spin it. Do your own editing." The only problem? My own personal shorthand and codes. A page from one day might only be a few lines, not even sentences, just details to jar my memory when I went back to read them. Conversations in Peter's office? That day we exchanged books? That page only had four words: *history books, first kiss.* I could look at those and everything would come back. But my shelves have other cryptic evidence too. Go find the stack of wall calendars I saved from 1964 through 1969. I always used calendars as a diary as well as appointment reminders. Look for the little blocks, the days of the week, notes of things I had to do in the near future, but pay attention to the small print in the corners, the roman numeral followed by a noun. Start with November 13, 1964. The Friday block, in my perfect cursive: *X-office.* It was the tenth time Peter and I had sex. We were in his office. Yes, I kept track of every time we had sex. For the first year, I recorded how many times were accumulating. Eventually I stopped keeping count, at CX, but I always wrote down the location. For evidence of how out-of-control two people in lust can be, go to May 16, 1965.

You want to see how really immature I was? Go find the blocks where I listed the date and location and drew, in the smallest writing I could, a tiny heart. By that time, I was twenty-three. And drawing stupid hearts. Is that a contradiction? Admitting that Dorothy was right, that I was too young to be making such serious decisions... mistakes...for myself. And still insisting that she was wrong. If you still think that, go find the locked metal box on the bottom shelf. If I could remember where I kept the key, I'd give it to you, but you have my permission to break it open. All the correspondence between him and me is in that box. Long before the internet and email and texting and all the other white noise makers of modern communication, we wrote letters and postcards to each other. I would send mine to his office address. And I lost those forever when he died. All I have are the notes and letters he wrote to me. Go read them. Smash the lock on that box. See if I was immature or he was not real. In the long run, I suppose, like most things, irrelevant.

Here's a mature hindsight: Peter James Jefferson was in my life, but he was not my life. We weren't Bronte material yet. I had to finish college. Which led to my first life-altering decision. Graduating would mean not seeing Peter every day, and I was not ready to go to work like any other adult. My student-teaching days as an undergraduate convinced me that I was not teacher material for teenagers. How did Miss Randall do it? Put up with all the drama? I went to graduate school for a Master's in English. Ninety miles away from Peter, an hour-and-a-half drive, but only twenty miles away from my parents. So, I was near them when the beginning of the end began for my mother.

I've been accused of being melodramatic. Among other kinds of behavior. Too self-conscious about the words I choose, the comparisons I make. Capital crimes, right? *The beginning of the end* for my mother. I suppose I could abbreviate and simply say that my mother got cancer and died. But her God is not getting off so easy in my world. My mother got cancer, suffered, and died. And her suffering made my father suffer. For their suffering, their God can go to Hell.

I was there when the first blood appeared. Home for a weekend, feeling heady because I was almost finished with my Master's thesis, I was also binge-eating to compensate for how I had been starving myself. It was all so calm, how she spoke to me after she came back to the kitchen from the bathroom.

"Well, that was odd."

So odd, indeed, to see blood in the toilet bowl after she urinated. She said "blood" and my first thought was proof that I had no idea how old my mother had become. She still looked thirty.

"Probably just a period thing," I said, not really thinking about her.

I was twenty-six.

"Emmy, I stopped having periods years ago."

Blood in urine? Once is odd. But again, and again, and blood becomes a symbol and a symptom. My father took my mother to a hospital two days after she told him about the blood, which had actually appeared a week before that. Her life had been so easy, remember what my father said? Bad things did not happen to my mother. I met them at the hospital and went with my mother into the examining room, my father's surrogate. The urologist was a man, as were all the interns and residents. My mother was the sixth of ten patients they would see that day. My job? To translate everything for my father, because he and I both knew that she would not tell him anything that would make him worry.

The good news? Except for the blood, my mother had had no worrisome symptoms. The bad news, in the unintentionally comic language of the doctor?

"There's a growth on the bladder wall that looks like a little mushroom cap. We clipped it out and will get the biopsy results soon."

My mother loved that.

"Emmy, I'm growing mushrooms. My bladder is a hothouse for fungus."

"Mother, I'm sure that Daddy will not be amused."

"It will be fine, Emmy. The doctor said that we probably got everything in the early stages."

My father was not amused. It was cancer. Cancer was not funny. But the doctors had been right. It was caught early. Surgery was not immediately required. No need to remove the bladder...yet. New treatments included chemo drugs to retard growth or new tumors. My mother was even amused when the doctor told her that her cancer was considered a "low-grade" form, not aggressive. My father was still unable to laugh about anything.

With my father still teaching, I became my mother's designated… everything. I took her to the hospital for her early chemo treatments, and I soon realized that my mother lied to my father all the time about how she felt. She would come out of the treatments noticeably weaker. I would get her home and she would describe the after-effects in terms that she never used with my father.

"Emmy, I feel like there's a burning bowling ball in my bladder. Excuse the alliteration. But a damn bowling bowl. Birthing you was apple pie compared to this." A rare profanity from her, although I never understood the apple pie and birth comparison. My father would come home and take over for me, and she would only say that she was feeling uncomfortable. The two days after the treatment were the worst, she would recover, and then go back for another round.

But she got better. The cancer did not recur. All that changed was my relationship with my parents. I was spending more time alone with my mother, not like after my high school graduation, when we spent time together without speaking, but this new phase was her talking all the time, very often about my father. She would talk about him and their life, and I would then look at him differently when I was alone with him. But he did the same too. My mother would be resting a lot while I was visiting, and he and I would talk…about her. Each would say things about the other to me that they would never say to each other. Not bad things, not disappointments or frustrations, but each would tell me stories about the other that I had never heard before, stories about their lives before I was born, their lives before they were married. Thing is, I did not have to ask them.

For that first year after her diagnosis, it was as if they wanted to relive their lives with each other, and telling me was re-living everything. I'm not sure now, but I wonder if they expected me to share more of my own life with them.

That's the sorrow of my own life. How could I share my life with them when I was living a life they could not accept? I was in love with, sleeping with, a married man. Every time I got back from taking care of my mother, I would call Peter. The voice, remember? I would be disappointed if there was not a letter waiting for me. I was juggling my schedule to finish school, take care of my mother, and see him. Admirable multitasking, right?

The problem with telling you all this now? How do I tell a story that is two stories? Back and forth in parallel narratives? Finish one, go back and restart the other? And Miss Randall? Where did she go? My writing career? Dorothy's baby dying? I know that I had that as part of a novel I wrote, heartbreak fictionalized, but Dorothy deserves more than that. I write too much about Peter James Jefferson but am not interested in writing about the man I actually married.

I guess I am telling a story that is many stories. What do you want from me? I'm not the goddam Bible. I'm not God. But, and this is a big but, but if I were the Bible, I would be required…required… to provide a Creation Myth. And then Paradise Lost. In my Bible there is no Flood, but there is a Fire. In my Bible, the Song of Solomon is Peter inside me. In my Bible, I write my own parables. In my Bible, I am Cain and Abel both. In my Bible, I die, crucified by my own hands, but I am not born again. Go away, leave me alone. Write your own story.

My parents are the Creation Myth. The Golden Age Myth. A line, the final line, from one of my favorite poems? "After the first death, there is no other."

One unintended lesson I learned from my parents? Or, perhaps from

George Carlin? We all have too much stuff in our life. Too much material crap. Ignore the stuff and life is better, certainly less expensive. I got a Master's in English and I suppose I could have searched for a job anywhere, but anywhere other than close to my parents *and* Peter was a nonstarter. Ocala had a community college, so newly minted me went there to teach comp and lit. The salary? For 1970, enough for a single white female. That was a plus. The minus? I had to teach comp and lit. I actually liked most of my students, but I hated teaching them. Contradiction? Peter would tell me that he loved teaching history. The difference between history and lit and comp? I loved lit, but I had no patience for teaching comp or lit. Teaching young adults to write? They should have learned it when they were in grade school, like I did. Comp in college was actually remedial comp. That was drudge work, but it did not threaten my soul like "teaching" lit did. Peter and Dorothy and even my parents agreed. Their consensus?

They're not like you. You were never young. They don't love stories and poems. Not their fault. Some of them will, eventually, if they are lucky. But when you're teaching, you are teaching something you love but which does not matter to them. Relax, this job now is not the end of the world for you, and it's probably only temporary.

Temporary? Like some sort of airplane holding pattern? That job at Harvard down there somewhere in the fog? Holding pattern? Stretch the metaphor. My life was in a holding pattern, but not because I was teaching kids who deserved a better teacher than I was. Everything was on hold because of Peter and my parents. Eventually, my parents outlasted Peter.

I was gainfully employed, using my degree. I was an English teacher, a reliable career path for a young woman. I was paying my bills. I bought a used car. I rented a studio apartment in Ocala. My biggest expense was gasoline, and this was back in the days when gas was forty cents a gallon. I was even saving some money for the future. My totally opaque future.

Dorothy married Jake, and I was the Maid of Honor. Peter was my guest. My father had met him when I graduated from college, but he seemed to be oblivious to him showing up a few years later at a wedding. At the reception afterwards, as Johnny Mathis sang "Ebb Tide," and the dance floor filled with people, Dorothy, keeper of all my secrets, still my Jiminy Cricket, saw Peter headed toward our table to ask me for a dance. She leaned over and whispered, "Don't be so fucking obvious. Your parents are here."

Were we really that obvious? So used to each other, so casual after years of sex and trips and long talks and music and books and…? The question you're probably thinking is not about me and Peter, but his wife. Was she that oblivious? Of course not. But that is a different story.

The cancer came back. Five years, the bladder had to be removed. My beautiful and pristine mother became a leaking vessel. She did her best to remain optimistic. My father did his best to ignore reality. I thought it was the cruelest of seasons. Already reclusive, my mother refused to leave the house, period. I would visit during the week, spend the night on Friday and Saturday. But she was alone during the weekdays. Writing notes that would eventually burn, sitting in her garden, but she told me that she heard the music less and less. Me, my voices had more company, and I was talking back.

Five more years, she felt a lump on her right breast. That old fucker…God. It of the infinite jest. Back to the hospital. Back to the language of "We caught it early" and "We know more and more, and the treatments are so much better." A small lump, so no mastectomy required, just a lumpectomy, but cutting open her breast to look for a small growth found something else, something spreading in the tissue, so close her up and start over. Mastectomy now the only option, and then the radiation.

I was in the room with my parents when the doctor explained the procedures. How do you describe the look on my mother's face? Was it the same as mine when I was told the same thing forty years later? Not at all, I can tell you that with a certainty. My mother was looking at my father, a look of despair on her face, as if, for the briefest of moments, she had disappointed him, that she would not be the same for him, that he would love her less? A few seconds, I watched her, then him. That thing they did, all the time I knew them, reading each other's minds, finishing thoughts. Her look changed. They were holding hands, and he leaned over to kiss her on her forehead, whispering to her, erasing me and the doctor, and she smiled.

How was my look different when I got the news? I had nobody to hold my hand. My oncologist was a woman, but she did not hold my hand.

Surgery done, now sans bladder and breasts, my mother shrank. She seemed shorter, frailer, certainly thinner. The first year after the surgery, with weekly chemo assaults, she began vanishing. She heard less and less music. My father was vanishing too. His own aging process was accelerated. But he was still too young to retire.

Dorothy's aunt, she of the Florida beach house, had died and Dorothy told me that her house was for sale. I had some money in the bank, and I really wanted that house. If I could buy it then, I could rent it out to pay for itself until I was ready to move over there. I told my parents my plan and they told me that they had some savings that they could contribute. I protested, but my father insisted.

"You would get it all eventually, why not now?"

"But, Daddy, you and Mother, you're going to need it for..."

"The future?"

"Daddy..."

"Buy it now and take your mother to the beach, just the two of you, and I'll come down later."

And here I am now, you and me, and my ghosts. Waiting for the sun to rise. Remembering my mother and me sitting here, telling secrets, laughing about my father and my grandmother. This is where my mother gave me the picture from my grandmother. This is where my mother told me about her breasts, how she missed them.

"Emmy, I knew I was lucky. I saw other girls growing up, my friends, whose breasts were okay, but they were not perfect. Mine were perfect. A few boys told me that when I was in high school."

"Mother!"

"Your father does not know. It's our secret, okay?"

"Mother, you were such a tramp."

We had been drinking. We were happy. We laughed.

"Even after you were born, I was proud of them. Of course, no one ever saw them but your father."

"Mother, this might be over-sharing."

"I know, surely I am. But something is different about me now. Not sure how to say it. Just, I am sad. I just assumed that..."

She stopped talking. Decades later, after my own mastectomy, I wanted to tell her that I finally understood. That night at my beach house, the conversation came back to me.

"So, Emmy, are you seeing anyone?"

"Mother, you ask me that all the time, you and Daddy, and the answer is always no. I'm very busy. And, evidently, my standards are too high."

I was trying to deflect the question. They had, indeed, been asking it for years. The truth? I was still thinking about Peter. Almost every day, even though I had not seen him for years. I had stopped saving my calendars. Between the last time I had last seen him and that night with my mother, I had dated a few men, had sex with fewer. Marriage and divorce were still ahead for me.

"Your father and I worry about you."

"About me not finding Mr. Right?"

"No, about you being alone. Your father and I are not going to live forever. We worry about you."

"Mother, I have friends. I'm thinking about working on some short stories. I'll get myself a dog. How about that?"

How did I miss what she was trying to say? It had nothing to do with love or loneliness. All my life my parents had been there for me. Even if they never knew about what happened to me on my graduation night, they had been there for me, taking me back in when I dropped out of college, always "there" for me. When the worst things happened to my mother, my father had been there to take care of her. Did my mother see my future when I didn't, that bad things would happen to me and I would need somebody there to take care of me, like they had done for me, like my father had done for her?

"Emmy, just take care of yourself, for me and your father, will you do that?"

After Jessica Wyman told me what Peter had done for her, I went to see him. I had questions. You want to know why I loved an older married man? Wrong question. You really want to know why I loved Peter James Jefferson.

"That was a good thing you did for her."

Peter was at his desk, tests and essays stacked in front of him. At first, he ignored me, raising his right hand and forefinger to motion for me to wait, not looking up. He was left-handed. It dawned on me that I did not remember anybody else in my life who was left-handed. I was twenty-one. There must have been hundreds of lefties in my life, but Peter's left hand fascinated me. He would hold a pencil in that hand and write, pausing, pencil tip still on paper, and he could use his forefinger to tap out some sort of rhythm that was happening in his mind as he thought about the words he was trying to jot down. I hear voices. My mother heard music. I imagined Peter as his own composer.

"Peter?"

With a flourish, he finished scribbling on the last page of a student bluebook and then looked up at me.

"I'm not sure what you mean."

I had thought he might have simply misunderstood me, that all I had to do was be more specific.

"Jessica, letting her go home but still keep her grade."

Focusing from a long distance, not everything is immediate. You have to zoom in slowly because there are always a lot of other important things to see before you get to the final image of the picture you want to take. Falling in love is not the same as being in love. I was falling, but I wasn't there yet. Peter looked back down at another bluebook. He was not going to talk to me about Jessica. He had sworn her to secrecy. She had violated that promise, but with me, and I was special, right? I was Peter's special student. I was safe with her secret. His secret. Peter had a lot of secrets, and I would know most of them eventually, but not that day. All I knew that day was that I was one of Peter's secrets, or so he thought.

"Peter, do you know that people are talking about us?"

That got his attention, but he still did not look up.

"People?"

"Oh, Peter, who do you think? Seriously? How about everybody in the state of Florida?"

I was falling in love.

"And how do you feel about that? People talking about you?"

"Us, Peter, us."

"How do you feel about that?"

How many times had I been in that office since the first time? How many times had I stayed after class to talk to him? How many times had we walked across campus to the dining hall? How did I feel about all that?

"I don't care. We're just friends, right? I'm your best student, even if I do say so myself."

"Yes, you are."

"But I do care about one thing, Peter."

I was about to lie and tell the truth at the same time.

"All we are is friends, but I still care what one person thinks. Your wife. I care what she thinks."

Peter had another mannerism that I will always remember. When he had something important to say, something that had been on his mind but held inside until the right moment, he would take a deep breath through his mouth but exhale through his nose. A tiny detail that I attached to a completely different character in a future book. That day in his office was when I first saw the pattern. Inhale deeply, exhale slowly. Rearrange my world.

"She knows about you. I told her."

It was my turn to inhale deeply, but I do not remember exhaling.

"Peter…I…uh…I…uh…"

"Would you like to meet her?"

Of course, I did not want to meet her. I wanted her to not exist, but not for the reason you might think. I did not want to marry Peter. I did not see myself as a wife to anybody. That insight about myself was validated when I did get married and made a good man miserable. I should have listened to myself. I merely wanted Peter all to myself. I didn't need to be his wife to have that. I could live a thousand miles away from him, as long as he and I loved only each other. That was my twenty-one-old woman fantasy. But I had another problem…my father. He had one philosophy in life that transcended God and my selfishness. How many times did he tell me, *Emmy, just be happy, but do it without hurting other people.*

"Emily?"

Four months from that moment, we would have sex for the first time. A scene? The two of us, facing each other, about to go into a hotel room for the first time. We had been playing baseball for months, bases being reached inning by inning, and I was, finally for the first time in my life, delirious with desire. Peter put the key in the lock and paused.

"Emily, all the moral questions about me and you have already been asked and answered."

I wanted him to turn the key.

"Older, younger. Teacher, student."

"Peter, I love you with all my heart, but sometimes you talk too much."

"And adultery."

That could have ruined it all, saying that at that moment, but it all made sense.

"Wasn't that your decision to make?"

"No, Emily, that was *our* decision. We're both cheating on her. I'm not doing this alone."

I looked at him, then past him, down the hallway, then turned around and looked behind me. I was a hundred years old, looking into the future and into the past. He was right. I was not an innocent bystander. She was no longer an abstraction to me. I had met her, eaten dinner with them, and lied to her when she wanted me to lie to her.

"I know that. We've processed ourselves forever, Peter. All I know right now is that once we go through that door…morality is irrelevant. Nothing that happens in there makes us a better or a worse person. I just want us to be happy. After this first time, I want us to want to do this again."

"Tell me again, how old are you?"

"Old enough."

"One last question."

Why did it seem like all our conversations were constructions, one question or comment leading to another, which eventually led to the real question? I once told him that talking to him was sometimes like playing chess. Each of us, old him and young me, wanting to make the last move. So, I should have thought more before I answered his question, a question that did not mean what it seemed to mean.

"Are you crazy…"

Was it the wrong thing to say at that moment and at that spot? I had asked myself variations of that question all my life. I thought I knew where he was going, but I was wrong. I snapped.

"Peter, you think I'm crazy, that I sleep around, that I am going to come haunt you at your house, expose you, stalk you, tell your wife, force you to choose, cry rape, that only a crazy woman would do this… that kind of crazy? Shouldn't you have figured that out before now?"

He was not defensive.

"No, Emily, I mean that most people would think you're crazy to do this. Get involved with no future…"

"Stop right now. If I'm crazy, so are you. So, stop it, stop looking for loopholes."

Another couple was walking down the hallway toward their room, an elderly couple, the man carrying two bags. I lowered my voice.

"Peter, I have one last question for you…before we go through that door."

The elderly couple walked slowly past us, the old man nodding at us. And then the old woman smiled at us and said, "Congratulations."

Peter and I looked at each other, and then he said to the old woman, "Thank you."

We were alone again.

"Your question?"

"Why did you want me to meet your wife? It was inevitable that we would cross paths, but you arranged it. Why? Some sort of test for me?"

The absurdity of it was becoming apparent to both of us, both of us desperately wanting to go into that room but having a Tony-worthy conversation that kept delaying the inevitable. But we had to talk, again, like we had talked for almost a year. As if there was a reason not to do what we were about to do, but a reason unique to us, him and me, and not our "situation." And the talk in that hallway was the first stage of finally undressing ourselves emotionally, to see if that reason actually existed or, possibly, whether Fate or Free Will had already determined what happened next.

"I wanted you to understand me. You had to meet her to understand me, and it was the last chance for you to change your mind. To decide that I was who you wanted."

"Or, for you to finally decide if I was who you wanted?"

"Emily…"

"Peter, I met her. I have never known anyone like her, and you caring for her means that I have never met anyone like you. And here we are, every bridge already crossed, and we both know that we are going into that room, and the future will sort itself out eventually. So, let's stop talking. At least until tomorrow, let's stop talking."

"Emily?"

"You told her about me?"

"I told her that I had met a totally unique student."

"Peter, unique or not, I'm old enough to know that most women have bullshit detectors. Wife of a teacher who hears about a *unique* female student is smelling bullshit."

"I want you to meet her."

"I don't want to meet your wife, Peter, ever."

"So, why are we doing this?"

He had me there. I wasn't even sure what *this* was. In my defense, I was still young. I was wise beyond my years, right? But that wisdom had a bad habit of being inconsistent. I was sure of myself. I was smart and *unique*, and the next day I was twelve years old reading *Tiger Beat* magazine. Okay, I never read *Tiger Beat*, but you get my point. I was brilliantly fucked up.

"Good question. Why are we?"

Where was the soundtrack theme music when I needed it? For that moment. For what happened, how I felt. I didn't hear it then, as he got up from his desk and came around to put his hands on my face. But I hear it now. I can go back and insert the music into my memory. An old Steve McQueen movie, him in a glider, *Like a circle in a spiral, like a wheel within a wheel. Never ending or beginning on an ever spinning reel.* I completely overwrite the scene and sometimes I find a different song. I can hear songs for the first time and they might take me back to that moment. And sometimes I think about my mother. The music she heard. Was she remembering something from her past?

He kissed me. Not the kiss for a friend, not a kiss of affection, but a kiss that erased every kiss I had ever had. My first kiss. A month later, I met his wife.

Another scene I put in a book: A young woman falling in love, calling the man she loved late at night, after midnight, knowing that he would be asleep in bed with his wife. But she could not stop herself. They had not even kissed. They had known each other only a few months. Four or five? She was drunk, out with drunk friends, a young couple she had known since high school. They would be her friends until the day she died decades in the future. Her girlfriend knew she had a "crush" on this older married man. Her girlfriend was amused, assuming it was a phase. The young woman had been driving her friends' car as they were making-out in the back seat. She could see them in the rearview mirror. She was happy for them. They were in love and did not have to hide it.

For the purposes of this scene, let's call the young woman Emily, and the married man we'll call Peter. Emily was driving in circles around their town. Her job was to simply keep driving, make the ride last as long as possible. There was no destination. Around and around, her job was to make time disappear for her friends. But she was thinking about Peter. She sensed that something was wrong, that he was in danger? Perhaps he was simply sad? She kept thinking about him. She wanted to talk to him…*had* to talk to him. She kept driving until she saw a phone booth outside an all-night convenience store. She told her friends that she had to stop. She would stop and leave them alone, but with the engine running, so they stayed warm, and there would still be the muffled sound of an idling engine, their own soundtrack for the moments they were left alone at the darkest corner of the store's parking lot. It was a cold night, and Emily walked quickly to the phone booth. She shut herself inside the booth, the folding glass door refusing to shut completely, so the cold air kept seeping in. She had Peter's home phone number on a slip of paper. She had written it on that paper a month ago and kept it in her small purse. She had no reason to write it down. He was married. She could always talk to him in his office.

He answered with the first ring, his voice a whisper.

"Hello?"

He described the scene to her later, from his point of view, soon after their first kiss. He was in bed with his wife, but not asleep. It was late, he assumed it was a wrong number, but he did not want the ringing to wake her up so he answered as quickly as possible. The phone was on a table by his side of the bed. He whispered, not wanting to disturb his wife.

"Hello?"

That was what she wanted to hear. His voice. His voice whispering to her. His wonderful voice, that even her girlfriend desired to hear.

"Peter..."

Without hesitation, he stopped her.

"Emily, is this you?"

One word and he knew her? Did that mean anything? But then she heard another voice, a sleepy woman's voice.

"Pete, is there a problem?"

Emily froze, her hand almost putting the phone back on its hanger. But she kept still, as if her being motionless also made her invisible, as if the call was not happening. She heard Peter whisper to the sleepy woman.

"My brother again, more problems at home. You go back to sleep and I'll take this downstairs. You need to sleep."

And then he spoke to the young woman.

"Jeff, call me back in about a minute. I need to change phones."

And then he hung up.

Emily looked frantically in her purse for another dime. She kept thinking to herself, *What am I doing? What am I doing?* How long did it take? But she found another dime and dialed again.

"Peter, I'm sorry."

He spoke quietly, not a breathy whisper, but quietly.

"Emily, are you okay?"

"I'm drunk, Peter, in a freezing phone booth, with my drunk friends in the back seat of a car somewhere around here. I have no idea why I called you. Just a feeling, I'm sorry. I should never have called you at home. I'm sorry, I'm sorry."

"It's okay, Emily. I'm glad you did. Now tell me, are you okay?"

"How can you be glad? Some deranged student of yours calls you at midnight! You should be pissed."

"No, it's okay. I can't talk long, so you come see me next week in my office. You can tell me more about what's on your mind, okay?"

Emily was sniffling and her hands were beginning to shake because she was so cold.

"Yes, yes, I will. I will come see you, and you can tell me what an idiot I was tonight."

"You be careful. Drive safely."

"Peter, I'm sorry..."

"Emily, it's okay. It's good to hear your voice. I'm glad you called. Seriously."

There is more to the scene, but Emily only found out much later. Peter told her. He had hung up the kitchen wall phone, but he did not go back to bed. He went into his den and sat in an old recliner, asking himself why he had ended the phone call as he did, with those words. He thought about his wife upstairs. She would not remember being awakened. He thought about Emily, not for the first time.

Is this true for you too? After the first kiss, the first real kiss, the rest is easy? Peter and I processed morality later, but the first kiss led to others. On the mouth, the throat, the breasts, stomach, and thighs, and, god-almighty, where those thighs met. Especially there. And then again. I look around at young men and women today, and I wonder if they ever kiss. Kiss as if the kiss is both the beginning and the end. Everything now seems so rushed. Some bar song: *Let's get drunk and screw*. America in the twenty-first century. The young are not only permitted, they are encouraged to have sex. Not a right, an obligation. Porn on your cellphone. "Save" yourself for what? Value only in the consumption, not the anticipation. No base traveling, a hundred home runs as a rookie and for every game. Jesus, I am starting to sound like I was born in the 1840s instead of the 1940s. I'm the oldest of old school. The most valuable things are the things you must wait to have. If you can get it anywhere from anybody, is it worth a copper penny? Are you laughing at me now? Bored with my rant? Social commentary from a breast-less dying woman who is angry and resentful? And lost, even on a good day, lost.

I speak now even though I haven't been kissed in a long time, and never again like Peter kissed me. But, if sex requires the actual touching and penetration of one body by another, how can it not begin with a kiss? And when it is over, kiss again. I miss that.

For the rest of that semester, I saw Peter every day during the week, and thought about him on the weekends, when he lived in another world. The agonizing part? Not the weekends, which were the price I paid for being in love with a married man. It was the time we were together at school, but we could not kiss. In the classroom, walking across the campus, eating lunch in public, times of no public displays of affection, right? How about public displays of desire? Performance art…not kissing or touching, that was the performance. But then there were moments when we would be in an empty hallway, or on an elevator, or in a car. Those kinds of moments. The danger of being seen. But we did not finish anything. How many orgasms could we have without having intercourse? Sorry, a clinical question for sure. The answer, of course, is…as many as we wanted. For both of us. As many as time and opportunity availed themselves. But we never went all the way. A quaint expression…all the way. It was his decision, not mine.

Peter James Jefferson was not only the only love-of-my-life, but also the most frustrating.

"Are you sure about this?"

How many variations of that question did I hear for the first few months? I figured it out eventually. Between us, he was the only one who had something to lose. I was falling in love, and I risked nothing. Even though I had once heard her sleepy voice in the background of a phone call, his wife was still an abstraction to me. You can say that he was the villain, like Dorothy said, but he was also the saddest man I ever knew. He was torn by the contradictions of his life. I think he would have had a happier life if he had never met me. Still, until he met me, was he really happy? If so, how was it possible for that happy man to fall in love with me? Was he deluding himself before, or me afterwards? Who you love, how you love, does that explain who you are?

Peter James Jefferson was not a saint. Emily Opal Sterling was the perfect match for him.

The recurring question.

"So, Emily, what do you want to be when you grow up?"

"Peter, do you realize how insulting that question is?"

We were soaking in a bathtub in Room 501 of the Dupont Circle Hotel in Washington, my back lying against his chest, his legs wrapped around me. He had just washed my hair and was running a brush through it to untangle the knots. Next to the tub was an iron-framed window that opened with a crank. We had been in that tub for an hour, window open, so we could hear cars and conversation from the street below. The only light in the bathroom was coming in from outside, streetlights below and unshaded windows from the brownstones across the street.

Hair brushing done, he began massaging my neck and shoulders with warm soapy water. I wanted to go to sleep right there in the tub with him. But then he asked that question.

"Wasn't meant to be, I'm sorry."

I was twenty-nine. He was thirty-nine.

"You didn't think that 'when you grow up' might be a little bit insulting? That I wasn't an adult, that all these years have simply been child's play for me?"

You can read these words now and you might think I was angry at him. No, it was just how we were. Almost ten years of processing the weight of casual thoughts.

"No, I meant that there is so much more ahead of you."

"I'm doing fine right now."

"No, Emily, you're not. You're too smart for the teaching job you have now."

"And you?"

"I am exactly where I should be."

The bathroom was almost dark, but we could see through the open door into the bedroom. The television had been left on, sound muted, blue and silver light seemed to bounce around a disheveled bed where an hour earlier we had almost fucked ourselves into a coma. Covers thrown aside, pillows on the floor. I wanted to take his words and turn them back on himself, saying that I, too, was where I should be, me pushing thirty, him pushing forty, both of us naked in a tub of warm soapy water. You know, some romantic comment like that. And then we could get out of the tub and go back to that bed and start again. I could have said that, but I didn't.

"Peter, this makes no sense, we both know that."

"So, Miss Sterling, why are we doing it?"

"How should I know? Remember, you're the adult here. You're supposed to have all the answers."

"All I know is that I thought you would go away a long time ago."

"So did I."

"I thought I was just somebody you wanted and needed at that time of your life, and then you told me about what happened to you in high school, and more about your parents, and..."

"And then I met your wife."

"And? This all adds up to what?"

"And I realized, soon enough, that you were never going to leave her. Hell, Peter, I eventually realized that if I were married to her, I wouldn't leave her either, not even for you."

Were there clues in that conversation? I can go back and see what was coming a year later?

"All I know is that we've been doing this for a long time, so it must mean something, right? All we have to do is figure out what."

Desire does not have to be explained. Or even understood. Peter and I were never going to be magazine models. He was an averagely attractive man. Imagine a handsome movie star, and then imagine that star's brother. The resemblance is obvious, but the brother is not handsome. Even Peter would admit that he looked better with his clothes on rather than off. But he had that voice, perfect for radio and lectures, a voice which made Dorothy envy me as soon as she calmed down and accepted the fact that Peter and I were having sex.

"Emmy, you bitch. You're fucking that voice."

"No, Dorothy, that voice is fucking me."

She raised her hands toward me as if she was going to choke me.

"I hate you, for the record, hate you."

I did not tell her what it was like to have him inside of me, talking to me softly as I fell further and further, those moments when his voice got lower and lower and his body went deeper and deeper into me, and we both became motionless, feeling each other pulse through us. Not every time, but more than enough. I told her a lot over the years, but not everything.

Desire does not have to be explained? Unlike Peter, I looked a lot better undressed than he did. I had my mother's body. A long time ago. I just needed to see it through somebody else's eyes. Peter's eyes.

The first time, after that talk about morality outside the hotel-room door, in a warm room at that overpriced hotel, we stood in front of a full-length mirror and undressed each other. It was too much for Peter. He had touched every part of my body, but he had never seen all of it at one time.

"I want you to do something for me."

He had gone to sit at the foot of the bed, leaving me in front of the mirror.

"I want you to let me look at you."

Who I was the year before...that Emily...would have hesitated, but I was not that Emily anymore. I stood there for a minute, looking at myself in the mirror, seeing him in that mirror too, sitting on the bed, leaning back and resting on his elbows, looking at me. I turned and looked at him, then I walked slowly around the room, stopping at the window, opening the curtains, looking down at the world from the seventh floor. My back was to Peter, there in that room lit only by dim lamp in the corner, and I stood there, leaning forward with my legs spread apart, feeling how I was making him feel. Was that how he was different, that he was the only man in my life whose pleasure was mine as well? I looked back over my shoulder and told him what I wanted.

"My turn. I want you to do something for me."

He stood up and began walking toward me, but I made him stop.

"I want you to do exactly what I want, for me."

He waited. I walked back to the mirror and looked at myself and then turned sideways, looking at my head-to-heel profile. Where did that come from, that desire, that confidence, that lack of inhibition? From graduation night to that moment, from hating myself and my body to being fascinated by my own desire, from agony to…joy? I took my breath away.

"I want you to come here and kneel down in front of me. I want you to kiss me between my legs. I want to watch you do that. And I want you to do it as long as I want, but you'll know when to stop. You always have."

"Emily…"

"And just be sure, when the time comes, you don't let me fall over, when I am totally limp and staggering. You hold on to me and keep me safe, okay? And when I get back to planet earth again, I will do the same for you, and I want you to watch us in the mirror, and if we're lucky, we'll remember this forever."

Remember? Forever? I've been told that we never really remember anything the way it actually happened. My time with Peter? I can take any moment, any of the thousand times we had sex, and remember it, but the next time I remember it, all I am doing is remembering the last version of it, with some detail forgotten or some other detail imagined, the facts of any experience eventually become a fantasy, and each memory gets more imprecise as we age. But I have an exceptional memory, right? I'm a writer. I made notes about my life. I was a prose witness. I can swear on a Bible about telling the truth. I have the receipts.

But I do not have videotapes or other witnesses. I have my notes. From years ago. That time in Peter's office, when we gave each other a copy of the same book? It happened. I remember it. But the note I wrote later only said *history books, first kiss.* When I described the scene to you, I told you that it was a Richard Hofstadter book. I think it was. I remember him quoting Hofstadter in class, I did some research and saw that Hofstadter had a new book published around the time I went to his office. Hofstadter and the memory are perfectly consistent. You're confused? I misled you? Only if you wanted this to be a memoir. It is not my life. It is just a story. Peter and me in front of that mirror? Of course, it happened, exactly as I described it. But, you, dear listener...reader?... only get the abridged and remembered version. And, of course, the revised and shortened version. A thousand pages of Peter notes consulted, a thousand pages of subsequent story-writing reduced to a hundred. I think my story, my life, has a three-hundred-page limit. I have to save space for my mother's death, my father's death, my rebirth as a writer, my death. My marriage and divorce? If I told you that I have decided to leave them on the cutting room floor, would you feel cheated? Trust me, if not telling my father about my mother's notes which were burned was a gift to him, not including my ex in this story is my gift to him too.

A writer's not so surprising secret? We are all our own therapists. For ourselves. Not all writers, and no insult intended, but only the seriously fucked up good writers are their own Freud and Adler and Joseph Campbell. I think I've covered one-half of why Peter is in my story. That was easy. I could have shown you a hundred other scenes of self-indulgent trips down memory lane, the porn paradise of my life. The physical singularity of Peter in my life. But I still owe you, and myself, an explanation...an attempt at an explanation... for why I spent ten years with a married man. The "meaning" that Peter and I constantly tried to understand for ourselves. That singularity, because he and I have to be an exception to that cliché of infidelity. Even if I cannot convince you, I have to believe it for myself. I have to find the right words.

I already wrote two drafts of that emotional relationship. I'll try a third. It might be all I can do.

"Emily, this is my wife. Amy, this is Emily, the young woman I've been telling you about."

He had told me that I was going to meet her that afternoon. I had spent the morning practicing my best false-face. I know that you would never do it, but if you ever had an affair with a married man and you met his wife, especially with him in the same room, you would, soon enough, think that you were giving yourself away, that it would be obvious to the wife that her husband was fucking the woman talking to her. Cloth scarlet A's be damned. Your entire face would be an admission of guilt. Me, that afternoon, I was on the red carpet about to pick up my Oscar. I was sure. I was such a good actress that I even disguised my total shock at how she looked. Peter had not prepared me for that. She was sitting in the chair next to his desk, only inches away from the two pictures of her that I had seen dozens of times. Peter could have prepared me for that, but he let me walk in unprepared. The difference in how she looked in the pictures and how she looked in the flesh in front of me…that was a story, a story that he had not told me, so what else had he not told me? How much, really, did I not know about her? And him. How much was left to discover?

The wife in the pictures was beautiful, with long wavy blond hair. The wife in front of me had short brown hair, barely to her shoulders, pale skin untouched by makeup. The wife in front of me looked like a woman who was once beautiful, but had gracefully aged into something else…and I kept looking for a word…and the only word that seemed to fit was how my Latin-loving father had once described older Roman women…they were *noble*. Was it true in history, they looked noble? I don't know, all I do know is what my father said. Until I met Peter's wife, I had never seen it in real life. *Noble*…is there a better word, more precise? Go find it, tell your own story. Telling you all this now, it occurs to me that I was absolutely not what I thought I was back then, calm and deceptive and in control of my emotions. I must have been transparently panicked. How did I react when I realized that she had streaks of gray in her hair? Did I blink like I was just waking up? For one brief moment, I felt intense anger toward Peter. How could he cheat on *this* woman? How could he let me be his accomplice? I knew nothing about her, except how she looked, her past in the pictures and her present in that office, meeting a young woman who obviously loved her husband. I was becoming unmoored. Soon enough, I would be completely out to sea.

I stuck out my hand, and with the last vestige of equilibrium I could muster, I spoke.

"It's a pleasure to meet you, Mrs. Jefferson. I've heard a lot about you."

It was a lie. It was not a pleasure and I obviously had heard almost nothing about her.

I was standing in front of her, hand extended, and she just looked up at me. I should have been paying more attention so I could remember more now. I should have paid attention to Peter, his expressions, but I couldn't take my eyes off his wife. She was beginning to etch herself into my memory. She smiled at me, the smile of someone who is amused, who is hearing or seeing something that amuses her, and amuses her even more because the other person has no idea what is so damn funny. No, it was more than a smile. It took me years to understand that she was not merely amused. She was *bemused.* No, I am not dicing words here. Go look it up: *having or showing feelings of wry amusement especially from something that is surprising or perplexing.* But that's not precisely it either. This woman was looking at me as if I was part of an absurd world that amused her. She was processing that moment. Thinking about Peter and me and the situation, amused because only she knew what was coming next, as if only she got the cosmic joke. She was amused by me, but more amused, I am sure now, by the delicious irony of finally meeting the interesting young student that her husband had told her about, and that interesting young student was... *me.* Years later, she would tell me, *I was afraid you would be a disappointment.* Would I have to spend my entire life meeting somebody else's expectations?

She had not extended her own hand toward mine, but she never lost eye contact with me. I would understand more as soon as she spoke.

"Oh, Emily, you don't have to call me Mrs. Jefferson. I never took Pete's last name. Please just call me Amy."

Revelations in Wonderland? She did not take his last name? It was still the '60s. Women did not do that, keep their own names. Hell, they couldn't get their own credit cards, much less keep their own names. But I did not think too much about that at that moment because I was overwhelmed by her voice. Revelations? The voice I heard when I called Peter at home, the sleepy voice of the wife in bed with him. It was the same. Amy had a sleepy voice. A sleepy slow voice. She talked quietly but precisely, as if she was not deciding on a thought to say but on each individual word to get to that thought. Haltingly, she spoke haltingly, as if English was her second language.

"Pete has promised a long quiet lunch for us, so we can talk. I suspect that he has tried to be a perfect gentleman around you all this time. But he's not as professorially dull as you might think."

Her *Pete* had already had his hand between my legs in that office.

"Here, Amy, let me help you up."

Hearing his voice, I realized that he was still there, in that tiny private world his wife had created for her and me in just a few sentences. I looked at him, then back at her, with another of those smiles on her face.

"That's okay, Pete." Looking up at me, finally extending her hand. "Emily, can you help me?"

I took her hand. She gripped mine like a vise and started to pull herself up and toward me. I instinctively started pulling her toward me, surprised at how light she was, thinking I was helping, extending my other hand, but she waved off my offer and put her free hand on the desk to steady herself. She rose up and stood, taking a deep breath, and then freed my hand.

"Some days are better than others. This is not one of them. Sorry."

Three of us, and only two of us knew what the hell was going on, and I was not one of them. I was confused, and then angry at Peter again. The woman in the two pictures on his desk did not exist, and the woman in front of me was a mystery. And this mysterious woman was obviously smarter than Peter and me. She was a goddam mind-reader.

"It's okay, Emily, I asked Pete to not say anything until you and I actually met. I'll tell you the story. I'm better at the details than he is."

Revelations? Even revelations have explanations.

Objective moral reality? Peter and I had not gone to bed together yet, but we were already committing adultery. In the first few months, even if we tried to take a step back, we always took two steps forward. The most puzzling thing? In all that time, we had never used the word "love." I was in love with him, but I could not say it out loud. He told me later, after I met his wife, that he had loved me for a long time. And then we finally had sex, all the way sex. It took time, but Dorothy finally believed me. But she was probably right.

"You grope each other for almost a year, and he never wanted you to go all the way? He, what, respected you? Please, both of you, not just you, both of you were fucked up."

A hotel hallway debate about morality was coming closer, and there was still no way for us to rationalize what we were doing. We were wrong. I as much as he. We did it anyway. Here I am a hundred years later, hindsight twenty-twenty, and I would still go back and do it again. I've known cheaters all my adult life, heard the self-justifications and hypocrisy. Some, at least, were honest enough to admit that it was simply about sex. Still wrong, right? Ten years, remember, me and Peter James Jefferson, so it must have meant something, been justified somehow. It would end before my life was half over, but I would live long enough to grieve Amy's death, and then his. From a distance. Wisdom comes from distance?

That afternoon, from the time we left his office until we met again at a restaurant, I drove alone, with Peter in my head, pointing my finger at him, yelling at him to tell me the truth, asking him why I felt like I was tricked. Peter in my mind, but Amy was there too, off to one side, that bemused smile of hers. She was not judging us, but, in my mind, she was vastly entertained by us. When I got to the restaurant, knowing they were inside waiting for me, I sat in my car and considered the possibility that everything was a mistake, that I was foolish and immature and selfish, and that I was…looking for a cliché…that I was *in over my head.* The best decision I could make right there and then was to turn the key and drive away. I looked in the rearview mirror: *Emily Opal Sterling, you will regret this as long as you live.* I got out of the car and went looking for Peter and Amy.

Until my mother's cancer caught up with her, and then a single candle turned her and my father into living cinders, the most tragic story I ever heard was Amy telling me about herself. My rape was brutal and mentally scarring, but it was not tragic. The damage was internal, and my life was always an evolving recovery. But my life did not stop the night I graduated from high school.

I had been pregnant once. Something was inside me, but it did not live long enough for me to feel it kick, long enough for me to love it before it was even born. Amy was eight months pregnant when her baby stopped kicking. The baby had a name. The baby had a crib waiting for it. The baby died in Amy's womb. That is a sad story, a tragedy. But it is not a horror story. The doctors tried to induce labor to help rid Amy of the corpse inside her. They failed, so they began cutting. It was the late '50s. C-sections were rare. But Peter and Amy had no choice. There were complications. Blood clots. And then a stroke. Peter buried his son while his wife was still in a coma. *That* is a horror story.

"I woke up, Emily, but I was dead. A dead cripple."

They sat together across the table from me. Food was on our plates, untouched. I was twenty-one. Peter was thirty-one. Amy was thirty. My great delusion? I was as old as they were.

She did most of the talking, and I focused on her, but I knew that

Peter was watching me. I remembered her pictures. What was she like when Peter fell in love with her? Was she different now? Which obviously led to the parallel questions. What was he like then? Would I have loved that version of him? Is he different now? Were she and I in love with the same man? Very adult questions, right? But it was still unavoidably obvious. The two people across from me loved each other. More adult questions. Not original with me, but I had never considered them before. Can a person love two different people at the same time? Then, not a question, but a conclusion occurred to me: Peter James Jefferson was never going to leave Amy for me. I had never really expected that. I was not seeing that far into the future when I started to fall in love with him. It was never supposed to last, right? But a perverse epiphany started knocking on the door. As I watched them, I realized that if he were a man who could leave *that* woman, he was not a man I could love. Seeing them together, I loved Peter more. So, sue me. Yes, I've been in therapy since then, for a lot of reasons, and all I understand better, after almost fifty years, is that I was right about Peter. Wrong about a lot of things, stupid about a lot of things, but not him.

Amy? She must have known. Even if she could not imagine me and Peter sleeping together, she was smarter than either one of us. How long before she figured out that we were in love? But I am sure she did. That first meeting? Even before we met, based simply on the way he talked about me? I knew her ten years. I took trips with them, and those were the rare days when Peter and I did not touch each other. No sneaking away. No furtive kisses in another room. I slept alone, knowing that they were in bed together in the room next to mine. Eventually, Amy and I could talk about loving Peter, but we never talked about sex. It all made sense to me.

Dorothy had a different opinion.

"You are incredibly fucked up, Emmy."

How fucked up? I told my mother what I was doing.

Five years after first meeting Amy, I was taking my mother to the urologist. She was beginning the long road to her breast cancer diagnosis, the bladder was just the minor leagues. My father had met Peter, my "favorite professor," at my college graduation, but Amy was not there. If Peter and I were giving off any signals about being in love, my father was oblivious. I hope.

But when my mother was diagnosed with cancer, I was desperate to talk to somebody other than my father. And here's where things get complicated. I knew that my father would be devastated and judgmental if he ever knew about me and Peter. I could not talk to him about *that*. But my parents knew about Peter and Amy, the life, their story. It had been the source of another rant by me about my parents' God. Even before that God killed my mother, I was pissed at *him*. None of that mushy ambivalence about God's sex. He was a man. Not an Earth Mother goddess knockoff. A deity that transcends sexual identity. Being called "Our Father" was wrong too. I wasn't an early feminist, but it was clear to me that the entire Christian theology was a smoke screen for sexist crap. To me, Jesus Christ did not represent God. My own father, Dewy Sterling, was a better god than God. For me, knowing Amy, dealing with my mother's decline, never getting over Miss Randall's exile, and remembering all the Chuck Warrens of the world…God was a man who hated women. That's how bitter I was when I walked out of that urologist's office with my doomed mother. I tried to explain it to Dorothy, but she seldom gave God a thought even on her worst days.

A year into my mother's treatments, my parents had defended their God when I described the horror of Amy's life. I raised my voice and my father said "Enough!" and walked out of the room. Cancerous mother and heretic daughter left alone in our kitchen, she looked at me and I began crying. For her, for Amy, for myself.

"Mother, I need to tell you something, but, please, you can never tell Daddy."

I started at the beginning. I did not go back to graduation night. I would never do that to her or my father. I started with the first day in Peter's class. His voice. My questions. The conversations. The books. The first kiss. Meeting Amy. The more I talked, the more it was obvious to me that I was lost. I had been lost and did not know it. I was in love with a man who would never be mine. I would never have what my mother had. I had been telling myself that it did not matter, that I was happy with what I had, and there was no logical connection between my mother's cancer and my affair with Peter. But as I ranted about God and Amy, it is obvious to me now, that I was also ranting about God and my mother. I was terrified of losing her. I needed her in my life. I needed her to help me understand what I was doing.

It was dark in the kitchen. My father was upstairs. My mother and I sat at the table, the only light coming from two candles at the center of the table. Why is it so clear to me now, looking back, how dark our house was? We had electricity. But my parents preferred candles. Those goddam candles.

"I would like to meet her," my mother said when I finished.

"Oh, mother, I don't think that's a good idea, for us all to get together."

"No, Emmy, just her."

My mother had been the topic of conversation many times between me and Amy, even though Peter had been more interested in my father. Sitting there in the dim light with my mother, I was feeling better about myself. She had not been upset. She had not admonished me. She had not judged me. She had not offered advice, did not say that I should protect myself and break off a relationship with a married man. I imagined my mother and Amy together. It was becoming a story in my mind. All they had in common was…me. I wanted to come up with a reason that they should not meet. My mother was aging. Amy had aged prematurely. A connection? No, not the same. But there was something that made me see more of the story develop.

"Mother, she loves to garden."

"Well, we'll have much to talk about, right?"

I brought Amy to visit while my father was at school. I was going to tell Peter, but she said I should not.

"Our secret, Emily, he doesn't have to know everything."

"Amy, we're not plotting a revolution, just small talk."

"I'll share him with you, Emily, but let me keep some things to myself."

Years ago, and all I have is half a page in my journal. My mother wanted to keep it a secret from my father. Amy wanted to keep it a secret from Peter. As you know by now, I'm okay with secrets. So, what they talked about will be their secret forever. But my journal left me enough details to draw a picture for you: Three women in a garden: young, older, oldest.

A gift. The older guest had brought some peonies to the oldest woman, pruned from her own garden, descendants of peonies first planted by the guest's mother years earlier. The youngest woman did not understand why the oldest woman was so moved by that particular gift. Significant only to ancient gardeners? Then, three women sitting in the dirt. The youngest woman had to help the older and oldest go from standing to sitting, each was so frail. Knees were stiff. Muscles weak. The youngest woman did their bidding. Go get some tea. Bring us a spade. That water bucket needs filling. Shears, we must have shears. Can you help me move closer to that bush? A Spring day, warmer than usual. Three women sweating. Only two sun-hats on hand, the youngest woman will get sunburned. The youngest woman will go to the house for something and she will pause as she walks back, looking at the other two women examining clods of dirt in their hands. The two women will wave at her. The youngest woman will get back down in the dirt with them, marveling that the two other women, at least twenty years' age difference between them, look the same age. The youngest woman will sit and listen to the older and oldest woman talk about their husbands. The youngest woman will learn many new things about each man that day. Each of the older women will ask questions of the other that the youngest woman had never thought to ask, about their husbands as they were when they were boys. The day must end. The youngest woman gets up first, and she helps the oldest woman up next. The oldest and the youngest women both have to help up the third woman. It has been one of those "better days" for that woman, but she is still weak. The oldest and the youngest woman each take an arm of the other woman and help her back into the house. Faces and hands are washed, dirt dusted off clothing. Embraces exchanged. Laughter. The oldest woman stands at the door and waves to the other two women as they drive off.

I apologize for being gone so long. Sometimes this is overwhelming, the effort to remember and write. It's called the *narrative thread*. I lose it sometimes. Dorothy is here with me now. Sometimes her children, all adults now, come to visit me. Others visit too, as if I mattered to them. Students, young once, now middle-aged, visit. Last week, Lorrie Knight came to see me, almost giddy as she handed me a copy of her new book, waiting for me to turn to the dedication page. My name in print: *For Emily Sterling, Teacher and Friend.*

I was her teacher, and I am her friend, but her tribute was a mystery to me. I deserve no credit for her success. But she insisted, "Emily, you've never understood, have you, how we all loved those classes? But this dedication is for more than that. The years afterwards, how you made me a better writer. You were my friend then, more than my teacher."

I still hear voices. Story voices. In my narrative thread, my life is not even half over. My teaching career, my writing career, still to come, but I only have time and space for perhaps another hundred pages. Those *Readers Digest* novels I read, the abridged versions, that's me now, trying to prune out the unnecessary parts of my life, save the essential.

Prune? My mother was an artist in her garden.

Definition: "Pruning, in horticulture, the removal or reduction of parts of a plant, tree, or vine that are not requisite to growth or production, are no longer visually pleasing, or are injurious to the health or development of the plant."

Dorothy teases me a lot now. I tell her what I am writing, let her read a few pages, and she will shake her head.

"Emmy, are you sure that happened? You never told me about it, and I sure remember some of these other things differently."

Pruning, an art form.

I had never been to New York City. It was a fictional place to me, seen in movies and television, too large, too tall, too busy for real people to live there. When we went, it was collapsing. Crime, racial tensions, fiscal mismanagement, Times Square a sewer of sex and burned-out neon. Okay, I might be exaggerating, but the truth is that when I told Dorothy that Peter and I were going to New York, she was less than enthusiastic.

"Do not drink the water!"

"Dorothy, you think you might be thinking about Mexico?"

"All I'm saying is don't you dare go out after dark."

Objectively, yes, it was not a good time for New York. But all I have are good memories of that trip. I've been back a few times since then, seen its transformation, but it was not the same as being there with Peter. The second-best time? My first novel, meeting my first editor and agent. I hope I have time to tell that story.

Peter was officially there for a conference of the Organization of American Historians. Our private joke? Knowing me, he became a better scholar, so to speak. He wrote more articles, got tenure, had his own dissertation updated and published. He went to a lot of conferences, and I went with him many times. He gave me credit for his success. He was full of shit, and we both laughed. But there *was* something different about him. Even Amy noticed, although she did not give me credit. In New York, he had morning panels, so we had afternoons and evenings. I called Dorothy every morning and gave her an update about the previous day. I told her about us going to the MOMA and Guggenheim, the Museum of Natural History, and...making her green with envy...going to see *Hair* and *Cabaret* on Broadway. I did not tell her about Peter and me walking across the Brooklyn Bridge with a full moon overhead, nor about the professional reception we attended together the first night of the conference. I could have told her more, perhaps parts of each experience, but those two times were the most important hours I spent with Peter, and I kept them to myself.

Crossing Brooklyn Bridge? I have written and rewritten that scene. The problem? It's a cliché. How many lovers have walked across that bridge? How many movie scenes have it in the background? And a full moon overhead on a cloudless night? How contrived. How did I describe it in my journal? *P and me on the BB. Full moon. GIANT moon. An hour? Cool. From Man to Brook, and then back to Man. Skyline. Stars in buildings. Kiss.*

The important thing to know about that night? I don't think Peter and I exchanged more than a few sentences for those two hours. "Cool"? It was a word to remind me how cool the breeze was that night. It started as a warm night, but the Bridge is high and over water, and the breeze was cooler than we expected. I had to wrap my arm around his and press as close as I could to stay warm. It was not unpleasant. There were hundreds of other people on the Bridge with us, some in groups, some alone, and some like us, holding on to each other. Was there any specific person I remember, some specific couple, some odd clothing or awkward gait, anything humanly specific I remember other than me and Peter? I could make something up, but it would be fiction for sure. I just remember me and Peter and that damn moon. A moon to make you stop and stare, a moon that nobody had ever seen or would ever see afterwards. Sometimes, now, as I walk on the beach late at night, I see something that looks like that moon. But the moon I see in the sky over the beach is just a memory of that moon over me and Peter, and we all know that memories might… just might…be untrustworthy, even for me, a writer with a perfect memory.

The other moment from that night? Walking back to Manhattan, about halfway across the Bridge, our first unobstructed view at the skyline of New York. *Stars in buildings.* We both stopped and stared, leaning against a rail, and we kissed. He did not kiss me. I did not kiss him. We kissed each other. You know what I mean, if you are lucky.

The reception? Unlike the Bridge, a lot of talk.

"First night of the conference, a meet and greet, renew old contacts, schmooze, drink, brag with faux humility about careers. You know, academics. Hundreds of them, being themselves."

That was how he prepared me for the evening. Peter and I had been to parties and gatherings as a couple a few times, but always out of town. We had actually developed roles for ourselves. Sometimes, with people we would never see again, I was his wife. Sometimes I was just a professional colleague. At the reception that night, I was...don't roll your eyes... his cousin who lived in the city. His guest. His cousin was a graduate student in history. But, here's the devil in the details. Peter went through the entire list of academics who were attending the conference, seeing where each was from, and then we would pick a school that was not listed. Why history, and not just say I was a graduate student in English, as I was? That was my idea. It was the role I chose to play, for no good reason except to...have them treat me as an odd junior future colleague? Peter loved the idea. It was odd because there were almost no female professors at the reception. There was always that first look as soon as I was introduced. The surprise, the squinty skepticism, the almost patronizing, "Well, you will make a lovely addition to our ranks." My talent? I could steer any conversation away from shoptalk. Since meeting Peter, I had finally developed an interest in politics, and I could go off on a tangent about Nixon with the best of them. I would even invent gossip about national politicians. "Did you know that..." And I was off. Historians, I learned, could be as voyeuristic and petty and salacious as...English majors?

I had expected a formal affair. Peter was wearing a suit, I was wearing my Sunday best. But the times they were a-changin, remember? Sport coats, dress shirts without ties, a few even wearing jeans. Turtleneck sweaters. Peter and I tried not to react when we saw the Nehru jackets and beads. Bell-bottoms, a few paisley shirts. Welcome to the Revolution, and not merely the French Revolution. Most of the crowd still looked like me and Peter, but the sartorial clash was itself a topic of conversation. I played both sides of the argument, depending on who I was talking to.

I was having a grand time. I was no longer bothered by our implied rule when we were out in public: No touching, no apparent intimacy. Time for that later. Back at the hotel. Peter and I would stand together at the reception, and we would also wander around on our own. He told me later that he would watch how the other men looked at me when I was by myself. I told him how some of them had actually asked me if I was there by myself, that perhaps I "... might be interested in a cocktail later." One professor from Michigan, pushing sixty, asked me if I was interested in "smoking some weed" back in his room. I wasn't offended, but the entire night was a revelation of how unintellectual the intellectuals were in the room, and thus they became much more interesting to me.

After two hours of mingling and drinking, Peter and I found our own public private space where we could watch the parade and talk to each other at the same time. We stood with our backs leaning against the wall, each of us with a glass in our hand. Somebody looking at us would have seen a man and a woman scanning the room as they talked, seldom actually facing each other, but obviously talking to each other.

"Peter James Jefferson, thank you for bringing me to this."

"Peter James Jefferson? Are you drink, Emily Opal Sterling?"

"Am I drink?"

"I mean..."

And then we both laughed. We were drunk and having a great time. So, why spoil it?

"Wait, look there!"

Music was playing. Couples were trying to do the Twist. It was not a pretty sight.

“That’s you and me in a couple of years,” I whispered.

“Only if I don’t shoot us both before then.”

“You’re such a romantic.”

More dancing. A few professors with younger women I had not noticed before then. Where did they come from? Two professors in some sort of argument, one pointing his finger at the other. The crowd was down to less than a hundred, the hard-core partiers. Peter and I imagined ourselves as reporters for the *New York Times*, waiting for fists to fly, our notepads open with pencils in hand.

Was it the best night, out of bed, we ever had? It was certainly one of the best. We were a couple. We were both happy. I was twenty-seven, he was thirty-seven. Nobody else in that room mattered to us. The people that mattered…they were a thousand miles away. But, of course, they were always with us.

I had enough alcohol in me to ask Peter a question I had wanted to ask after I had been around Amy a long time. Why not ask when I thought I was living a perfect moment with him, when even the truth would not change how I felt. Right? I knew that the Amy I knew was not the Amy he fell in love with. They had been high school sweethearts. Dated through two years of college and then gotten married. But then the horror happened. How could that not change a person? So, what was she like when their future did not include me? I had that question, but I began differently.

“Why did you keep Amy a secret from me so long?” Still looking straight ahead. “And, from everybody? All we ever knew was that you were married. Dorothy insists that you were sleeping with all your attractive female students. You know, the rumor mill.” We turned and caught a quick glimpse of each other, and then turned back to look at the merry-go-round of people in front of us. “Peter? Things were happening between us. Why did you wait?”

"It was what she wanted."

"Okay, can you be more cryptic?"

"Sorry, I mean it was never anybody's business except ours. I came to teach in Florida after it all happened. A few people knew, those who had to. But Amy was clear. It was nobody's business. And she was adamant...she hated pity. She didn't want anybody's pity."

I could see *that* in the Amy I knew. But he had still not answered the question I thought I was asking. I backtracked.

"Have you ever slept with any of your other students?"

"Yes."

So quickly, so casually.

"Did Amy know?"

"Yes, I think so."

"I could hate you, Peter. For you doing that to her." I was on a wave. "Have you slept with anybody else since you started sleeping with me?"

"Emily, I haven't thought about anybody else since I met you."

"Except for Amy, right?"

"Of course."

Why was I outside myself, listening to us talk, but not being hurt by it? It was if I was unraveling the greatest mystery of my life.

"But you wouldn't sleep with me until after I met Amy? A lot of other stuff, but you never let yourself go. Your choice, not mine. You must have known that I was willing to do it almost as soon as we started making out. But you wanted me to meet her face-to-face first? Hell, Peter, neither one of us actually said the word 'love' out loud until after I met Amy. But I loved you, and I think you loved me even before you admitted it to me."

"It was her idea, not mine."

"Peter..."

"She wanted to meet you. It was her idea. I didn't know what to do. I talked about you with her, probably too much. She's smart, Emily, smartest woman I have ever known. X-ray smart, I once told her, able to see through things."

That was also the Amy I had come to know. Was I smiling at that moment? I could never smile like her, that bemused all-knowing smile, but I was smiling my Emmy smile as Peter and I watched a conga line of drunk academics stumbling around the room. I was understanding Amy better, which all led back to me and Peter. He had not been testing me. It was her testing me. The child she had heard about. How would that child react to actually meeting her? The Wife. She had been studying me for sure, but the revelation in New York City was that she had also been studying Peter. She was testing him. How would the two of us act when she was in the middle? Would we pretend to be only friends? Was her intuition right? More importantly, why was this important to her, to see how Peter and I were with each other? What kind of woman, down deep, was Amy? Oh, to have been a proverbial fly on the proverbial wall as Amy and Peter were by themselves, after our lunch, after her meeting the "interesting" student he had told her about for months. Was everything spoken out loud, or did they simply both understand each other better, and still love each other?

"Peter, did she know when you and I finally went to bed with each other?"

"I doubt it."

"But she's known all along, since then, right? I mean, as much as she and I talk, we have never really gone…there. But I assume she knows. Hell, after what you just said, I assume she knew before we did, that it was going to happen."

"Probably."

The reception was winding down. Any pairings for future coupling had been made. Married couples were leaving together. Black waiters were bussing tables. The music had stopped. I had planned one question. What was Amy like before her stroke? But I ended up with another, more direct, and more consequential one, depending on Peter's answer. I knew he would be honest with me. That was the scary part. Honesty.

"Peter, are Amy and I the same person?"

He looked directly at me, obviously confused by the question.

"What...do...you...mean?"

"Bad choice of words. We seem to do that to each other, get it wrong and then revise. I'll get better. Bear with me. What I mean to ask is...is there anything about me that reminds you of the Amy you fell in love with? The old Amy. I mean, the young Amy."

He shook his head slowly, looked down, and then up, stifling a smile. He leaned down and kissed me on the forehead, in front of the nonexistent God of my world and the remnants of a reception.

"Emily, you are nothing like she was. You are not like anybody I have ever known in my life."

That would have been enough, but he finished my annunciation.

"And Amy thinks the same. We have never known anybody like you."

Have I said it before, the first rule of being a trial lawyer? Never ask a witness a question the answer to which you do not already know. I knew the answer to my final question, but I wanted to hear him say it.

"You're never going to leave her, are you?"

"No."

"And she's known that ever since you met me, right?"

"Emily, she's known that even before I met you."

We were still leaning against the wall, facing the almost empty room, almost empty enough to let us have unconsciously moved closer together, our shoulders touching. I felt his hand move behind me to find my waist and gently pull me even closer, our hips soon touching.

"Peter, you might not deserve it, but you're the luckiest goddam man in the universe."

"Amy says the same thing."

Two nights later, we walked across the Brooklyn Bridge.

I'm not sure I understand it now, so I shouldn't expect you to understand it at all. The thing between me and Peter...and Amy. I was young, but *youthful indiscretion* does not explain it. It lasted ten years. I had no expectations I would ever have him to myself. What the hell was I doing?

I was in therapy longer than I knew Peter and Amy. They weren't my only "issue." I started to see a therapist because I thought they *were* that singular unresolved thing that was keeping me from being happy. My first therapist was a man, but after a year of him not listening to me, him constantly trying to pigeonhole me into some Freudian case study, I gave up and just told myself that I would settle for being unhappy the rest of my life.

Dorothy went ballistic and found me a new therapist.

"You might be my bitch, but I'm tired of you acting like a whiny bitch around me all the time."

Once a week for five years, once a month for another five, board-certified Gretchen Laine and I talked. I had seen *Annie Hall* years earlier, and I made a joke to her about me being like the Woody Allen character who was always in therapy, and how it just seemed like he liked to talk about himself and was willing to pay for an audience, so the visits were as much social as clinical. She started tapping her notepad with her pen.

"Should I start calling you Alvy?"

"I'm sorry, who?"

"Alvy Singer, that character. Remember?"

"It's been a few years, Gretchen. All I remember is Woody Allen loving Diane Keaton."

"Well, remembering names of made-up people isn't important, as long as you remember the real things in your past. You've talked about Peter for years, so I think I understand him as you understood him. He seems real enough, but I'm still not clear about his wife."

"Gretchen, have you been listening? All I've done is talk about her and Peter."

"Emily, remember what I told you after your first few visits, about why you're here. It's as important that you listen to yourself just as I listen to you."

In other words, as she told me later, patients lie to their therapists because they lie to themselves. When they hear themselves, they hear lies. Not lies of commission, but often lies of omission. Before I had written my first book, she had also pegged the future me.

"I've had a few writers as clients, and they are the worst, especially the novelists. They lie for a living. And they want to tell everyone else their lies. Personally, I envy them. It must be a wonderful life, to tell stories. Professionally, they are often immune to honesty, especially being honest with themselves. I have to wait and wait for them to hear themselves."

The therapist's job? Gretchen was good at it. Ask the right questions, sense evasion or guilt, and ask again, from a different direction.

"So, tell me your favorite memory of Amy."

I'm not a dog-person. I'm more the crazy-lady-with-cats kind of person. If I thought anything was odd about my childhood, it was that we never had any pets. A hermit crab in a glass bowl does not count as a pet. Contrary to what my father always said, with a straight face, moths in a closet do not count as pets. Contrary to what my mother said, also with a straight face, birds that visited her garden were not pets. Everybody else around me in my childhood had a pet, even my grandmother, whose cats were always a mystery to me when I visited her house. Sometimes I would think they were simply stuffed animal dolls, but then a tail would twitch and swish and then all was still again. It took years, but they eventually took a liking to, or developed a tolerance for, me. My grandmother must have thought I would never learn.

"Emily, you must learn to sit still and let them come to you. If they like you, they will come to you. Of course, for a fidgety child such as yourself, it might take a few years."

But they did come, to my grandmother's great pleasure and pride. Augustus and Scribonia, ancient and noble calicos. I did not tell my grandmother that I had a secret. I had opened a can of sardines and rubbed oil on my hands. My grandmother's sense of smell was almost as bad as her sense of hearing. But as I sat on the couch in the living room with no television, I became a sardine, my fingers to be licked with cat-scratchy tongues. Eventually, I would bring little bits of American cheese with me, and I became Ceres, to be worshipped. Was I buying their adoration? Make no moral judgments against me. I was not even a teenager yet. Sometimes I would lie on my grandmother's couch and my two acolytes would cuddle up against me, their purring putting me to sleep. I would go home and ask, sometimes beg, to have my own kitten, but my parents were adamant. In the category of minor mysteries about them, their aversion to pets is number one. When Dorothy and I shared an apartment, she also banned pets. It was only when I got my own house, my beach house, that I indulged my childhood dream. I learned the hard way that the trouble with having cats as pets when you lived fifty yards away from the ocean is that those cats often disappeared if they were let outside. Sometimes the ocean air has as many predators as the ocean water. My two cats now, Livia and Claudia, are still with me because I have made them as reclusive as I am. When I walk on the beach at night, I have to double-check to make sure that all my doors are shut tight behind me.

Peter James Jefferson was a dog-person. A boy and his dog, always a good story. A boy and a big dog. Peter had a black Labrador about the size of the Trojan Horse. I first met it…I mean I met Ruff… when I first went to his home. Amy had called me and I could have sworn that I heard her bemused smile in the voice on the phone.

"I hope you like dogs."

The door opened and there were Peter and Ruff, side by side. I think that Ruff was almost chest-high to me. A beautiful big black dog who did not bark or jump or lunge or drool or pant. I could not tell who was prouder of the other, Peter or Ruff. Labs are wonderful dogs. They are calm and sweet and loyal. If I were a dog-person, a black Lab would go for walks with me on the beach and sleep at the foot of my bed at night…with Livia and Claudia on the bed with me. A Lab like Ruff.

Soon enough, Amy and I were in lounge chairs on the shaded patio, watching Ruff retrieve sticks thrown by Peter, over and over and over and over again.

Are you confused? You wanted a memory of mine about Amy, right?

Ruff had a history, and Amy was his historian. Sipping iced tea, watching the man we both loved, Amy and I spent the day in the past.

"You will absolutely believe this, because you know Pete. This is all *so* Pete. On our first anniversary, Ruff was Pete's gift to me. First-anniversary gifts are supposed to be something made out of paper. Some sort of symbolism. Not for Pete. A black Lab puppy he had already named Ruff. I had been trying to get pregnant for months, and he gives me a…puppy."

She stopped talking, to rest, but I could see it in her face, her remembering that moment, nodding to herself, and it was a pleasant memory.

"He said it was for me…and for the baby we would surely have. Time to get it trained and out of its puppy energy phase, but a Lab named Ruff was going to belong in a family of me and him and our inevitable child. He said he named it Ruff because it would be an easy name for a baby to learn. I pointed out to him that he had a name for our dog before we had a name for the baby. A dumb thing to say. He said we could name the baby Ruff too, and I jumped up out of my chair, back in those days when I could do that, and I hugged him. And you have to admit, Ruff is a great dog. Getting old now, a lot slower than usual. But still sweet, just like Pete."

Why weren't my feelings hurt? Amy so casually reminding me that she had loved Peter before I met him. But I sat there watching Peter and Ruff, remembering the story about how their baby died. The baby who never met Ruff.

"So here we are, eight years later, and Pete is still throwing sticks in the backyard. God, I love that dog."

That was my first visit, and I came to love that dog too. But, Amy? Who was she? I started hearing stories every time I talked to her. My second visit to their house was just me and her. She had called Peter to ask him to bring some prescription painkillers for her when he came home, but he was going to be trapped in one of those infamous sound-and-fury-signifying-nothing faculty meetings for who-the-hell-knows-how-long. He called me. He had called the pharmacy and made arrangements. Could I get the medicine for Amy? Well, of course I could. Be glad to.

I think about it now and it seems weird, but not back then. A married man calls his girlfriend to go get some medicine for his wife and take it to her. He'll be home late for dinner. Can she help with that too? Just another day in adultery land.

Amy was not having one of her "good" days. The front door was unlocked, and Ruff was waiting for me. He led me back to the patio, where Amy was in a lounge chair. If my parents lived most of their lives in our kitchen, Peter and Amy evidently lived most of their lives on that patio. He did all the cooking, and they would eat on the patio most of the year. There was even a desk in the corner, for Peter to grade papers while Amy worked in her garden.

"Emily, thank you so much. Pete owes you a favor for sure."

Alone with the wife of the man I was sleeping with. I started making obvious jokes in my mind about what kinds of favors we owed each other.

"He asked me to help start dinner."

"You certainly don't have to do that. I'm not an invalid."

She swung her legs around and put her feet on the ground and started to get up. It was a mistake. I saw it immediately and went to offer my hand. She looked up at me. I was so used to her bemused smile but all I saw that time was the pain.

"I suppose God got bored, Emily. A dead baby and a stroke weren't enough, I have calcium deposits in all my joints too."

It was all there, a hundred future stories, Amy and my mother's cursed bodies. I did not know that a Great Fire was coming. Illness was enough material for then. I got her up and she held my hands for a few more seconds.

"I'm sorry. Peter didn't tell me."

"I told him not to. I hate pity-parties, he probably told you that. And this is not as bad as it looks."

A bemused smile.

"Well, that's a lie."

My profound sympathetic response?

"Well, we all gotta die of something."

Her shoulders started shaking, then her chest began to heave, and then she burst out laughing. I had to pull her closer to me and hold on to her to keep her from falling down. And then I eased her back down into her chair and sat beside her.

"Just the two of us here until Pete gets home. Our own slumber party. You want to call the drugstore and ask them if they have Sir Walter Raleigh in a can and then tell them to let him out? I used to love that."

I was braver back then than I thought.

"Or we could play Twenty Questions."

"You go first."

"Okay, how did you and Peter meet? What was he like back then?"

Awkward silence?

"Ah, you want a serious conversation, right?"

"I'm sorry, I was just wondering about…"

"Oh, Emily, we're fine. But if I show you mine, you have to show me yours."

"Excuse me?"

"I'll tell you about meeting Pete and falling in love with him, but you have to do the same, tell me how you met."

My courage was wilting.

"Amy, you know how we met. At school."

"I know what he told me, but I want to know what you remember, how you would describe it. I want to put his version and yours together. You have to tell me like I was your one true friend. Everything."

We talked until Peter finally got home. This was still early in our relationship, a little bit over a year, and I was still trying to figure out Peter, so I wanted Amy to help me. New York and the conference reception were still to come, when I would ask Peter about Amy when he fell in love with her. By then, she was the only mystery, she and I.

In the two hours that Amy and I had talked, Peter James Jefferson became less mysterious. Amy and he fell in love in their junior year of high school. She had been a cheerleader. I was so *not* surprised at that. She still had their yearbooks, so I insisted that she show me everything. The shock? Peter had been a jock. Not scholarship material, a B-teamer, but a three-year letterman and captain of the football team his senior year. The other sports I could understand, but the image of him actually tackling somebody or hitting somebody or pushing somebody...that was not Peter to me.

"You should ask him about his parents, Emily. You want to understand him, you have to understand them."

"You could tell me, you know."

"No, I want you to ask him, and then tell me what he says. I knew those people up close. He could never fool me, but he might sugarcoat them around other people. Ask him, and then you and I can talk again."

"So, who raised us explains everything?"

Of course, it does, I knew that, a lot of things. I know that now, knew it then. You know about my parents. I am their child. You know what I am like, nothing mysterious about me. Peter was the oldest son of an abusive father and indifferent mother. He protected his younger brothers when he could, and finally fought back against his father when he was big enough. Amy was the only child of functioning alcoholics who doted on her. She loved her parents. When she told me about them that afternoon, they were still alive but living, barely, in a nursing home.

Amy told me all these things, but I still wanted more. I wanted to know why they loved each other. I wanted to understand how he could love her and love me too. I knew that I could not ask her *that* question, but I still wanted a story that I could tell myself when I was alone. Knowing about Peter's parents helped me understand him, but I wanted to understand *them*, the thing that was their marriage.

"Is he different now than when you married him?"

"Oh, just the opposite. He is slowly coming back to be that man again. Thank you."

Memories of Amy? Those two words. *Thank you.* And then that damn smile of hers. She knew what she had done with those two words.

"I didn't love Pete when we first met, for almost a year. He was uptight and angry. Oh, cute…and had that voice even back then…and smart, but not happy. Something changed by the time we were juniors. He told me it was because he loved me, that something about me had calmed him down. No more lashing out, no more resentments, he was starting to think that he actually had a future away from his home, and he wanted me to be part of it. You know, we had just turned seventeen when he asked me to marry him. No date set, no ring, just the commitment. And then, years later…the thing with me and the baby happened...and the Pete I married went away. He stopped laughing, stopped smiling, and it was rough for both of us."

"Amy, you said…"

"And then one day he started talking about this very odd girl in his class. I thought the worst thing I could think, you know. But he kept talking. He showed me your essays. He told me about the questions you would ask in those notes. He told me about those conversations the two of you would have in his office. And here's the important thing, Emily, he was utterly guileless about it all, a man telling his wife things that, if she were somebody else, would have sent her with a gun to that school, but he was sharing you with me. He wasn't confessing anything. It was all very odd to me at first, odd stories about an odd girl, but something else was happening too. He started being himself again, the man I fell in love with. Thank you for that."

I could not look at her as she talked. Surely, she knew what was going on between me and Peter. Surely.

"Emily, does this make any sense to you?"

I had turned twenty-two, prematurely mature and precociously smart Emily Opal Sterling. I finally looked at her and told the truth.

"No, I'm sorry, I'm lost here."

"No, Emily, just the opposite. This is the one place where you're not lost at all."

That is when Peter walked in on us. You ever walk into a room and the people there suddenly stop talking, and you realize that they were talking about you...how you must have looked, your expression? That was Peter when he found us together. Amy and I looked at him, then at each other, partners in gossip about her husband and my lover.

"Pete, start cooking, so I can finish telling your prodigy here all about your glory days in high school and how you were the apple of your parents' eyes."

"Oh, God, Amy, you didn't tell her about the time I stabbed my father, did you?"

He was not really upset. Me, I'm sure that I was blinking like a spastic.

"Pete, relax. We both know he deserved it, and, besides, it was only a flesh wound."

This is not the memory that I finally shared only with board-certified Gretchen Laine. Not Dorothy, not even my father as he was dying and wanted me to talk more about Peter and Amy. It is my private secret. How private? I've mined my life for fiction, scenes and people lifted and massaged into a new story. But this memory dies with me. And you? You die with me too.

Ruff died.

He was an old dog, and for over a year he had been stoically incontinent, forced to spend that last year on the patio or in the backyard because his bowels and bladder were the unpredictable bowels of a dying animal. I had been a weekly witness to his drift. Amy and I would sit on the patio and watch Peter and Ruff play fetch-a-stick. Ruff no longer ran for the stick, a slow walk was the best he could do, and sometimes Peter had to walk him over to where it was and pick it up for him. One time I had suggested the obvious…it was time to let Ruff go, to put him down. Amy agreed. Peter was adamantly opposed. And then he was back tossing sticks. Amy defended him when I told her that I thought it was almost cruel, to let Ruff suffer like he was suffering.

"Emily, Pete never had a dog when he was young. Ruff has been the one and only. And you should have seen him when he was a puppy. You could see it even then, how sweet he was."

Peter's wife and Peter's girlfriend sat and watched Peter play with a dog, a wonder dog named Ruff, who had been adopted as an anniversary gift for his wife and a future pet for their child who was to be eventually unborn.

A week later, I got the call from Amy. It was after midnight. She was crying, and she was frantic.

"Emily, I need you."

I was still waking up.

"Ruff is dead. He died an hour ago, as Pete was holding him."

"Amy, I'm sorry, so sorry, is there…"

"Pete's gone, Emily."

"Amy, what do you mean?"

The details of the memory began, details written not in shorthand in my journal the next night, but a story, five pages of details that would become this story. A story I wrote, but never published.

"He always told me what he was going to do, but I never believed him."

"Amy, I'm on my way. I'll be there as soon as I can."

"No, I need you to stop him."

She was almost hysterical, an emotion I had never imagined her capable of. Not even panicked, much less hysterical.

"He's taken Ruff to the cemetery where…our baby…is buried. He told me that was his plan, for weeks that was his plan, but I didn't believe him. I told him that we could bury Ruff here, but he said no. Emily, he's not okay. He's going to get himself arrested…or something…"

"Amy, what do you want me to do?"

"You have to stop him. You have to bring him and Ruff back here. I need you to do that for me. Will you do that for me, please."

It was the only thing in their life that they had not shared with me. Except for that first lunch when I met her and she explained why she was so crippled, their son was locked away in a world not shared with me. Or, as I knew, with anyone else. I had never been to the cemetery, so I had to listen very closely as a crying mother told me where it was, and then where in the cemetery the grave was. All I had to do was stop a grieving man from doing a foolish thing, right? Poetic gesture, or not, it was both futile and foolish.

My task was all so simple. Amy had granted me mystical powers to retrieve the dead from the land of the dead. So, what was I to do when I got there and discovered that the gate to the cemetery was locked? Apparently, access to the dead was ruled by office hours. I got out of my car and started rattling the iron gate, yelling Peter's name. Again and again. The dead were deaf. I was a falling tree, heard by no one, soundless. I yelled again. I think about this now, this memory, and I amaze myself. I hate cemeteries. No bucolic peace for me there. I had gone to a few funerals in my life, but I had never been in a cemetery at night, in the dark, alone. I was scared shitless, but I was Amy's knight. I got back in my car and began driving around the perimeter of the cemetery, looking for another gate. North and east, locked. Then I saw Peter's car, parked on an unlit service road, the trunk still open. There was no gate near his car, just a short stone fence along the back of the cemetery. I parked behind his car, got out, and went up to the fence. Three feet high? Almost up to my chest? I looked into the land of the dead. In the distance was the un-broachable front gate, and that part of the cemetery was lit by street lamps, casting shadows off a thousand tombstones and other monuments to death...obelisks, winged angels, stone crypts...every damn nightmare of my childhood. I yelled for Peter. Silence. I yelled again. Silence. Then I simply listened to the land of the dead. Enough of a wind to turn the tree limbs into the waving arms of a hundred maestros, the leaves an orchestra of strings. This is the best part, these words here that I am sharing with you. These were the words I was thinking at that moment. The words were coming to me at that moment and I would write them in my journal the next day before I forgot them. I was living in my own story that night.

I saw something moving in the distance, floating in the air, a slow bounding up and down, over the graves. If this were a ghost story, I could tell you about souls swirling in the shadowy light. But the truth is better. A family of deer was foraging in the land of the dead. A doe and two fawns, leaping, walking, stopping, heads turning as I yelled Peter's name one more time. Then bounding away. I was alone again.

The moral here? I had to stop looking so hard. So, I stood there, my hands on the top of the fence, and waited.

He was straight ahead. I saw a thin sliver of weak white light shooting across the ground. It had always been there, but I had been looking past it. Peter had found the spot he wanted and had put his flashlight down to start digging. Thirty yards away from me, closer to me then than the ocean is to my house now. He was close enough to have heard me, right? I yelled again. Silence.

I hoisted myself over the fence and walked toward him.

"Peter?"

I kept walking until I was standing over him.

"Peter, Amy sent me to bring you home."

He was sitting on the ground, a shovel beside him. Ruff was wrapped in a Tweety Bird beach towel next to him. There had been no digging. I imagined how hard it must have been for him to get over that fence with Ruff in his arms. I knew, just knew, that Peter would not have just dropped Ruff over the fence and then climbed over for himself. He was not going to do that, desecrate the thing he loved. He must have put Ruff over his shoulders and hoisted himself over the fence, gotten Ruff to that spot, and then gone back for the shovel.

I leaned down and kissed him on the top of his head, remembering the first time back in his office. Then I sat on the ground next to him, with Ruff between us.

"I tried, Emily, I really did try."

He was talking more to himself than to me.

"But I got here and I got tired. Very tired. I had a plan, but I got tired."

"Peter, it's okay. Let's go back home and I'll help you bury him in the backyard. Amy is worried."

He reached over and picked up the dying flashlight. The beam was then almost yellow. He pointed it to a tombstone about ten feet away. Then another. I suppose every cemetery has something comparable, the same space where Peter and I were. Dozens of small tombstones, etched with cherubs and lambs and tiny crosses, the land within the land of the dead, the land of dead children. Tombstones with names, but only one with *Peter Amelia Jefferson,* the stone closest to me and Peter.

"It all made sense to me. Bury Ruff here. Amy was still in a coma. We had a name picked out, but when I was filling out the death certificate, I gave him a new name. I had it put in stone, and then Amy came back to life."

"Peter, we have to go home."

It took a long time, us sitting there surrounded by dead children, me looking for deer, Peter looking at the ground, before he spoke again.

"You're right. We should go home."

I took the shovel and Peter carried Ruff back to the fence. I went over first, and then he lifted Ruff over and I took him with both my arms straining. But I held on until Peter was over the fence and carried Ruff back to his car. I followed him back to Amy. She had called me at midnight. We got back at four in the morning. The house was dark, but as soon as we walked in, we could see through the glass doors that opened onto the patio. The patio light was on, and we could see Amy in her garden. She was on her hands and knees, digging a grave.

My clearest memory of Amy? That's what my board-certified therapist wanted. As I was searching for her lost husband, she had begun digging. She had to rip out a newly planted section of flowers to get to the softest dirt. Wrecked and ravaged Amy could not even wield a short garden shovel, but she took a spade and began digging. As I was sitting with Peter hearing the story of his son's name, with no strength and every part of her frail body in pain, Amy had kept digging. Ruff was a big dog. His grave would have to be deep. Amy kept digging. Three hours, a square plot, four by four feet? Perhaps only a foot deep? She was inside the shallow hole when we arrived, tossing more dirt out. She saw us and stopped. Her smile was not bemused, but I could tell…she was happy to see us.

She tried to speak, but she was having trouble breathing. Peter put Ruff on the ground next to her and stepped into the hole with her, and then he kneeled down and picked her up and carried her past me back to the patio.

Me? I had the big shovel, remember? I walked over to where Amy had been, and I started digging, finishing her labor.

An hour? God, to be that young and strong again. An hour, two feet deeper. I was still in the dirt, in a hole higher than my waist, and all I could say was, "I can't do anymore."

Peter picked Amy up from her lounge chair and carried her back to me, setting her gently down next to the hole I was in. He then picked up Ruff and kneeled down at the edge of the hole, handing him over to me. Damn, even in death, that dog was a load. But I laid him down in the dirt as Peter got in the hole with me. He helped me up and out, and I sat next to Amy on the ground. We were both covered in dirt. Peter disappeared down into the hole, but I knew what he was doing. He was uncovering Ruff's sweet face one last time to pat him on the head. Then he was out of the hole and shoveling dirt back in. Amy finally spoke, quietly to me.

"Thank you for bringing them back to me."

Was I crying? Of course not, I was too tough for that. I was Dawn and Dewy's daughter.

I was crying like a baby. All I could say was something stupid.

"I'm sorry about your garden."

"No, no, Emily, this is perfect. I'll plant some more peonies. Ruff loved playing in the garden. Now he'll be part of it."

Don't you dare tell me that it is not possible to love two people at the same time. Peter loved me and he loved Amy, and I loved both of them.

I keep being told that I have to make some decisions about getting my "affairs" in order. I thought that was what I was doing, telling you all this. My singular affair. Getting it in order, making sense of it. I know, I know, a bad joke. Whistling past the graveyard? Thinking about something else while refusing, being too scared, to confront the obvious. But I am tired, as tired as Peter with a dead dog in a towel beside him, butt on the ground, in the dark. I had plans. I've almost gotten to the point where I could finish this story, but I am tired. A story about my life, that was the plan. But all I have told you so far are stories about my parents and Peter and Amy.

Somebody else said it first, but act like you've never heard it: *There are two important days in your life. The day you are born and the day you figure out why.*

I was born. I am close to figuring out why. But I only have a hundred more pages, and my remembered life is only half over. I'll be optimistic, even though the second half of my life, the last hundred pages, has less sex, you might still keep listening. Dorothy, however, is not a patient friend.

"Jesus, Emmy, you keep taking your sweet time. You just keep tripping down memory lane and I just keep getting older and fatter. And, by the way, I want all your journals. Because I know, just know, that the really good stuff is still in there."

Dorothy doesn't know it, but she is never going to get my journals. I have to be careful. I have to know when it is almost too late. I have to finish this story for you, and then I have to burn everything. I have a box of candles in my closet.

Movie analogy. The cutting room floor. A hundred hours of film in the cans, the Director has a two-hour limit. Audiences might get restless. Stars cry, "They left me on the cutting room floor." Writers are worse than stars. Every word we write is golden. My favorite lines from another writer? He had written the script for the movie adaptation of my first novel. We had corresponded for a long time, but we only met for the first time a year after the movie was released. Released and forgotten in one month. We met at a bar next to a bookstore, where he was reading from his latest, soon to be Pulitzer Prize-winning, third novel. He had written other adaptations, including for his own novels. He was a veteran of many writing wars, even though he was ten years younger than me. I was still a newbie, in awe of him. Three drinks down, he held court.

"Emily, that piece of shit had nothing to do with your book or my script. I went to a private screening a month before it was released, and I asked them to take my name off the credits."

I was mesmerized, as if I was finally being told who actually killed John Kennedy.

"Well, that would explain why you didn't come to the official premiere. I assumed you would be there. Our first face-to-face."

"Sorry about that. I should have warned you ahead of time. But I suppose it's time you heard how the sausage is made. My contract required a script and two rewrites if asked. Producers were happy with number one, asked for some tweaks, and *then* they hired the Director, a two-film veteran..." spoken as if he was about to spit, "...so I called her and asked if there was anything else she needed, but no no no she said...*this is exactly what I need to start with.* And then they hired the male lead. Remember him? Big star him, shit don't stink him. Director was so thrilled to have a big name on board, and the big name wanted daily script revisions, more lines and screen time for him. I was out of the loop. Hollywood, the fuckers. Sometimes a Buick script gets turned into a Cadillac movie. It can happen. But those fuckers turned my Buick script into a goddam Edsel."

It was, indeed, a bad movie. I was more than disappointed. I was shocked at how bad it was. More than the script...bad editing, irrelevant soundtrack, unimaginative cinematography. For the weeks leading up to the release, the book rating on Amazon was soaring up. After the release, the ratings dropped below where they were when the hype began, and kept dropping. Hollywood, the fuckers.

Dorothy agreed, as we both sat at the official premiere in Los Angeles, whispering to me, "What happened to your story?" A week later she found a T-shirt for me, black with white lettering: *Never judge a book by its movie*. Over the years, I've given the same T-shirt to a few other writer friends of mine, our very own exclusive club. Of course, my screenwriter friend reminded me of another Hollywood truism.

"We cashed our checks, Emily. A million other writers would trade places with us in a heartbeat. Hollywood paid us, and then it didn't belong to us anymore. Your book, my script, that's us. That movie is not us or ours. We took their money. We've got no high ground, no room to bitch, but still... fuck 'em."

All true, then and now, but I remember that movie for something else. It was being filmed in Georgia, not anywhere near the actual events, but filming in Georgia was notoriously less expensive than most other places, so my life was transferred to Georgia. My agent had gotten me permission to visit the set, but not while they were filming. I was not to disturb somebody else's creative process. Fair enough. Evidently, the presence of a book's writer on a set is considered some sort of jinx. A Hollywood urban myth? Me, I have always loved movies, in a theatre, not on TV. Peter and I had sex in a theatre balcony once, but that scene is being left on the cutting room floor.

I had a guide for my visit, to keep me out of trouble, I suppose. But she had read my book. She was a fan. She told me to show up at eight that night, instead of the afternoon when the day's shooting was scheduled. Shooting schedules, evidently, are subject to change on an actor or director's whim. I got there late and they were still filming. My guide, a barely-twenty "personal assistant" in the credits, introduced me as her mother. I was no longer the writer. I was free to see anything I wanted, as long as I stayed out of the way and did not open my mouth. Stars came and went, and I was a starstruck voyeur. But you all know enough about moviemaking to know that any set has dozens of people in motion, and then they become silent mimes as soon as "action" is shouted. They were craftsmen more than artists. I was thrilled. I looked at the young actress who was me. I was never that pretty. The Dorothy actress was busting out of her blouse. Perfect casting. My mother-actress was beautiful. My heart sank in joy.

The father-actor was a handsome man with too much makeup. The limp I had given my father in my novel was a caricature of a limp as the father-actor walked. I did not know at the time how much of an asshole the father-actor was and how he intimidated the Director. But, even there that night, I knew he was wrong for the part. Still, I had cashed the check.

I'm struggling for words here. What I was feeling. None of the actors looked like me or anybody else in my book, but I still heard bits and pieces of my own words come out of their mouths. But only bits and pieces, a phrase here or there.

But all that is irrelevant.

It was the material world of my past that I was experiencing that night. Had my book been that good? I wrote a novel, so I massaged real people and how they looked or talked, to hide them or protect myself from lawsuits. Fact to fiction. But I had been absolutely precise in my descriptions of all the things and places in my past that were not human. I did not think about it while I was doing it. It was unconscious writing by me, as I focused on the characters and dialogue.

The only screen credit that mattered to me when I saw the movie was not my name or my screenwriter friend's name. I looked for the set designer. He had read my book. He understood it better than me in many ways. He re-created the book's world as if he had seen it all firsthand, traveled back in time. But my words had created it for him, and he did not interpret them, did not polish them. Recreated, I'll say it again. That was his skill, his genius skill.

I stood on that set and all the actors disappeared, all the crew, the cameras and lights. All I saw was me and my parents at that table, all I heard was what we said that wasn't in my book. My mother and father were long dead, but there they were, at that table, reading poetry to their ten-year-old daughter. Then a blink, and Miss Randall was there at the table with us, having dinner, and my seventeen-year-old self was standing against the sink, watching them enjoy each other's adult company.

A few feet away from the kitchen set was the set for my grandmother's house. It was unlit and unpeopled, but I wandered over to it and saw her and me talking about her sister Opal. Ten again, holding the picture that was eventually hanging on the wall in my beach house. My past was a movie. Back to the future? How about that movie allusion?

I was on a movie set, hearing their voices again. Talking in my head to them. But then the other voices came back too. I closed my eyes and listened to Peter.

"You know, Emily, I'm disappointed that you never wrote a book about me."

I was standing on the set of a classroom. I saw myself in the back row, intently staring at an exam on my desk. Peter was talking, but it was as if nobody in the classroom could hear him, not even me.

"There was that time in New York, that time in Charleston..."

I watched myself look up from the exam, as if on cue, look around the classroom, and then stand up to walk toward Peter, talking to him as the other actors remained oblivious.

"That time in your office, that time...the first time...in front of that mirror."

I was on the set of a patio. Peter was standing next to Amy as she spoke.

"You know, Emily, I'm disappointed that you never wrote a book about me. That time I met your mother, that time we went to Atlanta by ourselves, that time I almost died from..."

I was on the set of Peter's office, him standing by his bookcase, Amy sitting where I first met her. I apologized to both of them.

"I should have written a book about both of you, and me, about us."

Amy braced herself with one hand on the desk and slowly stood up, walking toward me.

"You still have time, Emily. Turn us into a story. Will you do that for us?"

"I wish I could, Amy. I wish I had time."

"Emily, ssssh. You have to be quiet."

I was on the set of a movie based on a story I had written about my life, a story that was not the truth. My "personal assistant" guide was gently shaking my arm. An angry Director was storming toward me. I was about to be banished from my own movie.

If I ever wrote about Peter and Amy, would they like it? Would they even agree that it was, really, about them?

I call myself a writer now, even use that word on the occupation line of my tax returns. Nowadays, there are too many damn writers. Fewer major publishers, fewer reviewers, but too many damn self-published writers sucking up oxygen. Am I bitter? Not anymore. Down deep, I think we're all self-published. Every time we tell a story. Sometimes, I'll admit, a few self-published writers tell good stories. They found a way to put their stories in print, to outlive themselves. More power to them. They might dream of getting rich, but the real dream is seeing their words in print, in somebody else's hands. That is a noble dream. To exist outside of yourself.

I am sure this happens to other writers, those who seem to have real careers with real publishers, whose books are coveted by bookstores, not just reluctantly accepted on consignment from local writers who want to be a "writer." Those people are at least trying. But there's the other person who shows up at a bookstore event, the person with her own story who lingers after you sign her copy of your book, the lazy dreamer who says, "You want an idea for your next book? I could tell you all the things that have happened to me, all the things that my friends tell me ought to be a novel, and then you could write it."

You think I'm kidding? You think those people don't exist? They do, and every time one approached me, I always had the same answer: "You have to write your own story." It's very simple, I want to scream sometimes. *Write your own story.*

But in my story, I always exempt Peter and Amy from my anger at any stranger who wants me to write their story. Peter and Amy are different. They are my story. Only I can write it.

I met Peter in the Fall of 1963. I met Amy the Spring of 1964. The last time I saw them together was sometime in August of 1974. I did not see Peter again until April of 1986. Perhaps '87? I'm sure I wrote it down, the exact date, but it doesn't matter now, exactitude.

For ten years, Peter was almost a constant in my daily life. Not always physically present, but always there. Amy became a constant later. I could tell you more, but I need to finish our story. Contrary to what Amy told me on that movie set, I do not have time. But two scenes remain, when Amy almost died and when I lost them forever.

Lost? Peter might disagree. If he could read this now, he might tell me that I had never lost them at all.

I was in graduate school, first for a Master's and then working on a PhD. I wasn't working toward a career. I was postponing a life. Staying in school kept me closer to Peter and Amy. How to describe our threesome? I was his lover (girlfriend? mistress?), their friend, and I loved them both. Amy and I never ever talked about sex, but we talked about love a lot. But I don't think it was until she almost died that she understood how I felt about her. I had finished all my PhD course work and exams, and I was stringing out a dissertation as long as I could. I was ABD for years. I wrote and I wrote, but it was crap. I knew it was crap. I did not care. I was happy. My father was a bit distressed, but he had never pushed me to do anything except...be happy. And, he reminded me, pay my own bills.

I did not know it then, but those days were also fodder for future stories I would write. I was a Teaching Assistant in an English Department of drunks, womanizers, poets, sad scholars, future administrators, and pretentious assholes. Go read novel three. I'm the narrator. That narrator slept with two different professors. That wasn't me. That was fiction. I loved those days. Even though I wasn't writing the Great

American Dissertation, I loved the parties. Peter was my guest at a few of the bigger ones, so we did not appear out of the ordinary when everyone else was boozing and philandering. We were always more sober than everyone around us. Peter was there when one of my profs punched another, lifted him up and dumped him in the kitchen sink, and punched him again. Novel three, remember. Nixon was into his first term, the war he promised to end was going to last another four years. Chuck Warren died in Vietnam, not as painfully as I had always wished, but Dorothy and I still celebrated. Neither of us, we admitted, were forgiving people.

At the 1970 English Department Christmas party, I had two guests: Peter and Amy. The three of us were like me and Peter at that New York conference reception, lined up against the wall, watching the academics perform. Amy was in the middle, leaning against my shoulder. Peter was our go-fer. Another drink, some crepes, go tell Professor Bubba over there that his dick fell off at the last party and is looking for him, our own sophisticated humor. The fun part? Peter would walk over to that professor and start up a conversation. His special skill? What he would tell the professor, as he pointed back toward me and Amy, made that prof look back at us, wide-eyed, as if we had, indeed, said *something* weird. Then, back with us, he would not tell us what he said. He did it three times that night.

Amy was having fun, and then a small drop of the future fell on us. She coughed, then stifled another. She began trying to catch her breath.

"I'm fine, I'm fine," an obvious lie. "Just my same old cough."

Peter and I looked at each other, then her. An hour later, she was home in bed. A day later she was in the emergency room. For the next week, she was in the hospital, being treated for pneumonia. Just sick, right? A treatable disease. Some meds, some bed rest, some tender loving care from your husband and his mistress…a piece of cake, right? But, what if you've had a stroke, what if what you dismissed as arthritis years earlier had just been upgraded to rheumatoid arthritis? That old joker…my parents' God…might have poisoned that cake.

Amy was dying, I was sure. Peter disagreed.

"She'll make it, Emily. She always has."

Amy did not die, but she was never the same. Peter and I took turns staying with her in the hospital, sleeping in a chair in her room. Sometimes, I thought I was in a Medieval monastery, and the treatment for a sick soul was to beat the living devil out of them. A starched nurse would come in every four hours, regardless of the time of day or whether Amy had finally been able to fall asleep, and roust her awake and roll her over on her side and start thumping on her back. Didn't they understand how frail she already was, even when "healthy"? And those tubes in her nose, how secure were they? Nope, that congestion, it gotta go. I hated seeing it happen to her, but when we finally got her home, Peter and I took turns doing the same thing, pounding viral demons out of her, at least twice a day. Amy was utterly helpless to take care of herself. You want to see how much somebody loves you? See if they will take care of you when you can't go to the bathroom by yourself. Maybe even if they could pay somebody else to do it, they do it themselves. They clean up your shit and piss, and they will stand naked in a shower with you and hold you up while they wash you off. Peter did that for Amy. I did too.

A month, and she was able to sit up in bed. Six weeks, we could get her out of bed and on her feet for short walks. Two months, she could go to the bathroom by herself. I still hated my parents' God.

She was eventually well enough for me to make a confession. I told her that I was going to be pissed if she died.

"You and me both, Emily."

It was March, and we were sitting on the patio. Peter was at school. Ruff was pushing up peonies in the garden. Her bemused smile was back, but her voice was going away.

"Amy, I'm serious."

"And you think I'm not?" We stopped talking. A minute? "I'm good for a few more years, if my luck holds."

"Right, right, you and my mother, both of you with your good luck. Both of you, born under some lucky star."

Amy was sick. My mother was dying. I couldn't slap God, but if that damn Second Coming happened while I was alive, I had some serious abuse planned for the Son of God.

"How is your mother?"

Peter was right, Amy was a mindreader.

"Same old, same old."

"And?"

Of course, she was not going to let me be so glib.

"Slowly worse, and my father is faking optimism."

The irony I know now but which I would not have predicted then: My mother would outlive Amy by many years.

"I'd love to see her again. Do you think she would be okay with that?"

"Oh, absolutely. I can get her up here. She'd love to see your garden."

"Tell her that she and I can have a jolly good pity-party."

"Amy, one thing my mother and you have in common, other than a garden, is a complete lack of..."

"Self-pity. I know. That's what we have you for. To be sad for us."

"Dammit, Amy, I can't help it. This shouldn't happen to you, or to her."

"Or to Peter."

"That's another reason you can't die. It would kill him."

"He'll have you, and you will need to take care of him."

"Who's going to take care of me? What am I going to do if you die? Me? Selfish or not, who's going to take care of me? When you're gone, when my mother is gone? Lord love Peter, but who is going to take care of me?"

Amy did not have an answer for that.

You want a happy ending, right? Star-crossed lovers finally have each other. No, wait, that was Romeo and Juliet and it did not end too well for them. But this story is not life. It is fiction, and the writer can do anything she wants. I can tell you that Peter and I finally had only each other. I could lie to you. It would be a sad story because Amy had to die, but a happy story because Peter and I would have each other. That's one possible ending. Thing is, in a very romantic way, it would be plausible. It would make sense. It's not what happened, and what happened makes no sense.

Two years passed. Amy was turning into a living ghost, from limping cripple to wheelchair bound cripple. Peter and I stopped going on trips together. My mother's health seemed to stabilize, but even she admitted it was simply, "rearranging deck chairs on the *Titanic*."

I finished my dissertation. You will be absolutely shocked, surely, when I tell you that I wrote about Emily Dickinson. How many dissertations about Dickinson have been written since mine? Certainly, better ones. My committee was generous: *More interpretation than scholarship, but boldly written and powerful in its own way*. In other words, *here's your piece of parchment, now go away. Good luck finding a job at a junior college*. Remember all those stories I told you about that Department, and the scenes in my third novel? My alma mater was not Harvard or Yale. Give it a B-minus in scholarly reputation, but, damn, the parties were an education all by themselves. And, evidently, knowing what I do about some of the other dissertations that were approved, mine was not totally embarrassing. My favorite dissertation story? A certain grad student was sleeping with his dissertation director, an older woman who adored Dorothy Parker, and the student had "benefited" from her expertise. He wrote about Dorothy Parker. The problem? Too much of it was lifted from other sources without attribution. The solution? Reject the dissertation. The problem with the solution? The dissertation director was also sleeping with the Chair of the Department. I did not put that in my third novel. I was saving it. The ultimate solution? Every school keeps a copy of every dissertation in its library. You can go find mine if you are bored with your life. A dissertation in the library is acknowledgment of pride and/or complicity. The Dorothy Parker dissertation went on the shelf, a leather-bound hundred and eighty pages. And then it disappeared. Like some sort of Seal Team Six operation, the Chair and another faculty member went to the library when it was closed and stole the dissertation. The library was in on the fix. The conspiracy expanded. There is no listing of that dissertation in the library catalogs. The grad student went away, as everyone knew he would. He went to law school. I suppose he would have gone to some school for the rest of his life if he could. That was his career. Professional student. Me, I think that Dorothy Parker would have found the entire story so very...*delicious*?

And this academic comedy has what to do with Peter and me? Not one thing. It's just a story, a short story. Sometimes, especially lately, I start remembering things that I had forgotten. Irrelevant things. And they interfere with the important stories I need to tell.

Did I tell you about my own Dorothy's wedding? I was the Maid of Honor. Or, as she told me, "The Bitch of Honor." Complicity? English departments and libraries and universities all complicit in fraud?

By the time she got married, Dorothy had gone from being shocked that I was sleeping with Peter, to accepting it, and then to being... complicit? She had invited Peter to her wedding but did not tell me. It was her wedding gift to me. Her only regret, she told me later, was not being able to see my face as I walked down the aisle, arm-in-arm with her brother, my face when I saw Peter standing at the end of a row of seats. Peter, smiling at me. Is that what friends, best friends, do for each other? Ignore their stupidity and failures, aid and abet the crimes, care for them anyway? Dorothy was my best friend. One of our secrets from that wedding? I was at the altar as she was escorted up the aisle by her not-loved stepfather. I'm sure nobody else saw it, but I did...the smirk on her face as we made eye contact. The "You can thank me later, Bitch" smirk. But it was only a flash. Her real attention was focused on Jake waiting for her at the altar. I looked at her face and wondered if I would ever be that happy.

Peter only stayed an hour at the reception. Dorothy had invited some of her other teachers, so Peter being there did not seem out of the ordinary. He sat at a table with his colleagues. All so proper and invisible. I did my best to ignore him, torture that Dorothy also enjoyed. But we did have one dance together, in a ballroom lit by three blazing chandeliers and a hundred candles. First dance with the father, then the groom cuts in on him, and then everybody joins in. Rituals are important. Dorothy's dress looked like she was wearing a snowman that had exploded. It was garish and so totally perfect for her. I stood there and applauded with everyone else as Jake stepped in, and then Peter tapped me on the shoulder and asked me to dance. We had had sex a hundred times, but we had never danced with each other. And away we floated, my head resting on his chest as Johnny Mathis sang "Ebb Tide." How sappy is that? Johnny Mathis.

Years later, drunk with Dorothy at my beach house, me too weak to get out of bed, I told her that I wanted that Mathis song played at my funeral.

"Not a chance, honey. You're getting Van Halen, his hot for teacher song."

She thought she was funny, and I was used to her teasing me forever about my past, but it hit me wrong, and I started crying. Like a baby. She grabbed my hand and apologized.

"Emmy, I'm sorry. Just being myself. And here you are turning into a bucket of mush."

A memory. I remembered a question I had always wanted to ask her about her wedding.

"Dorothy, what did you say to Peter as he was leaving your wedding reception? I saw you follow him to the door."

"Oh, Emmy, I was a bit drunk that night. Hard to believe, right? But I just had to tell him to his face that you weren't as tough as you tried to act, that, even though I didn't understand it, you loved him. That you were my best friend and I would haunt him for the rest of his life if he ever broke your heart. You know, just casual small talk stuff."

"He never told me that."

"Well, let's assume the best…he knew I wasn't kidding."

There are eight million stories in the naked city. This has been one of them.

I don't have eight million, but I have too many. I'm down to my last one about Peter and Amy. The last time we were all three together. Forty years ago? You know what a rom-com is, romantic comedy? Why not have one for threesomes? Why not have couples' counseling for threesomes? I spent years with board-certified Gretchen. She actually helped me a lot. Would she have helped me and Peter and Amy stay together? Or, would she have agreed with Peter and Amy? It was time to end it.

I was thirty. Peter was forty. Amy was thirty-nine.

How many pages could I tell you about that last time? But, seriously, do any of us deserve your sympathy? And aren't these questions merely helping me delay the inevitable?

We need to talk.

I should have been shocked, right?

We need to stop doing this.

Between the opening *need* line and the *stop* line, we talked for an hour, mostly about our past, how long it had lasted, the singularly happy times we had. The three of us. Peter and I did not have to talk about *our* past. All we did was talk about our past *with* Amy. We even laughed about that first meeting in his office. Almost cried about Ruff the wonder dog. Amy seldom spoke, but it was obvious that she was in memory-mode with me and Peter, smiling as he and I riffed off the other's memories, finishing sentences the other started. The fact that Peter and I were acting like my mother and father when they were happy and having fun with each other…it popped in my head and did not bother me at all. Wasn't that what all happy couples do?

But, why were we even having that conversation? I had been invited to come talk about the past? Was there a fly buzzing around, some premonition that the conversation was headed toward bad news? Felt a funeral in my brain? How easy to use somebody else's image when you are lost for your own. I suddenly, sickeningly, knew why I was there. Bad news about Amy, some imminently awful news about Amy. I was sure. Wasn't all this misdirection, how parents broke the news to a child about a divorce or a terminal illness? Some goddam cosmic tear in the universe? I was half-right.

We need to stop doing this.

I thought it would be Peter, but it was Amy.

It's all gone, what she said. I did not go home and write it down.

I did not write for a year after that. Not a note to jar my memory. Just those six words from Amy. Not in print, just in the air. So, I can't really tell you *that* story.

Remember me saying that thing about two important days in your life, when you are born and when you figure out why. How about when you die and then figure out why? I died that day with Peter and Amy. I was dead for the next twenty years of my life. But, why did I die?

Amy died in 1974. Peter did not call me. I did not go to her funeral. Peter died in 1992. I did not go to his funeral. But I did see him one more time before he died. And I think I figured out the *why* of my death back in 1972.

A phone call, how could I forget that voice?

"I'd like to see you again."

He lived in the same house. We talked on the same patio. He was not the same person.

Peter tried to explain the past, but all I heard was Amy's voice, and she was much more honest than he was. No, that is unfair to Peter. He was honest, but he was wrong. The elusive *why*. I can tell you what Amy told me back then, but I might just be making it up, me still trying to make sense of everything. I listened to Peter, pushing sixty, more slouched, totally gray. But all I heard was Amy, and Amy had understood the future better than me and Peter combined.

Emily, we need to stop doing this. I am dying and Pete is tearing himself to pieces about you. I'm happy that it's not obvious to you, but I see it when we're alone. He wants both of us, he thought it was possible. I watched it all happen, how you came into his life and he came back into mine at the same time. You fell in love with the Peter I fell in love with. I wasn't jealous. I had him back too. But I'm dying, Emily, sooner rather than later. And the Pete you love is going to die with me too. I once thought that he would need you after I die, that you could take care of him. It took me awhile, things always get clearer near the end. I was wrong about you and him all by yourselves. He doesn't understand. I tried to tell him. But he's not thinking clearly. So, it's up to you, Emily. You need to have your own life. The Pete you love exists only as part of me. He and I are one person, and that's the person you love. You need to go away. You need to let us go before we die, or else it will be too late for you. After I'm gone, the person you love will be gone too. Emily, I love you as much as Pete does, but not as he does. But you need to go away...for Pete, for me...for yourself.

Amy said none of that, none of those words. They are my words, me trying to make sense of the past. Before I finish this story, I'm going to rewrite them, make them make more sense. All I need is time.

Peter and I talked for a few hours, but Amy had been right. Something was missing. Peter James Jefferson was missing. But he had one last gift for me, the key to a door.

"I saw this and thought of you."

He handed me a page which had been torn out of the *Atlantic Monthly*.

"It's a writing contest. But only for people who have never been published before. Twenty-five-hundred words, a profile of somebody important to the writer. I remember those stories you wrote about your parents. You should dig them out and submit something."

I thanked him. I put the page aside for a week. I wasn't a writer. I missed the submission deadline. But then my mother died. I thought I had died when Amy said good-bye to me, but I had simply been asleep. I woke up when my mother died.

Evidently, writing contests are like buses. You miss one, but another comes along. You might be late getting to your destination, but you eventually do get there.

III
Emmy: The End

Dorothy, in her own way, thought she was cheering me up.

"Emmy, I don't know which is more depressing, your life or the news."

"Would it make you happy if I told you that I won that contest I told you about?"

"Does the Pope shit in the woods?"

I said that I died. I said that I was only asleep. Does that mean I was just in a coma? More likely, being asleep, I was sleepwalking through life. All those metaphors, heavy symbolism.

I had a PhD and absolutely no ambition. I went to college thinking I would be a high school teacher. I met Peter and Amy. I kept going to school. I wrote a dissertation about Emily Dickinson, but I had no interest in becoming a Dickinson scholar. Title IX came along and helped millions of young women, those who wanted it. My problem was simple…I wasn't sure what I wanted. In my darkest private moments, I thought that Amy had been wrong about me. She said that she and Peter were one person, but I wanted to tell her that she and I and Peter were *that* one person. She might have thought she was doing me a favor, but she was wrong. I was becoming nobody, not even one complete person.

I became a traveling academic. Never considered for a tenure-track job…thankfully, since I would have been pressured to publish or perish…a lovely term, right? … cough up enough prose to be published in academic journals or by a university press… go as a supplicant to your professional peers and seek tenure…and, once granted, you could live your entire life on cruise control. Hell, my life was on cruise control already. A three-year Visiting Lectureship at one school, a string of short-term appointments with all sorts of euphemistic titles, but all meaning that I was…temporary, and replaceable. My greatest accomplishment? I managed to make a living and stay within a hundred miles of my parents.

Lessons I learned? I was a lousy teacher for most of my students. I was not a bad teacher. I was actually pretty good, but my secret was that I could have been better. I had grown up with good teachers. My father, Miss Randall, Peter, a few others…all I had to do was be them, right? I came to the conclusion that I lacked some essential goodness that they all had.

I talked to my father about my looming middle-age "drift" and he offered me a lifeline.

"Emmy, I love teaching, but I love what I teach too. I love it even when my students do not. You love what you teach, I know you do, books and poems, but you don't like teaching to those who don't love books and poems as much as you do. You want your students to be you. And, Emmy, *nobody* is like you."

A book I wish I had time to write? I want to write a book in which my father and Amy know each other, and I get to listen to them. That would be a wonderful story.

"And, in your defense, Emmy, teaching composition to college students must be a course designed by Satan to be taught in Hell. I hereby absolve you of any guilt you feel about your lack of enthusiasm about teaching eighteen-year-olds something they should have learned in grade school and junior high. By college, you are teaching the damned and the dead."

The damned and the dead? My father was usually not so harsh about young people, but he was still teaching when he should have retired, and he would sometimes mutter about how students had changed in the past fifty years. I would hear him and then shudder at the prospect that I might still be teaching for another twenty or more years.

But that *Atlantic* bus came around again and I hopped on board. Down deep, I think I assumed that I was just going along for the scenery of the route and would eventually be dropped off where I got on. I wasn't sure what they really wanted...that profile of somebody important in your life ... I pitied the editors who had to read thousands of entries. I wrote about Miss Randall. It did not do her justice. I wrote about my grandmother. It was better. Not good enough. I considered writing about Dorothy, but she would have killed me. I almost wrote about Peter and Amy, but they were still...I was still not ready to do that. My parents were the obvious choice. But what to say in twenty-five hundred words?

And then my mother died, and my father sat with me for a week, in agony from burns and grief, and told me about his journals and things that never got into those journals. And I wrote the first line.

He wondered what his parents would have named him if he had been born a girl.

"Emily Sterling? ... Are your parents Dawn and De Witt Sterling? ... I'm calling from the University Hospital Emergency Room ... You are listed as next of kin ... Your parents were involved in an accident and are in critical condition ... Yes, you can see them soon."

Remember the problem with time travel? You go back to the past to prevent a future tragedy or crime, but you are warned that if you alter any one thing in the past you also alter a million other things. Go back a hundred years and kill a butterfly. A possible chain of more important events might be irrevocably altered because that butterfly did not flutter one more hour. Fate or Free Will. Intelligent Design, that old hoax. What if it had nothing to do with any human decision. What if a single gust of wind…

An accident? How about a single goddam candle?

For the week after my mother died, my father and I talked every night. I let him try to absolve himself for his self-inflicted guilt about her death. A year later, he tried to remember other details for me. It was important to me, to understand. Important to him, for me to understand. But in that first week, I had enough for a story.

My mother was exhausted. The chemo had only slowed, not stopped, the spread of her cancer. My mother was depressed, my father told me, but then she recovered. She started hearing music again. She and my father went back to the silent Friends Sunday services.

One night, she had asked for an extra dose of the morphine she was using to numb the pain. My father told me that he was reluctant. But had he ever said no to her before? It was a warm night, almost no breeze. He helped her upstairs to bed and sat by the bed as she went to sleep. On the nightstand was a single candle. It was their night-light, a routine arrangement. He would sit and do a puzzle in the dimmest of light, and then he would snuff it out and get in bed with her. That night, the routine changed. He could not concentrate on the puzzle. He sat there and simply looked at her, looking for that tiny wet bubble that he had seen on her lip when she was born. Then he went back downstairs to close up the house. A task that should have only taken a few minutes, but then he reached the candlelit kitchen and sat down at the table, and wept. He was exhausted. He folded his arms on the table and put his head down and went to sleep.

What happened upstairs on that warm calm night? A story. Out of nowhere, a soft breeze came through the window, as if a breath, blowing a sheer curtain over a burning candle that was, for that night, too close to the window. An old curtain, probably from my grandmother's house, an old dry curtain, and with a quick poof it was on fire, and that burning curtain touched and torched another sheer curtain, which fell off the wooden rod and landed on the floor on top of the crumpled newspaper that my father had discarded earlier, and the burning paper lit the fringe of the old dry sheet that covered my pain-free sleeping mother, and, as the flames slowly overcame the numbness of my mother, the entire bed was aflame, and then the dry wood of the bed frame, and then the ceiling, and then my mother screamed. Thirty seconds from breeze to immolation? That long? More? Is that how it happened?

My father was asleep. He thought he was having a nightmare. Her scream, then the smoke and the crackling of an old wooden house burning down around him. He was upstairs in seconds, bursting into a room on fire, seeing my mother flailing about on the burning bed. He ran through the flames and pulled her burning body into his arms, embracing her as his own clothes caught fire, putting his hand over her eyes to protect her as he stumbled toward the door that was by then a blazing portal.

"And that's the last thing I remember, Emmy."

My father would process that night until the end of his own life. He would never say it aloud, but I knew his mind and heart. He blamed himself for what happened. If he had only not left her alone. That simple, right? He failed. His fault, not God's.

She died two weeks later, pain-free. My only wish? That she was conscious enough to hear my father whisper to her as she died. Her ugly husband charred into an abomination. It was all in my first novel. A fictional mother's death. But in that novel, it was a car accident. The fictional father was merely crippled more afterwards than he had been crippled before the accident, but, in my novel, he had never been ugly. She had died in his arms after he pulled her out of the overturned wreck. His last words to her, his fictional words, broke my heart to write. She was still beautiful. His fictional last words in the novel? I deleted them. Even in fiction, it was their secret.

Nowhere in my book are the notes she had written to him. They do not exist in fiction. In life, he never knew about them. I kept her secret for her.

Secrets.

I wrote about my parents and mailed it in. I was sure that it was not what they wanted, but it was what I wanted to write. A month later, the *Atlantic* wrote back. A gracious man I never met, named C. Michael Curtis, took my breath away.

"Dear Miss Sterling, it is my great pleasure and honor to inform you..."

I was soon in print, a thousand dollars richer, and awake.

One rare infinite pleasure of my life? Handing the magazine to my father and watching him read about himself and my mother, bringing her back to life and making her die all over again. He knew that something was coming, that I had written something, that it won a prize, but he did not know what.

As I handed him the magazine, I had a moment of abject terror. In the universe, he was the only reader who mattered. He was the only person who I could still hurt or disappoint, and it would matter. Sitting in a wheelchair, he could barely turn the pages, but I resisted the impulse to help him. I had to disappear while he read about himself, as much of a struggle as it might be. Ten minutes, or less? I was chewing on my lip. And then he looked up at me. I wish I could say that he smiled, but the fire made it impossible for him to ever smile again. He motioned for me to come closer, but he did not speak. I was collapsing. I walked over and kneeled down on the floor in front of him, laying my head on his leg and quickly pulling it back up, afraid that I had hurt him by touch more than by words. He was looking down at me, the magazine still in his right hand as he reached with his left to touch my face. I put my head back down on his leg. Neither one of us spoke as he stroked my hair.

I tell my writing students the story of how I got published and they are fascinated. If only it was all so easy. My first-ever submission wins a prize, and then I get a phone call from an agent in New York who read the *Atlantic* winner, and a year later the most famous editor in America buys my book. Publishing was a piece of cake, so I did not perish.

But then I tell them the full story of that year, and I become an example of what I would later title a talk I did on tour: *Dumb Luck and Perseverance: A Writer's Life.*

I did get a call from an agent. He loved my *Atlantic* profile, "showed I had talent," yadda yadda, and my head was inflating. But he was looking for a novel. Did I have anything in progress?

Was this how the business worked? I was being shown open doors, but I needed a novel to enter? That easy? Well, except for me not having a novel written. So, I lied. For whatever spur of the moment reason, I lied.

"Yessir, as a matter of fact, I've got a couple of hundred pages done."

"Terrific. You finish it, and I want first and exclusive rights to read it. Deal?"

I sat there at my desk, looking at a blank yellow page in a tablet. The door to my left was open. I could see the ocean. My father was staying with me, and the door to the bedroom was open. It was summer. I had two months of free time. Somewhere in New York City, where Peter and I had kissed on a bridge, a man had opened a door for me. All I needed was a story to write. The *Atlantic* issue was on my desk. I had a story. I started writing.

The great revelation I tell my writing students? As soon as I knew the story I wanted to write, a novel about my parents, I was free from reality, in a world with no rules except...tell a story. My magazine profile of them was true, and so were the details. But in a novel, I could tell the truth about them and still make up the details, as long as the story was true. That is the great drug of fiction. You can lie truthfully.

I hand-wrote three hundred pages in seven weeks. I turned those into three hundred and fifty typed pages in another two weeks. All this before I bought my first word processor.

My father was the perfect houseguest. Unobtrusive inspiration. I even let him read the first draft, making sure he understood that I was...sort of...just sort of...turning him and my mother into fiction, so he had to cut me a lot of slack. How good of a reader was he? He laughed every day. I never made him sad, until the very end, but that was unavoidable. My fictional mother still died, and he was a fictional cripple. But it was still a love story.

My Long-Distance Agent was thrilled. Dollar signs were in his voice. Dumb luck and perseverance? He was the dumb luck. I never met that agent. For nine months I got a weekly call from him about how close we were. And the perseverance began. My students love this story.

My book was rejected a dozen times in nine months. But, as my LDA told me, "These are not bad rejections. They all like your book, but, you know, it was not *a good fit* for them." Each rejection came with a short critique, some "issue" with the book that I might consider working on. My LDA was effusive. "Let's tinker with it and try again." I tinkered, he thought the tinkerings were terrific. I went back and looked at my LDA's record. He had A-list writers, was praised by them all, had started dozens of new careers. I was bound to be another success story for him. So, we persevered. My three-hundred-fifty-page manuscript became four hundred.

My favorite rejection?

I can see this story on a movie screen. I just don't see it in a bookstore.

I was teaching three courses a semester. The Fall term oozed into the Spring term. I was still tinkering. Persevering. My father was getting better, well enough to think about going back to teach in the next year. In between teaching, tinkering, and taking care of my father, I managed to supervise the building of a new house for my father. He loved me, he would laugh, but he wanted to go home. I did not point out the obvious fact that his home did not exist anymore. It did not matter to him anyway. He could go back to the *space* where they had lived, to a smaller house, built with an old-man resident in mind, but he could look out his windows and see what he and my mother had seen before. If that made him happy, I was going to make sure it happened for him.

Life went on without me winning the Nobel Prize for Literature. I looked around and discovered that my god-daughter Emily, Dorothy's oldest, had graduated from college and gone to New York City to work as an intern for the *New York Times*, an investment in the career she wanted as a journalist. I told her to walk across the Brooklyn Bridge. She told me to come visit and we could walk across it together.

Then the LDA called and gave me one of those break-up lines that every woman has heard when the guy she thought loved her tells her, "It's not you. It's me. You deserve better. I hope we can be friends." Some version of that, all about how we had both done our best and the business was so subjective anyway and another agent might just be the one for me that makes it all happen. I was angry and depressed, but it took me a couple of years to understand that he was a generous man, and that he was absolutely right about the business. He wasn't dumping me. He was letting me get a new start. So, here's a personal note to my old LDA: "Thank you. And, yes, I'd like to be your friend."

I had a four-hundred-page manuscript, and I was out of ideas. Did I tell you that my writing students love this part of the story?

But I wasn't out of dumb luck. My god-daughter worked for the *New York Times*. She called me a couple of months after my LDA and I parted company. In that short time, she had gone from intern to assistant copy editor.

"Aunt Emmy, Mama says you fired your agent. I asked around. You got a pencil and paper? Write this down and then let me tell you what you need to do."

A query letter, who was I, synopsis of book, first chapter enclosed. I had nothing to lose.

A form letter response two weeks later: *Thank you for your submission. Please allow six weeks for a more detailed evaluation. This letter is not an agreement to represent your work. Best Regards, Melissa Arens, Assistant to Sonny Schenker.*

Well, it wasn't quite a rejection, but I did not feel encouraged. How naïve was I? How much of the world outside of a classroom did I actually understand? I was about to go through menopause. Shouldn't I have been smarter?

The ghost of Mark Twain almost ruined my career. My god-daughter Emily was in on it too.

This is the part of my story where my writing students sometimes gasp, sometimes laugh, and by the end they usually agree: That was a dumb thing to do.

Dorothy and I went to New York to visit Emily. We were both proud of her promising start to her own career, and we went bearing gifts…ourselves. Emily was my favorite of Dorothy's kids. Dorothy knew it and agreed. Some kids have something special, and that was Emily. Even as a lippy and sulky teenager, she never disappointed her mother or me. Down deep, I invented a reason why she was so special. She had grown up as the second child, the one who came after Dorothy's first baby died of SIDS. Emily grew up knowing of her mother's heartbreak. She determined that she would be her dead sister's living spirit, to offer her mother some solace. Too contrived? Overthought and overwritten? Tough, I invented the story. I told Emily a long time ago that I was going to write about her and her mother. I was serious. I owed Dorothy her *own* story. And Emily was my favorite. She had become *my* Emily. I thought about the two of them together, and *that* story was evolving as Dorothy and I went to see her in New York.

On our agenda for New York was a "Ghost Tour." A lot of big cities have them, and New York is the biggest, so it had to have the most ghosts, right? And that is how we ended up in Greenwich Village. 14 West 10th, where Mark Twain's ghost often appeared.

"Anything familiar about this street, Aunt Emmy?"

I had been to New York a few times since I was there with Peter, but I had never been to Greenwich Village.

"Emily, you promised me some ghosts. All I'm seeing are brownstones."

"Your memory is obviously slipping. The agent I told you about. Sonny Schenker lives on this street. In fact, right over there..." pointing to the steps leading up to a brownstone that was two numbers away from Twain's ghost.

My future story about Dorothy and her daughter was being rewritten on the spot. Was all this a coincidence or premeditated? Stupid question, right? My god-daughter was not a person for whom coincidences just "happened."

"You should go introduce yourself. You know, connect a name and face. Be your charming self. Just happened to be in the neighborhood...that sort of thing."

Dorothy was as confused as I was, but she did not have to make the decision. Weren't these sorts of moments in a hundred movies? Move the plot along, get the lovers together? I knocked on Sonny Schenker's door. I waited. No answer. The door had a peephole. I assumed I was being studied. I knocked again. The door opened and a young woman looked at me, a young woman with a death stare and a single word.

"Yes?"

"I was wondering if Mister Schenker is here. My name is Emily Sterling. I sent a writing sample a few months ago. I was in the neighborhood and thought I should introduce myself."

Another death stare. Then, her head turned ever so slowly and slightly to the left, but she never lost eye contact with me. Then another expression...amusement?

"Wait here. I'll let Sonny...*Mister Schenker*... know that...Emily Sterling, correct? ... would like to introduce herself." The door closed. Why the smirk when she said *Mister Schenker*?

I was starting to worry. The door opened and I was face-to-face with Sonny Schenker, long and wavy silver hair, tortoise-shell round glasses, shorter than me. Not a simple death stare, a laser death stare. Sonny Schenker was a woman.

"This is my home as well as my agency. I was not expecting you. I have no idea who you are."

I saw my publishing future…the Hindenburg in 1937.

"I'm sorry. I, uh, I…"

"Who are you?"

"I'm Emily Sterling. I sent you a chapter of my new…"

"When?"

I had to think hard. How long had it been? Six weeks? More or less? I guessed.

"A month ago, I think."

Obviously, the wrong answer. And then I saw the young woman a few feet behind Sonny, and she was obviously enjoying herself.

"Melissa sent you a letter to acknowledge its receipt. Do you recall what that letter said?"

I shook my head. The young woman…Melissa… rolled her eyes.

"It said that we would respond within six weeks, and we have never missed that deadline. You have not heard from us, have you? No, you have not. It has not been six weeks. So, tell me again. Who are you and what is the title of your work?"

For some reason, counterintuitive to how I should have felt at that moment of my obvious evaporation, I found my voice and my spine and my heart and my courage. I locked eyes with Sonny Schenker and waited until she blinked.

"My name is Emily Opal Sterling, and the title of my book is *Once Upon a Time*."

Sonny Schenker crossed her arms, her laser death stare replaced by…curiosity?

"Well, Miss Emily Opal Sterling, you go home. I will find your chapter and let you know what I think in a week. And, regardless of what I think of your work, you should never, ever, come to my home uninvited."

She stepped back and shut the door. I was hearing doors slam all over the universe.

The next thing I knew, Dorothy and Emily had come up the steps and led me back down to earth.

"Well, I thought that went well," my Emily said, holding on to me as we walked past the brownstone with Twain's ghost. I stopped dead in my tracks.

"Emily, that was a disaster. She's probably already writing a rejection note dipped in poison. Hell, she's probably going to burn my chapter before reading it and then write the note. And why didn't you tell me that Sonny was a woman?"

"Aunt Emmy, there's always that possibility of rejection. But I asked around about this woman. The very fact that she agreed to accept your submission is an accomplishment. Most people get a different first response than you did. And, for the record, I did tell you that she was a woman, real name Sonia Schenker, but I guess you forgot all that."

"Oh sure, it's possible I forgot, but then I show up unannounced and shoot myself in the goddam foot. And you thought it would be a good idea to do that?"

"All I know is what I was told by a lot of reviewers at the *Times.* Sonny Schenker is a tough cookie…I love that expression…but the best agent in town."

Dorothy poked me.

"Emmy, I trust her."

More notes for their future story.

Emily took us back to her one-room apartment. She had been sleeping on the couch while Dorothy and I had been sleeping in her bed for the past two nights. It was the last night of our trip, and Emily had one last excursion planned.

"It's going to be a gorgeous night tonight. Let's go take that walk over the Brooklyn Bridge."

I tried to talk her out of it. I was tired. I was depressed. I did not want to remember Peter. But she was adamant, and then Dorothy chimed in.

"I've never done it, Emmy. Please, go with me."

How could I say no? It was the first week of September, and Emily was right. It was a gorgeous night. We went to City Hall in Manhattan and then headed for the Bridge. We started out together, side by side, but by the time we had reached Brooklyn and turned back, the crowds had gotten bigger, so I lagged behind mother and daughter as they walked arm in arm. How could anybody not envy them? Both adults, bonded for life, my Emily a perfect fusion of Dorothy and Jake in her looks, but Dorothy had obviously shaped her personality more. The two of them just so damn happy to be alive and together on a bridge crossing calm waters below.

Did I ever want to be a mother? I was pregnant once, but I did not want to be. I slept with Peter for ten years, popping birth control pills, and never thought about having his child. That would have been unfair to Amy. But, sometimes, just imagining what he and I would look like as one person…that sometimes intrigued me. But the past always came back to me…Amy's baby. *Peter Amelia Jefferson* was the only child that Peter wanted. His and Amy's baby. I was okay with that. You want to hear a story about when I actually thought I wanted a baby? I was married once, remember? My doomed-to-be-ignored husband. I was his great mistake, a story never to be written. For one brief year, we were happy, I thought. We actually talked about having a baby. We had sex a lot, more than before or after that time of our lives. We had sex on a schedule. We studied the art of positions. You ever do that…have sex on a schedule? Desire scheduled? I remember that time and I remember how that was when I realized that I did not really love my husband, nor did he love me. Why had we gotten married in the first place? Board-certified Gretchen tried her best to get me to answer that question for myself, but, down deep, the ugly truth was that the question did not matter to me anymore. It did not matter with Gretchen back then, nor that night with Dorothy and Emily on the Brooklyn Bridge. My ex-husband is safely out of my memory most of the time, and he should probably be thankful. The great irony from those days of scheduled sex? Sex did not produce a baby, so I went to another doctor. More tests. Evidently, I had some sort of T-boned uterus. I might be able to get pregnant, but my risk of having recurrent miscarriages was very high. More of that Grand Intelligent Design, right? Emmy Sterling was perfect Aunt material for Dorothy's kids.

Then again, as Dorothy always told me, "Emmy, I never thought you were mother material. Thank Jesus that some child of yours didn't have to find out the hard way."

I thought about all that as I watched Dorothy and Emily walk together in front of me. A quick flashback to my reproductive history, and then dismissed. I thought about Emily up ahead having her own children and then I would become a Great-Aunt. I started walking slower, and they started going further and further ahead of me.

I knew it was inevitable, as much as I told myself that I was *not* going to do it. I thought about Peter and me on that same bridge years earlier. I had written a novel about my past, and he was not in it. Neither he nor Amy. No, no, wait. He was in one paragraph, about the narrator's history teacher. But it wasn't Peter. It was just his voice given to a one-paragraph character. Dorothy knew who the voice really was, of course, but she was uncharacteristically gentle with me.

"He'll always be there if you want to write about him."

All a moot point, right? I had written a book and then screwed up my chances of getting it published by making an unannounced stop on West 10th in Greenwich Village. But I wanted to tell Peter anyway. To talk to him about it, even though he was not in it. I wanted to tell Peter how afraid I was to have to go back and tell my father that the story about him and my mother, the fictional story, was never going to be published. I wanted to be angry at Peter for not being there when my mother died, not there for me to cry with, since I could not cry in front of my father. I wanted him to be there and kiss me one more time. I was afraid to look up, afraid to look at the moon. So, I looked down at the water. Boats in the water, ferries and tugs and slow-moving barges. Dorothy and Emily were almost out of sight, oblivious to me slowly disappearing behind them, so lost in the pleasure of their own company. I started walking faster, catching up, afraid to be left behind. I had been looking for Peter, but he was not there. I had seen him when he had told me about the *Atlantic* contest. But, even then, Peter James Jefferson was gone. Amy had been right.

A week later, I got the letter from Sonny Schenker. Holding the envelope in my hand without opening, it seemed to me to be a very thin letter, a perfect size for a rejection.

Dear Miss Sterling, I read your chapter with great interest…

A classic yes/but introduction.

…but…

My students are frozen in their seats, waiting.

…I need to read the entire work before I can give you a definitive answer. Please send a complete manuscript to me at your convenience, and I

will get back to you as soon as possible.

Even I knew that was a good sign. Even I knew that most queries never get a response for more. Plus, and this was the big plus, I had sent her the first chapter only, the only part of the story that the other publishers had left alone. Sonny Schenker was going to get the revised and revised again version. It had to be better, right?

It was a pleasure meeting you, and I look forward to reading the rest of your story.

What?

My students applaud.

Two weeks later, another letter.

Dear Miss Sterling, I read your story with much interest. I was puzzled by some parts, but, overall, this shows much promise. However, I have a friend whose judgment I value in situations such as this. Let me get the manuscript to her and I will get back to you as soon as possible. Thank you for your patience. Best wishes, Sonny.

I called Dorothy. She called her daughter. Emily called me.

"Aunt Emmy, this is great news."

"But she's not sure. Seems like a gentle let down to me."

"You are such a Debbie-Downer. This letter says she wants to like it, but she wants one other person to give her permission. That is not what I hear from others about how she operates, so your book must be special. All I know is that I wonder who the hell this other woman is that she is asking for a second opinion."

My students are back to being nervous for me.

A week later, I got a phone call.

"Emily, this is Sonny Schenker. You might want to sit down. I have some good news for you."

Has it been almost twenty years? Surely not. That would mean it has almost been forty years since I knew Peter and Amy. Fifty, if I went back to the first time I saw Peter in that classroom. But, as much as I try, I can't make my life story into some sort of seamless thread. Gaps abound. Bursts of actually living, and years of merely existing. The year before Sonny's phone call had been utterly frustrating. I finally wrote a book that a lot of editors read but did not want. I was sinking like the proverbial stone. And then I had that call from Sonny and the next year was some sort of acid dream on meth. No, wrong analogy, it was like being in a spaceship leaving earth. Pure acceleration and exhilaration. One year down, next year up. But that up year was a bit more complicated.

So, was it actually two parallel Emily Sterlings, waving at each other in separate lives? I give up. You find the analogy.

As I was lifting off into space, menopause was turning me into a corn husk. Dorothy was my guide for that change, a misleading guide. She called herself the Queen of Hot Flashes. I was simply the Mistress of Night Sweats. Sex? I was like a lot of women. I was losing whatever little interest I already had in it. Dorothy was a monster of gender contradictions. She wanted more sex. Vaginal dryness? That's what medicine was for. Weight gain? She didn't care. Food was meant to be enjoyed. She gained thirty pounds, shedding neither tears nor pounds.

Desire?

"Emmy, I told Jake that he better be banging me every night or I was going to go find somebody who could."

For me, it was the headaches, those damn migraines. I had prescriptions, I even went to yoga classes to relax and meditate, until Dorothy found out. She had her own solution. I was coming into money with the new book, so I could afford what she was doing...weekly, sometimes daily, trips to a day spa for women with disposable income.

A First World white-bread solution for sure. But, saunas and massages and hot tubs got me through that year, and the old Emily Sterling finally disappeared.

I wonder how I would have felt about my book success in that first year if I had been feeling physically good. My public and professional life was so good, but it could have been better if my body had been in sync with my brain, right? The psychology of success.

And then my father died.

"Emily, I sold your book to a friend of mine at Windsor House. Sally Spencer..."

I'm sure that Sonny was waiting for me to be overwhelmed by that name, but I was clueless. My tone of voice gave me away.

"Sonny, this is amazing..."

"Sally Spencer," she repeated.

"Yes, I understand..."

I like to imagine her smiling as she realized that I was, indeed, clueless about the most important editor in America. As clueless as I had seemed to be about her being a woman.

"Emily, go to the store and get the latest issue of *Vanity Fair*. Sally is profiled this month. Pay attention to the pictures of her apartment. She wants you to come up here and sit down with her as she works through your manuscript. I'll let you know about the arrangements as soon as I can."

"Sonny, thank you very much. And I apologize again for showing up at your home without an invitation."

"Water under the bridge, Emily. You have my invitation now. You come to the City and come see me, and I will introduce you to Sally."

"This is all very..."

"Emily, you haven't asked me the question yet."

"The question?"

I did not have to imagine her smiling. I could hear her laughing.

"The money, Emily, the advance. Sally is offering you a two-hundred-thousand-dollar advance. I accepted for you. And, by the way, I changed the title, but we can talk about that when you get here. I'm not sure what you have written, but it is definitely not a fairy tale."

I called Dorothy, who called her daughter. I called my father. I wanted to call Peter, but I changed my mind, imagining a different meeting for us, where I gave him his own copy and thanked him. A final gesture?

I went to find that issue of *Vanity Fair*.

Who are the important people in your life? If you dropped dead today, could you name them? And explain them to your biographer?

Sally Spencer had graduated from the Oxford Divinity School when she was twenty-six and renounced God when she was thirty. That, alone, made me want to meet her. She had gone to work for Penguin in Britain as a sales rep to bookstores, did that for a year, jumped to Hachette as an assistant editor, did that for five years, and then jumped back to Penguin as senior editor, and in two years was editor in chief. Five years before I met Sonny, Sally had been lured by Windsor House to America. She was the daughter of an Ambassador in the British Foreign Office and had grown up in Australia and India. Married to a Colonel in the RAF at thirty, a widow by thirty-five. She was a chain-smoking, (almost raw) beef-eating, wine-drinking British blue-blood who had published more first-time novelists who became prize-winning best-selling novelists than anybody else in publishing. When I finally met her, she was past sixty. She was a legend. *Vanity Fair* had described a woman of enormous intimidating power. Every picture in the story reflected that power. Her New York penthouse had a library wall-to-wall, floor-to-ceiling, in every room. Just from the pictures, I wanted to be Sally Spencer. But there was a single line in the profile that made me realize that I could never be her.

"Sally rules a glittering world of art and literature, but she is shockingly humble and gracious in person."

Humility and grace, those were the exceptions in her world?

A week after I got the call from Sonny, Sally Spencer called me. Did I tell you that she was British? I thought I was talking to a whispering Queen Elizabeth.

"My dear Emily, it is such a pleasure to finally speak with you. Sonny has told me such glowing things about you, and, of course, I have read your story."

Was she lying to me or had Sonny been lying to her? Sonny knew almost nothing about me. But the story, my story, was real.

"Mrs. Spencer, it is my..."

"Sally, my child, please call me Sally."

"Sally, I cannot tell you how honored I am to have you and Windsor publish my book."

"Thank you, but it is our honor as well. I will see you soon, and then your real work begins. But we shall talk first. You must tell me where your story comes from. Such interesting people. I suspect you know them, as every author does. I would like to know them as well. You have a special talent, Emily. I seldom cry when I read the last page of a book. You did that for me."

A keen grasp of the obvious? Writing is art. Publishing is commerce.

Writing is craft, and sweat, and sometimes talent, but good writing is art. I think my first book was art. How good was it? How many friends, not just close friends, but friends, told me some version of the following:

"Emily, I always thought you were a bit of an asshole, or a bitch, likable and unlikable at the same time, but never lovable. But I read your book and I thought… Anybody who could write this book has to have something deep inside her that I missed. Where was it all these years?"

Those aren't the exact words, but that's what I heard.

Publishing as commerce? Editing, packaging, promoting…publishers make decisions and want to make money, so they can publish more books and make more money, and sometimes they publish works of monumental art. Sometimes they publish crap to pay for the monumental art that does not make money.

Dumb luck? I crossed paths with the right agent who knew the right editor. A million writers never get that lucky. Better writers than me. I got lucky. I know that. But I still wrote a good book. I made Sally Spencer cry.

A year of frustration with one agent led to Sonny Schenker, and it was another year before my book was in print. It had to be edited, then it had to be turned over to the publicity and promotion departments to find out how to sell it. Publishing schedules and catalogs had to be designed six months in advance. What gets published when? Sales reps have to be brought into the process. Media contacts are made. Advance review copies mailed out. Hollywood contacts are made. Other authors to blurb the book. Reviewers start to read it. Back in some office, somebody has to decide how many first-edition copies to print. Whatever the figure, the publicity department tells the media a higher number. Momentum has to be built. Hype and Buzz, the next Great American Novel is coming. First-time authors have to be careful, or else they believe they are the next Great American Writer, when the truth is simply that they got lucky.

Books have plots. A lot of genre fiction is plot-driven. A good mystery is harder to write than you might think. Books have characters. Stereotypical characters, or absolutely unique characters, but unique ones are rare. We're all versions of a type. And some books merely have...scenes.

And there's the rub in my writing. I'm at the point where all I have are scenes. All I have are memories, and memories are merely scenes from the past. Unlike fiction, life does not have a plot. You can look back and tell yourself that all the scenes were linear and leading to where you are. Not really. You can never remember all the scenes in your life. They are gone. You might think that what you do remember are the most important scenes of your life. They must be...because you remember them, right?

I'm not well this morning. Again. I know what I want to tell you, but I'm having problems.

Memories are a thousand dots on a piece of paper. Connect the dots, see the image.

Jackson Pollock. Splatter a canvas and call it art. It never made sense to me. My secret opinion? If a woman had done what he did, she would have been ignored or ridiculed. Is life merely a paint splatter? I might be wrong. Shouldn't I know more now, about art, about female painters? Surely, splattering was done as well by women too. Expressionists? Aren't we all?

Proust? It was always on my list to read. Sonny did not like my title, but Proust already stole the title I wanted.

Sally Spencer's penthouse had its own elevator that could only be accessed by the lobby clerk. I was confused when I got to the building. It was modern, glass and steel, and utterly boring. The pictures I had seen in *Vanity Fair* had to have been taken somewhere else. The building was cold. The pictures had been warm, as if she lived in an estate in the English countryside. There was even a stone fireplace, chopped wood stacked nearby, in a room with an ornate Persian rug that covered the floor, a room of wood paneling. That was what I saw as the elevator door opened directly into her living room.

Sally was standing there waiting for me, hand extended, as I stepped off the elevator. She was not wearing any shoes.

"My dear Emily, we meet at last. Here, let me help you with your coat."

It was January, snowing outside. I looked like a child bundled up by an overprotective mother. Intuitively, I turned around and unbuttoned my coat. I felt her hands on my shoulders as she slowly pulled the coat off. I turned around and took off my wool scarf and handed it to her. Instant insecurity. Was she judging my wardrobe? She was certainly studying something. I was so focused on her that I did not notice the India Indian servant in a white jacket standing deferentially off to the side. Sally, holding my coat and scarf, looking me up and down…she was all that existed. Evidently satisfied at the appearance of her guest, she turned to the servant and handed him my coat and scarf. She did not speak out loud, but I could read her lips as she looked at him.

Some tea for the two of us, thank you.

"And now, Emily, I apologize, but I have to return a few calls, and then we have the rest of the day to ourselves. Please, make yourself at home. You might relax and leave your shoes here by the door. This will only take a few minutes."

Make myself at home? I wished that were my home. Sally did not have the beach view that I had, but she had the skyline of New York City on a snowy day. More, she had *that* place, that room, and more rooms like it. A library in one room, and then I wandered into another. And another. I remembered the *Vanity Fair* spread. Sally with John Updike and Toni Morrison and Alice Walker and John Irving, posing with Sally in the middle, all in the room where I was. I walked around and around. Old and new books in some sort of arrangement undecipherable by me. Not alphabetically by title or name or, evidently, by date. Almost every one that I opened had been signed by the author. It was obvious that not every one of the books had been read, their spines still stiff, but the authors' inscriptions made them personal, a gift to be treasured. I ended back at the room where I began, standing in front of the fireplace, trying to connect me at eighteen with me then, me at thirty with me then. I wanted my mother and father to be there with me. I wanted Peter and Amy.

"I apologize for being gone so long. The National Book Critic Circle Award dinner is being held tonight. I have some books nominated, but I would rather relax here tonight and talk with you. And, besides, I was going to be seated next to John Updike and sometimes the man takes up too much oxygen, as much as I love him."

Sally was back, white-coated Indian servant behind her, holding a tray.

She had skipped the NBCC dinner to spend the evening with me?

"Let's have some tea and talk. You must tell me all about yourself."

I had talked to board-certified Gretchen for years, but I told Sally more in two hours. Had I always wanted to confess so much so quickly? All she had to say was, "Tell me why you wrote this story." My life from birth to snowy day in New York City. And the servant kept bringing tea. I ended up with how I had an agent for a year who could not sell the book even though I revised and revised, and then I found Sonny; that is, my Emily found her. Sally slowly nodded.

"Of course, our world is full of books that have been rejected and then accepted. We just don't like to admit we were wrong."

"Have you...."

"Of course, my dear, a hundred times, or more. I lose track. But I am happy for the author. He has found a home."

"Me, I just consider myself lucky."

"We all are, all of us, aren't we. Now, I have a few more questions, and then I shall walk you back to your hotel and we will meet at my office tomorrow and I will introduce you to my colleagues. They are all anxious to meet you. Most of them have read your manuscript."

A scene, or a moment? Sally bundled me up again, had her servant appear with her own winter coat, we donned our shoes, and the two of us descended to Fifth Avenue in New York City on a snowy night and walked back to my hotel, arm in arm.

A next-day scene. I was in her office, surrounded by her staff. Small talk mostly, pleasantries, champagne at ten in the morning. Was this how every first-timer was welcomed? A detail that nobody believed when I told them later? Sally did not wear shoes at her apartment, nor when she was at work. Ergo, neither did her staff. Why was that detail not in the *Vanity Fair* profile? Men in suits in sock feet. Women in black skirts and designer blouses, in their stocking feet. Thick carpets throughout the entire suite of offices, not a shoe in sight. Me? I was shoeless within thirty seconds of entering.

They had a secret, but it required me to see it in plain sight. I learned later that it was a ritual for every first-time writer of Sally's, but some of them never knew about it because they were too distracted at that first staff meeting. Me, I was more than distracted. I was in a daze, being the center of attention that morning. Because I was in a daze, I did not believe what I finally saw. I thought I was hallucinating. Surely, not.

On the bookshelf behind Sally's desk was a copy of my book, dust jacket facing out. I blinked. I was confused. It was not my title. It was Sonny's title, but my name was in silver print along the bottom. It was the image that stopped my breathing as I realized I was looking at a cover with a painting of the kitchen where I had grown up with my parents. Almost photographic in detail, but a painting it was, a painting that the Windsor House graphic artist had designed based on the description in my book. Still to come was the movie-set moment, when I was overwhelmed a second time, but there in Sally's office I froze and went away. I did not know it, but everyone in that office had been waiting for the moment when I would see the book cover. They told me later how disappointed they would be when a new writer did not see the gesture they had prepared. It was a pleasure of their work, to create that much joy for someone. And it was only for the first-time authors. Of course, it was not really my book, just a one-of-a-kind dust jacket wrapped around another book. Not a real book, but I'm tempted to say it was like an exhausted mother being handed her newborn child and seeing her creation for the first time, but that, I'll admit, would be a cliché. How could I be sure? Make that comparison? I was never a mother.

Sally had moved to the back of her office as I met her staff, not talking, simply sharing her new discovery with people who had over the years been part of her own success. It was a small family, and I was only visiting, because another new writer was out there waiting to be discovered, and commerce would go on. Still, the ritual required one more gesture. Me almost in tears, Sally went to the bookshelf and retrieved the book with my name on it, explaining how it was merely an early version of the cover, to be refined and polished and perhaps even discarded later, but…

"Please take this from us to you, a memento of this morning. And, welcome."

There's writing, then rewriting, and then there's editing. I spent three days with Sally Spencer as she edited my book.

After the morning visit with her staff, and then lunch with just her and the Publicity Director, Sally and I were back at her apartment. She led me into another room lined with bookcases, but the only furniture in this room was a table with two chairs side by side. On the table were two copies of my manuscript, side by side. Sally and I sat down, side by side.

"Shall we begin? Page one, line one."

Three days, line by line. Not every line merited a comment, but we had to get past the lines in sequence.

On the second day, her most memorable comment: "Emily, did you ever read your own book? I mean, finish it and read it as if for the first time, from the first page to the last, as if you were a reader, not a writer?"

Or perhaps it was what she said when I became exasperated and asked her, "Sally, with all these changes and corrections and deletions, why did you even buy this book in the first place?"

"Because, my dear, I knew there was a wonderful story in there, but it was being hidden by too much…"

She hesitated.

"…too much…crap."

It was becoming clear to me. The more we worked together, the more my story was returning to the version I had first sent to the Long Distance Agent. Bad analogy? A doctor reversing the inept plastic surgery of another doctor. Worse analogy? A beautiful woman gets fat and has to lose a hundred pounds. Sally had bought a four-hundred-page manuscript. When we finished, it was three hundred and forty pages.

I turned myself over to her and whenever we disagreed about a line or paragraph, she always won, except for one time. Near the end, as the crippled husband pulls his dying wife out of a burning car before the flames had touched her, I had the husband whispering to his wife as she died, but I did not have any dialogue. Sally wanted dialogue.

"Emily, it is a powerful moment. The reader will want to know what the husband said to his wife. A few words. I know you can do it. Tell us what he said to her."

She had been right on everything so far. I wanted to please her. But all I could think of was my father whispering to my mother as she was dying, the two of them so close to me, but his words were too quiet for me to hear. Sally was still seeing them as fictional characters. I was not.

"I'm sorry, Sally, but I can't do that. It was between them, not for me, or you, or anybody else. It's their secret. Let the reader write their dialogue."

I expected her to disagree. We were two pages from the end. One final tweak, right? She looked over the top of her reading glasses.

"You sure?"

I just nodded.

"Well, I suppose this is the one I give you."

"I'm sorry. I don't mean to be…"

"Emily, you should never apologize. It is *your* story, not mine. If anything I have done here helps you write your story, perhaps even makes it better, I'm happy." She reached for my hand. "As for that dialogue…you are absolutely right. I was wrong. Now, we're done here. It is a wonderful story, Emily. Thank you for letting me read it."

"We're done, but what about the last few pages?"

"Perfect, Emily, I wouldn't change a word. Remember, I cried at the end. Not two pages from the end, but as soon as I finished that last perfect line, I cried."

"So, we're done?" I was still pumping adrenaline. She stood up, extending her hand to help me up.

"Oh, you and I are done. I hand you off now. You still have to deal with Theresa Nolan, our copy editor, and if you think I was finicky, you will discover that Theresa can be a comma Nazi. And then the publicity and promotion people will be working with you about tours and interviews. Almost every writer I have known has told me that writing a book is easy compared to selling it. But I remind them that it is our job to sell it, it is their job to not embarrass us. Promise me, Emily, don't say something stupid to an interviewer."

"Yes ma'am."

I had one more question for her.

"Sally, have you ever thought about writing your own book. I mean, seriously, your life, this business, the people you have known."

"A question I am often asked. And my answer is always the same… no. I have files with thousands of pages, beginning with my birth certificate, then college essays, marriage certificate, and letters to lovers. A hundred people can be interviewed. Somebody else can write my life story. I am not a writer, Emily. I am a reader. You're a writer. You and I both know that this book is your life. However, the trick to having an actual career is to finally stop writing about yourself."

I was in Sally's apartment only one other time, when I brought my father to New York to meet her and Sonny. They had both insisted. My only stipulation was that we were to do nothing public. My father was frail. He had tried going back to teaching, as charred as he was, but it was too much for him. When I told him that there were people in New York who wanted to meet him, he was more excited than I expected.

"Should I buy a new suit?"

He was not serious. I knew that.

"No, Daddy, just be yourself. I've already told them all about you and Mama. *New Suit Dewy* is not who they want to meet."

"I assume they will want me to sign their copies of your book."

"Oh, surely, sign as *De Witt Clinton Sterling, Father of the Author.*"

Publication date was September 30. The early hype had been successful. A planned first print run of twenty thousand copies had been bumped up to forty thousand. *Today* was interested in an interview. Charlie Rose was starting a new talk show on PBS. Sonny told me that "People" from Mike Nichols' office had called her office wanting an advance copy. Paperback rights had been sold for more than the hardcover rights. Bidding for foreign rights was heating up. Bertelsmann evidently had money to burn. Little-Brown in Britain paid more than Windsor House had, just for World English Language rights. Even the Italians wanted their version. Even before the book was finally in print, the book advances and movie option passed a million dollars. Sonny got her fifteen percent, the government got thirty-five percent. I was still set for life. Dumb luck and perseverance.

Dinner and drinks with my father and Sonny were a bit oversaturated, with Melissa tending the bar in Sonny's home/office. The next night, my father and I were in Sally's apartment. He had seen the magazine pictures, read all the press about her, and I had talked incessantly with him about working with her.

Sitting in her apartment, watching him and Sally together, how could I not think of him and my mother? All the times I had listened to them joke with each other, talk about books and poems. I tried to go back as far as my memory would take me, wanting to grab the child that I was and describe her future to her.

You are not going to believe this, Emmy myself, you will become a writer and your father will live long enough to see you famous. You will go to

New York and sit in a room full of books, with the starry skyline just outside the windows, with servants in white jackets floating in and out, anticipating an empty glass, and the most brilliant woman in the world will be smitten by your father.

Of course, there were too many other things I would not tell myself, too many other things awaiting me in the future. No, *that* child would have to find out for herself.

Top ten moments of your life? So wonderful that even the memory is not enough? You wanted somebody to have been there with a camera because you did not want to forget a single tiny detail. Sally's cigarette smoke floating up, up in silver wisps and then evaporating. The overhead fan slowly turning. How ice rattled in a glass. The look on my father's stiff face when he was asked to remove his shoes, his eyes widening, but I knew him well enough to know that that was as much of a smile as his face allowed him. The memory of how he could not do it without help, so Sally knelt down and took them off for him. Later, the tilt of her body as she would lean toward my father as he spoke, her absolute attention on him. The way my father's hands would almost caress the arm of the sofa as he talked about my mother. The moment I looked around Sally's apartment as they talked, that moment when the fairy tale *Beauty and the Beast* wrapped itself around me and would not let go. My father was the beast, but the beauty was not Sally. It was the room we were in. *Beauty and the Beast.* But it was perfect because you know the truth of that fairy tale. The beast is not a beast. He is a Prince. My father was a Prince, surrounded by Beauty.

So much that night to remember. I wish I could do it, remember it all. One more moment. When my father casually dropped a Latin phrase into the conversation, something anybody would recognize, like a throwaway *et tu*, and Sally responded with a complete sentence in Latin, and my father responded to her in Latin, and they went to

Caesar's Rome, leaving me behind. More animated in Latin than they had been in English. How do you tell jokes in Latin? How do you laugh in Latin? I had not seen my father that happy in a long time. He was going to die soon, I expected that. I was so happy that night that he was with me in Sally's world. I wondered if he had ever imagined his future, his last conversation in Latin, in a room with thousands of books. I wanted to go back and talk to my father when he was a child. I wanted to tell him that everything was going to be okay. I was in his future. I would be there at the end.

Dumb luck and perseverance? When my book was published, dumb luck died and perseverance was a slow horse to ride, but it got me here.

It should have been the best day of my life, September 30, publication day. I had finally become the success story that Miss Randall had wanted me to be. I could finally tell Peter James Jefferson that I had finally grown up and become who I was supposed to be.

My father had been getting worse. The trip to New York had been his last trip. I was selfish. I had joked with him about staying well until I got back from my first tour. He had laughed. I had money. I arranged for a nurse to stay with him at my beach house for the days I would be on tour. I would call him every day. I thought I had things under control. I was wrong.

I was packed and ready to go to the airport in the morning, to fly to Miami for my first bookstore appearance. It was a big deal, that store, the most important independent bookstore in America, and the owner was a friend of Sally's who always got the first appearance of all her new writers. He was a legend. He had called early in the morning of the 29th and told me how much he looked forward to meeting me, and that he had loved my book. Six hours later, I called Sally and told her that I had to stay with my father. It was just a feeling, I told her, just a feeling. I apologized. Tours were set up long in advance, stores setting aside time and space and staff support, local media contacted, flights booked, money spent. But I had a bad feeling. Sally did not hesitate.

"Emily, do not worry about anything. My people will redo everything when you are ready. Just tell your father that I was honored to meet him, and you take care of yourself too."

An hour later, the bookstore owner in Miami called me.

"Emily, Sally just told me about your father. I'm very sorry. I feel like I know him just from your story. Do not give a second thought to tomorrow, okay? You and I will meet eventually, and you can tell me more about him. Take care, Emily, take care."

Were we both crying when the call was over? He seemed like a kind and gracious man. I think my father would have liked him.

My father had been having trouble breathing all day, unable to even lie down in bed. I had propped him up with pillows so he could finally go to sleep. I slept in a chair next to his bed, waking up early on publication day with him looking at me.

"Morning, Emmy."

"Morning, Daddy."

"Is Dawn here?"

How could I miss that? I looked out the window to see the sun barely peeping up on the horizon, the dark sky just starting to be tinged with orange.

"Almost," I said, and then I knew what he meant. I corrected myself.

"Yes, she's here."

My father had to take a breath between every sentence.

"You're still the sweetest daughter I ever had, Emmy...It's okay,

I know she's not really…I mean, she is…not like…not really here…"

"Daddy, you save your energy. I can…"

"Save it for what, Emmy?"

"Daddy, you are not allowed to die on me. I will not allow it. I can't lose you too."

He ignored me.

"Emmy, your mother and I wanted to give…you something once…for your birthday…but we never found the time…I've been thinking that maybe you and I could do it…but it's too late."

"Daddy, you get well, that's all I want."

"We were going to surprise you with a trip. The three of us. To go to Amherst, to Emily Dickinson's home. We thought you would like that."

Yes, I tell you now, it was too much. I am telling you this now, and I am crying now, at this very moment. It happens to you, I know that. A memory comes back and you are there again, and you cry.

"Daddy, you get well, and I will take *you* to Amherst, okay?"

"That's a deal, Emmy. You and me, and your mother."

"Absolutely, Daddy, absolutely."

"Any chance you and I can watch the sun rise? I always thought you and me and your mother would walk on the beach and do that, like we did a long time ago, when you were tiny, but I sorta think that my beach walking days are over."

It took more strength than I thought I had, but I got him up out of bed and then out to my deck patio and laid him in a lounge chair. It was a cool morning, so I covered his legs with a light blanket and sat next to him as he said the last words I would ever hear from him.

"You remember your promise, don't you?"

"Yes, Daddy."

I went back into my house and got the urn of my mother's ashes and took them to my father, to hold as he watched the sun rise. It was too much for me. I left them alone and went back inside to cry and feel sorry for myself. A few minutes, and then I went back to the patio. I stopped in the doorway. My father was talking to my mother, but I could not make out the words.

I just stood there, hoping I might hear my mother sing to herself again, even if only in my imagination. Hoping that I might hear them laugh one more time.

My father's voice went away. Publication Day.

My promise to him? It was not to bring my mother's ashes to him as he watched the sun rise. That was unplanned. I just had a feeling. The important promise had been made to him the night my mother died.

"Emmy, after I die, I want you to have my ashes mixed in with your mother's. Keep us together. Will you promise to do that for me?"

"Yes, Daddy, I promise."

Emily *redux*? I stayed in my beach house. I watched the sun come up every morning. Dorothy came and stayed with me for a week. God-daughter Emily came for a weekend. I thought about what Sonny had told me after meeting my father, that I should have written a memoir just about him and my mother. I told myself that I would do that eventually. Plenty of time.

My postponed tour began in Miami in November. The owner who had called me was everything I had imagined about him. Gracious and encouraging, and he delivered a full house at his store, almost a hundred book buyers. I was the center of attention. For the rest of my writing life, every bookstore appearance was a version of my first. Sure, the crowds dwindled with each book, and sometimes an embarrassed store owner would have to recruit employees to occupy a few seats, so

I would not be speaking to an empty room. But the faces remained the same. Especially the older women. I was surviving my own special menopause. Special to me. I think that some women knew it. Perhaps an offhand comment from me? But I also knew what else they were thinking. About their own stories they wanted to write, but which most of them would not even start. After awhile, even the audience questions became predictable. *What's your writing routine? Your favorite writers? Books that influenced you? Are there real people in your stories?* Questions I had asked writers when I went to bookstore events when I was young. But there was always one final question that I dreaded: *What are you working on now?*

I wanted to say, *You mean, the future? What is in my future?*

But I always had a book answer. I was always working on another book, and I would give them an outline and they would be intrigued. I think I described books that I was thinking about writing, but had not put a word to paper yet. They were just ideas, but I could not admit that I was not really sure where I was going. I admitted that to Sally, my indecisiveness about an actual second book, once when she called me to see how I was doing, three months after Miami.

"You must think of that as a compliment, Emily, their asking about your next project. It means they are looking forward to it. They want another book from you."

Sally was being generous, but I wonder now if she already knew then the truth about my future. She had not said that she was looking forward to my next book.

My first book was a minor bestseller for a few weeks. All the early hype had worked. But publishing is not science or math. Nothing is predictable. Some reviews were glowing and four-starred. Others were not. The *New Yorker* loved the book. The *New York Times* hated it. With a passion, they hated it. Were the two of them reading the same book? After seeing the *Times* review, the Windsor House Publicist had called me, trying to put cosmetics on a corpse by joking, "Who did you piss off at the *Times*?" He was laughing, assuring me that nobody batted a thousand in the book business. I had been scheduled for the new Charlie Rose show, but I was "postponed" the day after the *Times* review was published. Some reviews were tepid. Some greeted the dawn of my new career. Some missed the point of the book entirely. My darkest secret? For that first year, I did not care. The only opinion that mattered to me was Sally's.

All in all, the bottom-line truth about my first book is that it did not come close to earning back its advance money…anywhere. Windsor House lost money. Little-Brown in England lost money. The Italian publisher sent me a check in March for the advance, but they never printed a copy. It was cheaper for them to pay me and not pay for a few thousand books that would not, as all their projections showed, based on sales in other countries, be recouped. If I had gotten no advance for my book, and sold the same number of copies that I did with Windsor House, I would be a *Publisher's Weekly* success story. But an equal number of my books were sitting in a warehouse in New Jersey, destined to be pulped. Even when the movie was finally in theatres, my book was disappearing. But, a deal is a deal. I cashed the advance checks, all of them. Nobody asked for their money back. They just didn't offer any more.

Sonny did her best. But she was honest.

"Sally wants a second book from you, and we'll take whatever she offers, but it's got to be a sure thing, Emily. Not just as good as your first, but better. You can do that. Right?"

I could not.

I wrote a second book, stole shamelessly from my life, went back to high school and ended up writing a competent Young Adult novel even though I did not know it was YA. I sent it to Sonny and she sent it back to me.

"You can do better. I'll do you a favor and burn this one."

I rewrote it. Sonny was not fooled, nor was she calm.

"Goddam it, Emily, don't send me anything like this again. Focus, goddam it, focus."

Did we part ways then, and I just did not realize it? My first book had offered me two lessons, and I learned neither. First, trust my first impulse. Write what I wanted and truly felt, the book that was resurrected by Sally. And that's the lesson I misapplied. I was a good writer, but not the best in the world. It could all be better. Sally had not only restored my first version, she had made it better. I had to learn to be better before I went back for a second book, especially after the first was a ...commercial...failure. Second lesson? Money is a measure of success, and if you made a lot of money up front...your life was set. I am still living off the money I made on my first book, but I never wrote another one as good for a long long time. I didn't need to make money, but a publisher did.

Here I am, lecturing you like you are one of my students. All irrelevant. My second book never got published, but I still call it my second. But Sonny was right. It was stillborn. I wrote a third, finally focusing on something that I cared about, a time when I was surrounded by stories, that time between my life with Peter and my experience with Sally, when I was on my own, teaching in college.

But, in between? Between my first and third, I wasn't sure who I was anymore. It was some sort of adult version of the me in that period from graduation night to when I went to college and met Peter. I was in a shell, back at home with my parents. I grew up, turned fifty, and was back in a shell. I damn near lost Dorothy's friendship, but she was a better person than I was, and she stayed with me.

"Emmy, you'll always be my bitch, even when you're a real bitch. And you know as well as I do, you saved my life when I lost my baby."

Was that it? I was there when she found her baby dead in a crib, and I stayed with her for two months. I did not think I was doing anything extraordinary. It was just what you did for somebody you loved, your best friend. Who was I then?

I was between lives. Both times. Dorothy understood both times. It was not the commercial failure of my first book. The *book* did not fail. My father was gone, and as much as Dorothy and her daughter tried to console me, as much as Sally and Sonny tried to console me, as did the wonderful bookstore owner in Miami, and others, I was still lost. My parents, Peter and Amy, gone. I thought I had run out of stories.

God-daughter Emily took a hammer and cracked my shell. I had sent her a copy of my YA-ish book, and she sent me a New York City postcard: *I Read your book. Barfola. See you soon. You owe me for that three hours of my life.* She was, indeed, her mother's daughter first.

Mother and daughter came to my beach house, and they brought their own booze. That first night, Dorothy and I started reminiscing about our college days, and Emily sat mesmerized…stupefied?...as I revealed Peter and Amy to her. Her first response was to poke her mother: *And you never told me this? About my fairy godmother? The slut!*

A full moon night, three drunk dames. It was a good night.

My Emily was slurringly adamant, "You have to write about that, Aunt Emmy. It's too good of a story not to tell, and nobody can get hurt now."

"Thank you, Emily, for thinking that I'm a nobody."

Dorothy shrieked, her drink flying everywhere as she swung her glass at us.

"Oh, my God, Emmy, do you remember that poem?"

Her daughter was wide-eyed. I was clueless.

"The Dickinson poem, the one you suggested to me for Miss Randall. Christ, I loved that poem. Emily, you know I named you after Emmy, but did you know that Emmy was named after Emily Dickinson?"

As I was remembering that poem, my god-daughter picked another thread to unravel and went in another direction.

"Who is Miss Randall?"

Dorothy and I were back in high school again, telling stories about Miss Randall and Mike Migdalovich and Jake as a jock and all the adolescent world from whence we came. Young Emily was fascinated.

"Aunt Emmy, those are the stories you should have told in that godawful book you just wrote. Those people are real."

Dorothy chimed in, "You want school stories, Emily, you should ask Emmy about her college days and grad school and all the teaching jobs she had after that."

And off I went, recalling the parties and the profs and some of my most outrageous students. Soon enough, I was laughing as much as Dorothy and her daughter. I was remembering all of them, the good the bad and the ugly. I had forgotten how much fun I had had in those days. Post-Peter and Amy; Pre-Damn Death of Everyone I Loved.

"Aunt Emmy, that's the story you need to write. You can keep Peter and Amy in your little private chapel, but any story with stolen dissertations and professors punching other professors…I'd love to read that."

And that became my third novel: *Publish or Perish.*

I wrote it in six months, and I actually laughed out loud at the keyboard sometimes. It was a funny book, unlike my first, so I had to find the courage to send it to Sonny Schenker. I wasn't sure if that bridge had been burned. She did not call me, but she did send a letter: *Emily, thank you for sharing this with me. It is a delightful book, a real change of tone for you, and filled with vivid characters. I'm not sure to whom I can send it here. A lot is happening with the business. But let me make a call for you to a friend at a fairly new small press in Minnesota, and I will call you later. Just to be sure you understand, you should not expect any advance, but I will certainly not take a commission if it is accepted by them. I do this as a favor to you and to my friend at the press.*

I had underestimated Sonny. She was a better agent than I was a client. I suppose I could have tried another agent, but I knew that Sonny would make that Minnesota deal for me. I would be in print again, and my book might earn some money. I would not get rich again. But I would be published. I would be out of my shell. That was enough.

If it bleeds, it leads. Film at eleven.

Is that story-telling too? All just an effort to get attention? You watch enough cable news nowadays and you will be convinced that the world is going to hell in a handbasket and every hour is just "breaking news" to make us forget the past hour and get our attention again. Dorothy read everything I've said to you so far, and she was confused. Just imagine how much more confused she would be if she knew all the things that I have told you, not just what I've written.

"Emmy, all you do is remember the worst of your life. All of your stories should begin with a disclaimer: *In this book, everybody dies, usually in pain*. Any character close to being a surrogate for you is portrayed as a failure. Me, in the one story I am in, I'm wonderful, hard to screw that up. But sometimes I wonder if you were ever really happy. If not, you fooled me. As I recall, we had some good times together, sometimes just laughing about the bad times."

"I'm dying, Dorothy. Cut me some slack."

"You're not dying until you're in hospice, Emmy. Morphine drip and all your adoring fans gathered around your soon-to-be-gone soul."

"Well, I feel like I'm dying."

"Not the same, darlin', not the same."

"I have breast cancer."

"You had breast cancer. No signs for the past year."

"I'm living on borrowed time."

"Emmy, that is the dumbest goddam thing I've ever heard you say. And you're supposed to be a writer, remember? Borrowed time? Gag me with a cliché. Borrowed time? We're all living on borrowed fucking time."

Dorothy is right. I suppose that if any person older than sixty started writing about their life, there would be enough pain and misery to write about. Agony and Heartbreak are not my monopoly. A lot, a whole lot, of people have had more painful lives than me. I had wonderful parents. At least one true love in my life, a bit complicated because that true love involved a third person too. I have a best friend, and a brilliant god-daughter named after me. Got rich writing one book. Won an award for another book that sold less than a thousand copies. Before the cancer treatments, there were tens of thousands of days in my life when I was thrilled to just be alive, just the simple pleasure of being physically alive…smelling, touching, seeing, hearing, tasting…life. Crying not because my heart was broken, but because I was moved by music or sunrises or standing in front of a painting that I had only admired as a picture in a book, but then saw face-to-face on a wall in a museum, finally understanding what the artist had done. Hell, I cried at my god-daughter Emily's high school graduation because I was so happy.

I *have* been happy in my life, but I suppose those times do not make the most interesting stories.

My third book started the happiest decade of my life. With money in the bank, I was probably luckier than ninety percent of Americans, ninety-nine-point-nine percent of the world. That book opened doors that my first book did not. My small-press publisher, his small publicity budget spread thin over the ten writers a year that he published, compensated by letting me design my own covers, which he fine-tuned. Not a big deal, right? Wrong. Somehow, the book itself was more *mine* than when Windsor House had done all the work for me. It won awards for design. That made me happy. Touring? Not a jet in my life ever again, but I could drive, at my own expense, anywhere in a two-hundred-mile radius. I made friends in independent bookstores and small-town libraries. That Legendary Bookstore Owner, my LBO, in Miami hosted me for every book I ever had published, even though he never got another full house for me like he did with my first book. I was a writer with a first novel made into a movie…a weird, and totally invalid, validation that such a writer was somehow more important than another writer, more successful…and I was a writer with another novel that had won a PEN/Faulkner Award. So, I was an attractive candidate for visiting-writer fellowships and summer workshops.

All that, dumb luck…or simply more perseverance?

Regardless, touring and teaching and writing were my life for a decade, and I was happy.

A story that combines touring and teaching?

I was in Miami for *Publish or Perish*. My favorite bookstore owner, the LBO, had gotten me a good review in the *Herald*. In most of America, I was old and forgotten news. In Miami, I was the center of attention for fifty-two people. The next night, in Tampa, I chatted with twenty-seven. The other stops? Don't ask.

Sometimes…no, a lot of times, as you have probably figured out…I want to go back and relive a moment, but only as a spectator. You know, be the objective observer. As much as possible.

At the end of my reading in Miami, after the question-and-answer segment, the final ritual began. Half the crowd, or more, would leave, but the rest would line up to get a signed copy. Ask any writer on tour, most will tell you that the pleasure of signing books is sometimes problematic. First, in the secret realm of writer and reader, a personal connection is made, even if the reader has not yet read the book. *I wrote the book. You are going to read the book. We are in a relationship.* Readers are there because they want to meet you, see you, hear you, and many of them want to tell you how much your writing has meant to them or how much they are looking forward to your new book. Every reader is a story unto themselves. Each person in front of you, about to plunk down twenty-five dollars at the register, deserves more than your signature. They deserve a personal inscription, something from you that makes the book unique to them. I have tried to do that at every appearance I ever made. The problem? It is a slow process. You have one person absorbing your attention for a few minutes, with lots of other people in line. Down deep, the writer wants the inscription to mean something important to the reader. Okay, maybe not all writers. Maybe just the most insecure ones. Not naming names. But, individual attention for one reader means a longer wait for others. And I just realized…*this* is a *problem*? To have people lined up for your book?

Miami, I'm in Miami. I'm seated at a table, focused on the woman standing over me, the last woman in line, listening to her, conjuring up an inscription for her, and I see the LBO at the back of the room, talking to a young woman in denims and a plaid shirt who is holding two books in her hands. The LBO is leaning down to whisper to her, but pointing at me, making eye contact with me, holding up his finger as if to say, *One more, okay?*

I am exhausted. A book reading is also a performance. At least, it ought to be. You ever go to a reading and discover that the author is a wretched reader, and you rethink your interest in the book that brought you to the store? That's not me. I'm not sure how good a writer I am, but I know I'm a good reader. But I'm not a young reader. It's late. I am exhausted. The LBO knows I am exhausted, but he also knows I will sign one more book, as every writer would. The LBO leads the young girl to me.

"Emily, I want you to meet Lorrie Knight, one of my favorite customers, and a big fan of yours."

Lorrie Knight is the poster child for embarrassment. Perhaps scarlet-faced distress? The LBO winks at me, a wink that says, *She's all yours now. I think you're going to like her.*

"Hello, Lorrie," I said, extending my hand. How old was she? Twenty? Certainly not much older. "Have a seat."

The LBO steps away and begins helping one of his clerks start cleaning up the room, stacking chairs, picking up scattered programs, the after-event ritual. Lorrie and I might as well have been alone. She is still holding on to her books.

"Lorrie, I hope you enjoyed the reading tonight. Thank you for coming."

She finally spoke, haltingly.

"Ms. Sterling, I love your book."

There she is, part of my future, saying exactly the perfect thing to introduce herself. I am… *taken*?

"Oh, please, call me Emily. And let me sign your book."

She handed me the copy of the book *du jour*, my third, but kept the other in her hand.

"Thank you, you've already read it?"

"No, no, but I will start tonight. I meant your first book."

And that was the one in her hand.

"I was here for your first reading, a few years ago. I bought it then..."

"But I did not sign it?"

"No, I was...no, I just bought it. You were busy, a lot of people, and my mother wanted to leave."

I expected her to hand it over, but she held on.

"I read it three times. The girl in the story. I wanted to meet her in real life."

Was I tempted to be glib and say, *Well, let me introduce myself?* Yes, but I did not.

"Thank you...Lorrie...but she was just a character."

And there was a flash in her eyes that should have alerted me to the fact that Lorrie Knight was different. Different, sure, but no clue that she and I would be friends until I died.

"No, Emily, she was real. I don't know how you did it, but I wish I could write as good as you do. She was real."

The reading room did not have overhead lighting. Four large table lamps at each corner were enough to light the room, but keep it soft at the same time. The LBO had designed the room to be warm and intimate, even for a hundred people. One of the lamps went dark. Then another. The LBO came to the table.

"We've got to close this room up now, but I've reserved a table in our coffee shop for you. Get some coffee, have a snack. On the house. And don't worry about the clock. I'll be here and lock up whenever you want to leave. All the time you want to talk, my treat."

I think that Lorrie and I were both in love with the LBO at that moment.

Dorothy and Emily are coming to see me. Dorothy does not surprise me. She has always been a mother hen. But I never pegged Emily that way. Dorothy and I tease her about the lack of a man in her life. Dorothy's other children are grown and parents now. Emily is an odd bird. Never married, no long-term relationships, but a lot of boyfriends even as a middle-aged woman.

"Aunt Emmy, you're still living in the twentieth century. I don't need a man to make me happy. If one comes along…great…but I ain't looking."

Dorothy says that Emily has a surprise for me. I asked Dorothy if my god-daughter was finally getting married.

"From your lips to the Pope's ears, Emmy. But I've given up hope for that. She's more your daughter than mine. No, no wedding bells. But we have a birthday present for you. And, besides, if you would ever answer your phone, we could stop worrying about you. We're coming to see you to make sure you aren't dead and moldy in that damn deck chair of yours."

Lorrie Knight once told me that she was going to write a book in which I was a thinly veiled character. *Thinly veiled.* I love that. I told her that I was armor-veiled, thinking I was clever. She reminded me of something I had said years ago at a reading.

"X-ray vision…that's what you said we all have. Good writers have X-ray vision. We can even see though steel and stone."

Wasn't that what Amy had? X-ray vision?

"I said that…about steel and stone?"

"No, Emily, that's my own metaphor. But come to think of it, the book with you in it, I think I'll title it *Steel and Stone*."

A long time ago, Miss Randall told me that I was going to be *the* success story of her teaching career. Lorrie Knight is the success story of my career as a writing teacher. Not the only one, but *the* one. How many of my students went on to be published writers? Lorrie once did some research and told me that the number was more than I might have expected. She even found their books and read the acknowledgment page. I was mentioned in all but one.

"And you'll never guess who snubbed you."

"Lorrie, I'd hardly call an omission a snub."

"Guess."

I could tell by the look on her face that this was some sort of deep pleasure for her, this forcing me to remember a particular student who obviously had not made an impression on me.

"Lorrie, I haven't got a clue."

She rolled her eyes and then rubbed her fingers across her mouth, as if wiping off some leftover food crumbs on her lips. She was stifling a grin.

"You remember Ashley Brett?"

I did not.

And then I did.

Lorrie had a smirk on her face. Me? I was back in a classroom, about to punch Ashley Brett in the face.

Ashley Brett? Her real name? No way in hell is that her real name. But she knows who she is.

I was a lousy lit teacher, in love with the subject but impatient with my students. But for the past fifteen years I've been…and here's the problem…I can't call what I did *teaching* when I was *teaching* creative writing. A good writing teacher can teach writing. But a creative writing teacher cannot give you talent or desire or...X-ray vision. A good creative writing teacher ought to also have some empathy for her students, the good and bad and brilliant. How was I finally able to do that? Emily Opal Sterling, the know-it-all from my past. I suppose it would be a shock to my board-certified therapist Gretchen. She was in my rearview mirror by the time I had my first fiction-writing class. So, perhaps she deserves some credit for how different I was by then? Or was it the fact that all the people I had loved were dead by then? Sure, Dorothy was still my best friend, and I did love her, but...you know what I mean...it was not the same.

Lorrie came back into my life ten years after I had met her at that Miami bookstore. We had kept in contact off and on all that time. She would send me samples of her writing, and I would encourage her, even though a lot of it was not encouraging. But she got better, her writing. Encouragement became easier. When I got a one-year appointment at the University of Miami, I encouraged Lorrie to sign up. She was already my friend. She signed up for the Fall and Spring seminars both. It was in the Fall seminar that she had asked me if I was a virgin. A month after the Spring semester was over, she sold her first novel. She tried to give me credit, but the credit really belonged to Sonny Schenker. All I did was ask her to read Lorrie's manuscript.

You ever hear any horror stories about Writing Workshop seminars? The ego trips, the snark and sniping? I suppose those stories are true...sometimes. I wanted mine to be different. My format was simple: students exchange writing samples and respond to each other, with one or two students highlighted for each class. Standard operating procedure. Me, my job was to make sure nobody got ignored or was treated unfairly. I used the term *respect*...I expected my students to respect each other. I was as much implicit referee as explicit mentor. My own comments about a student's work were usually done in a private one-on-one conference out of class. Praise, however, was always issued in class.

To get admitted to my class, a student had to have submitted a writing sample ahead of time. So, when class started, I had students who had already shown some promise.

Lorrie's second seminar with me also included Ashley Brett. Twelve students, all good, but Lorrie and Ashley were...more than good. Twelve students, and only Ashley had any prior publications. Three short stories in lit journals...the best lit journals. I was impressed. Evidently, so was Ashley.

Was I bothered by the nagging feeling that I had about Ashley... that I was looking at me in a prior life, even before I was published, the Emily who ended up in therapy? No, certainly not. Ashley was dislikable all on her own. But, see, all that's irrelevant. The writing was supposed to matter, only the writing, not the writer. I was professionally bound to remain objective; at least, to try.

Ashley's writing was stellar. Dammit. She had cruised through her class critique with nothing but praise from the others, including Lorrie. I agreed with them. It was a story headed for publication somewhere. So, here's the mystery: Why was Ashley gunning for Lorrie? I asked Lorrie later, and she was as mystified as I was. Down deep, what did Ashley sense about Lorrie, right or wrong, that I had missed? Was it something about Lorrie, or something deep inside Ashley herself? Another mystery in my life, along with who really killed Kennedy.

In the next class, Lorrie was in the shooting gallery. Or...she was sitting on one of those spring-loaded chairs over a dunking tank at the carnival. Hit the bulls-eye and into the water goes the writer. Or... Whack-a-mole? Pick your analogy. All I know for sure is that her writing that day was a quantum leap beyond anything else I had seen from her in the past ten years. She had been working on it in secret, telling me later that she was afraid to show it to me until the last minute. I got my copy the night before class. I tried to call her, but all I could do was leave a message: *I just read your story. Do not let this go to your head, but this is brilliant. Tomorrow should be interesting.*

It *was* interesting. But not for the reasons I had expected. How to summarize a twenty-page stream-of-consciousness diatribe of an elderly black mother directed at her adult dead daughter? At the funeral home, standing over the open casket, a mother who stares at her dead daughter and goes back through time, from birth to death, reviving a lost life, angry at her daughter and the father who had forsaken them both, angry at herself, angry at God.

Eleven other writers-to-be in the room, and me. Ten of those writers were respectfully awed. *Respectfully awed*, how I had also felt when I read it and immediately called her the night before. I watched Lorrie as the others commented on her work. She kept her eyes down, her arms crossed across her chest. I was happy for her. It was as if she was trying to not burst wide open with joy and pride. I knew that feeling. I remembered that feeling. I was happy for her.

Ashley had been noticeably silent. With ten classmates down, we all waited for her. I had to give her credit. She knew how to make an entrance. Full of faux humility, she started excavating.

"Lorrie, I'm sorry, but I was a bit confused..."

Lorrie raised her head and looked directly at Ashley. I was conjuring Burr and Hamilton, and I knew Lorrie well enough to be thankful that guns were not allowed on campus.

"Ashley, I'm sorry, but it's still a work in progress. It can be made better. How is it confusing?"

"Again, it might just be me, but I was confused by your narrator."

"How so?"

"Her dialogue. It did not seem realistic to me, in that circumstance, that setting."

I blinked. Was Ashley that oblivious? I left Lorrie on her own. Before she could respond, however, little Minnie Martin…yes, her real name…all four-feet-eleven of her, jumped in.

"Ashley, it wasn't dialogue. The woman wasn't talking. She was thinking."

We all turned to look at Minnie. She had been the least talkative member of class all semester long. Then it dawned on me. *Nobody* in that class liked Ashley. That realization led to another. I was going to have to defend Ashley. I was the teacher, right? Dammit. Luckily for me, Ashley soon made herself indefensible.

"Yes, of course, perhaps I was imprecise in my language. Yes, her thinking. It seemed…too formal for that moment. Free-thought ought to be less comprehensible, perhaps? A free association of words and feelings, but not a coherent narrative."

None of us had any idea what she was talking about. And then Lorrie started playing with her.

"So, perhaps I should have the woman be drunk and thinking, almost incoherent with flashes of insight?"

Ashley was still loaded for bear.

"It is your decision. All I'm saying is that I think you could have had the same story in five fewer pages."

"And?"

"And what, Lorrie?"

"And what else? Do you have any other suggestions?"

"Actually, not a suggestion, since I have no alternative, and I'm reluctant to raise this issue, but it seems to me that you have put an alien voice in this black woman's head. How can you presume to write about the black experience in any form?"

Minnie Martin actually gasped. I was shocked as well…at how incredibly stupid Ashley was at that moment. How any serious writer could be that stupid. Ashley was a very smart young woman, I knew that, but she said a stupid thing. I looked at Lorrie, who was smarter. Lorrie was also holding four Aces and a King in her hand.

"Ashley, isn't that what a writer is supposed to do? Be somebody else. Live in somebody else's skin. Just me writing about me would be awfully boring, right? You writing about yourself, a small world, indeed."

It was time for me to step in, but I didn't. Lorrie was doing fine all by herself, but it occurred to me that Ashley's real target was not Lorrie's story, but Lorrie herself. The other students had withdrawn to the sidelines, no longer participants, merely spectators. Lorrie was on her own. Back and forth, Lorrie and Ashley traded barbs, never raising their voices, but in a war of attrition…Ashley, I thought, was slowly winning. Lorrie looked at me. I knew that I could have rebutted everything that Ashley had raised as an issue, but I did not want to win an argument. I wanted to destroy Ashley. I had taken sides. Forget about being a referee. Hell, forget about being a mentor.

Then I realized that I had been misreading Lorrie. Her face, in a smirky glance toward me, gave her away. She wasn't losing a debate or losing energy. She had been egging on Ashley to make even more petty comments, provoking her, but not really taking her seriously. Ashley Brett had become entertainment for Lorrie. She didn't care about the Ashley in front of her or all the Ashley Bretts she was going to meet in the future. *Fuck 'em.*

But I still cared. I spoke for the first time.

"Ashley, you have to remember…Lorrie is writing for adults."

Ten students leaned back in their chairs, pushing their chairs a few inches away from the conference-room table. Lorrie and Ashley turned to look at me, both leaning forward.

Was what I said fair? To Ashley, no. But I knew she would let it fester for the rest of her life. I had dismissed her. Said that she was not to be taken seriously. That Lorrie was an adult and that she was not.

You know, let me change my mind. Was what I said fair? Absolutely.

Ashley survived, of course. She went on to be very successful. But Lorrie went on to win the Pulitzer with her second novel. That award-winning book? She and I both knew which character was based on Ashley. We assumed that Ashley did too.

Was that it, the secret to life? Eventually, we all have to be adults? And being an adult means that you know when to simply...not give a fuck anymore? That's not to say that you quit caring, but that you know what is worth caring about? Who and what to care about?

I have no answers now. Ask me at the end.

Dorothy has something I wish I had: a sense of humor. I can laugh at jokes, even lame jokes. I can laugh at the absurdity of life. You know, that pretentious intellectual sense of humor. But I cannot make other people laugh. I do not even tell good jokes well. No sense of timing. Whatever.

Dorothy is funny, but she can't tell jokes either. Her real trick? She just improvises in the moment, calling in humor from the moon or another galaxy. She makes shit up. I might hear voices, but she can create them up in a split second, usually parodies of real voices, real people, and she can imitate their mannerisms. Her imitation of me makes me laugh, even when it is sometimes almost cruel in its truth.

My favorite Dorothy routine involved talking seagulls and breasts.

She had gone in for her first mammogram and was describing it to me and god-daughter Emily, telling it from the point of view of her breasts. Halfway through, as my Emily and I were laughing so hard that we asked to stop talking for a second while we caught our breaths,

Dorothy expressed disappointment in both of us.

"Neither one of you ever saw Red Skelton's bit about Gertrude and Heathcliffe?"

"Mom, who is Red Skelton?"

"Dorothy, you do remember that I did not have a television when I was growing up, right?"

"You're both cultural retards."

Gertrude and Heathcliffe were talking seagulls, and Skelton did his routine with his hands tucked in his armpits and his elbows flapping like wings. Talking seagulls who were less than brilliant, and each almost talked with a lisp. Future political incorrectness for sure, compounded by Dorothy, who gave Heathcliffe a gay lisp. Dorothy gave her breasts those voices and personalities, talking to each other after their first mammogram, describing the procedure in terms of a medieval torture chamber. Shocked at how poked and squeezed and abused they had been, lab technicians in black robes like some sort of sorcerer's apprentices. Two lisping breasts talking about being painfully flattened like pancakes. And then Dorothy riffed into Gertrude and Heathcliffe being in an Edgar Allan Poe story, the mammogram discs morphing into walls that were closing in and crushing their entire seagull-breast bodies. She started to make herself laugh so hard that even she had to stop to catch her breath.

Emily was aghast.

"I am never getting one of those things. They've got to come up with something better when I'm as old as you two."

Dorothy sighed, quietly serious, speaking to her daughter but looking at me.

"I hope so. I truly hope so."

My mother was diagnosed with breast cancer before mammograms were widely used. Would it have made a difference? In the long run, probably not. Perhaps a few extra years for her to be with me and my father. That might have been good, but would it also mean a few more years of suffering? My mother was not the same after her mastectomy. It's called a battle, battling cancer, losing a courageous battle. War metaphors abound.

God-daughter Emily is past forty and still swears she will never have a mammogram. She was right about science. It is getting better. I hope she is still right in the long run. Dorothy has had four mammograms. Cancer-free, she wins. I had two, went five years before the third. I am losing.

You can always tell that bad news is coming by how your doctor's tone of voice changes. I was there when my mother got her bladder cancer diagnosis. She won that battle. I was not there when she was told about her breast cancer. I wish I had been. I wish I could have seen her face as she heard the news, if she knew that she was not going to win that new battle.

"Emily, I'm afraid that the results are not what we had hoped for."

My oncologist was a woman in her fifties. A referral from my primary care doctor, a woman in her sixties. Both were good women. I was lucky to know both of them. I was still going to war by myself. I was still going to lose, by myself.

Sitting in her chilly office, surrounded by the paraphernalia of the medical trade...charts and boxes of rubber gloves and a reclining examination chair and a stethoscope hanging on the wall... I had a flashback and almost smiled. Not a flashback about my mother, or Peter and Amy, or my father. Those memories would not have made me smile at that moment. No, I was merely remembering Dorothy's lisping breasts.

T. W. Higginson, recounting in an 1891 issue of the *Atlantic Monthly*, meeting Emily Dickinson in her parlor on August 16, 1870:

After a little delay, I heard an extremely faint and pattering footstep like that of a child, in the hall, and in glided, almost noiselessly, a plain, shy little person, the face without a single good feature, but with eyes, as she herself said, "like the sherry the guest leaves in the glass," and with smooth bands of reddish chestnut hair. She had a quaint and nun-like look, as if she might be a German canoness of some religious order, whose prescribed garb was white piqué, with a blue net worsted shawl. She came toward me with two day-lilies, which she put in a childlike way into my hand, saying softly, under her breath, "These are my introduction," and adding, also, under her breath, in childlike fashion, "Forgive me if I am frightened; I never see strangers, and hardly know what I say." . . . .

She went on talking constantly and saying, in the midst of narrative, things quaint and aphoristic. "Is it oblivion or absorption when things pass from our minds?" "Truth is such a rare thing, it is delightful to tell it" . . . "How do most people live without any thoughts?" . . . Or this crowning extravaganza: "If I read a book and it makes my whole body so cold no fire can ever warm me, I know that is poetry. If I feel physically as if the top of my head were taken off, I know that is poetry. These are the only ways I know it. Is there any other way?"

I never was with anyone who drained my nerve power so much. Without touching me, she drew from me. I am glad not to live near her.

I'm back, not sure for how long. I've been resting, but also writing. Rereading my journals and even rereading all the correspondence Peter sent me. The last dots are being connected. I wrote another hundred pages, returned to Peter and Amy, had to stop myself from writing more about them, and your voice came back too. I promised you answers, right? What all this means, the big damn picture. All you have to do is be patient. *Penultimate*? I think this is the penultimate story.

How I finally met Emily Dickinson.

"You're going, whether you want to or not."

Was that Dorothy or my Emily? I had stopped writing, stopped reading, I was just waiting. For what? I was waiting in my beach house. *Beach house*? I say that all the time, but it is not necessary. I don't have two houses. I have one house. On the beach. It belonged to Dorothy's aunt. I bought it a long time ago. Dorothy's feelings had been hurt. She had always wanted the house, had even thought her aunt might have given it to her in the Will. But I bought it. Dorothy forgave me. It became her second home. I even let her put her own family pictures on the walls. Dorothy or Emily? I was sitting on the deck, looking east. They had arrived with a flourish, bearing gifts, let themselves in when I did not answer the door, and they began talking. A trip to Amherst?

"You said you always wanted to go."

It was my Emily, my favorite.

"And, hell, Aunt Emmy, I'm named after you, and you're named after her, so how could I not want to go too? A road trip, three nobody pilgrims headed to Lourdes."

Dorothy was there, but very tired. Had I never noticed how old she had become? I was dying, but she looked older and more worn than me. I looked at her, she looked at me, and we both looked at her daughter. My best friend and me, trying to keep up with our mutual responsibility. The more my Emily talked, the more I wanted her to slow down. I was not keeping up with her excitement. I wanted to tell her about my father, his own wish to take me, but I had to wait until she slowed down to catch her own breath.

"Did I ever tell you that my father wanted to take me to her house, but he died. Him and my mother, they both wanted to take me."

Emily blinked and beamed.

"Great minds, Aunt Emmy. We all think alike. So, it's settled. I'll get the plane tickets, or we can fly our brooms into Salem."

Dorothy always blamed me for her daughter's sense of humor. I always reminded her that she was the funny one, not me.

"Emily, I don't think I can fly anymore. Something about that. The airports, the nausea, the thought just exhausts me."

Emily was not deterred.

"You're going. I'm going. My Mom is going. This is for all of us, not just you, and I had always wanted to go with you anyway. You and me, mom as chaperone. You don't want to fly...fine...we'll take a three-day road trip. And you're going to do it because I'm your favorite godchild and you are my favorite weird aunt. You got me addicted to our namesake, this is the fix we need. And, besides, I've already paid for the room."

Dorothy and I both assumed she meant a hotel room, but Emily had one last surprise for me.

"Her bedroom, where she wrote most of her poems, her writing desk. Two hours, four hundred bucks, and you're only allowed a pencil and paper, no ink. And I arranged for us to have a private tour too, parts of the house not open to the public. I dropped your name."

"Are you serious?"

"As serious as death, Aunt Emmy, which seems appropriate since today is May fifteenth."

"Emily!"

Dorothy seemed upset. The mention of death?

Emily looked at us as if we were children complaining about having to drink castor oil. Infinite patience, adult amusement?

"For the record, I've been planning this a long time. I made the reservation for June first, *somebody's* birthday who happens to be on this deck right now..." phony frown directed toward me, "....and to tell *her* today because today is the date that Emily Dickinson died."

I wasn't about to let my god-daughter think that she knew more about Dickinson than I did.

"You know, she was born in December. That might have been a good time to go too."

Emily looked down, then up to look past me to see the Atlantic.

"Six months is a long time away."

She was right. I had forgotten. Six months was a very long time. I knew what she meant. I asked her to help me up so I could go back inside and talk to my parents. How long? A few minutes, hardly more, the three of us talked. I went back to Emily and asked a favor of her.

"Can I take them with me?"

Three days on the road, I-95 most of the time, Emily driving, the three of us cackling like old hens. How did I have that energy? We were in Dorothy's old minivan, Emily up front, me and Dorothy tourists in the back. Sometimes, Dorothy would sit up front with Emily while I stretched out in the back. Energy? I had bursts of energy, and then I would crash back to earth. Good days and bad days.

I-95 North, through Georgia, past the signs pointing to Atlanta, where Amy and I had spent two days by ourselves, me helping her visit her relatives, me and her acting like Peter did not exist. An hour on I-495, skirting Washington, but I still remembered me and Peter at the Dupont, and then two hundred more miles north to New York City. Emily had planned a route to go around the city and avoid the traffic, but I asked her to take me through one more time.

"Aunt Emmy, I live in the New York City. I don't own a car for a reason. Traffic is nothing but people who are always pissed about something, and the pedestrians are suicidal. But, it's your dime."

One more time. I just wanted to see the buildings again, even if only passing by, through a window, where I had been with Peter, where I had known Sonny and Sally, a side trip through Greenwich Village, but, no, not over the Brooklyn Bridge again. That would have been too much to bear.

I was in a minivan, headed to meet myself.

An hour away from Amherst, Dorothy and Emily changed places, in the minivan, in my life. Dorothy took over the driving while Emily sat with me in the back. When she had said that this trip was for her as much as for me, I had thought that it was a throwaway line. But she had been telling God's truth. For an hour she and I talked about Dickinson, an hour of "Did you know..." questions, and of course we did know. We were each an excuse for the other to tell stories about Dickinson, and Emily knew as much Dickinson...poetry and life... as I did. For all the previous years, I thought she had merely been humoring me about her interest in Dickinson, but for that last hour I started to see my god-daughter more and more as my daughter. She did not know it, but she was already in my Will, heir to my beach house. I had finally figured out who would want my pictures.

"Aunt Emmy, did you ever read Higginson's description of meeting her?"

"A long time ago."

"Me too. I read it again last week, and I remembered that the first time I read it, I thought he was describing meeting you."

"You mean weird and reclusive?"

"Weird maybe, but you have never been reclusive, as much as you try to be. No, it was how he said she had a *face without a single good feature.* A killer phrase. When I read it again last week, I thought of me trying to describe you to somebody else back when I was seventeen."

Is honesty the best policy? Emily said an honest thing about me, and I loved her for it. How old was I when I read the same thing? Younger than seventeen, surely.

"I did too. I thought he was describing me. But you do realize now, pay attention, that I have perfect lips. My mother told me. She wished she had my lips."

Emily actually leaned toward me, staring at my lips.

"I guess so."

Clap of thunder? Curtains parting? Some rip in the fabric of the universe? Or simply some slanted truth finally understood? My mother had lied to me. Not a bad lie, but a lifesaving lie, a mother's lie to her dying daughter? She had given her *without a single good feature* tormented daughter a thread with which to weave a new self-image. It did not matter that it was not true. It only mattered that I believed it. I looked out the car window to see a road sign. Amherst: 10 miles. Emily and I were approaching Lourdes.

"You know we're going to be in that same parlor in a while. We can take turns being her."

Our first stop in Amherst was not the home of Emily Dickinson, but her grave. Dorothy was in a good mood.

"You two just making sure that she is still dead?"

My Emily was a teenager again, with a teenager's glare at her mother. Me, I was looking at the inscription and the dates. Dickinson had died at fifty-five. I was going to last longer.

"Dorothy, just remember. You love her too."

"Emmy, close, but maybe I love her poetry more than I love her. You and my daughter, on the other hand…"

"Called Back."

My Emily was talking to herself, whispering the words on the tombstone before turning back to us.

"You know, Mom, they burned all her letters after she died. But those two words, they're from the last letter she wrote, her last written words."

Dorothy seemed uncharacteristically ungracious.

"Geez, and I thought I was a drama queen."

Her daughter and best friend were not happy. Dorothy saved herself.

"I mean that in a good way."

My Emily did not understand, but it made perfect sense to me. Then again, I knew Dorothy when she was a drama queen.

280 Main Street, Amherst, yellow brick Federal Style, hemlock hedges. Three pilgrims got out of a minivan and stood at the gate of a picket fence.

"Just like the pictures," Dorothy said.

Emily and I did not respond. Dorothy was wrong. She was not an Emily. It was Dickinson's home, original but also restored. You either understand, or you don't. Can you go back to the place you were born, and that same place is where you will die? Where I was born is gone. Where I'll die is still to be determined, but I have a pretty good idea.

Dorothy was ready to go inside. Emily and I were not. Afraid to meet a ghost? Afraid we might *not* meet a ghost?

"You must be Emily Sterling. I'm so very happy to meet you. My name is..."

If she had said *Emily*, I think that my Emily and I would have wet our pants.

"... Virginia Baker. I'll be your host this afternoon."

My Emily had done more than pay for two hours at Dickinson's desk. My Emily had bought all the tour slots for the hour before and the hour after our tour was scheduled. We had the house to ourselves. She had also added a thousand-dollar contribution to the Dickinson Foundation. We could wander as we pleased.

My first gasp? Walking in and seeing the stairway to the second floor. The red-and-gold carpet curving at the top. How many times had she been up and down those stairs? Virginia was giving us the history of the restoration, how most of the original black walnut balusters were found and refurbished and restored. Dorothy was listening. My Emily and I were looking for our Emily. Before we went upstairs, Virginia led us into the parlor and left us alone. I know, I know, a restored house is not exactly the same as the original house, but for me and my Emily, it was time travel. My Emily and I both seemed to have the same reaction. We wanted to giggle out of some sort of reverential giddiness. It was becoming surreal to us. To be in that spot. To be buzzing flies, settling on the mantel, to eavesdrop on Higginson and Dickinson.

In my purse was a small urn of my parents' ashes. I had left most of them in the big urn at my house. I looked around for Virginia, as did my Emily, and made sure it was okay to take the urn out of my purse and hold it in my lap. Hearing Virginia in the hallway, however, I quickly slid the urn back into my purse. My parents' voices were in the room with me. And then Peter's, reminding me about my essay on Lincoln and the Gettysburg Address, and then Miss Randall's voice, chastising me for picking that god-awful Marvel poem for a class assignment. I looked at my Emily, her face in a revery, and I wondered if she was hearing her own voices.

We finally got to the second level: the bedroom, the bed, the white dress, the white dress that she had actually worn, the desk, the window next to the desk. I was supposed to have it to myself, that was what my Emily had paid for, but I wanted her to stay with me, my Emily, in the corner in a straight-back wooden chair. Dorothy and Virginia disappeared. I sat at the desk and put the urn of my parents' ashes close to the window. I had a pencil and a notebook, and I thought I would be overwhelmed with words to write, but there were none. All I wanted to do was look out the window, to see what she would have seen, but I had to imagine the past, not the view I had, but the view she must have had. She must have written about that experience, looking out her window, but I could not remember anything. I used to recite her at the drop of a hat. Not then. What had Virginia said, that there were seventy-five windows in the house? Four big ones in the bedroom. But Virginia gave me one fact about windows that suddenly made sense at that moment. Window glass-making in Dickinson's time was not uniform, panes were seldom totally smooth. Light and colors were often refracted and distorted. *I'll tell you how the Sun rose/A ribbon at a time.* Just some opening lines, all I could remember. Then I remembered how bad my vision was when I was a child, how I did not see things as others did. I also remembered how bad of a poet I was. I looked at my Emily, a woman with a spiral notepad and a pencil.

"Emily, let's change places. You sit here and I'll rest over there."

"Seriously?"

"Seriously. And bring your notepad."

Two hours gone, Virginia led us outside, thanked us again for visiting, and said, "Feel free to wander around the grounds. I have a group lining up out front, but they will have to wait awhile."

My Emily and I were still in a daze, an exhilarated daze. We stood there, looking back at the house. Me, knowing I would never see it again. Emily, making plans to come back. Dorothy was more tired than we were, that was obvious, even though she had remained in the background most of the day. I thought that I and her daughter might have to hold her up as we walked. My Emily and I had one last place we wanted to see, the garden.

The Garden of Eden? The Garden of Earthly Delights? No, better. Emily Dickinson's garden. If you did not know it was the Dickinson garden, you would have still admired it, enjoyed it, but it would just be a garden. Roses, lilacs, peonies, sweet Williams, daisies, foxgloves, zinnias, and more. Just a garden. But my Emily knew what I knew. About a third of her poems revolve around gardening. We were not in front of her flowers, but we were on her ground. It had been a long day, but there on that ground was the first time I felt like I was about to cry. I felt sorry for myself, staggeringly sorry for myself. I remembered my mother's garden, her hearing music in her garden, the dirt on her hands, the day that Amy came to visit, two dirt-women sharing me. I remembered Amy's garden. Amy on her hands and knees before the sun came up, frail and failing Amy, digging a home for Ruff the Wonder Dog, a home finished by me as Peter held Amy's hand.

I was in Amherst with Dorothy and my Emily. It was all making sense to me, and I'll write that down when I get back to the beach. I promised you some answers.

I stood there, figuring it out, and I did not care that Dorothy took my purse away from me. I felt lighter. So light that I wanted to sink down on my knees and put my hands in the dirt.

"Mother!"

My Emily was almost shouting at her mother, loud at first and then a furtive whisper.

"You can't do that!"

Dorothy had taken the urn of my parents' ashes and scattered them in the garden. I woke up and saw the last of them floating down over the flowers.

"Dorothy?"

"Mother?"

She was crying.

"Emmy, I love you with all my heart. I don't want you to die."

I looked around the grounds. We were alone. I looked up to the second floor of the house, finding the bedroom window. I could not see anybody looking down at us. Perhaps a glimpse? Me at the desk, looking down toward the garden?

"Emmy, remember, you made me promise to put your ashes in with your parents, all together, remember?"

I nodded, wanting to put my arms around her.

"You know I'm going to do that for you, right?"

"Yes, I know. I know."

"Here's my other promise to you, Emmy. I'm going to save some of your ashes and bring them back here, to this same spot, and I'm going to put you with your parents here. And your god-daughter is going to be my lookout as I do it. Right, Emily? You're going to make sure that nobody stops me, right?"

It was too much for my Emily, who could only nod and cry at the same time, too much for me, too much for even Dorothy. How three weeping and crippled pilgrims got back to their minivan...I do not remember.

I am putting words together as Dorothy and my Emily sit up front. It has been a wonderful birthday, but I am tired. I have a thousand other pages I could write, but I think you've gotten the Emily Opal Sterling highlight reel. When I get home, I'll finish this for you. All the answers I promised. The Big Picture answers.

I had a dream last night. My father was telling me a story, about how he and my mother had taken me to the beach when I was a tiny girl, holding me as they watched the sun come up. It was a very vivid dream, as if it was real. Not just my father telling me the story, but me actually with them as the sun rose. It was real. But then something happened in the dream. I was in this minivan, just me and you, and you were driving. Too slow, and I kept telling you to speed up, but all you did was nod and keep looking straight ahead. I was in a hurry to get home. You kept ignoring me. And that damn dream got weirder. We passed the elementary school where Dorothy and I first met. She tormented me then, but in the dream, we were best friends, playing together in some sort of wet dirt, almost mud, and we were a mess, but we were laughing. And then…

I'm sorry. I'm very tired right now. Very tired. I have to rest. Thank you for listening.

Acknowledgments

I feel like the guy who won an Oscar but only has forty-five seconds to thank everybody. So, up front, my apologies to a lot of deserving people. The orchestra is trying to play me off right now.

First, to Nat Sobel and Sonny Mehta, who put me in print a long time ago, and then to Steve Semken, who kept me in print ever since. If you like my books, thank them.

Even a curmudgeon like me has friends who read all my books and kept me writing. I've been lucky to know the likes of Dan Campion, Julie Tallman, Mike and Sonia Schenker, Charles Yates, David Levy (whose teaching provided one key scene of this book), Jim and Sharon Hiett, Chris and Sharon Bullard, Linda Lake, Anthony Buysse, Harold George, and ... more.

For my children, especially the son I failed, you have my love.

Finally, most importantly, Ginger. In my third book, A GOOD MAN, I wrote about her: "Singular love and thanks to Ginger Russell. Of all the people I have known, and I include myself in that group, only she is truly unique. The biggest mistake of my life was not understanding that simple truth from the very beginning." True then, and truer now. Even if her own memory is not as good as it used to be, she will always be truly and uniquely memorable.

The Ice Cube Press began publishing in 1991 to focus on how to live with the natural world and to better understand how people can best live together in the communities they share and inhabit. Using the literary arts to explore life and experiences in the heartland of the United States we have been recognized by so many well-known writers including: Bill Bradley, Gary Snyder, Gene Logsdon, Wes Jackson, Patricia Hampl, Greg Brown, Jim Harrison, Annie Dillard, Ken Burns, Roz Chast, Jane Hamilton, Daniel Menaker, Kathleen Norris, Janisse Ray, Craig Lesley, Alison Deming, Harriet Lerner, Richard Lynn Stegner, Richard Rhodes, Michael Pollan, David Abram, David Orr, and Barry Lopez. We've published a number of well-known authors including: Mary Swander, Jim Heynen, Mary Pipher, Bill Holm, Connie Mutel, John T. Price, Carol Bly, Marvin Bell, Debra Marquart, Ted Kooser, Stephanie Mills, Bill McKibben, Craig Lesley, Elizabeth McCracken, Derrick Jensen, Dean Bakopoulos, Rick Bass, Linda Hogan, Pam Houston, and Paul Gruchow. Check out Ice Cube Press books on our web site, join our email list, Facebook group, or follow us on Substack. Visit booksellers, museum shops, or any place you can find good books and support our truly honest to goodness independent publishing projects and discover why we continue striving to hear the other side. We are the revolution!

Ice Cube Press, LLC (Est. 1991)
North Liberty & Soldier's Grove Midwest, USA
Resting sometimes above the Silurian and Jordan aquifers
and other times within the driftless
steve@icecubepress.com
Check us out on Facebook
Order direct: www.icecubepress.com

Subscribe to our Substack:
Ice Cube Press: Publishing, Writing, and Smart Life Secrets
Check out our Community Supported Literature (CSL) program.

Celebrating Thirty-five Years of Independent Publishing.
We are the revolution.

To Fenna Marie—
reading and more reading has
served you well. And I didn't
want this to be the one without this